The Saint of Incipient Insanities

The Saint

of

Incipient

Insanities

Elif Shafak

Farrar, Straus and Giroux

New York

Farrar, Straus and Giroux
19 Union Square West, New York 10003

Copyright © 2004 by Elif Shafak
Distributed in Canada by Douglas & McIntyre Ltd.
Printed in the United States of America
First edition, 2004

Library of Congress Cataloging-in-Publication Data
Shafak, Elif, 1971–
  The saint of incipient insanities / Elif Shafak.— 1st ed.
    p.   cm.
  ISBN-13: 978-0-374-25357-8
  ISBN-10: 0-374-25357-9 (alk. paper)
  1. Students, Foreign—United States—Fiction.   2. Graduate
students—Fiction.   3. Young adults—Fiction.   4. Immigrants—Fiction.
5. Friendship—Fiction.   I. Title.

PS3619.H328S25 2004
813'.6—dc22

                                                    2003027975

Designed by Patrice Sheridan

www.fsgbooks.com

1   3   5   7   9   10   8   6   4   2

I saw a crow running about with a stork
I marveled long and investigated their case,
In order that I might find the clue
As to what it was that they had in common . . .

When amazed and bewildered, I approached them,
Then indeed I saw that both of them were lame.

—Rumi, Mathnawi, Book II, "The Cause of a Bird's Flying and
Feeding with a Bird That Is Not of Its Own Kind"

The Saint of Incipient Insanities

Started Drinking Again

Only two customers are left at the bar. Two graduate students whose combined tuitions and rents far exceed their grants, both foreigners in this city, both from Muslim countries. Despite the apparent similarity, and despite being close friends, they might not have that much in common, at least not at this particular moment, not by 2:36 a.m., when one of them is drunk as a skunk, the other as sober as always. They have been sitting side by side in increasingly coruscating contrast for hours. Five hours, to be more precise.

But now it is time for them to leave, and in a few minutes, the sober one, who happens to be shorter, darker, and far more garrulous than the other, will come out of the restroom, smile apologetically at the waiter sweeping his boredom off the floor, and walk stiffly toward the ossified figure of his friend glued on a stool. His friend, meanwhile, pouts with ouzo-fogged eyes at the writing on a napkin. He is utterly motionless, utterly unaware of the ferocious gaze of the Puerto Rican bartender standing right across from him.

Date: March 16, 2004
Location: BOSTON
Time: 2:24 a.m.
Temperature: COLD
Subject: OMER OZSIPAHIOGLU

Extract: Started drinking again . . . after fourteen months sixteen days of absolute sobriety . . . (14 months 16 days = 439
days = 10,536 hrs = 632,160 minutes = 37,929,600 seconds =
101,145 times Nick Cave's "As I Sat Sadly by Her Side")

"What are you writing on that napkin?"

"My feelings," murmured the figure on the stool, now looking less
ossified. "I am summarizing my feelings . . . so that I won't forget."

The burly, broad-shouldered bartender shot both a nervy glance,
looked at the clock on the wall dramatically to make it clear that he
was on the verge—but the very verge—of sacking them out. To tell
the truth, the man's manners had changed tremendously. He had
once been an exceptionally polite bartender, especially at the beginning, and had remained so during the following four hours, after
which his graciousness had begun to thaw steadily, visibly, and irreversibly. For the last twenty minutes he had been anything but polite.

"Haven't you summarized them enough? It's been five hours,
man. Come on, move, let's go," the short guy bellowed. His name
was Abed. His English was brushed with a thick, guttural yet most
inconsistent accent oscillating madly between nonpresence and
omni-presence. One moment it was almost gone, and the next it
loomed in every word.

"Come on, they are gonna close this place." Abed elbowed his
friend as he glanced around tensely, trying to avoid eye contact with
the waiter and the bartender, failing in both. Being the sober next to
the bibulous, he concluded, was a most tedious job. The latter was
entitled to all sorts of absurdity, every one of which he'd simply get
away with the next morning while the former could only and
painfully be the spectator to a farce that was both external to him
and yet had no chance to remain so.

Abed inhaled between his teeth, scratched the cleft in his chin as he always did under tension, and pulled down a curl from his extremely curly hair, as he always did when scratching his cleft didn't help. He jerked his head in the direction of the restrooms but once again found himself staring against his wish at the pair of beamlike, crimson eyes, watching them fixedly from the shelf it had been placed upon, congealed in an abstruse dignity that made it look more like a creepy toy than a magpie that once soared high and twittered with life. How people could take pride in displaying stuffed birds Abed would never understand. In escalating discomfort, he turned to his friend only to find him this time making huge holes in the napkin with his fountain pen.

"What the hell are you doing now?"

"I am putting the dots of my name back to their place," groaned the other guy, peering desolately at the cobalt ink spots spinning upon the letters of his name, each dot dissolving softly on the napkin, getting bigger as it disintegrated, as if to prove that one way of becoming more visible to the eyes of others in this life was to get as far as possible from your innermost seed: . • ● ●

When you leave your homeland behind, they say, you have to renounce at least one part of you. If that was the case, Ömer knew exactly what he had left behind: his dots!

Back in Turkey, he used to be ÖMER ÖZSİPAHİOĞLU.

Here in America, he had become an OMAR OZSIPAHIOGLU.

His dots were excluded for him to be better included. After all, Americans, just like everyone else, relished familiarity—in names they could pronounce, sounds they could resonate, even if they didn't make much sense one way or the other. Yet, few nations could perhaps be as self-assured as the Americans in reprocessing the names and surnames of foreigners. When a Turk, for instance, realizes he has just mispronounced the name of an American in Turkey, he will be embarrassed and in all likelihood consider this his own mistake, or in any case, as something to do with himself. When an American realizes he has just mispronounced the name of a Turk in the United States, however, in all likelihood, it won't be him but rather the name itself that will be held responsible for that mistake.

As names adjust to a foreign country, something is always lost—
be it a dot, a letter, or an accent. What happens to your name in another territory is similar to what happens to a voluminous pack of
spinach when cooked—some new taste can be added to the main ingredient, but its size shrinks visibly. It is this cutback a foreigner
learns first. The primary requirement of accommodation in a strange
land is the estrangement of the hitherto most familiar: your name.

Playing around with pronunciation, curbing letters, modifying
sounds, looking for the best substitute, and if you happen to have
more than one name, altogether abandoning the one less presentable
to native speakers . . . Foreigners are people with either one or more
parts of their names in the dark. Likewise, in his case, too, *Ömer* had
replaced his name with the less arduous and more presentable *Omar*
or *Omer*, depending on the speaker's choice.

Standing still on the stool, the world whirling around him, he
whirling around cobalt spots dissolving on a napkin, Ömer felt inspired, almost elated, and perfectly competent to philosophize about
a dot of ink for hours and hours. But Abed must not have felt the
same way because he harshly yanked Ömer's arm to bring him down
from the stool. With that impetus, they managed to get out of the
place, just before the bartender went homicidal.

Outside the night was chilly. Too chilly for March 16 in Boston.
Still, as they plowed through Somerville Avenue, they did not seem
to mind the temperature. It wasn't the cold that made them frown
like that. It was something else. Something less blustery and rheumy,
more diffuse and hideous . . . something that, if asked, they might
have defined as *a sudden sense of sulky solitude*, though probably not in
these words, and surely not in this specific order. For despite being
loyal company to each other for the past five hours, and all the way
through lewd pleasantries and lewder jokes, manly chuckles, and
brotherly oaths of solidarity, as they finally dashed out of the bar's
swinging doors into the night-slick street with a rush reminiscent of
a drowning man's panic to reach the water's surface, each simultaneously, and yet separately, had recognized his own desperate loneliness. Along with the gust of fresh air, the sharp discrepancy between
their states of mind and mood, not to mention their respective scores

in a Breathalyzer were they given one, must have played a role in this unexpected aloofness.

Yet, after a moment of unwieldy silence, it was not, as might be expected, the drunk, but the sober one who blurted out, delivering cloudlets of steam before cloudlets of words:

"Did you notice the name of the bar you forced me to sit in for five hours, *dostum?**** Do you know what that depressing dive was called? Five precious hours of our lives!" Abed sniffed. "The Laughing Magpie, that's what the damn name was! But magpies do not laugh, they chatter! There is even an expression, an American one: 'To chatter like a magpie!' You might think, what an irrelevant detail! I mean, maybe you do not think so at this moment but that's because you are too drunk to think. But listen, if Americans heard some foreigner say, 'Oh, that girl laughs like a magpie,' they would've immediately corrected the mistake. Right? Then, why don't they correct it when they see it on a fancy brass sign? Or on the coasters? Which gives me the right to ask, if they don't correct it there, why do they correct the foreigner? See what I mean?"

Subject Ömer Özsipahioğlu stopped and squinted at his friend, as if hoping to see better this way.

"Of course, this is just a small example." Abed went on walking and talking vigorously before he realized Ömer had stayed behind. "Just a miniature of a greater flaw that operates in the society at large."

"Gail says . . ." came Ömer's quavering voice from behind as he tried to catch up. But then he had to stop and swallow a couple of times, as if pronouncing this name for the hundredth time tonight had eventually left an acidic taste in his mouth. "She . . . she says the crow is the venerated elder of the venerated fowl family. And if you find a crow old enough, the chances are it might have once looked right into the eyes of your great-grandmother."

"Gail! Gail! Gail!" hollered Abed turning back and opening his hands in despair. "You've been babbling about her for five hours. I was the one who sat next to you and listened all ears, remember? So

*My friend

have some pity, give me a few Gail-less minutes. No pinch of Gail in my magpie monologue, please. No preservatives, no chemicals, no Gails, until I walk you home safe and sound, OK?"

Ömer caught up with him and heaved a doleful sigh. Those glasses of ouzo he had downed tonight, along with grapes, star anise, coriander, cloves, angelica root, and the like, had added a certain touch of "exaggeration" to his manners.

"Besides, I'm not at all surprised to learn about Gail's eye con-tacts with crows. Weird is her middle name. If you haven't learned this by now, you'll never learn it, brother. She is the weirdest woman who has entered our lives, and if all these people sleeping in all these houses had the chance to get to know her, she'd surely be the weird-est woman in their lives, too." He tilted his head slightly backward and thundered into the empty streets: "So sleep, you lucky people! Sleep well!"

And asleep they indeed must be, as there came no response from the dingy buildings, tawdry stores, homely homes. Only a pricey topaz car passed by, sizzling, as if made of butter melting in a saucepan soon to disappear, to leave behind only a liquefied replica of what it once had been. Before it vanished, though, Ömer caught sight of a girl with dark hair peering out the back window, looking startlingly calm despite the ghastly whiteness of her small, round, sick face. As the car slowed down before turning the corner, he leaned forward to see better, but the girl wasn't there anymore. Ömer felt uneasy as to how to interpret this. If Gail was here, she'd surely take it as a sign, but he couldn't decide if it'd be a positive or a negative one. He looked around in vexation, feeling a headache coming on. Not that he minded the deluge of complaints that accom-panied him. Abed was always like this, always cantankerous, a fer-vent agitator who left less impact on his audience than on himself. Worse yet, alcohol seemed to bring out the frustrated orator in him, through some sort of a sight effect rather than a side effect. Each time Abed witnessed so much drink being consumed by someone next to him, he almost automatically got all the more feisty and pas-sionate to criticize *the society at large*. At those times Ömer likened him to people who cannot possibly sit still in a room where the picture frames are not symmetrical. Just like them, he desperately needed to correct every asymmetry he noticed, even when he sensed they were intended to remain like that. Unlike them, however, Abed's interventions were purely verbal rather than physical. Talking and complaining constituted his primary way of amending wrongs. And the more he saw he failed to do so, the more he had something to complain about.

"This must be the worst night I've had in a year, ever since that Halloween catastrophe," Abed's voice echoed deep in the throes of a temper tantrum. "You babbling Gail-this-Gail-that on my right, that baritone goof blubbering Doris-this-Doris-that on my left, and mister bartender making silly jokes about all womankind . . . Do you have any idea how ridiculous you three looked? No wonder the place is called The Laughing Magpie! And as to whose idea this *marvelous* name was, although Gail would not like me to say this, I'm gonna say it all the same: *Cherchez la femme!* I am sure it was a woman's idea. That rosy-cheeked wife of the boss, probably. 'Honeybunch,' she says one day, 'I've got the name for our bar!' The guy is probably doing some serious arithmetic at that moment, trying to understand why costs exceed revenues. So he says, 'That's a nice name, honey,' just for the sake of having said something, 'but do you really think it is appropriate for a bar?' 'Sure,' she replies, 'it will give the place a cheerful atmosphere.' The guy doesn't say anything, hoping she'll soon forget about it. But that's a grave mistake! In the meantime, the wife has already baptized the bar The Laughing Magpie!"

It was at these particular moments that it became extremely difficult to estimate Abed's age. He was supposedly a young man, young enough to fit into the "20–30" box in personal questionnaires, but in the eyes of those listening to his motley monologues longer than half an hour, that category started to blur, wavering from "40–45" or "60 and above" down to "below license age." Sometimes he sounded like an old, obstinate man with a skin so hardened no gale of provocation whatsoever could possibly touch him, whereas at some other times he sounded like a thin-skinned teenager easily inflamed by even the faintest puff of nuisance. And yet he always

looked a lot younger on those rare occasions when he managed to remain quiet than at those hours of talking. Once he started to protest,
his line of thinking headed directly to the heart of the matter as he
saw it, oblivious to all alternate routes and byways on his way there.
Such straightforwardness might be said to have a double effect, generously embracing both meanings of the word. Unlike many, Abed
was always candid, having no boxes of discontentment in the base-
ment of his soul in which to store up *better-not-declared* remarks until
they'd begin to rot and stink. And he was straightforward, too, in the
second sense of the word, being too to-the-point, or too *phallocentric*,
as Gail liked to remind him every now and then.

As the thought of Gail traversed his mind once again, Ömer's
face grew dim and his steps fumbled. He wondered what she was
doing at this moment alone with the cats at home. He wondered
what would be her reaction when she saw that he had started drinking again. Had she missed him, and would she tell him if she had,
and if she did not tell him anything would that mean she had not
missed him at all . . . Ömer wanted to keep wondering aloud and
would probably do so, if Abed could be interrupted.

"Then ta-ta-ta-ta . . . here comes the opening day. What do you
call it in English when a new bar or a store is opened to the public
for the first time?"

"I don't know." Ömer glowered.

That, indeed, was the best thing about a foreigner conversing
with another foreigner in a language that was foreign to both. When
one couldn't find a particular word, it turned out that the other
couldn't either.

"OK, but you understand," Abed went on confidently.

That was the second best thing about a foreigner conversing
with another foreigner in a language that was foreign to both. When
one of them couldn't find a particular word and neither could the
other, still they would be able to understand each other entirely.

Like a ghost interrupting earthly matters without actually being
here in flesh and blood, that never-captured word would still find a
way to convey its meaning without appearing on the stage in person.

Among people conversing in a common foreign language, words develop an abstruse ability to speak through silences, to exist in their very absences. Some sort of a lingual phantom limb effect. Just like patients still feeling their amputated limbs long after the surgery, people who have been entirely and brusquely cut from their native tongue, and have henceforth learned to survive in a foreign language, somehow continue sensing the disjointed words of their distant past, and try to construct sentences with words they no longer possess.

"Since it is the opening day, first drinks are free. No wonder the entire neighborhood is here. The boss is too happy, too busy, and probably too drunk. Then the only sober man within eye range approaches and says: 'Sir, forgive my curiosity, but why did you name your bar The Laughing Magpie?' The boss is perplexed. He has just realized he doesn't have an answer! Then he recalls his wife's words: 'Because it gives the place a cheerful atmosphere.' The employees overhear his explanation and instantly imitate, because they, too, had been trying to solve the mystery of the silly name. And so it goes, like a contagious disease. Years later, you drag me into this burrow, I ask the same question, and guess what the bartender replies: 'Because it gives the place a cheerful atmosphere!' *Ouaghauogh!*"

That might not precisely echo the very last sound he had unleashed but it is the closest any idiom could get to it. *Ouaghauogh* was a wholesale sound effect for a variety of things Abed refused to relish. It was an umbrella term under which omnifarious personal belongings could be efficiently piled, including numerous disgruntlements and a mélange of sounds (guffaws, roars, snorts, and groans of varying decibels). Whatever the particular feeling it was intended to designate, *ouaghauogh* was, in practice, less a final exclamation than a starting pistol. The moment he heard himself shoot the sound, Abed launched a new attack in his restless marathon of talking.

"Why are you complaining all the time?" sniped Ömer in a croaky voice. "What is it to you anyhow? You never drink! Damn you, Abed! You didn't drink the day you learned your girlfriend was still waiting for you in Morocco. You didn't drink when I proposed to Gail in front of your eyes. If joy is not a good enough occasion for

you, what about sorrow then? You didn't drink the day you learned
your girlfriend was getting married to your cousin! If you don't drink
at this age, you'll end up swimming in alcohol when you get old."

"So that's what you've done tonight? Invested in a better future!" Abed snarled, his eyes flashing with scorn. But the frown that
accompanied the scorn instantly took a clement turn. "Omar, my
friend, why did you start to drink again? Last year this time you lay
comatose at a hospital, vomiting your stomach out under a Christmas tree. You promised never to drink again. And now look at you!"

"Fourteen months sixteen days." Ömer nodded and chuckled as
if he'd just shared a joke with himself. "You know what I've realized? If eleven months before I had just put on my headphones, and
played this Nick Cave song continuously . . ." He paused, searching
for the information on the napkin, ". . . after 99,533 rounds, I could
just take my headphones off, and fourteen months would have
passed. For me it'd be just one song."

Abed's eyes narrowed as he stared back, half-flabbergasted:
"Omar, that's the most reasonable thing that came out of your mouth
this evening. Why don't we make it two years? Let me see . . . in the
past two years, you left Istanbul and came to the States to get a
Ph.D.; you forgot about the Ph.D., and specialized instead on *girlfriends*, but failed in all of them; you killed your stomach and then
your stomach almost killed you . . . and then, of course, you either
got sick or fell in love, nobody could tell the difference; after that
you got married, and on top of that you got married to Gail and ru-
ined your whole life! Yes, it'd certainly be much better if the moment
you arrived in America you had just put on your headphones and
kept listening to whatever song you wanted to listen to a billion
times. If you had done that we'd all be at peace now."

He stopped, took a handkerchief out of his pocket and wiped his
runny nose, and then wiped it some more. Ömer waited, knowing
too well that when Abed's hay fever–stricken nose began running,
time quit doing so.

"As to my nondrinking," Abed nasaled when his nose had finally
let him continue. "You can be totally open and totally aggressive.
That's what Gail does to us all the time, no? So if you think I am an

outdated, boring asshole trying to secure a nice little pasture in
heaven to wave down at you, just say it aloud. Let your protests flow
freely!"

Impatiently and queasily they stood staring in each other's eyes.
Abed was impatient as he waited for the deluge of remarks to come.
Ömer was queasy as he tightened his lips with the sudden fear that
something much nastier than that could escape his mouth. It was an
old pattern recurring. In the past, whenever he drank, he drank too
much, and whenever he drank too much, he used to finish the night
throwing up.

"All right, if this is what you want to hear." Ömer felt compelled
to say a few things when it was clear to him that *impatience* would
win over *queasiness*: "I'll tell you how spider-minded you are!"

"What what what?"

"That's the Turkish expression for people like you. When somebody is long-behind-the-times, conservative, old-style, traditionalist . . .
we call him spider-minded."

"But why?"

"*Why?* There is no why!"

An ersatz query was "*why?*," a dead currency used nowhere and
by no one once you stepped in the tranquil valleys, orderly parishes
of that vast and yet familiar land called Mother-tongue. There you
could live your entire life taking for granted having all answers to all
sorts of "why?" until someone asked you one.

"I mean is it like saying 'Your brain is as small as a spider'? Or
is it more the cobweb than the spider itself? Like saying 'Your brain
is so dusty for being unused for ages.' But even then, I tell you, it
doesn't make sense unless you say *cobweb-minded* instead of *spider-
minded*."

Ömer unleashed a desperate sound as he fought back another
surge of nausea. He would have thought of going out for fresh air, if
he weren't already there.

"Anyway." Abed shrugged. "Your point is well taken. At least
you tried to say something reasonable for the first . . . actually, *second*
time this evening. I am indeed spider-minded. Tarantula or something. But that doesn't offend me. No, not at all, 'cause it precisely

means 'pious' in my book. I am a pious Muslim whereas you are a *lost* one."

"A lost Muslim . . ." Ömer gallantly repeated, closing his eyes in some kind of an ecstasy as if expecting a "lost Muslim animation" to appear before his eyes and tell him about the tragedies of mortals.

As nothing appeared, he had to reopen his eyes, and observe some deep sense of wretchedness filling the void where he had expected the image to appear. While the wretchedness intensified, he first felt a paternal compassion, then a comradely empathy, and finally an escalating pity for his humble existence on earth. "Lost" was precisely what he was, and what he had been more than anything for the last five, ten, fifteen years of his life . . . a graduate student of political science unable to accommodate himself either inside the torrent of *politics* or on the little island of *scientists*; a new-to-the-job husband finding it hard to breathe amid the flora and fauna of the marital institution; an expatriate who retained a deep sense of not being home here, but not knowing where that home was anymore, even if he had had one sometime in the past; a born Muslim who wanted to have nothing to do with Islam or with any other religion whatsoever; a staunch agnostic less because he denied knowledge of God than because he denied God knowledge of himself . . .

"I do not drink, no sir. And the more I'm ridiculed for not drinking, the more honored I am. When I'm dead, I'll tell them up there that I have nothing to declare. I don't know the taste of Chardonnay or Scotch. I don't know the taste of that *rakı** thing. But I do know how all that stuff smells on people. And thanks to you, I also learned how it smells when it comes out of their mouths! *Ouaghauogh!*"

Ömer's face paled as he suddenly realized that hearing someone talk about vomiting, at this delicate gastrointestinal state, might have a provocative effect on him.

"I just don't get it. If you are going to throw it all up at the end," Abed went on without realizing the physical aggravation he was about to cause, "why do you bother drinking it anyway?"

"Abed . . . stop it . . . will you?"

*Rakı: a strong spirit made from grape and anise

"Why should I? I've been listening to you patiently for five hours, and now that you have slightly sobered thanks to fresh air, cold weather, whatever, I, too, will have a few things to say . . . Let me at least ask you this: Provided that I've never consumed alcohol in the past and given the hypothesis that I'll never ever drink in the future, can you please be kind enough to tell me what on earth am I doing in bars?"

"I don't know," Ömer grunted impatiently. But his wrong answer only bumped up the pressure for the right one.

"You *certainly* do!"

Although soundly battered by the ouzo for five hours, even with his bruised eyes Ömer's common sense was still able to see that any objection to such an acid *certainly* was bound to shatter *certainly*.

"You were there because of me," Ömer gasped half to himself, as if on the brink of confessing a sin—or rather a series of sins. "Because I called you and said I wasn't feeling well this evening . . ."

"Is that all? You said something else, remember?"

"I said I was . . . I felt . . . like I was thrown into a dry well."

"That's right. *The well!*" Abed cackled as he jumped up with his arms agitatedly flapping in the air.

The jumping act was some sort of a victory sign. Every time he got the confirmation he yearned for in an ongoing dispute, he repeated the act, partly because he was always overloaded with energy, but mostly because deep down in his soul, he wasn't content with his height. He could be called quite handsome, and was indeed thankful to God for his appearance, if only he were a little bit taller. Not as tall as Ömer the Stork, of course, but just a little . . . twelve inches to be more precise. Because he wasn't just twelve inches taller, Abed suspected the features that could have dressed him up with charisma—a high forehead, curly hair, dark dazzling eyes, a faintly aquiline nose, and the cleft in his chin—instead made him look like a second-year Ph.D. candidate studying the use of a cerium oxide catalyst to make hydrogen from water vapor and carbon monoxide.

Discovering the elaborately latent drives behind his friend's blatantly simple gestures was, however, the last thing on Ömer's mind, as he continued with his free flow of protests:

". . . I was so depressed because Gail was depressed. That's been
going on for a long time and today finally I had to have a drink, so I
called you . . . By the way, do you see the connection, Abed? First
you feel like being thrown into a dry well and the next thing you
know you long for a drink! . . ."

His eyes flashing with mock puzzlement, Abed looked baffled,
torn between placidly enduring, if not secretly enjoying, the *free flow
of claptrap*, and blocking it by an abatis of counterarguments.

". . . You begged me not to start drinking again but you knew I
would do it all the same, and you must have thought I'd be safer
with you. So you came. Then we had to go around all the bars in the
neighborhood because I convinced you that a fermented spirit would
not harm my stomach, and that specific spirit had to be rakı. But we
couldn't find any. Instead we found this place where they served
ouzo. That was kind of ironic because people presume Greeks and
Turks have nothing in common. But let me tell you this: The likelihood of a Turk substituting his national drink with ouzo is greater
than . . . someone of another nationality to substitute his national
drink with ouzo. Likewise, although they unashamedly call Turkish
coffee a 'Greek coffee' over there, still the chances of a Greek to prefer Turkish coffee to any other coffee are greater than the chances
for . . . of someone from . . . another nation . . . nationality to . . .
to . . . to prefer . . . Turkish coffee . . . ugh!"

Ömer let out a moan as he acknowledged in dismay that the
level of his English would never allow him to shepherd all these
words he had been carelessly scattering around.

"See what I mean?" he wailed.

But he knew Abed would. That was the third best thing about a
foreigner talking with another foreigner in a language that was foreign to both. Whatever inconvenience one of them might face in
speaking English, the other was bound to give at least some credit
to the tacit claim of "I-sure-could-have-sounded-wiser-than-this-if-
only-I-had-the-vocabulary-and-the-grammar."

". . . So I told you ouzo was fine with me but then of course you
must've felt angry because if I was going to be content with ouzo
eventually, why had I made you walk all that way for rakı . . ."

"Omar, my friend . . . that's all right," Abed tried to placate in vain.

"No, it isn't! Nothing is right anymore. Gail is entirely beyond my reach. When she's unhappy, she is so extremely unhappy that I'm worried. When she's happy, she's so extremely happy that I'm worried again. There is nothing I can do about it . . . I'm hopeless . . ." Ömer went on spinning round and round in circles of whimpers as he plunged deeper and deeper into a whirl of self-disparagement.

"Gail will be all right and we'll help each other, *dostum.*" Abed looked confused as to what else to say, searched for a proverb as he always did at times of confusion but couldn't come up with anything finer than: "*A good friend is better than milk.*"

"Even better than milk," Ömer squawked heartily, the proverb making remarkably perfect sense to his remarkably pixilated cognitive process.

Then, startlingly, not a single word was uttered for the next ten minutes or more, until they arrived at a brick building steps from Davis Square. Once there, Ömer's face twisted in a sudden grimace as if what they'd finally reached after an arduous, adventurous walk wasn't his own apartment where the night came to an end but the arc of the rainbow, where the world did. Knowing him well enough to recognize his capacity to exercise increasingly severe methods of schmaltziness on his wobbly body and wobblier soul, at the moment of farewell, Abed couldn't help giving his friend a bear hug, which only helped to make the other all the more schmaltzy.

When he got out of the hug rhubarb-red agitated, Ömer repeated in a ten-minute-delayed echo: "Even better than milk!"

Then he was gone.

Abed stood on the pavement, watching his friend's long-limbed, willowy body disappear behind the gargantuan doors, wondering what Gail would say when she saw he had started drinking again, feeling guilty for not trying harder to prevent it, worrying about him, about her, and before he knew it, worrying about all of them.

An Assyro-Babylonian
Pregnant Goddess

Inside, the building had an odd smell. Though hard to say it was pleasant, it wasn't a bad smell either. A sour smell of its own, which meant that it possessed, Gail claimed, a sour story of its own. She liked those kinds of stories.

They had moved into this place early last fall.

Early last fall, they had moved in with far too many more belongings than they had initially planned to bring along—including the simplest furniture of a twin-size bed, two oak desks, a bamboo chest, and then the rest: a few thousand CDs (Ömer's), four different coffee machines (Ömer's, though more like a tribute to the good old days when his stomach was still functioning), incenses of every sort (Gail's), bundles and bunches of plants-spices-herbs-teas (Gail's), dozens of goddess pictures, one of them bearded (Gail's definitely), a collection of silver spoons (Gail's most definitely), then books (Ömer's) and books (Gail's) and books again . . . and a public notice in Turkish used in the ferryboats in Istanbul in the late 1920s, forbidding the passengers to spit. Ömer had slightly distorted, poeticized, and venerated the notice as his lifelong motto of coruscating wisdom:

Oh passenger, do not ever spit on the ferryboat that carries you!

At the outset, Ömer and Gail had agreed in ostentatious unison to take nothing, literally *nothing*, with them, just their humble mortal selves and the two Persian cats (though until the very last minute Ömer had secretly hoped that they, too, would be left behind).

They had stoically agreed to move to a completely empty house, and once there, make a fresh start *as light as a feather.* It was a great scheme, simple but exalted. Ömer had unleashed a scintillating speech on the Turks' long-forgotten ancestors scattered somewhere in the steppes of Central Asia, where they used to live a happily nomadic, shamanist life, long before they arrived at the land that would become modern-day Turkey; concluding how deeply he regretted that somewhere along their history they had lost that wanton spirit and chosen to settle down instead, only to lag behind in the crazy race of civilization. Nomads were noble and restless. They were neither infatuated with the doctrine of a "better future" that kept gorging on the insatiable lust of capitalist consumption, nor entrapped in a good-old-days fetishism that required piling up sentimental relics of an unsentimental past. On the saddle of a nomad's horse there was no room for *memento mori*, family albums, childhood photos, love letters, or adolescence diaries—each dead long ago but never allowed to rest in peace. No, none of those sappy shackles. Only freedom that merits the name, so pure and plain, could ride a nomad's horse.

A few days after that speech, as Ömer was struggling to find a place for a quotation he had once taken from a book—a quotation that must've made more sense at that time than it did now—amid the maze of paragraphs that were supposed to mold into the second chapter of his thesis, the door had banged open and in had rammed an amorphous box on wheels followed by Gail followed by the female cat followed by the male cat.

"What's that for?"

"Oh, soaps and things like that. Nothing much . . ."

No objection. Nomads carried a bar of soap with them, didn't they? And if they could take soaps, there was no harm in taking a few CDs either. That was on Tuesday morning. Before the day was over, other cherished items followed—possessions too dear to be left

behind sneaked into the Box of Exceptions, and when there was no
room in it anymore, they simply made another box. As the list of exceptional items expanded, so did the number of boxes to carry into
their brand-new *light-as-a-feather* life. On Friday they were looking
for a moving company. They took the first, smallest, cheapest company that offered itself. Fortuitously, its name was Galloping Horse
Van Lines.

Still sniffing the building, Ömer moved toward the mailboxes at
the entrance and peered at all the surnames written on all the tags,
until he finally found his own. There it was—without the dots! If
Gail, doing who-knows-what on the fourth floor now, knew that he
was spending his postcarousel time here pondering the problem of
his surname being dotless and far too long to fit into a tag on a mailbox, she would have bitterly mocked and interpreted the whole
scene as yet another example of fear of castration. Men, she argued
pompously, were scared of losing their names, more so than women,
who already knew about the volatility of surnames even when they
were little girls.

Was that why she had not wanted her surname to be written
here? Ömer Özsipahioğlu was in no position to ponder the question
at this instant. He opened the mailbox and pulled out a handful of
mail. It was always the same junk; sale ads, flyers, credit card offers
pouring in from everywhere. Among the pile there was also a catalog
from a bookstore nearby, the second issue of *If Ain't in Pain, Not Alive
Enough*, an ultranihilist journal by a hyperconfused bunch of DJs
with incredibly antagonistic musical preferences but postpunk in
common—a journal Ömer had subscribed to annually though he
knew too well it wouldn't survive a year. However, because the
chances of its survival were so slim, every month the journal provided a supplementary joy to its readers when they received the new
issue, and saw that, yes, they'd made it again!

Under the journal there were more and more ads, and an envelope for a certain . . . a certain *Zarpandit*?! Normally Ömer handed
all misplaced envelopes to a short gaunt man who happened to be

the most lackadaisical Korean in the world and also their concierge, but this one had Gail's surname on it.

Did Gail have another name?

All of a sudden that taxing question he more often than not avoided asking himself darted back and seized his mind. *How well did he know his wife?* Was the uncovering of the secrets buried between them just a matter of time, or was it fundamentally, realistically, epistemologically impossible, even if they spent a long time together, even if a whole life?

Second floor. He puffed and panted as he rattled the stairs. He rattled the stairs as he wondered how deeply Gail was connected to her past. Ömer sure wasn't! It was only that from time to time he caught himself longing for his bachelor days, especially of the part when he used to live with his two housemates, Abed and Piyu.

It wasn't that Gail wouldn't understand what Piyu and Abed meant to him, because she would, and it wasn't that he couldn't go and stay there overnight whenever he wanted, because he could. Missing those days, in spite of being merrier and married now, was, somehow, much more obscure and difficult to handle than that. Guilt, he supposed. It felt like keeping on with the same old constant pace of masturbation though you now had the super, steady sex you had always craved. Actually he was keeping on with the same old constant pace of masturbation though he now had the super, steady sex he had always craved, but this didn't make him feel guilty. Missing the life of a grad student he used to lead on 8 Pearl Street definitely did.

But there was more to the matter than *this*. For the real danger that resided in telling your wife that every now and then you missed your premarital life was not that she might not understand what you were talking about, but that she might understand it too well. Could Gail, too, be missing the life of a spinster she used to lead with Debra Ellen Thompson, her all-time housemate? Because if she did, in that case, *this* could mean far more than just *that*!

At the outset, Ömer used to think that he did not care about this matter, and when he found out that he actually did, he decided not to think about it anymore. Not only because these were acerbic mat-

ters, which it therefore seemed better not to touch, but also because
he simply was in love with Gail, and as she had once whispered in
his ear, "We tend to resist being changed by our lovers for fear of
losing them, but maybe the alteration that comes with love is our
only saving grace."

Ömer was ready to let her remold his habits, standards, and
even beliefs, if he had any left in store. But getting rid of the suspicion had proved to be the most grueling of all. After all this time, he
still couldn't help wondering if it could be true that it was more than
a house that those two had shared? Was it some kind of a "Boston
marriage" as rumors traced back? Were Debra Ellen Thompson and
Gail lovers once, and if yes, how had it come to an end, if it ever
had? Half of him craved the answers, while the other half simply
wanted to avoid them. Better take your hands off. Though they
might have been jointly despondent in the last days, still, theirs was
a sunny marriage. Better not upset.

Do not spit on the ferryboat that carries you, oh passenger!

Not that he minded her past affairs as long as they were past affairs. And that was exactly how he wanted to see Gail's bisexuality:
a rickety candlelight that had long flickered out—somewhat like a
childhood illness that left behind no trace, similar to measles or small-
pox, though probably less glum—whatever the analogy, in any case,
as some other *belonging* that she had excluded from the boxes Galloping Horse Van Lines had grubbily carried into their matrimonial life.

Fourth floor. Number eighteen. Ömer chose a key from the
bunch, stood expressionless for a few seconds as if confused about
what to do next, and failing to come up with a better alternative,
opened the door.

"Gail!" he hooted as he tumbled inside.

Falling in love is an appropriation of the names of the beloved,
and so is falling out of love a reappropriation. Names are the bridges
to people's castles of existence. It is via them that others, friends and
foes alike, can find a way to tiptoe in. To learn someone's name is to
capture half of her existence, the rest is a matter of pieces and details. Children know this deep down in their soul. That is why they

instinctively refuse to answer back when a stranger asks their name. Children comprehend the power of names, and once they grow up, they simply forget.

History of religions is a roll call of the names to revere, as well as a testimony to the reverence of names. Jews professed the arcane tradition of naming, particularly at the moment of death. They changed the names of the ones on their deathbeds to give them a second chance to live. Muslims, too, professed the tradition, particularly at the moment of birth. They whispered into a newborn baby's soft ears what her name would be, echoing the name three times to ensure that it sank deeply onto her soul. And the Orthodox Christians who, still to this day, refuse to utter the name "Istanbul" instead of "Constantinople," professed the tradition, too. After all, the conquest of a city resembles losing your lover to someone else. In both cases, no matter how much time passes by, you will remember her with the name you used to call her, never with the one she acquired after your departure.

"So you've started drinking again?"

There she was, sipping a late-night herbal tea, the female cat attached to her, the male cat attached to her female.

"Maybe yes," Ömer beamed with ouzo pride, "maybe no. I decided to treat myself to a drink, but I don't have the foggiest idea if I've started drinking anew or not."

An uncanny smile flickered across Gail's lips as she headed to the kitchen, followed by the extremely thick-coated smoke-gray female Persian cat, followed by the even thicker-coated male cat of the same breed but tabby color.

"There is an envelope here . . ." Ömer faltered as he stared at the silver spoon hanging from that amazingly black hair of hers. In rational moments he'd wonder why on earth Gail attached a silver spoon to her hair. But this being none of those moments, he postponed that question and instead asked: "Do you happen to know of anyone named . . . *Zar-pan-ðit*?"

"Yes I do," came the answer from the kitchen. "It's me."

True, names are the welcoming bridges to the significant other's

castle of existence, but they are not necessarily the only way to get in
or out of there. There might always be, and usually are, some other
routes too buried to be noticed at the first glance. Some other
names, nicknames, or appellations most definitely from another time
and of another consciousness, unofficial, undocumented, unidenti-
fied names, part bygone forever, part eternal, each a hidden subway
in the labyrinth of love through which the beloved can walk away
before the lover has even realized her absence. That is how it is with
names, the easiest thing to learn about human beings, yet the most
difficult to possess.

She walked out of the kitchen with a glass of milk, seized the
envelope on the way, and without wasting time to open it, directly
headed to the bathroom, once again in a mind-numbing wagon walk.
It was pathetic what these cats were doing. Besides, it was totally
at odds with the "cats-are-fond-of-their-independence-whereas-dogs-
are-not" myth.

"That wacky thing is your name?"

Gail nodded with a sigh before she pulled her pants down and
sat on the toilet. Ömer's eyes slid across her and focused on the mirror behind to avoid the discomfort of watching her as she peed. He
scanned the horde of bottles and pitchers in front of the mirror, all
the towels on the shelves, and every single pink octopus smiling on
the shower curtain—everything in the bathroom but her. How and
why she insisted on publicly peeing in front of the cats, in front of
him, he'd never understand. Not that *he* was ashamed of or bothered
by it, but how come *she* wasn't?

As she went on peeing, Gail reached down to rub the female
cat's stomach. She instantly started purring in an absurd echo, with
the male cat purring next to her, as if they were one single body
and his pleasure depended on her pleasure. Ömer frowned at this
chunky creature with a flat nose and a flat face. He had never managed to like him. He had never managed to like the female cat either,
but the female cat didn't seem to be in the business of being liked. As
she never demanded love from anyone, even a simple caress rewarded her with more than she had asked for. Unlike her, however,

the male cat solicited more love from every organism around, particularly from the female cat, and therefore always ended up getting
less than what he had initially wanted.

"Are you talking to yourself? Why do you keep calling them
male cat and female cat? They have names, you know," Gail said
tonelessly.

Ömer blinked twice, one for each name. *West* and *The Rest*. The
female cat was named *West*, coined by Gail as a critique of the constant feminization of the East by Orientalist discourse, which was
fine, had the male cat not been named respectively, *The Rest*. It was
he that annoyed Ömer most, with his insatiable hunger to be adored
by the female cat. By the time he completed his second blinking, his
fury had slid from the male cat to his wife. If she was so carefree as
to pee publicly, why had she cared to conceal from her husband her
name and *Godknowswhatelse*? The implications were subtle and edgy.
Once again, part of him wanted to probe the answer now, *right now*,
while the other part preferred not to spit on the ferryboat that carried him, and do instead something more worthwhile, like going into
deep, delicious slumber *right now*.

"Why didn't you ever tell me?" he groaned when he figured out
which part of him had won over the other.

"Probably because you never asked."

The female cat gazed fixedly at some invisible company, Ömer
stared at a mauve bottle of tonic in front of the mirror and wondered
if it was new, the male cat watched his own tail move, and Gail
looked at nothing in particular.

"And what was I supposed to ask? *By the way Gail, do you happen to
have a most ridiculous name?* Or should I have asked instead, *What was
in your parents' mind when they named their child that wacky thing?*"

"You know what," Gail said, "people mocked it so much in the
past that I've had enough. So if you, too, want to sneer at my name,
go ahead, be my guest. I really don't mind it anymore."

"What about Debra Ellen Thompson?" Ömer caught himself
yelling. "Will this funny name of yours shock her, too, or does she
already know it? You two were very close in the past, right?"

There followed a minute of embarrassing silence as Gail stared at him in astonishment. "Are you trying to ask something?"

"Like what?" Ömer squealed, still frowning at the annoyingly mauve bottle, then at the annoyingly hilarious octopuses on the shower curtain, then at the annoyingly itself male cat . . . once again, basically everything in the bathroom except her.

"Like if we were a lesbian couple or not?"

Gail stood up, flushed the toilet, and squinted as she leaned close to inspect him.

"Because if that's what you are asking, you will have to go through a memory restoration! You're the one who told me that you wanted to know nothing about my past, unless I wanted to tell it myself, that we should make a fresh new start, live just like nomads, and whatever my personal history, it was fine with you, as long as you knew I loved you . . . blah-blah-blah! And look at you now. You start drinking again and fog your brain with Abed, come back home smashed, and all of a sudden you realize your most tragic distress in this miserable mortal life is whether your wife and some Debra Ellen Thompson had a lesbian affair in the past. So tell me, what happened to that legendary progressiveness of yours? Did you leave it at the bar counter?"

Ömer looked at her with pitiful fawn eyes he could barely keep open. He sure had a counterargument but couldn't remember what it was. Besides, there was too much light around. It hurt his eyes. Minutes later, when he reopened his eyes, he was alone on the bathroom floor, rolled in a fetal position. It was warm and comfortable down here, the only problem being some nasty smell from nearby. Somebody had vomited on the mat.

The required link between that happily-lying-on-the-bathroom-floor stage and the one in which he found himself clean and in pajamas in bed, was missing. He had no idea how or when Gail had brought him here. A smile cracked his stern face as he watched her taking out the silver spoon from her amazingly thick, frenziedly wavy, ravenly black hair. After almost twelve months of intimate company, how on earth she managed to attach a spoon in her hair every morning was a question Ömer still found peculiarly baffling, and how she took it out every night without spoiling the shape of her hair was even more so.

"Tell me, does that name . . . *Zarpandit*," he mumbled vaguely, near oblivion, "does it have a meaning?"

"Yes it does," she said as she lit her reading lamp, which was supposed to modestly illuminate only her half of the bed but was never pleased until it had invaded the other half, too. Trying to avoid the light and ogle Gail simultaneously, Ömer caught a blurry glimpse of her face focused on a book titled *Did Somebody Say Totalitarianism?*

Ömer sank his face into his pillow and muted his own voice as he screamed desperately: *"Oh no, not Zizek again!"*

His thesis adviser being a staunch Zizek hater and his wife a staunch Zizek fan, nobody, not even Zizek himself in all his cerebral subtlety, could ever understand the torment Ömer had been going through for months now, listening to the same man being condemned and venerated, venerated and condemned subsequently within the same day, oftentimes for exactly the same reasons.

"Isn't he brilliant! Shall I read you a few pages before you go to sleep?" Gail enthused miles away from reality.

"Nooo!" Ömer answered—shrieked, in point of fact, as he had forgotten to sink his face into the pillow this time.

Gail turned aside with a quizzical smile and tenderly caressed his face, his lips, then glided her hands softly toward his chest down to his penis as if to check how drowsy he really was. The answer must have been obvious to her, for she stopped the endeavor in a few seconds, slightly disappointed.

"Zarpandit is an ancient name," she whiffed out the explanation after a brief pause. "It belonged to an early Assyro-Babylonian pregnant goddess who was worshiped each night as the moon rose. It means silver-shining."

"Really? It is poetic!" murmured Ömer half-asleep, a grudging compassion creeping into his voice, as if *poetic* meant that which was no longer here.

Suddenly he felt ashamed of all the fuss he had made tonight. Bit by bit everything was connected to every other thing, and startlingly,

all made sense. Glasses of ouzo on a bar counter, dots of ink dissolving on a napkin, an early Assyro-Babylonian pregnant goddess worshiped each serene night as the moon rose, a laughing magpie, and
the ghastly face of a small child alone in a taxi late at night . . . everything made sense in pure harmony. He got the impression that if he
managed to wait long enough, quietly and patiently, all the wonders
of the cosmos would be connected into a momentously meaningful
whole, and then altogether offered to him.

"If it surprises you so much, I better tell you I have some other
names, too."

"Like what?" Ömer asked automatically, but before he could
reach his own question mark, let alone her answer, his body plunged
into the silky slumber it had been craving.

It was hot here, very hot. His mouth went dry, and he longed for
a drink. A few steps ahead he noticed the glitzy entrance of a bar.
The light was annoying but he entered nevertheless. As they
watched him coming, the Puerto Rican bartender who had now become the waiter and the waiter who had now become the bartender
gave him a reluctant smile. All the shelves behind the counter were
full of boxes and stuffed birds.

"Is there coffee in all these boxes?" Ömer asked as he sat on the
nearest stool. "What are they named?"

"Oh, it depends which one you are asking about. There are so
many different names . . ."

Ömer turned his head to avoid the sunlight intruding from the
huge windows.

"This one, for instance, is called *coffee latte*," the bartender continued plaintively as he put on the counter a frothy cocktail decorated with pineapple slices. "But I definitely recommend . . ." he
twirled, scampered back to the bottles on the shelves, and pulled out
all at once three, four glasses of cocktail, ". . . *coffee mocha* or also this
one here, our specialty, *coffee Zanzibar*."

Zanzibar . . . Remember this name, Ömer thought to himself. *Zanzibar . . . Remember this . . . name . . .*

As he served his only customer distinct coffees from the shelves behind, the bartender's hand gestures became tremendously swift, as if he were tricking Ömer into something.

No matter how hard Ömer tried to follow him, each cocktail put on the counter was no more than a glimpse in a carousel of ever-changing mirrors and every name uttered remained a sprinkle in the air.

THE CROW

The Letter Inside the Banana

If anything akin to obsessive-compulsive disorders, panic attacks, or episodes of social phobia shines among your personal deeds, then presumably, a having-your-picture-taken-to-get-a-student-ID line winding and winding through the Office of Social Services on the first day of the semester, wouldn't be the right place for you to be trapped for more than an hour. For others it might not be that bad. Boring but still tolerable. While some others can even enjoy the situation, seeing it as an opportunity to meet new people, chitchat, exchange information and learn the ways and hows of things.

She definitely was not one of those.

The only solace she could think of to help her endure was the comfort of knowing she had another chocolate bar somewhere in the depths of her bag. When she'd finished with this, she would start eating that. By then, she hoped, the line would have proceeded enough for her to reach the edgy-looking lady at the counter who repeatedly shrieked, "Can I help the next please?" in a ringing voice that sounded more like a command than a question.

She checked her hair tightened into a pitch-black ponytail. It wasn't the waiting-in-a-line part that tortured her most, but the waiting-in-a-line-with-other-people part. It was always people. The way they talked, the way they joked, the ways they just were . . . it was always them, the same old problem. She took another bite, as petite as possible to make her panacea last longer. Ever since she'd arrived at this campus, she had been feeding on two elements, which she liked to think had more in common than they seemed to have: chocolates and bananas. Both were consumed with similar practicality, peeled off as they were nibbled down. All day long she could go on without eating anything else. Sometimes she ate chocolates for dinner and bananas for dessert, and sometimes she ate bananas for dinner and chocolates for dessert.

Right in front of her eyes was a pair of elephantine ears attached to a tall, slim girl with hair as short as newly mown grass and as red as an oak leaf. It was hard to tell what her face was like, but as spotless and white as her neck was, it gave the impression of something edible. The redhead was energetically talking with a group of girls surrounding her, and every now and then they all burst into laughter.

She started looking for the other chocolate bar in her bag, while the line proceeded one step farther. Among the multitude of junk in her bag, she found a half-eaten banana instead, gone almost entirely black inside. She recalled how it had gotten in there. It was her first time on the shuttle, she was sitting next to the driver calmly munching a banana, this banana, when her eye had caught the three signs above. The first sign asked: "Did you know hate language is a crime?" She knew. The second sign was an ad for a Women's Care Center with the picture of a young smiling woman jumping in the air. This she didn't understand. She couldn't think of any woman hopping like that after paying a visit to a gynecologist, however jaunty that place or the news received might be. The third sign commanded: "No Drinking, No Eating on the Bus." She had put the banana back into her bag, watching from the corner of her eye the gestures of the driver who couldn't care less. That was two days ago. Now the banana had darkened inside, and there was a sparkling contrast between its deep blackness and the pure whiteness of the neck she stood looking at. She decided to take the contrast as a good sign. Exactly at the same time, the girl in front turned back and smiled.

"You like chocolate, huh?"

She blushed in panic as if the words had come from the bus driver under the "No Drinking, No Eating" sign.

"Debra Ellen Thompson is the name," the redhead said, reaching out her hand. Right upon her forehead a threadlike cowlick grew in the opposite direction from the rest of her hair.

But before she could say anything back, "Can I help the next please?" asked a familiar voice.

The next in line to have her picture taken was Debra Ellen Thompson, which meant that she would be going afterward. That was fine, she thought, as she finally pulled out the spare chocolate bar from her bag, and instantly peeled it, hastening to gobble it down before it was her turn. Experience had taught her that the overwhelming majority of chocolate bars could be finished in two and a half bites, but now she was going to try reducing her usual score to one and a half bites. With this purpose in mind, she took the biggest possible bite, while watching indifferently a dark-goateed man that had just then appeared at the other side of the counter.

"Sorry for being late," the man mumbled in a meek voice.

"I wouldn't mind if it were any other day but this afternoon, with so much work to do . . ." the edgy-looking woman yelled at him, looking even more edgy.

Being scolded so badly in front of a horde of students, all girls, the man's face darkened into a color akin to his mustache. He rolled his sleeves up and bellowed icily: "Next please!"

Next please? But she had at least ten more minutes to be next-pleased! A groan spurted from the depths of her throat as she tried in panic to swallow the colossal bite, now filling up her cheeks. She failed and shivered a bit.

"Next please!" the man yelled looking at her.

That was it. That was the ominous moment for someone with anything akin to obsessive-compulsive disorders, panic attacks, or episodes of social phobia shining among her personal deeds.

"Are you going to move or what?" The goateed man narrowed

his eyes as if she were rapidly shrinking right before him. Maybe she was. Already she felt reduced to pin-size.

It's definitely not my fault that you came late from lunch and were scolded by that boorish woman in front of everyone, she wanted to say, with a perfectly calm and cool air, but instead only managed to unleash a snort. She was petrified, like a deer caught in headlights. The girls in front of her began to sneer and giggle. But it made no difference, not anymore. She couldn't hear them when she was frozen.

It was then that Debra Ellen Thompson turned back and stared in wonder at the girl behind, now turned into a sculpture with half a chocolate bar in her hand. After a brief hesitation she dared to touch her, and shook her a little but no way, the girl seemed unable to detach from her congealed dread. Debra Ellen Thompson cautiously opened the sacklike bag sagging on the other's shoulder. There, among chocolate papers, oak leaves, chestnuts, campus maps, stones, pebbles, and a mind-numbing collection of junk, she managed to find the girl's papers and handed them to the dark-goateed man before he went berserk.

Then they made her sit on a stool and took a picture to put on her Mount Holyoke College student ID card.

With all said and done, Debra Ellen Thompson carefully guided the sculpture through the still-giggling crowd of girls right into the fresh air outside, where they sat silently on the nearest bench.

"What happened to you in there?"

"I panic under pressure," the statue replied, as she visibly relaxed.

There they sat for half an hour canopied by a mist of tranquillity that always arrives after emotional upheavals, watching new girls come out of the line in synchronized steps. They didn't talk much. The statue didn't seem the talkative type.

"Are you sure you're all right?"

"Sure, thanks!"

"Listen, once you've settled down, don't forget to give me a call." Debra Ellen Thompson smiled solicitously as she scribbled her dorm name and room number on a piece of paper. "And if you need anything . . . and I mean it, any problem whatsoever, don't hesitate to call me anytime."

"Sure, thanks!"

She watched Debra Ellen Thompson walk until her red head disappeared behind Abbey Chapel. When alone again, she gave a deep sigh of relief and plunked the piece of paper into the left side pocket of her gritty bag, fishing out a banana from there, this time an entire one. She had no idea how or when it'd gotten in there, but decided to take it as a sign, a positive one presumably, but you never know before you look inside. She took a bite, a small one, and observed the dark, jagged stain in the middle of the soft, white fruit. As always, there was a letter inside the banana and this time it resembled a *P*—just like in *pixie*, *peppy*, or *placebo*, which was a good sign. And yet, it also looked like an *R*—as in *resentment*, *renegade*, or *rage*, which was not that good.

It was a childhood game she and her mother used to play. They played it because sometime in the past God up there in heaven had cooked himself an alphabet soup and let it cool down in a huge bowl near his kitchen window. But then a strong, insolent gale, or a mischievous, rotten angel, or perhaps the devil himself had either accidentally or intentionally (this specific component of the story was subject to change each time it was retold) dropped the bowl to the floor, that is to say to the skies, and all the letters inside the soup were scattered far and wide across the universe, never to be gathered back again. Letters were everywhere, waiting to be noticed and picked up, wishing to be matched to the words they could have written had they remained inside their Bowl of Eden.

The game was supposed to be entertaining and educating at the same time. Educating perhaps, but entertaining it never was. Yet never in her life had she given up playing; not even when she had sent her mother into exile from her childhood paradise, and not even when she'd painfully realized in her absence that even if she admitted the fallen Mater back, her childhood had never been a paradise. To this day she played the game and refused to ask herself why. In unruffled silence she finished the banana, still undecided what the letter inside was.

But it must have been an *R*, for the following weeks were awful. Not that the classes were tedious, because they were not, though she still didn't attend most of them. Not that the food served on campus was unsavory, because it was not, though she still didn't eat it. Not that all of a sudden she had found herself in bottomless solitude, because she was already there. Be that as it may, she could do much better. It was beautiful down here, plus the trees were gorgeous. The town was too small but it could still be enjoyed, and the only deli did not sell bananas but she could always walk to the local market . . . She sure could do better than this, were it not for the people, the same problem as always. It was always the people, all of whom happened to be girls in this case. Mount Holyoke was swarming with girls, and also with squirrels.

Squirrels and girls composed the campus population with similar alertness and agility. Unlike squirrels, though, girls roamed in groups, and smiled all the time. They kept smiling at everyone, and basically everything with a face on it. They wrote silly notes on multihued papers, drew shining suns and wrote ostentatious statements on their notebooks, Scotch-taped say-cheese faces on their walls, downloaded aphorisms from the Internet, and then passed these to each other as a sign of their intimacy and profundity. If for some reason they failed to see each other for a few days, at their next encounter they ran toward one another screaming, and kept doing so even after they collided in the middle. They exclaimed abundantly, talked in a baffling code Zarpandit pretended to understand, and fetishized some abstruse notion of a friendship they deemed *very special*. On their walls, desks, shelves, and even exam papers, Zarpandit saw a deluge of maxims venerating friendship. What she couldn't possibly fathom was how come something deemed so unique was so widespread at the same time. Friendship was the easiest thing to erect in this campus. In order to confide in each other these girls didn't have to become friends first, for they were already. As they bumped into each other for the first time, traveled together for fifteen minutes to Hampshire College on the same bus, happened to walk in the same direction at the same time, or stood side by side as they ordered food, they became buddies, gossiped, and chattered, obviously having no difficulty in revealing their innermost secrets to someone they'd met only a few minutes ago. They were so quick to draw conclusions, and then so sure of the conclusions they had just drawn, Zarpandit felt embarrassed by her incessant uncertainties. It was these girls, and the agony of observing them so obviously succeed where she so obviously failed, that upset her inner balance, for which chocolates or bananas could offer little solace.

In the weeks that followed, she went from a chronically anxiety-drenched antisocial youngster fresh out of her family home certain she didn't belong there and that some college education might do her good, to a chronically anxiety-drenched antisocial youngster convinced she was stuck in the middle of a campus life she was certain she didn't belong to and that nothing could do her good.

It was some time before she gave serious thought to calling her redheaded savior. Though the piece of paper she was so sure of having put in the right side pocket of her bag that day could not be found anywhere, surprisingly enough, she could still remember the name of Debra's dorm.

Her Name Is Zarpandit

Four girls wearing sweatshirts in different shades of blue turned the corner smiling in unison while she was lingering in front of Brigham Hall. Seeing them coming this way, she hurried, or at least made an attempt to do so. She took her ID card out and slid it through the machine attached next to the door. But the door refused to let her in. She tried sliding it again, almost robotically, and then again, fanatically, turning the ID card with that awesome picture of hers on it upside down, in every different way she could think of. But the door declined. She could see the girls heading toward the dorm, which by now looked definitely like *their* dorm. She felt her face burn as she realized what a fool she'd been to think she could use her ID card to enter someone else's dormitory. Nobody would believe her, and even if somebody did, that special person would not be one of these girls, each an eyewitness to her efforts of intrusion. Of course, she could tell the truth, explain to them that she'd come to visit a friend, but the girls would presumably ask why she had tried to intrude with her own card then. Or she could tell them she'd confused the dorms but nobody would buy this. Or maybe she could just walk away, but that would be like admitting her guilt. Unable to choose among these unfeasabilities, she chose to stay firm. Firm and frozen.

But doors, after all, do not only open from outside, they are capable of being opened from the inside, too. Right at the instant the girls in blues had reached the scene, somebody pushed Brigham Hall's door from inside and out came a bright-red head, almost glowing.

Coincidences have a spell of their own. And if they are abrupt and amiable enough, they can shine like mortal-made miniature-size miracles, but miracles nonetheless, to the eyes of their recipients, especially to those of the hopeless.

"Hellooo, hiii!" she exclaimed in ecstasy. "I was looking for you!"

The four girls passed by smiling in deepening shades of blue, totally unaware of the panic they had caused.

"Oh, hi," Debra Ellen Thompson faltered, not knowing quite what to say in return for such an excited greeting. "I'm so sorry, I forgot your name."

"No, you didn't!" she squealed, still not back from the thrill of the coincidence. "I mean, you didn't forget. I *never* told . . ."

The expression on the other's face told her to cut it short and, perhaps, start anew. "My name is . . . Zarpandit."

"Zır-pın-deeet???" Debra Ellen Thompson rolled the name over her tongue like a sour candy. "That's an interesting name."

That is what they always said. But by now she knew too well that *interesting* was the most hard-shelled of all adjectives circulating in everyday human interaction, hard-shelled and well concealed, which did not necessarily mean there was anything pleasant inside. The shell was difficult to crack but even when you were able to do that and peep inside, it would be empty most of the time. There was nothing interesting about the word *interesting*.

Seeing her immerse little by little into tenebrous silence before her eyes, Debra Ellen Thompson felt she should say something, so she ventured to ask: "Does it have a meaning?"

"Oh, yes, the name belongs to an Assyro-Babylonian goddess," Zarpandit replied, but she didn't feel like going through the explanation.

"Gee, I'm afraid to ask what your siblings are named."

Shaking her head in a rehearsed pulse, Zarpandit seemed to be waiting for this question to come up. "I don't have any."

Debra Ellen Thompson smiled consolingly, as if forgiving her for that—that and everything else, including not being whatever she couldn't be and being instead whoever she was.

"You should definitely come to our meetings, I think it'd do you good. Did you have anything special to do on Wednesday, two o'clock?"

But they both knew she did not.

Despondency! Despondency! Despondency!

"Debra! Hi Debra!"

Debra Ellen Thompson lifted her pointed chin above the ongoing hassle around her and scanned across the room crowded with almost thirty bodies until her eyes focused on that dark-haired, weird-named girl now enthusiastically windmilling her hands as she kept shouting her name. She walked directly toward her but had to stop a dozen times on the way to speak to other girls. When she'd finally reached there, she forced herself into a smile: "Zarpandit, how nice to see you! I'm glad you came. Listen, will you do me a favor?"

This could be, Zarpandit thought instantly, the crossroads in her career as a chronically anxiety-drenched antisocial youngster. Not only had Debra Ellen Thompson invited her to this meeting, which she was obviously leading, not only was she glad to see her here, but she was also asking a favor of her. "Sure," she beamed, delighted that so much progress had been made in so little time.

"Don't call me that again, please."

"Sure," Zarpandit replied, fully perplexed as to what it was that she'd called her.

"Everyone here calls me by my full name, Debra-Ellen-Thompson. I'd rather all three of 'em. I hope you don't mind."

Zarpandit blushed in deep regret and yet deeper acquiescence. She, too, would have preferred to be called by her full name, were that name anything that sounded as magnetic as *Debra Ellen Thompson*.

The meeting lasted all afternoon but only brief moments would be carved in Zarpandit's mind. The pesky moment when newcomers were asked to introduce themselves, and the peskier moment when it was her turn to do so; the stirring moment when Debra Ellen Thompson welcomed all to discuss the urge to bring out the yet-to-be-realized in every woman, and asked for any suggestions that could serve this purpose; the hard-to-believe moment when a girl with caramel-brown pigtails proposed to everyone in the room to loudly expose the self-hating woman in her, the even-harder-to-believe moment when this suggestion was jumped at by all; the dreadful moment Zarpandit bitterly deduced, with the only exit blocked by more and more girls, she was stuck here; and the moment of relief when Debra Ellen Thompson intervened, apologizing that not everyone could be given a chance to vent the self-hating woman in her as the meeting had to be finished at five o'clock. Before they left the room the day of the next meeting was announced, and everyone asked to volunteer for the division of labor for the forthcoming events.

The share Zarpandit received in the division of labor was doing the chores, which turned out to be far more wearisome than she was ready for. In the days to follow, she increasingly found herself preparing, coloring, photocopying flyers, and then running from one place to another with pins and tapes to distribute these all around the campus. But that was not all. There was one more task she had to perform: to read!

Once it had become apparent that Zarpandit would be a permanent member, the leading heads of the group led by Debra Ellen Thompson unanimously agreed that there was indeed much to bring out in her if only she could overcome her shyness, nervousness, or whatever it was that impeded her from expressing herself within collectivities, and that the best fuel to launch this grueling process of consciousness-raising would be "books." Zarpandit *should* read more. Somewhere somebody somehow had confused introvertedness with introversion, and introversion with ignorance. Zarpandit didn't mind the confusion, though, being a bookaholic herself. There followed days and weeks during which everyone brought her books and booklets they deemed she *should* read. And indeed she did; with no hesitation whatsoever she kept reading, gorging on books, but also on bananas and chocolates.

She was used to it. Feeding her with books had also been one of her mother's treasured projects, and actually the only one that succeeded with her. Zarpandit couldn't understand how people could remember so little of their childhood when she could trace hers as far back as her second year on this planet. Too many details were tattered but the general framework of her very first memory was always fresh in her mind. For her first memory happened to be about her first attempt at "suicide."

Zarpandit remembered the kitchen vaguely, and some other things clearly, including the vomitlike puree inside the bowl on the table, and the pureelike vomit on her chin. She remembered her mother, the corona of her hair, dazzlingly black and soft, and her father, a man with a forlorn smile, and the grandpa, though by that time he had begun to forget who he was. She recalled her mother shoveling into her mouth the dubious substance in the bowl, and she constantly giving it back. Her mother had always been a terrible cook. She then remembered her father trying a new food on her, the taste of an omelet, the heavy smell of melting butter, and a piece of pepperoni, spicy and hot, unreturnable, unswallowable, stuck somewhere in her baby throat.

"Press her chest, press her chest," she remembered her mother yelling.

With her chest pressed by a pair of strapping hands and her wall-calendar-size body tucked upside down like a chicken clutched before its head is chopped off, while floating right at the epicenter of a whirl of screams spinning and swirling, she felt she was falling with enormous speed, and a swifter release, into someplace where it

didn't matter anymore if she breathed or not. Looking back at the
scene repeatedly in the years to come, Zarpandit had drawn three
conclusions of life-long company.

1. Even if something stalwart is firmly holding one part of your
   body, you might still be falling.
2. The act of falling does not necessarily mean going downward; if
   you are turned upside down enough, you might manage to fall
   upward, too.
3. Despite all the bias to the contrary, falling upward into death
   might not be a bad experience after all.

One, two . . . three more seconds had passed, three more shrieks
her mother unleashed, three more pressures on her chest, and the
piece of pepperoni had popped out of Zarpandit's mouth like a cork
out of champagne.

"There's no way you can remember all that," her mother used to
object whenever the issue was brought up. "It's because we've talked
about that day over and over again, you think you remember it, too."

But Zarpandit was quite sure that wasn't the case. She remembered details her mother would never tell—details too real to be
imaginary, too worthless to have a role anywhere in a postconstrued
reality, like the big brownish stain on Grandpa's cardigan, the re-
proachful grimace on her father's face, or like her mother crying
next to the popcorn popper on the counter, grateful to have her baby
back, and her life remain the same, sincerely grateful for that and
secretly sad.

Hence, at some point in the fourth general meeting, when Debra
Ellen Thompson began to talk about the strategy of DD—Deliberate Distortion to turn patriarchal linguistic codes upside down—it
was the fervor of her first memory on this planet that attracted
Zarpandit to the subject.

"We're going to play a game of squash with patriarchy," Debra
Ellen Thompson declared. "We'll voluntarily become the wall patriarchal rackets hit with their balls!"

A ripple of laughter followed when Debra Ellen Thompson imitated Zarpandit flushing. "What's wrong?" She smirked. "You never heard anyone say *balls*? Gee, I sometimes get the impression you were raised in a monastery or something. But cheer up Zarpandit, and don't feel bad 'cause this is what the whole strategy is about."

The whole strategy was about hitting the enemy back with its own arrows. Arrows being slanders in this case, the whole strategy was about embracing antiwomen terms, until they'd be neither anti nor related to women.

"And the stronger it hits us, the stronger we'll hit back. For so long women have been accused, attacked, targeted for being hysteric, right? Hysteria was yet another name for femaleness. In return, some women remained on the defensive, trying to prove they had nothing to do with this illness. Some others sought to prove that men, too, are hysterical. None of these will do us any good. I propose instead to embrace every single accusation targeted at women. The moment we've willingly accepted all its slanders, patriarchy won't have any more power to insult. You see how simple it is and yet how complicated?"

Zarpandit stared fretfully at Debra Ellen Thompson's ears, as if she had just noticed how big they were.

"Appropriate their tools," Debra Ellen Thompson continued, "embrace the poisoned arrows that were meant to knock you down. Don't run for shelter or protection, stay firm where you are. So if they call you a bitch, don't try to prove your chastity, don't ever try to be the virgin type. Every virgin is the cause of yet another whore on the streets. The latter is only a corollary of the former. The strategy of DD follows a completely different path. We take derogatory words from patriarchy's hairy hands and use it to honor people, women and men alike."

When the meeting was over, Zarpandit asked Debra Ellen Thompson in private to make sure she'd gotten it right: "You're telling me to use offensive words favorably?"

"That's right. And also to use patriarchal compliments pejoratively. Make *slut* a compliment, *maiden* an insult!" beamed Debra Ellen Thompson. "We're extracting terms targeted against women out of their soil. Stealing the enemy's dirty property is quaint robbery!"

Quaint robbery! At the moment Zarpandit could only think of Robin Hood.

"Well, yeah, in a way, I guess. Like stealing from the privileged in the name of the deprived." Debra Ellen Thompson pondered awhile. "But rather than Robin Hood, I'd say more like magpies. You know what magpies do? They steal every shining, glittery object from the world of humans. We are feminist magpies stealing patriarchy's words so that they won't be used against women anymore."

On her first day as a feminist magpie, Zarpandit woke at nine, ate a banana before getting out of bed and another banana when she was outside, and then attended Tracy Harley's class at 10:30 a.m. "Justice, Injustice and Everything" might not be an unpresumptuous title for a first-year course, but Harley herself was not your type of an unpresumptuous instructor either. If anything, she was a legend; half of the girls were busy imitating her, while the other half were busy imitating the imitators. Feisty and lyrical she always was. Feisty and lyrical today, even as she recited passages from *The Prince*, so inspired and nifty in her interpretations, such a powerful orator with an electrifying presence that had he heard her talk, even Machiavelli would be enthralled by himself.

When the class was over, Zarpandit found a table to sit at in the open air, recalling to herself the maxim of the day: *The best way for the Prince not to be overthrown is to avoid being hated.* Sagacious counsel indeed, she thought, as she took out the last banana in her daily stock. She would have to go to the local market.

The letter inside the banana looked like a *B*, which was good because it immediately reminded her of *banana*. But the problem with *B* was that it could also be a *D*, as in *doldrum*, *doom*, or *destitute*. As she stood there inspecting the mushy fruit, a skinny Indian girl she knew from Harley's class approached with a reserved smile and asked permission to sit at the same table. Her hands were bedecked with rings and bracelets. "Gee, that class was something," she said as she took out a big sandwich with a sad-looking lettuce leaf hanging out. "Don't you think Harley is terrific?"

"Yes, she is terrific," blurted Zarpandit, gnawing eagerly. "*Quite a fuckin' black cunt*, I'd say."

The girl looked at her with amazement that soon widened into horror.

"No, please, don't take me wrong!" Zarpandit panicked as she noticed in dismay that the other girl was absolutely unaware of the strategy of DD. "I like her a lot . . . I mean it . . . I really love her . . . I said those pejorative words deliberately. I think she is . . . she is . . . great!"

A shadow passed across the girl's face—forgiveness, or maybe compliance, Zarpandit hoped, but knew it was none of these when she saw her leave the table and sit somewhere else, jingling her bracelets nervously.

Hence it must be a *D*. It was a *D*. And that specific letter made her think of only one word: *Despondency! Despondency! Despondency!*

The first day she began as a feminist magpie she ended up as a chauvinist swine.

And she had never liked swines, not even as a child.

When she was eight Zarpandit decided time was ripe to reexperience falling upward into death again. She remembered that day well for it was her birthday. Her mother had made a cake, and baptized it "Piggy-near-a-Pear-Tree-Cake." As to the question of what on earth was a pig doing next to a pear tree, Zarpandit had no definite answer. She guessed it had to do with the ingredients at hand. Perhaps her mother had first coated the cake, then colored the pear tree, and though initially had intended to create some animal that would match well with the tree, a partridge or something, she had suddenly found out that the only color left for the dough was pink. And the only pinky pink animal she could invent happened to be a pig.

The moment she saw it, Zarpandit hated the cake as much as she hated the party and being the birthday girl. There was nothing more depressing in life, she deduced, than being obliged to have fun. That afternoon as she stood there chewing some pizza, a piece of pepperoni winked at her in recognition. It looked exactly the same as the piece she had choked on six years before. Zarpandit twirled the piece in her mouth and tried to stop it somewhere in her throat. To no avail. All the pieces of pepperoni she intended to stop halfway through she ended up gulping down. In the meantime, she'd surmised that even if she could not stop swallowing, she could instead hold her breath, which might basically serve the same end.

"You'll die if you keep doing that," a small boy with a tie the color of his freckles murmured calmly, without shifting his eyes from Piggy-near-a-Pear-Tree-Cake as if trying to understand how much his share would increase if she died. There were more than fifteen children in the party. The absence of one could make only a slight increase in the slice of cake each would get. He made a whiny noise and rushed inside to find Zarpandit's mother.

It wasn't like the first time. It was more difficult. For some reason her breath did not like the idea of being incarcerated. It oozed away every time she attempted to hold it. But she wouldn't give up that easily.

"What the hell do you think you're doing?"

She opened her eyes to face a mother boiling with rage, and to be shaken harshly as if she were a tree in blossom, not a pear tree, she hoped. With so much fuss going on, her concentration was shattered to pieces. In bitter resentment she started to cry. Why was it so difficult, God, to die?

Every Saturday morning they gathered in The Thirsty Mind to discuss a book, an article, a movie, or the life of a woman of unusual personality based on the presentations all girls were expected to make one by one. When it became too evident she could no longer postpone her turn, Zarpandit announced, to everyone's delight, she was willing to present to the group the fascinating story of a fascinating woman: Lou Andreas Salome.

True, that was her intention, but as she delved deeper into her subject she ended up instead preparing a presentation on Rilke. Lou was semigod, Nietzsche was semibug, but Rilke was both, a double-mutant, semigod-semibug.

It's true, it's strange not living on earth
Anymore, not using customs you hardly learned,
Not giving the meaning of a human future

Zarpandit swallowed a couple of times as if cautiously slurping from a cup full of coffee, either too hot or too bitter. It was going to be harder than she'd thought.

To roses and other things that promise so much;
No longer being what you used to be
In hands that were always anxious,
Throwing out even your name like a broken toy.

Daring to raise her head she met pairs of painfully bored eyes staring at her as if she were something close to a total ignoramus. She lowered her head immediately.

It's strange not to wish your wishes anymore.

There followed an embarrassing silence. What was expected to be a presentation on the feisty figure of Lou Andreas Salome had turned into sappy poetry reciting. Zarpandit regretted the mistake but it was too late. She started to sweat, yet her body was freezing.
    "It was a very good contribution to bring up Rilke *and* Lou, thank you." Debra Ellen Thompson ran to her rescue. "Now, from this stage we can proceed to Nietzsche, whose misogyny is something we should seriously ponder."
    Ponder they did indeed. That semester they pondered the problem of misogyny and the prospects for an antithesis, the problem of pornography and the prospects for an antithesis, the problem of masculine ego and the prospects for an antithesis, and surreptitiously and hopelessly in smaller groups did they also ponder on the problem of Zarpandit and the prospects for an antithesis.
    Sometime after Thanksgiving break Zarpandit deduced once again that the time had ripened to reexperience, and perhaps finalize, that unfinished fall in her oldest memory on earth. She sure

wasn't planning an *Omen*-like scene in which her body would all of a sudden dash out from the windows of an old building in the background as Debra Ellen Thompson and the other girls were having fun outside in the garden, and her last gasp would be muffled by the screams of horror and sobs of regret flooding below. That was not her plan. There were no plans actually, only this abysmal lure of death that was already here, inside her soul, keeping her loyal company wherever she went, pummeling and pulsing, sometimes less acutely than at other times but never entirely absent.

This time, she happened to be alone in the dorm room with a gym rope in her hand.

"What are you doing up there?"

The cleaning lady was gaping at her, with a frown on her face, a mop in her hand, and gum in her open mouth. She looked shorter from up here and that chewing gum of hers might or might not be cinnamon. She should not be in the student rooms at this time of the day, but being where she shouldn't be either, Zarpandit was in no position to question her.

"Nothing," she replied calmly. Like many of the hyperanxious who panicked over nothing, she had the ability to remain calm and cool when there really was something to panic about. "Just looking for the best spot to hang a new poster."

"Well, I can't see a single spot on those walls even for a Post-it honey, so you better come down!"

Though a naysayer and a nitpicker, the cleaning lady still had a point. The walls of the room Zarpandit shared with two other girls were overbedecked with pictures and posters and a lunar calendar as big as the half-moon itself. She came down from on top of the encyclopedias she'd piled on top of a chair she'd placed on top of a desk. As to why she had a rope in her hand rather than a poster, the cleaning lady had not bothered to ask. Zarpandit pulled open a drawer, put the rope in, took her notes out, and got ready to make another presentation, this time on the history of the gay movement in America.

✿   ✿   ✿

The history of the gay movement in America being lengthy, onerous, and meticulous, Zarpandit had felt no need to make her presentation on the same topic any different. After fifty-five minutes of detailed speech she was still talking, albeit in a huskier voice, bombarding the thirty girls, now slightly groggy but still attentive, with the prosaic details and encroaching facts pouring from her notes.

"The rainbow flag has been one of the most popular symbols of lesbian and gay pride. The flag's original eight stripes were meant to represent diversity. Hot pink stood for sex, red for life, orange for healing, yellow for sun, green for nature, turquoise for art, indigo for harmony, and violet for spirit. In 1979 when it was decided to mass-produce the flag, pink was removed and indigo was replaced by royal blue, due to production constraints. The colors were, of course, hand-dyed originally. Since hot pink was not commercially preferable, the stripes were reduced to seven. After San Francisco's first openly gay supervisor, Harvey Milk, was assassinated, the Pride Parade Committee eliminated the indigo stripe, so they could divide the colors evenly on each side of the parade route. I mean, three colors on the one side and three colors on the other side of the road. This way, very soon the rainbow flag became a six-color version. But if you ask my personal opinion, I don't understand why the committee took the seventh stripe out. I mean, I can see the difficulty in dividing seven into two but still a solution could be found, like three on each side and then somebody could walk in the middle as the seventh stripe. My other objection is: Why was indigo sacrificed for mass production? I like that color, I think it stood well for harmony. I know I should pay less attention to these details, but I just can't help lamenting the loss of indigo. Besides, this royal blue does not fit. What's royal blue got to do with harmony?"

The answer came in a chorus of sighs.

Debra Ellen Thompson was a resident lesbian, to use her own words, and not one of those visiting tourists eager to learn the ways of the locals while they are around, just to leave it all behind the moment they go back home upon graduation. The world was replete with such unquestionably heterosexual wives of questionable pasts.

Being a lesbian was not, Debra Ellen Thompson argued, primarily a matter of sex or sexuality, but of something more abstract and cerebral: *clarity of mind*. In order to attain such clarity you had to make a choice, less to distinguish who you were than to distinguish who you weren't. For Zarpandit, however, that was easier said than done. Who she wasn't, she wasn't that sure of. To choose sides between heterosexuality or homosexuality made no sense to her. If possible she'd rather choose not to choose, be the seventh stripe, the excluded color from either side of the road, follow the destiny of indigo.

Men and women, all the same, she had been loved by none. Men and women, all the same, she had never loved someone. What was the use of separating them when all types of failing to love were essentially intertwined?

"Zarpandit, do you have a spare moment?" asked Miriam after the talk. Behind her stood Debra Ellen Thompson stiffly. Together they seemed to have worked themselves into a wu-ry, some sore combination of worry and fury. "We've been having quite a think about you, as we believe you needed us to do."

Once they'd profusely hoped and doggedly believed that Zarpandit could be changed and liberated into an independent woman, and that they would be the achievers of this radical transformation. After so many months of watching her lack of progress, however, they seemed to have lost faith in her. But this they didn't let slip. Instead Miriam said: "We found this card and thought it could be of some interest to you."

"Take the card," Debra Ellen Thompson intervened with a tired smile. "She is a professional. Go and see her."

What Zarpandit asked in return, what else was uttered that day, she wouldn't remember. Maybe it was nothing significant to remember, or maybe, far too significant. Whatever the mnemonic mystery, the foggy words of that talk faded away, but the card remained.

On the front:

Ava O'Connell, M.Ed., LMHC

FEMINIST JUNGIAN PSYCHOTHERAPY

Experienced therapist committed to integrating the
principles of feminism with the practice of therapy

Fees negotiable

On the back:

Low self-esteem / self-hatred / stress / grief / co-
dependency / anxiety / depression / lack of will / relationship problems / everyday life concerns /
trauma recovery / sexual identity concerns / public speaking fears / shyness / eating disorders . . .

If you think one or more of these are relevant to
you, we can help, give us a chance.

Zarpandit thrust the card into her bag, and to her surprise, had
no difficulty in finding it whenever she wanted to give it a second
thought. Two weeks later, as she was sitting on a bench munching a
chocolate bar and frowning at squirrels, still unsure what to do with
the card, a chestnut fell from up above the highest branches right
under her feet. The thorny shell cracked open, like a mouth forced
into a sad-sack smile on the verge of a confession. She took the
chestnut's message as an affirmation, and decided to give this Ava
O'Connell a chance, until she received any sign to the contrary.

Old Wine in New Bottles

Ava O'Connell looked "less" of everything her card made one visualize, especially when she crossed her stick-thin legs as she did now. Less aged, less rigorous, less sturdy, less tall . . . she certainly looked less *professional* than Zarpandit was expecting.

"There's a set of questions I'd like you to reply to before we start. It's pretty much routine, we'll go over them as quickly as possible. But the information is essential for me to get a glimpse of your personal history. Will that be OK? How does that sound to you?"

"How does that sound to you?" was Ava O'Connell's refrain. But Zarpandit did not know this yet. All she knew at this point was, it sounded fine so far. So they went through a set of personal questions, including her age (nineteen), her place of birth (Massachusetts), her religious/ethnic background (half Jewish, but since it was her father and not her mother who was Jewish, Zarpandit didn't know what that made her in total), any medications she had been prescribed in the past (there was a delicious cough syrup she used to fake a sore throat to deserve, but she couldn't recall the name), any childhood diseases (sore throat), any heart problems (none), any genetic illnesses recurring in family history (cancers of various types), any mental illnesses in family (there was a paranoid schizophrenic racist uncle who over the last ten years of his life couldn't walk on the streets without changing the side of the road whenever he came across a bank, for he deeply feared crashing into muscular black robbers with masks on their faces and guns at hand—more a suppressed fantasy than an open fear, Zarpandit suspected; there was a cousin who couldn't drink water in restaurants or from tubs because she firmly believed that if anybody decided to poison her one day this would be the way; there was an aunt treated for several psychosomatic illnesses for her constant complaint of feeling deep inside like she was being suffocated by everything around her, but that might not count, for after long years of mistreatment it was discovered that she had an unusual type of asthma. Apart from those, of course, her mother didn't look sane at all, and Grandpa had died with Alzheimer's but Zarpandit kept the last two pieces of information to herself).

When the questions were over, Ava O'Connell wrote in capital letters at the top of the page, slurring the words melodically: "And your name is . . . Deb-ra El-len Thomp-son."

"That's right," Zarpandit beamed, fully enjoying her new identity.

Somewhere in the middle of that session a crow perched on the window, and Zarpandit paused to wonder whether it was a good sign or not. She couldn't decide with so little data. Meanwhile, however, her fixation was detected by Ava O'Connell, and already turned into a source of inquiry. Hence, in the ensuing minutes, Zarpandit found herself floundering with a new set of questions, which gradually drifted her toward a muddled monologue on the signs and premonitions scattered all around us. When she sensed it didn't make much sense to proceed in this vein, she switched to an even more muddled monologue, this time on birds.

"I guess I envy birds, like many people do. But I envy them in a different way. It's not their wings that I'm after. I mean, flying can be interesting, but I'm not particularly attracted to that. I envy birds because of their names. We've only one name, or maybe two. But birds have hundreds of them. Even a single species of fowl has so many different names."

"But tell me, Debra, why do you think having so many different names is so *good*?" Ava O'Connell asked, crossing her legs once again.

Zarpandit noticed a funny thing about her. When she crossed her legs, her face got cross, too, or maybe it was the other way around, maybe when her face got cross she crossed her legs. Anyway. She would never learn.

Why having so many names was so good?

But why is it that a person is given a once-and-for-all name when she or he might have been called any other thing, even with the same letters of that name huddled in a different order? When was the opportunity to rename everything around us, including ourselves, taken from our hands? How can I manage not to worry about being permanently stuck to my name, when my only consolation for being me is a chance to the contrary?

I am anchored in a world that fixes names forever, where letters are not permitted to be in frenzy. But every time I thrust my spoon into the alphabet soup, I hope to fish out new letters to recompose my name, and along with that, recompose my fate. I long for the possibility of *no longer being what you used to be in hands that were always anxious . . . throwing out even your name like a broken toy . . .*

That was the most eloquent speech Zarpandit had made in a long time. But it was hard to tell that Ava O'Connell looked impressed. "I would like you to talk a little bit about your mother," she declared, obviously seeing no harm in wrenching her from the reverie back into her own reality. "How does that sound to you?"

"My mother . . ." Zarpandit gasped and tried to gain some time, scanning every single object in the room. Alas, the room was minimalistically furnitured. " . . . is a terrible cook."

Any other, any further information about her mother, she felt deep inside, would be like revealing a secret of hers, which she didn't think she had a right to do. As to her being a terrible cook, there was no harm in mentioning that. It was no secret.

Speaking of secrets, however, not everybody was just as sensitive to privacy. Before the week was over, all the girls and squirrels back in Mount Holyoke College seemed to have learned that Zarpandit was "under psychotherapeutic supervision." That being roughly the outline of the gossip circulating, its embellishment depended on the taste of the recipient. Hence, as rumors twirled, Zarpandit was victimized as a child, sexually harassed by her father/brother/uncle/neighbors, battered by stepmother(s), adopted at differing ages between one and ten, accidentally learned about her adoption at differing ages between ten and twenty, had been addicted to this imaginary drug with ever-changing names that was responsible for her superego defects in the long run, and so it went. The fact that nobody fully trusted the fragment of the story she'd heard of only made the urge to discover the rest all the more irresistible.

Whatever the yet-to-be deciphered reality, and how grave it might turn out in the end, everyone conceded Zarpandit *must be* going through a tough phase. Nonetheless, that was not the only reason why they had started to treat her better, for in her absence, the group had noticed . . . well, nobody quite knew how to put this but it looked like . . . they'd missed her!

Bizarre are the ways of collectivities. Though in the final instance it is popularity that everyone is after, the overall demand for the one who is unpopular and introverted can exceed that for the one who is popular and extroverted. The former are pretty much like oxygen, of no definite value while they are around, but urgently craved in their absence. Hence after being distanced from the group and cordially delegated to a therapist, in the ensuing stage of her student life, Zarpandit found herself welcomed by those who had ousted her, now benefiting from a tenebrous tolerance that she, in turn, used not to get closer to them but to distance herself further and better. Her "deviance" being finally acknowledged and astoundingly appreciated, she could keep on the same track and enjoy the autonomy. So far, that was the basic change Ava O'Connell had brought to her life. This, of course, she wouldn't reveal when asked about the course of her therapy sessions. For that specific question Zarpandit had a specific answer in reserve. "We're making progress," she would say, and then add broodingly: "But it'll take time."

They would benignly nod. Somehow it made sense. *Progress*

seemed to be the golden key to the gateways of collaboration. Once considered *in progress*, anything, anyone, could be generously credited. What was so sinister about the illusion of "being in progress" was, however, less what it made others expect from you than what it made you expect from yourself. For if you repeat the word often enough, you might end up believing in it. With this drive, one windy day as they had stopped to look at a pair of ducks by the Lower Lake, Zarpandit made her first notable attempt to criticize Debra Ellen Thompson.

"You object to *everything*," she sniped out of the blue. She'd intended this as a tiny teasing, but dithered in the middle, and panicked toward the end, ". . . just for the sake of . . . objecting to *everything*."

But Debra Ellen Thompson didn't look offended at all as she slouched solicitously after a second of silence: "I appreciate what you've said."

"You do?" Zarpandit gasped.

"I definitely do. Self-criticism is always the most difficult to fabricate in any type of human collectivity. We as a group have to be careful not to live in a state of constant self-approval, and encourage instead self-criticism, no matter how thorny and hurtful it might turn out. I know you've doubts about the group. But I also know your doubts are going to be much more contributive than the blind devotion of many others."

Zarpandit was taken aback, more by the tone of crunchy mildness on crispy kindness than by the things she'd heard.

"Listen, why don't you bring this up in the next meeting? Make another presentation, but not on one of your studies this time. Give us a critique of ourselves."

A critique of *them*? No way. But Ava O'Connell would sure like the *sound* of that.

And yet she made it. Next week, in the next meeting, there she was in front of the group, criticizing *them*. Grievously doubting everything that was about to come out of her mouth, Zarpandit felt she should dip her words into a murky sauce of "maybe" as often as she could: "Maybe emancipation should not be imposed from the outside . . . The project to bring out the best in every woman can be damaging sometimes . . . for some of us maybe. Not that it is a bad idea in itself, but maybe if we drag it too forcefully, what comes out may not be the best in that woman . . ."

May it be or not, something miraculous happened when she gave a pause. They agreed! All of them.

She didn't know, and thereby had quite a hard time snatching a reasonable handle out of the hubhub that followed, that there was already a splinter in the group, which preceded her presentation and actually had nothing to do with it. Her role in this stage was trivial. Like when a newly washed tablecloth, pure white and silky, accidentally falls from the balcony where it was left to dry right on top of a bike rider passing underneath, covering his head and eyes for a few seconds, enough to direct him right in front of a bus coming from the other side, and causing the driver to steer the wheel until the bus rammed with its thirty passengers into a pet shop, heaving the puppies and kittens in their cages, and shattering the tanks in which Japanese fish peacefully swam. That kind of trivial. Within seconds following the picayune stimulus of Zarpandit-the-tablecloth, a chain reaction was on its way unearthing the long-covered-up power conflicts in the group. As easily as a huge, juicy, and ripened watermelon heaved to the ground, the group cracked into two major parts and one slim slice. What had gathered as a cohesive group came out of that room as three new clusters, each of which took a new name to differentiate itself from the others.

The first group, led by Miriam, was called *Hush-Hush Daughters*. By its nature, the "love that dare not speak its name" required not to be articulated, they claimed, and instead, advocated integrating lesbians into the larger heterosexual society. To a certain extent they might be said to have already achieved some success in that end, for even though lesbians were constantly mentioned, there were none in the group.

The second faction named themselves *Capists*, an abbreviation for *Concerned About the Preservation of the Embryo*—a term borrowed from Kant, who was bold enough to assert that a woman's character, in contrast to a man's, was totally defined by natural needs, and concerned about the preservation of the embryo, which in turn implanted fear into her character and made her in need of masculine protection most of her life. The Capists, instead of attacking Kant, genially embraced his biased diagnosis along with the strategy of deliberate distortion. Unavoidably, Debra Ellen Thompson was at the center of this group. So was Zarpandit somewhere in its periphery.

The third group, the smallest of all despite the name *Femini Mundi*, voiced the need to organize along broader lines, in the name of a sisterhood that transcended class, ethnic, religious, and national boundaries. This all-encompassingness, however, was more a result of the group's population than a cause of it because here was gathered a motley composition with little in common except perhaps those that did not want to take a part in the power struggle between Debra Ellen Thompson and Miriam, as well as some others who wished to stay aside at the moment, in order not to lose their bargaining chances with each group in the foreseeable future.

As usual, the split had radicalized each faction in its own way. Radicalized and reembittered, Zarpandit would add, since they all seemed to have drifted back to their customary coldness toward her, as if she were some kind of an agent provocateur, the walking incentive behind the Great Crack.

"In our first session, you'd said something very interesting about yourself. Something like . . . *letters in frenzy*. Do you remember that, Debra?"

That was the worst part of therapy. First they encouraged you to prattle lavishly, without any reservation whatsoever, and then they noted down everything you said, so that they could judge you on each and every one of them.

"The other day I was having lunch with Helen Lehman, a close friend of mine who publishes this local magazine in Northampton. She was telling me how desperate she is because the woman who used to reply to readers' letters has all of a sudden left the job. So, she urgently needs someone to replace her . . . then, as I was listening to her, I recalled what you'd said the other day: 'letters in frenzy.'"

People with difficulties speaking in front of the public can be quite skillful in writing, you know? Now look, you owe me for the last five sessions, I owe Helen a favor from the past, Helen owes us nothing. So here is the deal. Go and visit her sometime, see what this job is about. How does that sound, Debra?"

Zarpandit took a deep breath, almost a sigh.

"Actually she can see you today. Did you have anything special to do this afternoon?"

No, she didn't have anything special to do this afternoon, nor the one after. But why did they always care to ask when they already knew the answer?

Letters in Frenzy

Zarpandit took her time roaming around Northampton, watched the spectators contentedly watching a street pantomime, ate a banana but avoided the letter inside, drank hot chocolate at HayMarket observing families and couples, mused on what good Ava O'Connell had brought to her life, couldn't find much of an answer, and ate another banana. In a local newspaper, on the sports page, she read about the story of the first group of Holyoke Catholic High cheerleaders from 1947–48, the year Sacred Heart, Our Lady of the Rosary, and St. Jerome schools had combined for sports. There was also a photograph of the "Cheerleading Pioneers"—eleven girls, six standing, five sitting. Beneath the photograph the names of the girls were written, back row, front row from left to right. At the end of that list there was a sentence that attracted Zarpandit's attention more than anything. It said: "Missing from the picture is Gartheride Keith."

Zarpandit tried to imagine her. Was she any different than the others? Why was she missing from the picture? Had she not wanted to have her picture taken or had something prevented her from doing so? But perhaps it simply was the way things were and had always been. The law of absences required that there always be a cavity, a loss, something missing from each and every entirety. While she mused, she finished two more bananas and drank another hot chocolate. Despite all the lingering, she was still at the given address on time.

Inside, she found a tasteless office, world-weary workers, and a Helen Lehman, just as she had expected, except that Helen Lehman didn't seem to be expecting her.

"Oh sure, I was waiting for you," she finally nodded as the blaze of confusion marring her face disappeared at hearing Ava O'Connell's name being pronounced. She was bony and shortish, just like Ava, but also stern, unlike her. Her gaze was abrasive, her voice not at all. "I must have your name wrong, sorry, honey. Wednesdays are hell in this job. Every Wednesday I forget who I am . . . but never do I forget who my husband is!!"

Zarpandit unchained the chortle she felt she should.

"To be honest with you . . ." Helen gaped suspiciously at this dark-haired, plump girl, with a brownish stain of chocolate to the left of her upper lip.

"Gartheride," Zarpandit said, her voice slightly wavering.

"To be honest with you, Gartheride, I'd never give this job to someone who just walks in. Especially not after what that bitch did to me. I come here one day, where is Ilena, nobody knows. Vanished! Can you imagine?" She snorted her disapproval in an inflated sigh. "But Ava is a good friend, she wants you to try this, and she gave me her word. Now look, honey, we might not be *The New York Times*, but we got readers that confide in us. Confiding in . . . *you* . . . oh, but you are so young . . ." Another sigh.

Zarpandit thought that must be it. She would now be kindly shown the way. But the way Helen Lehman showed led her into a room where a fairly modest pile of letters was waiting for her. Having always suspected it was the editors that made up all those readers' letters in these magazines, she was surprised to see the ones in the pile were from real people, with real names.

"She was a clever bitch, that Ilena. Terrific. I mean, I wouldn't give a damn about her personality, but she did her job well. I don't know how you'll be able to replace her."

Zarpandit tried to feel snubbed, but something in this woman's smile, so quirky and impish, made her unsure if she should.

"Please don't take it personally." Helen Lehman noticed the confusion on the other side. "OK, listen, let's give it a try. But we don't have to let our readers know what's going on here. Readers are conservative people who expect to be treated as if they were not. They won't like to see their correspondent change. Ilena had been answering their letters for more than six years now, giving hundreds of responses, which I can assure you, honey, people *do* take seriously. She is supposed to be ideal, out of time. Now we can't tell them, she was, as a matter of fact, an asshole! That bitch took two months' payment in advance and vanished with her creepy boyfriend. No, dear, we cannot bother our readers with these details. We need to retain Ilena's name. You got it?"

Not yet. But she sure had begun to enjoy it.

"We cannot expect people to confide in us if they are made to write to someone different every month. That'll be like saying 'Sorry folks, we screwed up here.' Can they trust us when it's 'Dear Ilena' one week, and the next week it's 'Dear . . .'?"

Zarpandit ran to her aid: "Gartheride."

"Yes, listen, we don't have to inform our readers that from now on they'll be corresponding with a young girl with no experience in life because the preceding correspondent ran away with the editor's money. We'll pretend Ilena is still here, but not alone anymore. She's got an assistant: Gartheride! You got it?"

She had. Almost.

"Of course, we might need to make a few arrangements first. Why don't you two, for instance, reply to the same letters from two different angles, like the optimist-pessimist duality? Because Ilena was a bitch, she should reflect the dark side of life. And then Gartheride will speak in the name of the bright side. It'll be like hearing your angel dispute with the devil. And we'll let the readers decide! They'll love it!" she beamed, becoming more and more enthusiastic about the idea the more she heard herself talk about it. "Believe me, honey, I know my readers, I know women, and I sure understand their needs better than those bunch of therapists, including dearest Ava, but don't be so mean as to tell her this!"

Zarpandit smiled at this wiry little woman full of life, full of profanities, none of them deconstructed in accordance with the strategy of Deliberate Distortion, suddenly sensing they were going to be the most unlikely of friends.

"Honey, why don't you take a seat and start working . . . on . . . this one here, for instance." She picked up a letter from the pile, patted Zarpandit on the shoulder, brought her a cup of tea, and then left her alone in that besmirched room.

Dear Ilena,
Three weeks ago I met this guy. He changed my life. We
instantly fell in love. Last week I moved into his apartment.
It's breathtaking, he's everything I wanted. Except for a
small problem. It turns out there are three of us in his
apartment. He lives with an iguana. This sorry, ugly, green
creature moves on chairs, carpets, as if it was the owner of
the house. Every time I look at it I feel like I'm going to
throw up. To cap it all, Stephen (that's my boyfriend) wants
Edgar Allan Poe (that's the iguana) to sit at the dinner
table. It has its own plate and eats lettuce with us. It really
turns me off but I can't say anything.
    What shall I do? Shall I move back to my house? But
we were so perfect. Shall I stay here, and try to love Edgar
Allan Poe? Do you think love can be learned in time, as our
mums wanted to make us believe?
                                                Annie Lee

Zarpandit stood stone-faced for a minute. But why not, she then thought, communicate with this Annie Lee from another planet. To concentrate better, she drew a shining sun, tried to recall a few aphorisms the girls back in Mount Holyoke Scotch-taped on their doors, and then began to write.

Dearest Annie,

Love that merits its name is a priceless gift from God. When
you believe this gift has been given to you, you shall be
utterly honest toward it and also toward yourself. If Stephen
is as wonderful as you say he is, he should try to understand
your feelings. Talk to him. Tell him how much you love him
and how much you enjoy being in this house with him, but
also tell him it has been hard for you to live with Edgar
Allan Poe, and ask him to show you a way. Be frank. Love
needs no curtains. And do not forget that if you'll always be
sincere with him, he'll always be sincere with you, too. I am
sure you both will figure out the best solution.

Blessings,
Gartheride

That done, Zarpandit sketched a dark moon to help her focus on
the next stage, and tried to reckon what Ilena would write if she
were here. As she pondered, the image of Ilena in her mind's eye began to blur with familiar female faces — a pinch of Professor Harley,
a pinch of Miriam, a pinch of her mother, and spoonfuls of Debra
Ellen Thompson.

Annie honey,

I really have a hard time understanding young American
women these days. How could you move in with a guy
you've only known for three weeks? Anyway, there is no
use in crying over spilled milk, so let's see what you can do
now.

Obviously, talking to Stephen is one option you might
consider. But let me tell you in advance that it will *not* work.
He will be offended. Even if he does his best, there will
always remain a stain of resentment deep down in his soul.
And that malicious seed, honey, will grow and grow there,
until one day, while discussing something completely
irrelevant, you'll notice you are in fact quarreling over the
iguana case that you'd thought was long forgotten.

So, here is my suggestion. Keep this a secret and
pretend not to mind living with an iguana. Do not
exaggerate. Do not go around giving kisses to the animal
when Stephen is around. Don't try to fool him. Just be cool
and act as if you really don't mind. Let some time pass, be
patient. And when time has ripened and the right day
comes, here are your two options:

a. Leave the door open, let Edgar Allan Poe run out. It may
    work, though Stephen might still be resentful, and accuse
    you of being careless.
b. Put a sleeping pill, some barbiturate, whatever, in Edgar Al-
    lan Poe's food. This will help to slow down its motions.
    When it is dizzy enough, put the creature under a cushion
    where Stephen is likely to sit, and make him *eradicate* his own
    iguana. All guilt will fall upon him, and your role will be to
    console and comfort. Promise him you'll get him another
    iguana. He'll probably tell you, it'll never be the same, that
    Poe was so special, and not a replaceable commodity. All the
    better.

But I'd still advise you not to leave it there, and get a
pet you two can get along with. Why not a cat? You'll be
three in that apartment again, but on your terms this time.
You are a big girl. Use your mind.

Good luck in all your deeds,
Ilena

P.S.: What sort of a person would name an iguana after
the revered Edgar Allan Poe? Are you sure this is the
right guy?

In the following days, and weeks, and months, Zarpandit
the feminist magpie, Zarpandit the chauvinist swine, Zarpandit the
gullible tablecloth, Debra the therapy subject, Gartheride the agile
correspondent, and her many other apathetic names under camou-

flage, Balkanized selves in constant clash, all staggeringly, startlingly, miraculously found a room, warm and secure, in this new
role of assisting a woman who was only a name to answer the private
letters of people who were no more than names. So much elusiveness
did her so much good. The relief of watching the real and the imaginary blur serenely, the relief of being surrounded with ever-changing
names, the relief of being able to speak simultaneously in two voices
ceaselessly veering from one to another, the relief *of throwing out even
your name like a broken toy, of no longer being what you used to be in hands
that were always anxious* . . . It was this ambivalence that helped her to
handle her anfractuous world of angst. Being given an opportunity
to swing freely between two poles soothed her bipolar pendulum.
After all, the cure might be of the same essence as the illness sometimes, just like the counterpoison is soul sister to the poison.

   Toward the end of the second semester, while sitting alone on a
bench near the Lower Lake, watching the once frozen waters now
spurt deliriously, seeing the world from behind her dual imaginary,
imaginary duality, Ilena and Gartheride, Gartheride and Ilena, she
poured the letters at hand inside the Bowl of Eden, and stirred and
stirred the alphabet soup until all letters were in frenzy again. As the
metaphorical spoon of evanescence drew circles, the idea of henceforth attaching a real spoon somewhere on her costume, perhaps
onto her wavy hair, crossed her mind. That spoon would constantly
remind her that whatever name she found herself attached to, could
be erased and replaced with the letters of another name.

   When the whirl of her thoughts had finally soothed, she took the
spoon out to see what it had brought her. On it was a new combination of letters that read: GAIL. She liked the *sound* of it and decided
to keep it as her new name.

   The name Ömer Özsipahioğlu would marry seven years later.

THE STORK

Newcomer in the
New Continent

Ömer Özsipahioğlu first set foot in America in mid-June 2002. Just like countless newcomers to the new continent before him, he felt simultaneously a foreigner in a foreign land and yet that the place he'd arrived at was somehow *not that foreign*. What America did to the conventional stranger-in-a-strange-land correlation was to kindly twist it upside down. In other parts of the world, to be a newcomer meant you had now arrived at a new place where you didn't know the ways and hows, but would probably and hopefully learn most, if not all, in the fullness of time. In coming to America for the first time, however, you retained a sense of arriving at a place not *that* new, since you felt you already knew most, if not all, there was to know about it, and ended up unlearning your initial knowledge in the fullness of time. Probably in a similar vein, before he started living here, Ömer Özsipahioğlu had the country's snapshot and chronicle clear and trim in his mind; all he needed was to fill in the holes, to work on the shady parts, and to catch the details. Before his second month was over, all he was left with were those holes and parts and details, the general text having evaporated sometime somewhere.

Before, he used to perceive America as a despite-its-vastness-and-variety-simple-in-essence land, somewhat like a diluted solution that came in all sorts of bottles with more or less the same basic ingredient in each. After he started living in it, his perception of America was altered to despite-its-simplicity-too-vast-of-a-variety land, more like a concentrated powder you could turn into myriad drinks depending on how you diluted it. And then there followed a third stage, when the clumsiness and curiosity of the early days had oozed away, leaving him within a blunt riddle of foreignness that did not necessarily demand to be solved, at last accommodated but not as attentive to facts and details as he was before. This, he assumed, must be his "personal adaptation to cultural adaptation."

Various factors must have facilitated this process, particularly the *S*-factors. After all, he already was an avid fan of *Seinfeld*, a devoted *Sandman* reader, addicted to *The Simpsons*, and to *Saturday Night Live* to a lesser degree; pretty much aware of the significance of the Sundance Film Festival, an ever-great devotee of *South Park* and everything in and around it, and a well-trained admirer of the queen of punk, Patti Smith. He fully respected Art Spiegelman's *Maus*, the Tupac Shakur legend, Steppenwolf's "Born to Be Wild," especially in the opening sequence of *Easy Rider*, liked Sean Penn, and everything Stanley Kubrick had produced, though he could also understand why the distinguished director had largely disowned *Spartacus*, despite the *S*. But he could always cover that loss of *S* with his affection for Susan Sarandon. Given his relentless coffee-holism, he was ready to become an insatiable customer of Starbucks. Though from a distance, he'd sure kept a keen eye on Steven Spielberg and Stephen King, and had been interested in news of sex scandals and serial killers. While he mostly enjoyed making analyses of each of the series of *Star Wars*, he was usually silent on *One Flew Over the Cuckoo's Nest*, the movie that he utterly adored, and made him curious about Salem. Deep down in his soul, Ömer Özsipahioğlu felt ready to contend against any authoritarian Nurse Ratched–like figure blocking his way in the new continent. As the list expanded in a similar vein, he seemed relatively well-equipped with regard to *S*-factors. In spite of what many Americans would presume, this foreigner was better acquainted with their culture than with his own.

The *S* no doubt is a prolific letter, but the alphabet is far ahead. Soon he would find out the little he knew and the many other letters he had to become skilled at. There certainly was a lot to catch up on, quite an array of daily practices to wonder and learn about. It was, however, not the learning part that irritated him eventually but the catching up part. Ömer Özsipahioğlu was, in every single layer down to the lowest echelons of his soul, demoralized and unsettled, poo-scared and exhausted into slow motion by the hyperspeed of that crepuscular hologram called "time." Anyhow, *what was time?* Though he appreciated the point St. Augustine had raised, he still doubted the saint really knew the answer even when no one asked him what that was. Ömer sure didn't. And yet, it wasn't the definition, and not even time per se that got on his nerves, but what she was supposed to be doing all the time: flow . . . and flow . . . and flow . . . It was precisely this flowing part, and flowing not as in lyrical meandering but as in galloping at full speed, that made him so tense about it. Time, to his slightly myopic hazed squint, was constantly to be problematized, compartmentalized, analyzed, stigmatized, and measured, never accumulating into a meaningful whole, never getting anywhere. There was no way of stepping off time. It was this all-engulfing womb giving birth to dead babies, and immediately impregnating new others without even mourning for the ones passed away. She suffocated little by little, careful to give enough air to breathe, so that she could suffocate you longer.

When he was a child, and his brother was a child, and when after a too-early heart attack their father had been advised some leisure for which he could only think of hiring a sullen fisherman to take him and his sons every Sunday at dawn right into the open sea where they would all sit shivering for hours and hours silently staring at the dark waters of the Bosphorus, back in one of those old days, Ömer had seen the swollen corpse of a cat flowing along the tide before it got caught in the net. Having fished out a dead cat, his brother had thrown up, Ömer had stopped eating fish, and maybe then, maybe after a while, their father had renounced the idea of recreation. To his knowledge, nothing had happened to the sullen fisherman. Looking back at the incident now, he likened the idea of time to that rabid tide in which dead and living bodies swam together.

And since time itself was intolerable, Ömer Özsipahioğlu found it all the more intolerable to measure it with time. Hence, he wore no watches, needed no alarm clocks to wake up early, and ended up failing to wake up early. Punctuality had never been among his merits. Meetings, classes, schedules, duties . . . he was usually late for all. If there were any clocks in the public places he happened to pass through, he glanced nervously at them, failing to understand why they were scattered everywhere and how come nobody was disturbed by the constant obligation of having to mind something that did not mind being minded at all.

That's how he had been living back in Istanbul, and once in Boston, the old habit did not fade. And yet, though the practice remained the same, the ways in which it was practiced had slightly changed. In order to learn what time it was in Turkish, you asked people if they had a "watch." In order to learn what time it was in English, however, you asked people if they had the "time." It was as if in the latter you possessed time or at least the possibility of possessing it, whereas in the former, you possessed the means to measure time but never time itself. Having observed this cultural-linguistic distinction, Ömer didn't know what to make of it. All he knew was that like many who end up engrossed by what they try to avoid most, behind his mind's rim he couldn't help gauging the pace of time. Disgruntled with the conventional time-measuring system, unable to abandon the idea altogether, he had developed some sort of an alternative measurement, which he used wherever and whenever he could. The idea was simple: To redress the balance, in measuring what he liked least, he utilized what he loved most: music!

Rather than hours, minutes, and seconds, he used albums, songs, and beats. The length of a period between two succeeding things was tantamount to the length of a certain song played over and over again. Basically, it was good to be reminded that unlike time, music could always be rewound, forwarded, paused, and replayed. Music was no swollen corpse. It did not glue itself to the one-way current of time heading toward a phony notion of progress. The circular loop of songs eased the burden of the irreversibility of linear time.

So his flight from Istanbul to New York did not last eleven hours fifteen minutes; it lasted dozens of albums and hundreds of repetitive songs. The plane took off with a ten-minute delay at 10:45. Facing huge screens spangling flight and time information, this Ömer couldn't help noticing. At 10:46, the child in the front row started to cry, and Ömer put on his headphones, listening to Roger McGuinn's "It's Alright Ma" twelve times until the tea service. Thirty thousand feet somewhere above the Balkans not much had changed in their lives, with he still playing the same song, the child still crying the same cry. The time between his first request for extra coffee and the second must have lasted four minutes, ten seconds because that was precisely what The Stone Roses' "Made of Stone" lasted. And after the stewardess made that joke about handing him the whole jar of coffee, the time he needed to soothe his anger lasted twice as long as Barry Adamson's "Save Me from My Hand."

Once he had calmed down, he started pondering. But pondering is no ordinary process on a transcontinental flight. It is an ontological trigger. Soon Ömer found himself wallowing in a set of existential questions, such as what was he doing (not in this plane but in life), where was he going (again for that matter), why was he leaving his country, what difference would it make to have a Ph.D. in political science in America, was that the real reason why he was on this plane or was he sort of running away from the person he was, and so on. Somewhere above the Atlantic Ocean, the set of dragging-down questions was replaced by a set of uplifting decisions. Broadly, he decided not to be himself anymore. Particularly, he decided to be more tolerant, which also entailed that he be less tense and more tranquil, to concentrate on his work, to strive for his lifelong goals, and if he didn't have any to find a decent one soon, to make some sort of an inner peace with his past, to stop trying to change his parents and being frustrated when they would not, to stop confusing quasi-love with love and to refrain from jumping into new affairs until the latter arrived, to be less skeptical toward others and more sure of himself . . . in short, to mature as quickly as possible.

The feeling that arose afterward was so peaceful and soothing that he felt like the transformation had already begun, that he was already a more mature person. He sure could have flown the rest of the three thousand miles with this conviction, had the child in the front row not turned back at one point, still crying as loud as he could, still with no visible tears in his round, hazel, hypocrite eyes, and for some wry reason, tugged Ömer's headphones as he was listening to The Pixies' "Where's My Mind" for the sixth time. Ömer yanked the headphones back, perhaps a bit too harshly, but given the child's personal history, did not feel responsible for the crying that ensued. Still, after a few minutes, he would feel bad about the incident, looking retrospectively at the poor score he'd obtained in his first maturity exam. Though from then on he kept an eye on the child and his painfully bored mother, just like linear time, they, too, refrained from giving him a second chance to be a better man. The sign to fasten seat belts turned on, and in this state of mind he landed in America.

Once in JFK Airport he didn't score any better when the brand-new personality he'd become found itself in a phone booth making calls to Istanbul only to decipher the mess left by his predecessor.

"It's me!" he said and then paused, as if those two words had epitomized all he wanted to say and he could thereby hang up. But Defne was too excited to notice anything.

It was ironic in a way. They had been dating for two years now, in the last six months of which they had been breaking up slyly, slowly but steadily. And then, before or after he couldn't tell, but sometime around the day she learned Ömer had received an acceptance from Boston University, Defne's love had suddenly undergone an epistemological break, only to come out of it all the more intensified and deepened, doubling her resentment when the moment of farewell arrived. "Why didn't you go before?" she had asked and reasked. Although she had specified no precise date for that "before," they both knew it could be any time in between their mutual infidelities, habitual breakups, or following that postabortion crisis when she had confessed it wasn't his baby, and they had spent weeks and weeks of him torturing her to learn the name of the father, her torturing him with her silence, him torturing her some more, her eventually confessing it was him and no one else, that she'd been lying all this time to make him jealous, him never believing her, her never forgiving him for not believing her, on and on and on. They could have parted at any one of those crossroads but not now, Defne seemed to presume, not now.

Once it had become clear that he'd be leaving in the summer, they had spent the rest of their time together feigning he would not, and thereby avoiding the pain of making plans about a dubious future, when Ömer would come back with a Ph.D. degree in hand. Just like peppers left in the sun to dry, a child's tooth expected to fall anytime, they had delegated the task of bringing this affair to its long-awaited end to Ömer's lifelong antagonist: time!

"I know I shouldn't have, but I missed you," she said.

Ömer instantly passed the case to his new mature personality who after an edgy, ponderous silence, finally murmured: "What time is it there?"

It was noon in Istanbul.

"I missed you, too," he then added, as if learning it was noon there had made it easier for him to reveal this here.

Next he called home. Talked to his brother. Ömer didn't need to ask him anything to ascertain that his mother was not at home at the moment; otherwise, she'd never let anyone else answer the phone.

After the calls, he had twelve more minutes before the check-in for the New York–Boston flight. He put on his headphones and listened to David Bowie's "I'm Afraid of Americans" subsequently five times. But there were more urgent things to be afraid of, as he would immediately grasp once on the next plane. The nightmare child and his mother were passengers on the same flight, sitting next to him, even closer this time. The child looked startlingly calm and cute, though, as he kept licking a huge lollipop of a pinky pink that reminded one of nothing but chemicals. Every time he lifted his head from the lollipop, Ömer expected him to start crying again, but he simply did not. This, Ömer Özsipahioğlu found all the more annoying, and drew the conclusion that aberrant serenities in life were harder to handle than expected disruptions.

In Boston, he was welcomed by a friend of a friend who took him to a friend of his who had a spare room in his MIT dorm to stay in for a couple of days. On the way there, they took the T, and only then a taxi, to save money. How unwise Ömer had been to make this long trip with wheelless suitcases would be unveiled once down at the T. As they struggled to drag along his three huge suitcases through the rush-worn corridors under the pitying gaze of nocturnal passengers, Ömer thought to himself, it was sort of ironic that his very first act in this new city should be sweeping off its dirt.

When they'd finally arrived at the MIT dorm, all three suitcases had been damaged here and there, one of them badly torn at the bottom. As they entered the spacious building, Ömer caught sight of a pretty brunette shimmering an enchanting smile of a perfect set of white teeth to her cell phone while she stared in the direction of the door. Though the smile was obviously reserved for the person at the end of the line, for the one unable to see it, Ömer still felt glorified, and smiled back. The brunette's almond eyes flashed with a brief surprise as she was torn from her talk to see what she was already staring at, distinguishing this tall, slender, comely guy struggling in visible pain to push inside two huge suitcases and smile at her at the same time. Seeing that much of an effort there, she felt obliged to correspond, give another enchanting smile, this time to him directly.

The friend of the friend of a friend was a short, scrawny, to-be-genetic-engineer, who seemed too-full-of-his-too-fond-self, and eager to introduce Ömer into a network of Turkish friends or friends of Turks. A wide range of information (from everyday details, like how to make calls home cheaper, or where to buy good-quality black olives for breakfast, to sharing academic interests and personal gossip) seemed to circulate through this network of shaky solidarity, occasionally causing minute explosions here and there, in a chain reaction. Once you introduced yourself, whatever problem you might face here as a foreigner, you could always find some friend of a friend of a friend that could be of help, and give valuable advice, and whom you were expected to help back one day.

It wasn't solely the Turks doing that. All other international students were entangled in similar national networks, some of which overlapped, crisscrossed, or simply collaborated with some others, therein creating further networks of even shakier solidarities. Still, the farther the country of origin or the harder the conditions met here, the swifter these networks seemed to mushroom, albeit less rhizomic in their burgeoning. Birds of migration were the most peculiar of all fowl. Initially, they detached from their own flocks to migrate to faraway lands, and once there, they flocked into detachments.

To find a place to stay in for a few days, Ömer had already laid his fingers on the network and touched it for the first time. But the moment he felt the tepid, humid organism aspiring to engulf him in return for the sense of security it promised to provide, he'd instantly stepped aside. Whatever the outcome, despite the threat of lonesomeness, he preferred to remain outside flocks, his and others' alike. That being no easy resolution to expound to the to-be-genetic-engineer friend, though, to avoid the trouble Ömer could only think of taking shelter in a flaccid, jet-lag slumber. Hence, he basically spent his first two days in America sleeping-dreaming that he was in America.

On the third day he opened his swollen eyes, and though he instantly tried to close them back, he soon had to accept the surly fact that he simply couldn't sleep anymore. He dragged his sacklike body out of bed, put on his headphones, and went for a stroll to see what the city that would foster him for the following four or more Ph.D. years was like. As he sat absentmindedly sipping large mugs of dark coffee at a café in Harvard Square, listening to Patti Smith sing "Paths That Cross," he watched the motley multitude of people pouring from side streets, buoyant stores, the T, and everywhere. Suddenly an increasingly captivating sense of revelation descended over him. Here he was, surrounded by hundreds of faces of dazzling variety, and not even one of them looked familiar. None of these individuals had any idea who he was. Not even one single soul. He

was a nobody to each and all of them, so pure and immaculate—
absolutely nameless, pastless, and, thereby, faultless. And because he
was a nobody, he could be anybody. So wonderful was his azonal
void, of a substance so translucent almost invisible under the veneer
of anonymousness; such a consummate stranger he had become in a
world of suffocating familiarities, where too many were recognized
down to the minor details of their personal histories. He finished the
coffee and glided toward the door with a touch of superciliousness
added to his long, thin legs and storklike walk, fully enjoying the
exclusiveness of being a total eclipse, the unique freedom of being
here, right in front of everyone, and yet seen by no one. The freedom
of . . .

"Ömer! *Abi naber ya, n'apıyoуun burда?*"*

Tossed out from the poetic glaze of his delusions, Ömer frowned
in the direction of the voice. His vision-fogged eyes needed some extra seconds to recognize the tubby man in shorts happily yelling at
him. Back in Istanbul, long long before, a family of four but capable
of making the noise of ten had been their neighbors for several years.
Their two teenaged children were twins so much alike you could
never tell who was who. Now, standing in front of him was a grown-
up replica of one of those boys with a huge grin on his no-longer-
slim face. Ömer didn't bother to pretend he was delighted, though he
managed to turn on a semiamiable smile, as he stood there listening
to him babble about his life as a petroleum engineer, his American
wife, and projections for the future. The guy wrote down a bunch of
phone numbers saying he should definitely call, definitely come to
dinner sometime, and definitely meet a network of good Turkish
friends.

Henceforth robbed of the privileged pleasure of being a nobody
on his way back to the MIT dorm, Ömer decided it was time to start
looking for a house. And to find a house to live in in Boston as a grad
student required finding housemates to live with.

---

*Ömer! What ya doin' here, brother?

Housemates

The first thing Ömer noticed when looking for a house and housemates was being late again. Most ads seemed to have been circulated
in the past weeks, and an overwhelming majority of them answered
back within the same period. Hence, by the time he started the
search, his choices had been rather reduced to the pulp of the business, including the most expensive homes or the cheap but in dire
shape, and the most demanding housemates or the demand-nothing-
provide-nothing types. Then he came across this:

Two Ordinary Guys and a No Ordinary Dog Looking for
Clean & tidy, environmentally conscious, & spiri-
tually reflective & psychologically balanced &
well mannered, & respectful (or at least trying to
be), but most of all

FRIENDLY HOUSEMATE

To share 3 BDRM Apartment
Pearl St. Somerville Convenient Location
Hardwood Floors/High Ceiling/Big Windows/ Yummy Pies
750/MO PLUS UTILITIES

Leaving all others aside for the moment, Ömer decided friendly he was not, housemate he could learn to be. Besides, after days of restless search, he was tired of reading the ads in the papers, surfing the Net, going all around the city. It had to be this one. He called the number. A sleepy male voice with a heavy accent answered the phone. He spoke with short, curt, edgy sentences as if about to go back to sleep any second.

"You've got the address," the voice hurried. "Come tomorrow! No, no! Come today! Seven o'clock!"

"Aren't you gonna ask me anything?" Ömer stammered with all the experience he had gained so far.

"Like what?" the voice grunted impatiently. A loud crinkle came from the end of the line, like a bag of potato chips being opened.

"I don't know, how about asking my name?"

"No need to!" responded the voice now escorted by grinding effects. Definitely potato chips, Ömer thought. If he waited long enough on the line, he could even tell what particular kind. "We've got a questionnaire here for all those things, if you don't mind. OK?"

Ömer gave a reluctant "OK," more a quizzical prologue than a toning resolution, but before he had the chance to ask what was meant by *questionnaire*, the voice was gone.

Still in the booth, he inserted the phone card for long-distance calls to the Middle East. When checking the lists for each phone card to decipher which one to buy, he was disappointed, in a way typical of Turks, to detect Turkey excluded from the list of European countries on whose card a glamorous night image of the Eiffel Tower shone, and included instead among Middle Eastern countries on whose card glowed a camel. It looked like a blissful camel, with that smirk on its face. Having seen none before, Ömer wondered if a camel could ever smile like that. And with that particular doubt in mind he reached Istanbul.

"Hi Ma! Did I wake you up?"

Though he obviously had, she would obviously deny it. But it was better this way, Ömer thought, much better. She would be more confused and thereby less instructive when pulled out from deep slumber.

"Are you all right? What happened in the typhoon?"

"What typhoon, Ma?"

The day before, some tropical storm had caused colossal dam-age, tattering roofs, spoiling crops, shattering windows in some city or maybe small town. She couldn't recall the name of the storm-hit settlement but was sure it was somewhere in America.

"It is nothing to worry about," Ömer sighed. What difference would it make to tell her he had not even heard about it.

"Be careful," her voice dwindled into a compassionate whisper. "Promise me you will be very careful."

He did. He promised he'd be very careful with cyclones and tor-nados, natural disasters, terrorist attacks, serial killers, gang wars, or a single bullet that could come out of nowhere for no reason at all.

Then, with whatever was left in the smirking camel's stockpile, he dialed Defne's cell phone. Unlike his mother, Defne was awake. Awake and drinking with friends, hers and his, somewhere among one of those small, white-clothed tables in the most bacchanalian street of Istanbul where everyone sat side by side, and drank and chattered, drank and grimaced, drank and sang, the whole street af-ter a while, floating featherlike on a rampage of verbal blunders. That's where she was, carousing at one of those tables. There was so much noise in the background, Ömer had to keep shouting at the uproar she was in, getting nervous by the echo of his own voice in the small booth, under the partly curious, partly chiding but fully distant gaze of the pedestrians passing by. On the other end of the line, a gurgle of laughter was unleashed as the rest of the table learned it was he calling. Next, Defne's cell phone was transmitted from one to another as everyone seemed to have something to say to Ömer in their cigarette-tainted alcohol-blurred voices. Some were close friends but now sounded aloof, others previously aloof now sounded close. Still he could sense a dose of an obscure, quashed re-sentment in the tones of most; a resentment that those left behind tend to feel for the one who has gone.

A torrent of images flooded Ömer's brain. He could see the table they were sitting at down to its minor details—an assortment of small, appetizing dishes, the smell of fried calamari and grilled fish, eggplants in olive oil, little triangular pieces of white cheese, and the

lavish garden salads waiters kept refurbishing, and a bottle of rakı
swiftly shrinking while the talks deepened even more quickly. And
the ice . . . he could spot the small cubes of ice melting furtively in a
metallic bucket at one end of the table. He could spy on the commencement of a long night, every particular stage of which he could
more or less presage from this phone booth in Harvard Square.

"Hey *Ömer the Johnny*, the first sip is for you," yelled someone at
the table but Ömer couldn't recognize the voice.

He could predict the aftermath, too. After the final bottle of rakı
had been emptied, brains too much fogged, and the food congealed
into a sad squander on the once-pure-white plates, after the Gypsy
musicians had been paid, and each coffee cup used to divine the future of its drinker, he could stalk them as they'd leave the table, only
to be engulfed by the snaky side streets of Istanbul.

"E-mail me tonight," Defne hollered when she finally managed
to tow her phone back from intruders. "Tell me everything. I'll read
it when I wake up."

He said he would. She said she would be waiting. He didn't
understand what exactly she would be waiting for, his e-mail or
homecoming. An awkward pause. Another blast of laughter in the
background. She started telling him what the joke was about but
the line was cut off.

When he came out of the phone booth Ömer looked at the
crowd in Harvard Square absentmindedly, losing the sense of continuity in time. On his way back to the dorm, he listened to Leftfield's
"Open Up" seven times as he chain-smoked three cigarettes. At the
entrance of the building he saw the gorgeous brunette again, exactly
where she was standing the first time. She was talking to an elderly
woman who looked like her mother, a mother pleased to see her
daughter's pleasant room. Ömer walked to the elevator, this time
turning his head slightly to avoid any eye contact.

He was planning to have a nap, then take a shower and e-mail
Defne before going out to see what this ad was about. But because
he overslept he was able to accomplish only the first task on the list.
He dressed in a panic, rushed out to the street, took the T, sat down
next to a pregnant black teenager, and tried not to feel lonely, not to

feel anything in particular at this moment. The ride must have lasted ten minutes fifty-six seconds, tantamount to four times Cypress Hill's "Hits from the Bong." He got off in Davis Square, asked someone the time, heard it was 7:38 p.m., walked Pearl Street from one end to the other, asked someone the address, then walked all the way back, and finally found the house: a typical ashen wood frame house.

"You are late," said the guy who opened the door, smiling affably despite the tinge of scolding in his voice. He was shortish, had dark, bright eyes, quite curly russet hair, and a funny cleft in his chin that softened the frown on his wide forehead. Ömer thought he might be an Arab, but he couldn't be sure. The only thing he could be sure of was that this wasn't the guy he had spoken with.

Inside, the door opened into a small porch, leading them directly into a spacious kitchen that looked extremely clean and buoyantly colorful. As he took a quick glance around, Ömer couldn't help wondering if it was the creation of a female's taste, but kept the suspicion to himself.

"Welcome!" called another guy from the other door. He was a bit taller than the other, and certainly much more bulky, almost chubby. He had gentle hazel eyes behind round glasses, and dimpled, almost crimson blushed cheeks germane to the diabetics or to the uncomforted. Ömer liked him instantly.

A few words of courtesy and many more glances of curiosity were exchanged as they stood in the kitchen, which Ömer was now starting to notice had a spicy faint smell of its own. In the living room, they asked him where he came from, and once they heard "Turkey," in unison they delivered: "Oh, Turkey?"

By this time Ömer had already gotten used to it. People in America asked him frequently where he came from, and once they got the answer, too often they bounced it back either in an instruction format—"Oh, Turkey!"—or in a question format—"Oh, Turkey?"—inspecting his face with affable curiosity in the meantime, as if saying respectively, either "Oh, that is too bad!" or "Oh, is that too bad?"

"So, is it possible to see the house?" Ömer asked.

"Sure, you can see the house," the ruddy-cheeked one nodded, his voice now revealing it was he on the phone. Ömer thought he might be Hispanic, but couldn't be sure. "But first things first. We have a small questionnaire. It doesn't take much time."

"Just to see if we'll get along well. Why the rush?" confirmed the short guy. "As they say, we are not eating eggplant, are we?"

Ömer couldn't think of an answer to that. Neither could he think of a housemate questionnaire until he saw one.

HOUSEMATE QUESTIONNAIRE

The following questions are not intended to judge your personality or morality but only to gauge how well we'll get along, for the benefit of all. Thereby, please answer them frankly.

1. People who know me well enough will tell you I am:
   a. Deeply, if not pathetically, obsessed with cleanliness & order
   b. Neat & tidy
   c. Neither tidy, nor worryingly untidy
   d. A bit disordered
   e. A mess!

2. Concerning *The Sopranos*, my policy is:
   a. Miss no episode
   b. Suffice it to say, I have the James Gandolfini Hand-Signed Pasta Photograph
   c. To watch it as long as I can spare some time for the petty things in life
   d. I'd love to see it on DVD someday, but gotta study now
   e. I don't like opera

3. If one day I have an overnight guest, that person would most probably be:
   a. A relative
   b. A close friend

c.   My fiancée/long-term partner
d.   A one-night stand
e.   It might be anyone, as long as I enjoy the company

Ömer inhaled through his teeth, struggling to make sense of whether it was some sort of a joke or they were serious about this absurdity, so that he could decipher what exactly he should hate them for. If the latter he would hate them for their arrogance, if the former, for their sense of humor. He shot a probing look at the two guys but spotting in return that nerve-wrackingly kindhearted smile on the faces of each, he doubted if they'd decoded his glare-message correctly. He then decided to go for it as quickly as possible. Why bother with reading it all through? Just mark the same answer for each question, and then see what happens next. After a shred of hesitation, he chose that fixed answer to be "e" and started e-ing everything they asked.

---

4.   If a show notorious for its religious/ethnic/racist/sexist/national-
     ist bigotry appears on TV, my next step will probably be:
     a.   To turn it off immediately and prevent others from seeing it
     b.   To watch it for a while and give myself a chance, perhaps I'll
          enjoy it
     c.   To watch it all through with scientific neutrality so that I
          might analyze this social phenomenon better
     d.   To watch it all the same, no big deal
     e.   I don't watch TV!

5.   Concerning music my preference is:
          i.   classical/ii. blues&jazz/iii. rock/iv. heavy metal/v. new
          age/vi. ethnic, which I relish listening
     a.   With headphones all the time
     b.   Without headphones but as low as possible
     c.   Only as loud as it can be heard in my own room
     d.   Perhaps loud enough to be heard from upstairs
     e.   LOUD!!! The way music should be if it is to merit the name

6. Concerning sleep, my habits can be likened to:
    a. Hens. Sleep early, wake early, save the day
    b. Owls. Stay up late at night, wake late
    c. I sleep late but wake early enough, and don't know which particular animal does this
    d. Cats on sofa. I luv sleep
    e. A dog named Arroz the Insomniac

7. If one night all of a sudden I decide to invite a whole bunch of friends with whom I'd been lingering the whole evening, my very next step would probably be:
    a. Call home first, get permission from housemates
    b. Invite people, and then call home to inform my housemates
    c. Invite the people and make them call my housemates
    d. Invite people, skip the calling home part, but arrive at the house before others and inform housemates about the group on the way
    e. To pop up with all those people and surprise my housemates

8. Concerning horror movies, my basic opinion of them is:
    a. They are a visual opium astutely disseminated by the hegemonic powers to keep young people away from all sorts of critical thinking that might disrupt the status quo
    b. They are just a waste of time
    c. Not very favorable but still might watch 'em every now and then
    d. Might watch them only if they are cinematographically good enough
    e. What's wrong with horror movies, I luv 'em

9. Concerning Rita Hayworth's performance in *Casablanca*, my honest opinion is:
    a. It was one of her best performances
    b. Classic I guess, like in all classic movies
    c. I've no particular memories of Rita Hayworth
    d. I've no particular memories of *Casablanca*

   e.   The movie was pleasant to watch but also replete with sugar-coated Orientalist bigotry

10. Concerning garlic, my general approach is:
   a.   Negative. I can't stand its smell in food, and not on people please!
   b.   Indifferent. It makes no difference to me as long as the food is tasty
   c.   Democrat. I never consume garlic but do *not* mind when others do
   d.   Affirmative. I don't mind people eating garlic and I do eat too
   e.   Partisan. I luv garlic!

That was it. That was the whole stupid thing. Ömer leaned back, crossed his arms, frowned his brow, and so badly wished he could light a cigarette now, so deeply longed for a dark dark dark coffee.

"We'll evaluate it immediately," the Arabic-looking guy uttered jovially as he took the form and added: "Speak the truth, even if it's as tough as the feet of an old retired washing-lady, they say."

Who are *they*? Ömer tried hard to avoid asking. Who else on earth was reiterating these phrases? But his nerves were quick to be appeased with a generous platter of blueberry pie put in front of him, which he hoped would be accompanied by a hot drink, coffee for instance.

"It's delicious, my girlfriend is a great cook," the Hispanic-looking guy bobbed his head, flushing a deeper hue as he pronounced the word *girlfriend*.

And then they disappeared.

When alone and upset that there was no coffee on the way, Ömer scanned the room but couldn't find much on which to focus. A huge, comfy couch, a buffet, a big-screen TV, a pile of videocassettes, the one at the top of which read *Texas Chain Saw Massacre*, some magazines in Spanish here and there, comic books everywhere. Ömer sighed and took a bite from the pie, and immediately took another one. He wasn't expecting it to taste so good. The first slice had been almost finished when the door behind yawned, and in slipped the biggest, gawkiest, black-and-white Newfoundland with the most crinkly face he'd ever seen. Just under the left eye he had a nutlike, black stain, which made him look like he'd been beaten badly in some street fight. And whatever the fight, it must have left him starving, for after a pithy, reluctant sniff to get to know the stranger inside, the dog's entire attention was focused on the blueberry pie. He mostly welcomed the piece offered, instantly chomped it, and looked back at Ömer all the more coveting with those miserably black, miserably ravenous eyes.

Fortunately, they didn't make him wait too long. "Has the jury decided?" asked Ömer as he saw the guys coming, his voice sounding more edgy than he'd intended, with the tension of being torn between handing the whole pie to the dog, or bearing that heartbreaking stare for the last five minutes.

"Congratulations! You have scored the highest in our garlic test."

"What garlic test?" Ömer asked puzzled but almost sensed the answer. "Was all that nonsense for garlic? Why didn't you ask me directly if I had anything against garlic?"

"Oh, but then it would be too obvious," came the answer.

They introduced themselves. The Hispanic-looking one turned out to be from Spain. His name was Joaquin but for some reason he preferred to be called Piyu. He had a fellowship from Tufts School of Dental Medicine. The Arabic-looking one turned out to be Moroccan. His name was Abed and that was exactly what he wanted to be called. And he, too, was affiliated with the same university, working on a degree in biotechnology engineering.

"What about the dog?"

"Don't ask me," Abed bellowed. "Ask Piyu and only him. That giant stomach over there is his dog."

"He is the Arroz in the questionnaire." Piyu appeared with a small broom in his hand, sweeping in a blink of an eye a few crumbs that Arroz had dribbled on the carpet. "Arroz the Insomniac. Don't let him deceive you, he is always hungry."

So, whatever was left of the blueberry pie they kept to themselves. Ömer asked for something to drink, coffee for instance, and Abed brought him a large a cup of tea that smelled like Vicks.

After that, having decided to sleep in his new house tonight, Ömer went back to the MIT dorm, grabbed a few things, left a note to the to-be-genetic-engineer Turk, and discovered that when you knew the way, the road from the T to his new house lasted four times System of a Down's "Chop Suey." Once back at his new house, he found his three new housemates glued to the TV screen, watching *The Sopranos*, the questionnaire now making more sense, at least with respect to one question. There was a new pie on the buffet, and when he asked for something to drink with it, coffee for instance, Piyu brought him a large mug of hot chocolate.

"There is one other thing you forgot to include in your questionnaire," Ömer said as he inspected the creamy sauce seeping from the pastry after a bite. It was apple and cinnamon this time. "I am a smoker and if you don't mind, I'd like to smoke in my own room."

"Our rooms are our rooms," said Piyu, without tearing his gaze from the screen.

"By the way," beamed Ömer, visibly relaxed now that he had the smoking permit, "are you sure it was Rita Hayworth in *Casablanca*?"

"No, you are damn right," Abed said shrugging his shoulders to double the effect. "That was the trick question."

So it turned out that they liked tricks.

Tricks, they surely liked. Even as to the issue of garlic it was hard to say they had been completely honest. In order to be able to fully understand the depth of the leak in the information alluded to him, however, Ömer had to start living with them. Not too much time though, even one week was enough to get a clearer picture.

Hence, during his first seven days in the house, Ömer found out his new housemates were neither garlic-consumers as they'd claimed to be, nor garlic-lovers as they'd hinted, but merely *garlic-worshipers*, whatever they maintained their true religion was. Garlic was deemed almost holy here, the master signifier in the house.

Speaking of distorted facts, that didn't seem to be the only item on the list. First of all, there were things about the house they had forgotten to mention. Nobody had told Ömer that, like many homes in this part of East Somerville, this one, too, was pretty rough and worn out. The good news was that a renovation had been going on for some time. The bad news was that it would be going on for some more time, implying that he might have to endure a ruckus every morning when the workers appeared on the stairs sloped onto the facade, with a hammer in each hand. Likewise nobody had warned him about filling the bathtub on the second floor because then all the water in the tub dripped downstairs, right down from the kitchen ceiling. These and the like were still a mystery to Ömer Özsipahioğlu.

At the moment he was learning other things. Take this Abed, for instance. Ömer sure didn't know the guy was so tremendously garrulous, overflowing with protests, comments, and proverbs to toss out on almost every topic. Oddly enough, so much talking did not seem to exhaust him at the end of the day. Every night he still had nearly enough energy to watch two horror movies so he could sleep with composure. Most of the time, in the midst of the second video, he fell asleep on the couch, snoring peacefully while the characters in the movie met all kinds of awful deaths. As to that thunderous snoring of his, it seemed to be yet another encumbrance Abed's faintly aquiline nose brought into his life. Suffering from a most hectic hay fever, his whole life, past and present and future, seemed to be under the yoke of his nose. Vicks, mint vapor, inhalers, nasal sprays . . . and a whole lot of stuff that might not mean anything to many others, were lifelong buddies to Abed.

And about the other guy, Piyu, there were things to learn, too. He was obsessed with cleanliness and hygiene. As if long before having given up hope about others, he did all the cleaning himself, which was fine at first glance but a bit tedious in the long run. A buck, a crumb, a wad . . . the instant they fell to the floor Piyu started cleaning, terrorizing everyone around, and making them feel like dirty pigs. In addition to his obsession, he had a remarkably odd phobia for pointed objects, even for those slightly bristled. He could not stand the sight of a knife, let alone touching one. It was because of him that there were so few knives in the kitchen, and most food was eaten with chopsticks or spoons. As to the question of how then would he be able to practice his profession as a dentist, at first Ömer did not feel close enough to ask him, and when he did, he sensed that Piyu would rather he did not ask. Piyu liked neatness and orderliness not only in the kitchen, but in every aspect of his life, striving to keep things under control at any cost. Was that the reason he preferred to sleep on the third floor? Ömer couldn't tell, but it looked like he wanted to be as near as possible to God. He was a devout Catholic, and his girlfriend even more so. A young Mexican American as thin as ice despite the great cook she was, and with deep, saturnine eyes, unlike her name: Alegre.

There were facts to discover about Arroz, too. Concise, brute, and unconditionally muted facts, for Arroz was deaf. His ears clogged, his eyesight never that good, Arroz had delegated his nose his one and only guide in life. And in this, he was exceptionally competent. He might not be able to hear sounds, not even screams, but he could *smell* ticks, tinkles, zings, and even the faintest susurrus. Day and night made no difference to him because this contemplative looking nine-year-old male Newfoundland did not sleep. All night long he patrolled the house, looked pensively out of each window, ate every edible thing within his reach, and stood watching each house member in his deepest sleep for hours, trying to sniff where they'd gone when their bodies were nailed here.

So on the last day of June 2002, Ömer fell asleep feeling lucky to have a pleasant home in a pleasant neighborhood, with three housemates each minding his own business in his own walk of life. And as days and nights evolved, he gradually woke into another reality where he was this foreigner in America who lived with an exceptionally talkative Moroccan and an exceptionally phobic Spaniard, not to mention the exceptional hunger of the dog, in this worn-out Somerville house beaten by mallets and hammers every morning. All of this for $750 a month, plus utilities.

Alegre and Agony

Monday morning sitting at her desk in Doctor Marc Fitzpatrick's office, Alegre had already finished reading all the new issues of all the weekly women's magazines. Now, on the page open in front of her, a six-year-old girl smiled in toothless pride under the headline "The Girl Who Can't Stop Reading!" The girl was said to have learned to read at the age of five, and from that day up to the moment of the interview had finished reading 2,278 books, a sum she planned to increase to 4,000 by the end of the year, reading six books a day. "We can't keep up!" her mother feigned to whine, and her father heartily confessed they lugged the books home from local libraries and bookstores in a huge bin. On the next page, there was another picture of the girl, this time in pajamas in her bed with the parents sitting on each side as if she was ill but they were all happy for that.

Alegre took another magazine and peered inside. Over six hundred women had been surveyed to find a strong connection between a woman's favorite soup and the way she interacted with her partner. Preference of chicken noodle indicated you were more like a mother hen in your affairs with men; if minestrone, you wanted to get things out in the open; if vegetable soup, you were always resourceful and self-sufficient; and if you'd rather have tomato soup, that made you an active adventurer. Alegre, on the other hand, had her own favorites. She would fancy spicy gazpacho or lentil soup with chorizo when she cooked for friends or family; when in a soup kitchen she'd rather have bean and beef soup to distribute to the homeless; if alone at home her preference would be plain-zucchini-boiled-in-plain-water soup for herself, and when dining with others at restaurants she'd choose sweet-and-sour soup to binge and vomit. The survey did not include any of these options, so she skipped the page.

Besides, she'd rather avoid thinking about her affairs with men. As a matter of fact, that meant only one true affair with one man so far, but Piyu and she had split and reunited so many times that she felt like she'd had numerous affairs. On the next page, the five surprising ways to get ahead at work were presented. First: *Speak slowly!* A survey had proved that speakers who spoke slowly were rated as 38 percent more knowledgeable about the topic than those who spoke more quickly. Alegre put a check mark on that. Unlike *las tías*, she had always been a slow speaker. Second: *Be polite.* Another check mark. Third: *Volunteer for charity.* Volunteers for charity were 25 percent more satisfied with their jobs and had more self-esteem another survey had found out. Several check marks. Last summer Alegre had bowled with veterans in April, one-on-one tutored the children of a Somali refugee family throughout May, sorted dry goods for distribution to area shelters in June, and since early July she had served food at Kate's Soup Kitchen to those in need. Suggestion four was to *keep a journal* in accordance with another survey that had proved people who regularly kept a journal of their hopes and dreams were 32 percent more likely to reach them. Another check mark.

Fifth: *Get in with the right crowd.* "If you go out to lunch with the slackers," said a psychologist with confidence, "then your boss will associate you with them and consider you a slacker, too, even if you work hard." Alegre put the pen down, pouted at the photo of the psychologist, and gave that some thought. At lunchtime, three days a week, she joined a therapeutic reading group designed to help women with eating disorders. Certainly not the right crowd, the usual suspects this psychologist here was telling you never to be identified with in the eyes of your boss. And yet, the situation was somewhat more complex for it was no other than her boss, Doctor Marc Fitzpatrick, who compelled Alegre to go there. She skipped the page.

"I wonder how long it'll take you to notice I'm standing here."

Alegre slumped in the chair, but quickly restored a smile at Doctor Marc Fitzpatrick standing right behind her. The doctor, in return, adjusted his lips into a line that could have been confused with a smile by people who didn't know him, and perhaps even by Alegre herself, were it not for that familiar scowl in his eyes. "I see you worried these days; you look thinner, too. Are you losing weight again?"

Alegre swallowed hard, her face cramping as if she'd just gulped down a top-secret microchip to be digested rather than handed to the enemy. For a few seconds she remained pensively silent. There was no use in denying, for then he would make her step on the weighing scale. She lamented more than anything that ominous afternoon she'd confessed to him that yes, *sometimes* she did have *concerns* about her body. That was all she'd said, nothing more. And the very next day she'd found herself irretrievably subscribed to this therapeutic reading group where three times a week she had to sit in a circle of insanely bored women with boringly sane Connie and read all the more boring books written by women who'd overcome their eating disorders, women "with stories to tell." Discussions of chapters of these books were followed by lengthy, grueling, and usually gloomy passages from world literature. As these were read aloud, they all had lunch together, on a dish cooked by someone in the group assigned with the task of "up-cooking"—a term coined by Connie.

The whole project was developed by Connie, an ambitious psychology graduate determined to win some eminent psychology award before pursuing a career in neuropsychology. She proposed that the gravest problem that women with eating disorders faced was not *food* but *loneliness*. Eating, for them, was an act of solitude. Mostly, they had few people around and dined alone. Thereby, Connie suggested bringing these women together in three expanding circles. The inner circle: The reading group where each member was proof to every other that she was not the only one. Circle two: Through books written by women in similar circumstances all around the United States, the members were made to realize how nationally widespread were the problems they had long been suffering all alone. Circle three: The circle of recognition was expanded to a global level via passages from world literature, specifically chosen to challenge cultural notions of "food" and "body." To this end, they regularly read about countries that suffered from hunger or famine, or cultures that valued plump women. Once they had read a story about this African boy, Chiamaka, and another time a story about an Arab woman trying to gain weight to be the sheikh's favorite in the harem. To be a part of Connie's project to get the award she so rigorously pined for did not make Alegre feel any better. Meanwhile, she doubted deep inside that this collaboration between Connie and the infantile neuropsychiatrist Marc Fitzpatrick was merely *professional.*

"So how is Alegre doing in the group," he asks in the chic serenity of a hotel room (for he was married and so was she) as Connie kisses, licks, sucks, and nibbles his nipples, adoring his not-even-one-gram-of-fat body. (The doctor went to the gym regularly and three days a week at noon breaks he went to the sauna, at the time Alegre was in the reading group.)

"Oh, you know how Alegre is. Her chances are so slim, surrounded with that mega-macho Latino culture. On top of all that, her great-grandaunt is a terrible role model for her. Alegre cannot possibly challenge her aunts. She has no control of her own life!"

"I know, sweetie, I know," Doctor Marc Fitzpatrick coos, his voice lilting with pleasure, holding Connie's head tight between his hands before pushing it downward. At the thought of that, Alegre instantly lowered her eyes as if she'd feared her boss would see in them the voluptuous fantasy she was building around him and Connie.

"You'll be at the reading today, won't you? You can leave early if you need to," the doctor gasped as he peered thoughtfully at the cheap snow globe on her desk, which he otherwise liked for its tidiness.

In the snow globe Nuestra Señora de San Juan de los Lagos

stood in a lagoon-blue cloak, with pink-red flowers under her feet.
Every time you shook the globe, a blizzard of gilded snow calmly enveloped her. Alegre kept the snow globe on her desk all the time but
she seldom shook it.

"And please, Alegre, try harder to open up. Connie is brilliant.
You can trust her. Not everyone has to be a Catholic priest to deserve your confidence, no?"

That was typical of him. Doctor Marc Fitzpatrick liked to think
of himself as an open-minded Christian respectful toward every religion and creed in the world, provided they were not dogmatic. The
problem with Catholicism (and Islam, and Judaism, and Hinduism)
was that they failed to comply to this standard. However, he was always careful not to discuss these matters with people of these creeds.
He never passed judgment on Alegre. Instead he preferred to help
her *find the truth herself*. Many a time over the last weeks, Alegre had
found periodicals on her desk with news of the Catholic Church con-
troversy in Boston. That sort of indirectness, too, was typical of
Doctor Marc Fitzpatrick.

A minute later, right when they seemed to be on the verge of
tumbling into a prickly silence, the doorbell rang, to Alegre's relief.
It was Mrs. Serrano with her mentally disabled six-year-old son,
Manuel. While his mother was inside having a private talk about his
situation with the doctor, Manuel stayed with Alegre in the waiting
room, silent and compliant, with a colorful book in each hand.

Manuel adored books. Everywhere he went, he took five or six
of them with him. And books, too, must like him, for they let him
scribble iridescent whirls on their pages, scribble and scribble until
he finally got bored of doing that, and tore them all into a thousand
pieces. He liked confetti more than anything.

Only when alone with Manuel did Alegre shake the snow globe
on her desk.

Between 10:33 and 10:35 a.m., a UPS van loaded with letters
and boxes, a hacker on his way to break into the computer of one of

his professors who he heard had accused him of being a "hacker," a Norwegian tourist lost on his way to the Museum of Modern Art, and a pizza delivery boy who had just received two phone calls from people unknown to him—the first from someone ordering a large vegetarian pizza with extra mushrooms, the second from someone informing him his girlfriend had dumped him last night—plowed through Pearl Street, each in his own rhythm but similarly pensive and quiet. As they passed by one after another, a brawny, buoyant worker on a ladder leaned against a three-floor house under reconstruction sedately watched them all from up there, whistled a tune he'd heard back at Joe's this morning, took out the hammer from his belt, and started hitting on the slack nails of the front. Exactly at the same time, on the other side of the wall, Ömer slumped in his sleep as if smacked on the face and opened his eyes in panic to his first morning in his first house in the U.S.A.

After the noise, what struck him even harder was the sharp smell in the house, a smell that got more intense at each step toward the kitchen. There they were. The three of them. Piyu frying sausages, Abed stirring eggs, and between them Arroz with his dark, miserable, hungry eyes waiting to be fed.

"Good morning!" chorused his new housemates in unison.

Ömer threw an irritated look at them. Always a little nervous in the mornings, how people could manage to be so meaninglessly merry and endlessly energetic when they woke up was a puzzle to him.

"We couldn't figure how you would like your eggs, so we're making an omelet." Piyu smiled assuredly. "This sausage is not pig."

Ömer felt a slight headache coming on: "I don't mind pig. I don't like omelet. Where is the coffee?"

"You don't like omelet?" wondered Piyu.

"You don't mind pig?" wondered Abed.

And then they wondered together: "Coffee? Do you want coffee?!"

But it was more an inauspicious exclamation than a promising question. For it turned out the new housemates had a coffee machine

(it must be in the cupboards) but no coffee at home (they remembered seeing some somewhere). But if he changed his mind, he was
more than welcome to share some mint tea or hot chocolate.

Thus, on his first morning in his new house, Ömer had to make
several discoveries, including that the nearest place to buy a bag of
coffee beans was a deli on the other block, the walk from home to
there and back lasted five times Barry Adamson's "The Vibes Ain't
Nothin' but the Vibes," there was indeed a coffee machine in the
cupboards, a pretty good one surprisingly, but the coffee mill had
tired out long before, and that it was so stupid of him not to have
bought a cup of coffee with the beans that would at least have helped
to trounce this emergency. He passed the rest of the morning repair-
ing the mill, and he managed to convert the beans into a gritty grainy
powder before the brawny, buoyant worker on the ladder took his
first break. He then reverentially carried a cup full of this pitch-
black steaming creation back to his room.

Having finally calmed down, he pouted thoughtfully at a
wrapped piece of paper. Before he had left the MIT dorm, he'd introduced himself to the brunette, asked her name, learned it was
Tracey, and then told her that as he was moving to a house, his only
chance of getting to know her was to exchange their numbers now,
which he was more than willing to do if only he had a telephone, so
why didn't she instead give him her own number? To his disbelief
she had.

After all, just as Piyu and Abed had misinformed Ömer about
themselves, he, too, had concealed certain truths. Not that he had
lied about the fundamental issue of garlic, or anything. He was easy
to get along with generally . . . theoretically . . . as long as he got his
coffee, and cigarettes, and weed, and alcohol. A good housemate he
could turn out to be, for sure, under normal addiction conditions.
What he had failed to notify ahead was the likelihood of a range of
women visiting the house in an endless chain of succession. More
precisely, what he hadn't preinformed, or even prehinted, was this
glaringly fallible but incessantly duplicable attraction and repulsion
of his life: girlfriends!

Ömer's temptation toward the opposite sex could be likened to a toy car's pathetic tussle in front of every obstruction that it bumped into as it hurtled confidently on its path. Just like those battery cars, each time he failed to climb over the block and tumbled on his back, he tussled hard like a turtle turned head-over-heels, and when he finally managed to complete the somersault, he reclimbed and retoppled, again and again, never considering changing his ways, until his batteries were totally exhausted or some external force would pull him out of the loop. To complicate it further, that external factor to haul him out of the loop of a woman too often happened to be another woman.

"I am so sorry," Alegre puffed as she dashed in.

"It's OK, Alegre, we'd just begun," said Connie, smiling circularly to integrate everyone in the circle into her smile. "Amy was telling us about her interpretation of Maureen's journal."

Amy Alberts had gained some sort of a reputation and quite a bit of money selling the dog biscuits she made at home before she was harshly swept off the market by her own daughter and hospitalized for a nervous breakdown. Ever since that day she could not eat, not even stand the sight of wheat, bran, rye . . . anything that resembled the color or ingredients of the dog biscuits she was once so proud of producing. This food therapy was part of her recovery, that's what she said, but Alegre too often thought she came here just to poke her nose into other people's lives, and that was probably why her own daughter had turned away from her. In any case, she was undoubtedly the feistiest of the group, the apple of Connie's eye. In order not to lose this superiority she worked hard, interpreting every detail in every entry of *My Food Journal of This Week* that every group member was vehemently *encouraged* to make. Alegre thought herein resided the main problem with group therapies. Some group members ended up confusing themselves with the therapist.

"When I saw Maureen's journal, when I saw the things she ate this weekend, I felt sad and angry . . . Sad and angry," Amy repeated, in case she hadn't been understood the first time. "Look at her Saturday. Fried potatoes, onion rings, double hamburger! Junk food. The same on Sunday. Obviously because Ken is at home on weekends, and this is what he feeds on. When Ken is around, Maureen can't be herself."

Ken, as they all knew by now, was Maureen's second husband. Every session, he drove her here and then picked her up when it was over. Alegre wondered if he had any idea how deeply he was disparaged by complete strangers, and if not, would he still heartily bring his wife when he learned.

"What about you, Alegre? Did you bring your journal?" asked Connie.

Alegre smiled politely as she distributed a photocopy of her last-week's journal to every member of the group, and lastly to Connie.

Monday 24th: I came to work decisive and energetic. Dr. Marc Fitzpatrick had seven appointments, it was a busy day. Turkey sandwich at lunch. Dinner at home.

Tuesday 25th: I visited *la* Tía Piedad at the hospital. She wanted me to bring her gazpacho, and to come with Piyu next time.

Wednesday 26th: At work all day. A ham sandwich at lunch.

Despite Connie's insistent warnings, Alegre's journals were curt and cryptic, revealing little about her inner soul, and even less about the food she binged on, and certainly nothing about what she vomited shortly afterward. The group looked at each other not knowing quite how to start the interpretation process. One woman volunteered to talk but was immediately shushed by others when she confused gazpacho with a man, searching for a love triangle in Alegre's life.

"Would you like to up-cook one of these days?" Connie asked when it was clear no one had any other interpretation to make.

Alegre nodded affably, as polite as always. Cooking was, after all, what she did best in life, and the only good thing about being here. She put down her journal and took out her To-Do List of the Next Week and wrote down: Up-cook for the next session!

During the rest of the session Connie read the confessions of a man who called himself Fat Chic Admirer. The guy had always dated fat women, and then one day had written this manifesto to tell the whole world the reason why. He fervently criticized the Western culture for imposing this bony straitjacket on women, and favored instead other cultures where girls were fattened up to make them desirable. He gave the example of Latino men who, he said, were fond of *las chicas gorditas*, for they were wise enough to know "the bone is for the dog, the meat is for the man."

Alegre, meanwhile, sat silently, pretending not to have noticed several group members inspecting her skinny breasts with a scathing smile.

Americans!!!

It wasn't the fault of the bold, burly man, a local beekeeper who had come to Boston from Amherst to renew his contract with several store owners here, that he poured a large cup of no-milk no-sugar dark coffee on Ömer's trousers when both were standing in line in the deli. The beekeeper, of course, could have been more careful had his mind not been elsewhere—his trade partners had told him they were quite content with the quality of the honey and maple syrup he provided, but they would not buy any more cider doughnuts from him. *What was wrong with his cider doughnuts*, the man was trying to figure out when he turned around, maybe a bit careless, and ran over the tall, willowy young man standing right behind him with a dour look on his face, a large cup of coffee in his hand. If anyone were to be blamed for the incident it should be Ömer and not the man, for he was standing too close to the counter, not leaving the customer in front of him any room to move. Ömer, no doubt, could have been more wary, and certainly less dour, had Elaine, his second American girlfriend, after two weeks of middling dating but promising sex, not told him half an hour ago that this *thing* between them wasn't getting anywhere. Therefore, although it looked like the local beekeeper and

Ömer that collided, it was actually the trade partners and Elaine that had done so.

When he came out of the deli with a new cup of coffee (bought by the local beekeeper), a big brown stain on his trousers, and an even darker expression on his face, Ömer walked a little bit, chain-smoking three cigarettes, listening to Alabama 3's "Mansion of the Gods" incessantly. To cheer up a bit, he decided to buy himself something nice to eat, and then decided to turn that into something nice for his housemates to eat. From a Moroccan restaurant he bought couscous with lamb and sweetened figs as a favor to Abed, and though he couldn't find a place nearby that had paella on the menu, he hoped the soft beef tacos with salsa he had bought would make Piyu half as happy as Alegre's tacos did. As for himself, he had gotten three bottles of red wine.

"Hey, what are we celebrating?" Piyu smiled his soft dimpled smile.

If truth be told, there were still eight more days to count but they decided all the same to celebrate their first month together in this house. The dinner table was cordial in its plainness and unfussiness. While Piyu curiously observed each of them, Abed turned a blind eye to Ömer's drinking, and Ömer disregarded Abed's non-drinking, both draped in a semitolerant, semi-ignorant hush that people from Muslim backgrounds reserved for one another whenever they sensed their discrepancy could be sharper than they wished to face at the moment, or perhaps ever. During the dinner, as he told them a series of hilarious stories, each galvanizing the next one, Ömer looked quite unlike the man he was in the mornings, and he got even higher when the second bottle of wine had vanished.

Soon after, however, he began to talk about less amusing things, the miseries and misdemeanors of the past, and the fear of those on the way. The sudden switch in his tone was not as out of the blue as it seemed to be, or solely attributable to the merits of wine, or not even to the acrimony caused by Elaine. The reason was somewhere else in his soul. For no matter how detached he could feel from Turkey from time to time, Ömer had absorbed the cultural ethos in which he was raised; an ethos that deemed it no good to laugh too much, or too loud, for fear that a deluge of gaiety would be followed by a deluge of agony. If you laugh so much that tears come from your eyes, the Eastern ethos advises you not to forget the simple fact that "tears of laughter" are closer to tears than to laughs.

But to listen to someone talk about his fears is like watching him yawn repeatedly. Before he finishes his stock, you find yourself going through yours. Soon Abed and Piyu had joined Ömer in contemplating what fate had in store for each. And yet, since the utmost denominator of the motley worries poured on the table was being "a stranger in a strange land," after a while the conversation irreversibly headed toward the common area of interest: "Americans!"

"Have you seen the flashy yellow CAUTION stripes they put everywhere around the library? I thought someone was stabbed or something," Piyu blurted. "And then I learn it was only the rain they were cautioning against!!!"

WATCH THE STAIRS! it flashed on the stairs. ATTENTION LOW CEILING! it said on the ceiling in every floor of Student Affairs. On the cups of coffee it read: CAUTION: CONTENTS HOT! And on fruits: SOFT WHEN RIPE! On side mirrors of cars, stickers informed: OBJECTS IN MIRROR ARE CLOSER THAN THEY APPEAR, and doors in the public buses warned that they MIGHT OPEN! Only in America could you read signs that informed SNOW SLIDES.

"My favorite is their passion for giving meticulous names to every little thing," Abed said when he came back from his room with a pile of color stripes in his hand. Each stripe was of a different color, moving from darker hues to fainter ones. "Take a look at these. They are used by people planning to redecorate their homes. Back at the store where I found them there are hundreds of them. And every single shade has been given a weird name!"

A tone of beige was named *Desert Dawn Echo*, of brown *Sand Castles of Childhood*, of blue *Celestial Riddles*, of pink *Pillow Talk*, of white *Only Yesterday*, of orange *Aron's Freckles* . . . As they squinted at the peculiar names on the stripes, the three of them bobbed their heads in collective astonishment: "Americans!"

Before they knew how, they were painting their chitchat with this common shade named *The Difficulty of Being a Non-American in*

America. A darker tone along the same stripe might be called *Anguishes of Daily Life*. All in all, the principal teachings of Buddha are pertinent to the particular cases of foreigners all around the world. For them, too, "the easiest is the most difficult to achieve."

How to make a phone call and not go homicidal when you hear the mechanical lady repeat her mantra: "We-are-sorry-your-call-cannot-be-completed" even when you are 100 percent sure this time you dialed the correct area code, inserted the right coin at the right time. How to operate a photocopy machine that works with some sort of a special card that you keep confusing with other special cards. How to decipher in a few seconds what kind of cheese (there are more than ten in the showcase) you want on which bagel (there are more than twenty different types over there) while the aproned saleslady gives you acidic looks. How to talk to a pharmacist about the itch on your penis. How to steer the intricately blatant machinery of the routine through the serpentine paths of daily life and manage not to look like an idiot as you crash over and over again? It was daily life that humiliated most, mortified like nothing else.

"It was my first month here," Abed murmured half to himself. "I went to this supermarket to buy some tomatoes. But then I saw these two dressy ladies there, chattering right in front of the tomatoes. I didn't want to disturb them, so I went in circles in the market and got some stuff I didn't even need to, and when I came back, they were still there. When they saw me coming closer once again, they stopped talking and began to watch my moves as if I was a threat or something. You can see it in their eyes. I started selecting tomatoes, but they were still staring at me. And then this awful thing happened. God, I hate my nose! I leaned forward to pick a tomato, suddenly I see my nose dripping and I know the women are seeing it too, I panic, I can't find my Kleenex, I panic more, and before I know it my nose drips on the box of tomatoes. *Ouaghauogh!* It was so embarrassing. And the only thing you see is how they see you. Here comes this fishy guy, looks like an Arab, his nose drips on tomatoes, he must be an Arab!"

Piyu and Ömer smiled amiably, knowing exactly what he meant, each in his own way. Abed seemed relaxed now, glad to have told them about this incident. And yet still, there were things he'd rather keep to himself. He wouldn't tell anyone, for instance, how nervous he'd gotten when three Muslim girls wearing head scarves entered some chic café he was sitting in. One of the girls had a baby boy in her arms, such a young mother. From the moment he saw them, Abed had started to keep an eye on their moves, and the other eye on all other customers. It was ironic in a way, for his inquisitiveness to decipher whether the people around were staring at the girls and if yes, what did they see, had instead made *him* fix his eyes on them. Then the baby had slid down from his mother's lap and started to crawl on the floor, eager to discover what was going on at other tables while the girls continued chattering vigorously. Nothing bad had happened. Nothing extraordinary. After a while the mother had fetched the baby and when they had finished their teas, the girls had left. Nobody had mistreated them, nobody was hostile or anything. What Abed couldn't explain to himself was this incredible tension he had felt until the Muslim girls had left the café. Trying to see how they were seen in the eyes of Americans, Abed's own stare had dwindled to a judgmental gaze toward the girls, especially toward the mother, getting furious at her for letting the baby crawl like that on the dirty floor. No, he wouldn't narrate this incident. Nor would he talk about Jamal, a friend of his, who had this habit of going to this store every month to complain about the shoes he'd bought from there just because every time he did that, they took the shoes back and gave him a new pair. Abed would not let slip how ashamed he was of Jamal's insatiable need to exploit the system of consumer rights—a system that many non-Westerners arriving in the rational capitalist Western world too often found *irrational*!

A prickly silence loomed until Ömer mumbled: "When you are a foreigner, you can't be your humble self anymore. I am my nation, my place of birth. I am everything except me."

It was good to share this feeling with them. But he would never tell them what had happened with Tracey a month ago, when they had begun to make love for the first time, galloping toward what seemed to them a long-postponed crescendo of desire. Still on top of her, Ömer had fetched a condom from his pocket, and whispered in her ear to help him put it on. But she had suddenly drawn herself back, exclaiming: "Is that a Turkish condom? Check if there is a slit before putting it on." Was that a joke? Was she serious? Ömer didn't know. All he knew was though he had feigned not to be offended his penis had been more honest, shrinking rapidly inside the *Turkish condom*. No, he wouldn't mention this to his housemates.

"With Latinos it is neither this nor that. They are a part of this country, but the less integrated in a way. People think all immigrants made it here, why can't Hispanics? Alegre says when she was nine the headmaster sent a letter to her mother, asking if they could speak English at home with the child as she was making no progress at school. When *la* Tía Piedad heard about it, she took it so seriously, she ordered everyone in the family to speak English when Alegre was around. Can you imagine? Ahora *we speak* con la niña *in English!* Language is power in America. Latinos know this better than anyone. Whatever you say you have to say it in the victor's language, if you want to be heard."

Piyu seemed relieved to unleash his sullenness, but there were things he'd rather keep to himself. He would never confess that no matter how much he loved Alegre and her extended family of *tías*, still from time to time he had difficulty in adjusting to their ways, and that as a highly skilled Spaniard, seeing his culture as definitely part of the European civilization, if not what spiced its otherwise somewhat dull taste, at times he felt incredibly aloof to the Hispanic communities here, especially to the Tex-Mex and their ways. *Bailes, bautismos, lotería, misa, bar-b-ques, posadas, fiestas de cumpleaños, quinceañaras, velorios* . . . they seemed to miss no opportunity to socialize among themselves. A pace Piyu didn't know how to keep up, and wasn't even sure he wanted to. No, he wouldn't mention such things.

"Well, since our problem is common we can help each other." Ömer rose up from his chair, his face flushing in a manic flame, and seized the brick-thick English-English Dictionary on the bookcase behind, lifting it above his head as boastful as a champion lifting his prize. He took a deep breath as if to highlight the magnitude of the proposition he was about to make. "In our daily life we use few words in English. We need more. More words, more power to us!"

The idea that had occurred to him as he was listening to Piyu was a game of idiom that required three persons to play. Shifting turns, each time one would ask a word, and the other two would respectively try to find the antonym and the synonym, using exemplary sentences. With the help of a scoreboard, they could make the game quite competitive.

"What if the other two don't know the meaning of the word?" Piyu wondered.

Ömer shrugged: "Then the one who asks the question gets all the scores."

That principle, however, proved to be highly noxious once they agreed to give the game a try. For the sake of that score, questions could be blown up out of all proportion. Hence in the ensuing days and weeks, they found themselves learning against their will that the attraction to ants exhibited by certain plants and insects was called *myrmecophilism*; that collecting Camembert cheese labels was a real concern for some and even had a name: *tyrosemiophily*; that *potanadromous* stood for movements of fish up and down the stream in a single watershed; that *floccinaucinihilipilification* was the categorizing of something as valueless trivia or that somebody had created the word *alectryomancy* for a special form of divination based on recording the corn-covered letters revealed as a cock eats corn, and since that was what *copoclephily* stood for, there were people on this planet collecting key rings containing some sort of an advertising, and if they went on playing the game in this way they were all bound to *sesquipedalianism*, a long word to define the lust for long words.

Before it went berserk, the game had to be revised, and a new rule introduced: the *have-mercy rule*! The innovation was lucid and simple: Whoever asked the question was expected to *have some mercy for God's sake*!

Ever-Cooking

Even if she hadn't been assigned the task of up-cooking for the next session, on her way back to the clinic Alegre would still be constantly and compulsively thinking about food. Food was a business-class traveler on the flight of her thoughts, always in the front rows, more privileged and better cared for than other passengers. And it was a lonesome traveler, too, never at ease among multitudes. After all, Alegre barely ate in front of other people, especially if they were not strangers enough, and when she was compelled to sit at a table with friends and relatives, she did eat, but too often banished this greasy burden from her body immediately after. If this was some kind of a loop she wallowed in, she was pretty much aware of the recurrences in it, aware that the less she ate the more she thought about food, which in turn incited her to eat incredible amounts of low-calorie food that eventually generated high sums of carbohydrate, and big amounts of guilt, thus requiring it to be vomited, after which she always felt clean and all the more hungry. She recognized her problem, and certainly was not ignorant. She was *working* on it. While the construction of her soul continued restlessly, there was one thing that really helped her: the pleasure of feeding others. She enjoyed feeding the homeless at Kate's Soup Kitchen, frequently cooked for *las tías*, relished more than anything feeding Piyu and the housemates who were always hungry, and besides, of course, there was Arroz. There was no plea for food that Alegre could possibly turn down. That was her brief culinary history when she spotted the ad at her usual bus stop.

> **HELP! HELP! HELP!** wanted for approximately 4 hours between 6:00 and 10:00 p.m. this Saturday evening, October 12, at a party at my home for approx. 20–30 people. It will be a casual affair!
> I am looking for someone to help me with the **FOOD**, which includes: easy party cuisine, cocktail snack, pâtés, spring rolls, cheese balls, and everything yummy & savory (and not costly) you suggest to make.
> I will pay a minimum of 4 hours to make the evening worth your while and am prepared to offer a fair hourly wage. If this is something you might be interested in please give me a call. Only serious cooks need apply.

What Alegre liked most about the ad was the concomitant sight of the words in capital letters: *HELP!* and *FOOD.* These two words being already a flawless match in the uncharted depths of her subconscious, she didn't hesitate to note down the number and the address.

Abed was heading to get the kettle running when he halted in panic and tried to get away. But it was too late. He had already been noticed by the girl in the kitchen. Detected by *another toothbrush holder.*

"Good morning!" she exclaimed.

After two and a half months of living in the same house and sharing the same bathroom with Ömer, Abed was firmly convinced that a toothbrush was no ordinary item. It was, first and foremost, a modern girlfriend's dowry. In this relentless roundabout of affairs that Ömer was wallowing in, a new toothbrush in the bathroom was a messenger heralding that some fresh brand-new affair had been launched. For they always came with their toothbrush. The toothbrush always came first. All other things, cleaning cottons, lotions, moisturizers, avocado and wild raspberry tonics to be applied after oatmeal and whatever masques and the unidentifiable liquids in all those bottles, simply followed the footsteps of the toothbrush. Nevertheless, what was first to come was the last to go. For some reason, girlfriends never took their toothbrush back when they split, thus making it hard to decipher the ends of affairs, unlike the beginnings. They did take the cosmetics stuff but left the toothbrush. Abed simply hated having to share the bathroom with Ömer. But still, he could have tolerated it better, if it were not for the meeting-the-face-behind-the-toothbrush phase, from which he now knew, there was no escape.

"I am Lynn!" the girl in the kitchen beamed. She wore shredded jeans and had her bottom lip pierced.

"Hi, Lynn." Abed forced himself to smile. That could be a more genuine smile if he weren't so sure of what was coming next.

"And you must be . . . Halid!?"

There it was again! Obviously, Ömer had a habit of talking about his housemates to his actual or potential girlfriends before bringing them to his house. And whatever he said, once the girlfriends came here and bumped into Abed, for some incomprehensible reason they felt compelled to reveal what little dubious information they had, starting with his name. That wouldn't be so dreadful, if they could remember his name correctly, or simply ask what it was when they couldn't. But they preferred to guess. To make a shot. A slipshod shot. To distort freely, just because the detritus of the name they came up with sounded as alien as the original one.

"Actually it is Abed," he corrected with practiced courtesy, and spelled it for her.

The first girlfriend to come was the worst of them all. This health-addicted, tall brunette from MIT. To this day Abed had not been able to solve the puzzle as to how on earth such a toxic-free girl could get along with the smoker, drinker, and *Godknowswhatelse* that

Ömer was. No big surprise it hadn't lasted long. But with Ömer no-body seemed to last anyhow. Meeting that girl had been more shock-ing for Abed than meeting any one of those to follow. Probably because in time he simply had gotten used to running into unknown girlfriends in the house, different types of toothbrushes in the bath-room. Back then, however, Tracey had totally caught him by sur-prise. "Hi! I am Tracey . . ." she had energetically hollered between puffs and huffs, as she dashed into the kitchen while Abed was calmly waiting for the tea kettle to boil. She seemed to be back from jogging or something. "And you must be . . . Law-ren-ce?!"

Abed had gaped at her, his face twisted in utter confusion, and could more or less have remained in that position had the kettle not started to whistle. Obviously there was a confusion somewhere but he'd wondered what else was she confusing? Had the unmapped rims of the human brain played her some sort of a trick, connecting the sight of an Arab to *Lawrence of Arabia*? That was and still lingered as the only plausible explanation Abed had been able to come up with.

Never again had any other girl made such a peculiar guess. Ac-tually, when compared to Tracey, others had come pretty close. Not that Abed had anything against any one of them. He might even be-come good friends with some, had they met elsewhere, in any other context but *this*. Under these specific circumstances, however, all in-terest from whichever side remained fallacious, if not bogus. For nei-ther Abed nor Piyu, nor the girlfriends really, sincerely talked; they only exchanged syrupy words of either routine courtesy or courte-ous routine. Initially, all girlfriends perceived Abed and Piyu, as well as Arroz, only through and as gratuitous extensions of their new boyfriend. Once they started having an affair with Ömer, they em-braced him as an entire entity, together with the bunch of friends, relatives, hobbies, and whatever else he had in store. It was pretty much like ordering a well-cooked steak, and gladly welcoming the mashed potatoes and brussels sprouts that came along with it. Maybe what they all needed was some time. Nevertheless, before any progress could be made, and either Piyu or Abed, or Arroz, could be elevated to a better role, the affair would be over, the cosmetics gone, after which there came a brief moment of tranquillity only to be followed by the arrival of another toothbrush in the bathroom. Given this recurrent history, and with no hopes for any improvement in the foreseeable future, Abed gently but doggedly discarded Lynn's attempts to chat, and with a quickly done pot of mint tea in hand, ran back to his room.

Poison in the Chocolate Cake

At 5:30 p.m. in Boston, 10:30 p.m. in Marrakesh, 11:30 p.m. in Madrid, 12:30 a.m. in Istanbul, like a plumber going to work with his box of tools, Alegre arrived at the party house with her bag full of cookbooks and favorite spices. She rang the bell and got ready to smile to a stranger. But to her surprise, it was someone familiar who opened the door. The redheaded woman from the therapeutic reading group. They looked at each other in what was more discomfort than amazement. In point of fact, people in the same therapy group should never meet outside. The characters and events in group therapies should always remain at least partly fictional; any resemblance to real life, even if coincidental, should better not coincide. The same with the therapist. You should never ever spy your therapist in a supermarket languorously choosing her third cauliflower from a pile in discount for three, or among the rows in a pharmacy voluptuously looking for a vaginal moisturizing gel. Therapists should never enter into the public zone where daily life meekly rotates, and neither should therapy mates.

But here they were. Staring at each other in the doorway, with a half-smile on their faces, the rest of which was complemented with a half-scowl. Next thing they did was, again simultaneously, a quick memory search. Each woman instantly went through the jumbled files in her memory to recall what the heck she knew about the other. But both came up with very little. As to the woman who had opened the door, all she could recollect about Alegre was that she was this ultrathin, petite, baggy-eyed Catholic girl with hordes of aunts all with similar names, and with some boyfriend with whom she had an assortment of problems, and that she constantly failed to update her calendars, disappointing Connie, but also that she cooked so well that each time she was assigned cooking task, all group members feasted on something pleasant in the next session. That was all the information she had about her.

As for Alegre, all she could remember about the other was that she was a jittery, flour-white-skin, gigantic-ears, and red-red-red-hair Debra with a cowlick that made her look more high-spirited than she really was, and a set of problems with some close girlfriend of hers, and could not endure not being loved by her anymore, a problem Alegre had never fully understood why it was a *problem*, and also, that she could eat neither bananas nor chocolates, for some ob-scure reason. That was all. That was all the attention Alegre had paid to her all throughout the sessions they'd been sharing for six months now.

"What a nice coincidence." Debra forced herself into a smile. "I'm so glad. I know what a wonderful cook you are." She seemed different somehow, much more self-confident than she looked back in the reading group. "Would you mind if we start working right away, time is running out and nothing is ready yet."

She led Alegre to an indigo kitchen, wall-to-wall stuffed with packets, boxes, tins, and cans of food, food, and more food. The guests, she said, would show up after seven o'clock, and would pre-sumably be very hungry by eight-thirty. In total, there were twenty-two people expected to come. "And we are two in the house. That makes twenty-four mouths to feed. What do you think? Can we manage it?"

But as it'd soon be revealed, there was no "we." There was only Alegre. Never in her cooking history had she been in the position to

cook so much food in so little time for so many people. Yet, this culinary dependability must have had a calming effect on her nerves, for
she felt fully capable of the task, at ease here. While she stood inspecting her materials and ingredients, Debra Ellen Thompson had
time to inspect her. Somehow Alegre looked different now, much
less timorous than she was in the reading group.

She did, indeed, feel sure of herself and would be even more so
when Debra left her alone, finally running to help a constantly complaining female voice on the other side of the kitchen door, a voice
that sounded like somebody there was trying to make the living
room nice and ready for the evening but did not really want to do
this, did not even care. When alone in the kitchen, Alegre felt no curiosity as to what was going on in the living room, just like she
wasn't interested in the rest of the house or what the guests were going to turn out to be like. She was where she needed to be: the kitchen.
Even if it belonged to someone else, this was *her* kitchen now. All she
wanted to learn was what precisely she was expected to cook. But nobody turned up to clarify that matter for her. Instead a chubby,
smoke-gray cat with a flat, funny nose and an extremely long, thick
coat walked in imperiously, and right after it, another cat of the same
breed, only this one a tabby and perhaps less bumptious, came in to
check what she was up to. Bored of waiting for the hosts to be ac-
countable enough to give her a clue as to what the menu would be,
bored of watching the cats, Alegre decided that she alone was the
captain of this culinary boat, and as such, the choices fell upon her.

There was goat cheese in the fridge, which she crumbled on pita
rounds. She found lots of canned tuna in the cupboards and turned
them into lots of tuna noodle fettuccine. The meat in the freezer was
quick to develop into meatballs; the cabbage on the counter became
coleslaw salad with red beans; some of the leftover corn evolved into
pudding, and the rest into corn and zucchini sauté. Potatoes, as always, were an exceptional help. Alegre boiled and baked and oven-
roasted and mashed them with different sauces and spices. She
stuffed the rest with bacon and cheese. She made chicken burritos,
though none of the taco sauces she found in the cupboards were
among her favorites. She prepared peanut dipping sauce, and

chicken liver pâté. She made the usual appetizers — shrimp with garlic sauce, crudités, and cheeses. There were two huge bowls of Caesar salad with walnuts, and in case somebody was still hungry, she had in store twenty-four turkey club sandwiches. The remaining eggs and lemon juice she used for a lemon meringue tart. She was planning to make a banana split pie with the oodles of bananas she encountered in the fridge, but had to give up and sit down for a while, utterly wiped out.

She desired to eat none of this food, nor even to taste it. She took out the red grapefruits she had in her bag, and started to count as she gnawed and gnawed: 13 red grapefruits, 70 calories each, 910 calories in total.

"Look at you, I can't believe this!" Debra Ellen Thompson screeched when she finally stepped back into the kitchen after being absent for more than two hours. She halted reverentially in front of every single dish on the counter as if saluting them one by one. "God, I don't know what to say. You've done a marvelous job. This is gorgeous! Gorgeous!"

But she herself didn't look "gorgeous! gorgeous!" not even "gorgeous!" Instead, she looked as if she'd been crying for hours.

"Are you OK?" asked Alegre, in a flash hiding the pile of grapefruit peelings.

"Yes . . . actually no . . . my housemate was in the doldrums lately and you know what I did to cheer her up . . . I painted the kitchen indigo, that's her favorite color . . . it didn't help much, though, then I thought it'd be a good idea to throw a party but now I see what a fool I've been . . . this crowd won't do her any good."

Alegre wanted to ask her why was it so important to make her housemate happy, but she suddenly felt that would sound too Connie-like. Besides this was really not a time to chat. The guests had already begun to arrive.

After all the trays and plates were carried to the living room, Alegre was once again left alone in the kitchen. She'd promised Debra she would come inside to meet the people and eat with them, but this she knew she would not do. Instead, she tidied up the kitchen, cleaned the counters, took out the trash, and scrubbed a few pans. And then ate three more grapefruits, 210 more calories, listening to the voices inside multiply into a mélange of serene music, jovial chitchat, tentative jokes, blithe guffaws; but also now and then nervous sneers and hoarse snipes. Then somehow, somewhere started the drumbeats and the music went into hyperspeed. The house began to quake as if everyone had at the same time decided to mistake dancing with cavorting and cavorting with bucking and vaulting.

By 11:33 p.m. in Boston, 4:33 a.m. in Marrakesh, 5:33 a.m. in Madrid, and 6:33 a.m. in Istanbul, Alegre decided it was time to leave her kitchen and be paid. She warily opened the door and peered inside. But what she then gaped at was a living room so utterly unlike the one she'd seen there six hours before that it made her feel as if she'd sneaked into the twilight zone and from there into an alternate house, a ravaged village. Debra was nowhere in the picture. Instead she saw alcohol-drenched faces, opium-fogged gazes, and wobbly bodies exhausted into slow motion, some couples still dancing a slothful swoon sway as if though they really wanted to detach and stop, an invisible hand had glued them forever, while some others were conversing faintly on the couches or around the table, still nibbling the flotsam and jetsam that was once the *gorgeous! gorgeous!* food she cooked. Alegre walked around the room cautiously, but no one seemed to be awake enough to take notice of her. All these people looked like they had experienced some big shock and were now trying to recover.

When Alegre returned to the kitchen, the scene she found there was even more confounding than the one she had left behind in the living room. There was a woman on her knees with her head ducked into the oven. The cats stood next to her, as if the stove were a clandestine passageway to the underground, and they, too, wanted to follow her in there.

"Ex-cu-se me," Alegre stuttered with a barely hearable voice.

But the young woman in the oven must have heard her, for she instantly came out, at least tried to, bumping her head in the endeavor.

"Geez, you scared me to death! Who are you?" she squawked

when she finally managed to stand on her legs. But then her ice-blue eyes brightened with a sudden flash of recognition. "Oh I know who you are! You are Debra Ellen Thompson's guardian angel. Alegre right? Alegre the party savior! Our Lady of Miracles!"

"What . . . were . . . you doing there?" Alegre couldn't help stammering as she gaped at the other's head suspiciously. There was a silver spoon with a long handle hanging from that pitch-black hair of hers, and she smelled funny, and pungent like . . . like . . . gas.

"Dying, but obviously I failed." She grinned, tilting the large beer can in her hand as if to indicate she'd toast to that had Alegre a can, too—but the truth is, even if she had one, Alegre could not possibly tell what exactly they would be drinking to, the "dying" part or her having failed to do so.

"Or maybe I didn't fail . . . do you think you might be a real angel?"

Alegre snorted a tense chuckle, that being the only reaction she could think of after all the things she had heard. "I am glad you didn't die," she then murmured cordially. "Do you know where Debra is?"

"Don't you ever make that mistake!" The girl bobbed her head broodingly from side to side, tinkling the spoon in her hair. "Deb-ra-El-len-Thomp-son is the name. Never call her half-baked name! She'll get angry!"

Alegre's face struggled with stupefaction but lost instantly. In a voice as absentminded as the look on her face she felt the need to ask: "Are you her friend?"

"Am I her *friend*!?" The girl's jarring laughter lasted awhile, halting only when she guzzled some more beer. "Well, let me think . . . I guess I am . . . oops, I *was*, more than that . . . but not anymore . . . so that makes us *friends* now . . . I guess."

Alegre warbled in an attempt to change the subject. "These cats are so pretty. What are they called?"

As she looked down at the cats stuck to her feet, the girl's face softened, and when she spoke, her voice too had somewhat softened. "This beauty here is called West," she caroled after briskly lifting the tremendously plump, tremendously furry, smoke-gray cat above her head and giving her a sloppy kiss on the nose. Once at the same eye level, the girl and the cat stayed entirely motionless for a few seconds, staring directly at each other's pupils. Then she gently put her back, and patted the other cat on the head. "And this one here is called The Rest. That's why we treat him worse."

"I better go now." Alegre snatched a troubled glance at her coat. "It was nice to meet you."

"No, it wasn't. You don't mean that, Alegre, but that's OK," the other intervened, suddenly starting to hiccup. "Don't go now. We should find Debra *hic* Ellen Thompson and get your *hic* money first. You've done a *hic* great job tonight. I am really sorry if I upset *hic* you girl, I mean it. You *hic* are a great cook. The very best!" She lowered her voice into a confidential murmur. "You know *hic* I, too, made a cake, banana and chocolate, my *hic* favorite, I wish I could offer you some but don't think *hic* there is any left. They loved it!" She sniggered curtly, sharing a joke with herself.

Alegre brought her a glass of water. She held her breath, took a big sip from the water in her left hand, and a bigger sip from the beer in her right hand. They waited in reverential silence for one hiccup life span to pass, inspecting one another in the meantime. The girl had her ice-blue eyes fixed on the golden Jesus sagging from Alegre's necklace, but as she was still motionlessly holding her breath, it was hard to tell what she thought of it. Alegre, in turn, had concentrated on the other's hair, wondering how it could be so voluminous and so black, whether she was dyeing it or not, and what on earth a silver spoon was doing there. When she decided she had defeated a hiccup interval successfully, the suicidal girl interrupted this thick silence:

"Listen, you should give me a chance to apologize. Come to our store. Come tomorrow, or whenever you want." She took a card out of a drawer and handed it to Alegre. "We make chocolates. Actually, I make them, and Debra Ellen Thompson does the marketing. Will you come? I'll make a delicious Jesus for you, of hazelnut chocolate."

Before Alegre could figure out how to respond, the girl reached out for her hand. "By the way . . . ," she said, still smelling of gas and hiccuping anew, "my name is Gail and I'm *hic* pleased to meet you."

By midnight, as Alegre was still struggling to get out of the party house, back at 8 Pearl Street, on the third floor, Piyu's worries as to her whereabouts had reached a piercing level. He had called *las tías* four times to learn if she had arrived, and alas each time it was *la* Tía Piedad who had picked up the phone, and in her twisted logic implacably asked Piyu where the hell Alegre was. A fifth call he could not endure.

Meanwhile on the second floor, Lynn was trying to cuddle her postorgasmic sleep, which had been continuously slipping out of her hands for the last thirty minutes. She exhaled deeply as she looked at the barely hairy chest unfairly sleeping next to her, the body she'd passionately desired an hour ago but now felt like an utter stranger. She elbowed him several times: "Are you awake? Can you bring me some water?"

Ömer turned toward her, opened his eyes, murmured something that sounded like "sure," and went on snoring. Lynn cursed him, got up, puffed out glaringly, and didn't stop doing that until she had stepped out of the room into the dark corridor. Still trying to find the light switch, she first heard glass being broken somewhere too close, and then all of a sudden this horrendous scream. Her first reaction was awe. For though Lynn had met *Halid* and had been preinformed on some of his ways, nobody had warned her against the horror movies. She stood there, face taut, body tense, eyes wide open in the dark before she could shake off her daze, convinced that the ogreish chomps from downstairs were *only a movie*. Still, it was not *only a movie* that had made her hesitate to proceed. Some sudden grip had seized her abdomen, more like a suspicion than a feeling, the suspicion that though content and loved in this new affair, she wasn't with the right guy right now. There followed the mordant intuition that the person she should really be with was somewhere outside, and she by being here inside, was missing her chance, missing her destiny, missing *him*. When she finally found the switch and turned it on, her eyes were irritated by the luminosity of this new reality.

Exactly at the same time downstairs on the first floor, after spending one and a half years in America and years of practicing English much before that, Abed, for the first time in his life, began to dream in English. Indeed the meaning of *every* dream might be the fulfillment of a wish. But had Freud lived the life of an expatriate, immigrant, or a humble non-Western Ph.D. student cut off from his native tongue, he might have added to this that at times it's not mainly the subject per se but the very form of the dream that fulfills that wish. Not the message but the medium. The latter can follow a path of its own and may even blatantly contradict the former. That's why, that's how, every so often foreigners in a country wake up from pleasant dreams with a glum feeling as if having lost something (not knowing that particular loss was a wedge of their mother tongue), or from gloomy nightmares with an inexplicable delight as if they had acquired something novel (not knowing that was a boon from the nonnative language). Dreaming in English for the first time is a threshold, a sign of a bigger change on the way, a change that won't let you be the same person anymore. You wake up in the middle of the night and try to remember, not the theme of the dream but the words with which the story was told to you. You might be surprised to find out that some of those words you do not happen to have learned yet. For dreams, unlike us, are capable of living simultaneously in more time zones than one, and in the terra firma of Morpheus, the past and the future are one and the same.

Unaware of all this, and probably uninterested in any speculation on dreams, Lynn walked warily, almost on her toes, as she breezed through the living room glaring at *Halið* snoring in an armchair, and then at the lettuce-green ogre on the screen. She didn't want to turn off the TV. She didn't even want to approach the TV. She softly slid into the kitchen, opened the fridge, and peered inside.

Exactly at the same time, upstairs on the third floor, Arroz raised his head, sniffing a suspicious metallic sound among the usual voices and noises canopying 8 Pearl Street at this time of the night, and instantly jumped out of the bed. He caught Lynn tiptoeing behind

Abed's armchair, this time with a glass of milk in her hand and her eyes fixed on the screen at the body of the heroine now slaughtering the lettuce-green ogre with an ax. Lost in the depths of her thoughts, besotted by the scene she was watching, when she crashed into the menacing body of Arroz, out of reflex Lynn unleashed a shriek but amazingly managed not to spill even a drop of milk. Abed instantly woke up and squinched his eyes at the ogre on the screen now choking on blood. He didn't notice either Lynn or Arroz behind him, sighed deeply, and tried to go back to sleep. But no matter how desperately he rummaged around, he couldn't find the gate to the path back; his first dream in English was ripped apart.

Step by step Arroz guardedly followed Lynn's tense body until she had sneaked back into Ömer's bedroom. Once inside the bed again, Lynn rolled herself into a fretful fetal position, listening to Ömer's steady pace of respiration, her feeling of *being-in-the-wrong-place-with-the-wrong-guy-while-the-right-guy-is-miles-away-or-perhaps-just-down-on-the-next-street-right-now* intensifying with each breath of his.

She had a most nasty sleep and forgot to drink the milk.

"So I see you two have met," Debra Ellen Thompson spoke in a voice as sober as the expression on her face, when she finally showed up in the kitchen carrying a tray full of dirty glasses and a messy pile of plastic plates.

Either her nose was still crimson from the outburst hours ago or recently she had cried again. "I am terribly sorry, Alegre, for leaving you alone here for so long. But *everything* went out of control. I had to carry the drunk to the bathroom, help them throw up, and drag those that had passed out. This party has been a disaster. The only good thing was your food, you know? I owe you so much . . . and, hum, I will pay you double the amount."

"It's OK, you don't need to . . ." Alegre smiled warmly but hesitated to pronounce her name. *Debra* or *Debra-Ellen-Thompson*, either way, she was glad to see her again. "Why did the party go so wrong?"

"Ask her," Debra squealed, pointing at Gail, now sitting on the floor in a lotus position, with the cats at each side, meditatively squinting at the creased ball that until a minute ago was still the empty can of beer she crumpled and recrumpled between her palms.

"Gail brought this giant chocolate and banana cake to the table, gosh, how was I to know? I thought it was one of yours. Everyone ate, can you imagine? She made every one of us eat at least two slices. Only I survived because I don't eat bananas or chocolates. But then people started to act in this weird wacky way, and I assumed they had drunk too much. Which was true, they were drinking nonstop, but that was not the reason. It was the outcome. They drank so much because of the cake they had eaten. God, Gail, how could you do this . . ." Perhaps she wanted to say "to me?" but instead chose to say "to all these people?"

Under the inquiring gaze of two pairs of eyes, one ferocious, the other dazed, Gail lifted her chin, grinned at them both, and continued to inspect her metallic creation.

"Did she poison them?" Alegre asked, her eyes widened with affronted awe.

There came a gurgle of raucous chuckles from Gail. Debra grimaced, Alegre flushed. West shot them all a patronizing stare, The Rest licked a paw.

"I better go, I am so late." Alegre panicked.

"Oh, please let me drive you home." Debra Ellen Thompson tried to placate her while scolding Gail at the same time. "Don't worry, I am not intoxicated, unlike the rest of us."

But Gail wasn't paying any attention to them anymore, or to her crinkled creation. She had sunk into a deep slumber, with a gleeful smile on her face as if it were not the cold kitchen floor but a comfy, balmy mattress she slept on. Four times they attempted to carry her back to her bed, but each time she woke up with an increasing tension, and at first pleaded, then groused, scolded, and finally decreed not to be moved an inch. Consequently, they covered her with a blanket and left her to sleep there with the cats as guards on each side.

The car was a huge indigo Jeep. Once inside, Alegre let out a sigh of relief, Debra Ellen Thompson started to cry.

The first ten minutes on the road they spoke not a word. But then, as they slowed down for a pedestrian on the crosswalk, Debra Ellen Thompson broke her own silence: "She has changed so much, sometimes I doubt I recognize her at all. Like a metamorphosis . . ."

Alegre stared at the pedestrian, a homeless midfortyish woman she had never seen at the charity, passing right in front of them at an enormously slow pace, her sagging face blatantly illumined and painted sick white under the streetlight. She wore a cerulean velvet hat and pulled along an old, badly tattered suitcase on wheels as if she were still on some trip she'd embarked on ages ago.

"What do you mean by metamorphosis?"

"Well, maybe even that is too light of a word for this," whined Debra Ellen Thompson and sniffed twice. "Can you imagine, Gail was this distant, ultratimid girl with a funny name back in the college days. She was so shy, she couldn't even move when a stranger asked her something. And then in some mysterious way, she turns into this other person. Furious, fierce, fuming . . ." She stopped and looked around in anguish as if to see any other *F* words coming. "I lost track of her, you know." She bit her lip painfully. "When she is manic, I can't keep up with her. When she is depressive, she can't keep up with life. Two weeks before, she tried to kill herself. She took a whole bottle of Valium. God . . . it was so frightening . . ."

The good girl in Alegre felt she should say something positive, effective: "It's my birthday tomorrow. We are going to eat Chinese with a few friends. Would you like to come?" She added automatically, though less enthusiastically: "You can bring Gail, too."

But speaking of a birthday party instantly reminded her of a birthday cake, which in turn prompted a puzzle still unsolved for her: "What was in that cake that Gail had made?"

"Banana and chocolate mainly, and lots of cannabis." Debra Ellen Thompson smiled bitterly.

The homeless woman had finally stepped onto the other pavement, but once there she briskly stopped and looked back, as if to see if she had dropped something, *anything*, behind. Even if she had dropped an invisible item of hers, the Jeep didn't wait for her to find out what that might be and roared into the night in a glistening indigo light.

"Lynn, are you okaaay?"

Ömer knocked gently on the bathroom door, leaning forward to hear better the answer coming from inside, but the only thing he heard was a gurgling.

He knocked again, this time less gentle. "Breakfast downstairs. I made coffeeee!"

"It is Abed here! Stop banging," a gruff voice hollered. A few seconds later, the door was opened and Abed's head popped out with a roguish smile. "Lynn has gone, *dostum*, she went early in the morning. If you don't want to drink that tar of coffee alone, you gotta wake up earlier . . . I can keep you company in the breakfast part, though. After the shower!" And the door was slammed shut on his face, only to be reopened in a split second. "Omar! I hope you didn't forget the dinner tonight."

Ömer pretended he hadn't but the initial flare on his face was too obvious.

"It's Alegre's birthday, so you better remember it. She has invited people we've never met before. Don't leave me alone in that chic restaurant among strangers. I don't even like Chinese food! You better be there on time!" And the door was closed again.

Ömer went downstairs befuddled as to why Lynn had left so suddenly, only to become more befuddled to find a woman in the kitchen as petite as an elf, as old as ages, sitting calmly at the breakfast table.

"So you are the new tenant, are you?" she chirped in a clipped, slight voice with a sharp, stark accent. She was white and wrinkled from head to toe. Her hair, her skin, her clothes, her hands . . . even her shadow must be white and wrinkled. "And this is Oksana Sergiyenko, I am your landlord. I know I shouldn't have come in like this, but maybe you wouldn't mind offering me a cup of morning coffee. It smells wonderful."

"Sure." Ömer perked up. "I'm so glad to have a coffee mate at last."

She had her coffee with cream and sugar, Ömer had none as usual.

"Tell me where your parents live; are they far away?" she asked, raising her white-wrinkled arm languidly in the air to point at the window, as if *far away* were so close.

When Abed came back from the shower he encountered Ömer eagerly talking about his childhood days in Istanbul, and the landlord's long-senile mother listening with an attentive smile, both smoking like chimneys while placidly sipping their third cups of coffee.

Las Tías

Cultures supposedly dissimilar are remarkably similar in their depiction, if not derision, of fortune. In the scripts of church fathers, pretty much as in Islamic folk parables, Fortune was depicted with two basic characteristics: blindness and femininity. That she had no sense of justice when the moment came to bestow upon each and every soul his share in life from her wheel was no big surprise to the ancients, who took this wrong as a natural outcome of her being a woman rather than her being blind. Misogyny aside, the ancients had a point. Gratuitous in her generosity, Fortune always made excesses, and still does; she brings loads of luck to some, heaps of health, piles of power, oodles of opulence to others. In Alegre's case, too, there was one particular thing Fortune had lavishly conferred: *las tías*.

First, there was the eldest. The great-grandaunt, *la* Tía Piedad. There was *always la* Tía Piedad, preceding everyone and everything. To Alegre, to this day, *la* Tía Piedad was a chosen cryptic being, the epitome of eternity, past, present, and future alike, an indomitable woman warrior accidentally fallen onto this planet from another dimension, most definitely from out of the cosmos. And yet still, *la* Tía

Piedad had always been here, deeply anchored in this world. She was here much before the First World War, or the assassination of the archduke of Austria, the San Francisco earthquake, or even the Spanish-American War. She was here when pineapples were canned for the first time, the Harley-Davidson motorcycle was introduced, the ideal waist for women was announced to be eighteen inches, the first Ford motorcar was road tested, and Jack the Ripper committed his sixth crime in London. She was estimated to be at least in her midforties at a time when life expectancy nationwide was estimated to be forty-something, and the concept of the "weekend" as a time of rest had started to gain popularity. That is how old she was.

A more precise estimation of her age, however, was a constant concern for all her relatives, young and old alike. At family reunions, amid gossiping and chattering, someone would bring up the question of *la* Tía Piedad's age, and in tumultuous cooperation they would all try to calculate it for the nth time, though by now everyone had bowed to the impossibility of the task. There were bits and pieces of information in family archives: anecdotes, testimonies, photographs. But no precise dates. All those who had eyewitnessed *la* Tía Piedad's childhood, or even her youth, having long passed away, there was no one left to help solve the riddle of her date of birth. Even the oldest memories of the eldest in the family depicted *la* Tía Piedad as a "mature" woman. It was pretty well recorded, for instance, that she used to listen regularly to the spiritual stories broadcast by KDCE, and would compel her grandchildren to listen, too; a piece of information insinuating she was already beyond middle age by the 1950s, the implications of which slyly hinted that she'd been an "old woman" for at least the last five decades.

The only person who could respond to the question of *la* Tía Piedad's age was, no doubt, *la* Tía Piedad herself, but by now everyone knew she wouldn't respond. Not that she was suffering from Alzheimer's or any other memory defect expectable *at her age*, just that she simply preferred to keep her lips tight and her mouth shut. For like many who could never tell how they'd managed to survive and grow older and even older in an age of exiles and expatriations, wars and genocides, catastrophes and mass destructions, *la*

Tía Piedad's heart, too, was beset with a subtle sense of guilt. A guilt aggravated even deeper as the mother of a lively daughter and a son-in-law never back from their road trip to the South, crashing in plain midday, for no reason at all, into a parked caravan somewhere in Arizona; the grandaunt of a newlywed niece raped and beaten to death on her jogging track, a charming daughter-in-law whose only fault was to be on the same road with a drunk driver, of a newborn baby with a heart deficiency, and of two nephews who couldn't survive long with AIDS. About, and to, every single one of them she felt culpable, as if by having lived so long and still lingering around, she had somehow been stealing from the life spans of every relative that had departed way too early.

What *la* Tía Piedad didn't know was the damage she had given to the mental stability of her family members in keeping her age a secret so far, becoming in their eyes a nebulous combination of death and life, of forlornness and hope, and of resentment and reverence. On the one hand, she was no doubt a harbinger of long life, and as such, benignly insinuated that a similar length of life span could be awaiting her relatives. If she had managed to live so long, they, too, could make it to there. The thought of it made them feel somewhat indebted to her, as if she'd bequeathed something precious to them, her genes or whatever that might be. Being the direct receiver of those genes, her four daughters were the most expectant of all, even though the soul of a fifth sister lost in a car accident warned them against expecting anything from life. No matter what, when asked about the medical history of their family they couldn't help feeling good, and really good, to reveal their centennarian mother, still bursting with health. They felt even better when they shared this piece of information with insurance companies.

That indeed was true, but only part of the truth. For *la* Tía Piedad was also a cause of deep resentment, if not sheer indignation, as if there were an ongoing blunder, some sort of a celestial muddle, or maybe even favoritism, up there in the ninth floor of heaven, and that she down here had been for so long unashamedly benefiting from it. Consequently, numerous members of *la* Tía Piedad's family, inexorably, obdurately, and desperately failed to love but loved to envy her.

And then, there came *las otras tías.** Four of them (Tía Tuta, Tía Flaca, Tía Licha, and Tía Graciela) were sisters of Alegre's late mother and the other four (Tía Chita, Tía Cata, Tía Bertha, and Tía Martha) of her late father; distributed equally on each side, as if to prove that not only useless generosity but also useless fairness stood out among Fortune's plenteous virtues. Yet, whatever favor Fortune might have made to them fizzled out when it came to the husbands of *las tías*, given that all but one had passed away, each facing a separate end but all with similar suddenness. Losing their husbands so unexpectedly, so soon, had buttressed the resentment of *las otras tías* toward not only *la* Tía Piedad, whom they could never bite, but also toward the only husband alive, *el* Tío Ramon, whom they always could.

Thus, Alegre came from a crammed-full family of *tías*, where women composed the overwhelming majority, where women suffered more but definitely survived better. A family of never-settling resettlements, past-ablaze still-fumy commotions, of children that were made to learn the taste of almond soap when they failed to speak English, and sent to speech therapists when soaps didn't help. A family of solitary mothers unable to communicate with their own children, but certainly able to understand the times they were mocked by them for their mispronunciation of English words. A family of women and children with gaps of silences between them, tributes for those words that were lost somewhere, sometime on the road to a better future.

Being of the fifth generation, born and raised in the U.S.A., her past, present, and future fused in a sense of continuum, Alegre had never had to experience similar difficulties, nor had her younger cousins. One bad thing about being one of the less suffering in a family where too many people have suffered too much, however, is that your own family might help to redress the balance for you. The

*The other aunts

intention behind it is *good*, of course. But the intention to do good should not be confused with doing good. Likewise, the simplicity and sincerity of buying a special gift to make someone happy will not necessarily generate special happiness on the side of the other. Cause is not consequence, however sophisticated yours may be over the primordial deductions of pure logic.

With a family so passionately assiduous, she never had had to be either passionate or assiduous herself. *Las tías* had always been with her, in whisper range, ever since her birth. In a shielding mist their affection had enveloped her and her younger cousins—balmy and accustomed no doubt, but a mist nevertheless, and like every mist, one that doesn't permit one to see that far. Then, when the news of the ghastly accident in Arizona had reached Boston, that gossamer mist had in a blink of an eye evolved into a rock-solid armor of love and devotion clenched around Alegre. Having lost her mother and father, Alegre had found each and every one of her aunts trying to be both parents to her, *la* Tía Piedad ranking first, as the stanch head of the armor. Since none of *las tías* wanted to recede from her position, Alegre had ended up with eight mothers, eight fathers, and a mega-mother-father, all henceforth devotedly, tenderly, ceaselessly intervening into every crack and crevice of her life.

Her mother had never been pushy. Born into a family that had suffered too much in the past but was now well off and well known, Alegre, she thought, had all she needed. There was no need for her daughter to be competent, and certainly no need to be more ambitious than would look good on a young woman. Still, however, she used to remind Alegre every now and then: "*Tienes que hacer concha, hija.*"*

It was ironic that the *concha* that her mother had so badly wanted Alegre to attain had automatically arrived upon her death. Ever since that day Alegre had been living behind a fortification of care and love that intended to block all the passages through which outside life could perchance touch her. It was too much. It was too much love that smothered her, and this she could never confess. *Las*

---

*You need to build yourself a shell, child.

tías were so benevolent they could not be fought. *La* Tía Piedad was so truly unique and invigorating in her electrifying presence, there was no way of stepping aside from her caring orbit.

The effects of relocations are bizarre. If flying for half a day through several time zones is expected to cause "disruption of circadian rhythms in the individual body" (dictionary definition of jet lag), to take off once and forever from the homeland and soar through several culture zones can be plausibly expected to yield "disruption of centenarian rhythms in the collective memory" (suggested definition of sorrow). Undergoing undesired changes that bring an end to the past can prompt a desire to bring an end to change per se in the future. Those with less to conserve end up all the more conservative.

Like many other immigrants of past decades, in *la* Tía Piedad's case, too, replacements meant irreplaceable losses before anything else. Moving to the Big Apple from Hargill, a land itself perplexed enough by five subsequent rulers, from Spain to Mexico, and to the United States, she had lost the wood-frame house and the vegetable garden she cherished so much. On the way there, most of the few pieces she had been able to take along had disappeared somehow, somewhere; embroidered linens, rosaries, *retablos*, crocheted doilies gone. Once in New York, she had lost an adored husband, and too many unknowns. Never marrying again, moving six times to different neighborhoods of similar look, losing more items each time, she had finally moved to Boston with five daughters to raise, unaware of the bigger losses on the way. All through this sodden record, there was one thing she had managed not to lose, actually eighty-seven things in total. A dinner china set painted by her. And the pattern she chose, sardonically, a tiny blue flower with a yellow smile at the core, the fabulous Myosotis, commonly known as *forget-me-not*.

Twelve bread-and-butter plates, twelve soup bowls, twelve dessert bowls, three salad plates, a covered casserole, a teapot, a coffeepot, platters, and cups and saucers . . . all eighty-seven of them coming along with her all the way through the vicissitudes and peregrinations that Fortune had in reserve, following her faithfully, miraculously, without even a scratch on even a single one of them.

The history of the china set being so imperative, its future was even more so. The essential question was: "Who would take the china set upon *la* Tía Piedad's death?" It was the great-grandaunt herself that had turned this into a burning issue, never to be fully resolved. Every now and then, for this or that reason, she would announce her heir but then simply change her mind and favor another one.

Being the apple of *la* Tía Piedad's eye, Alegre was the most likely to inherit the china set. And this she desired deeply. In every piece it entailed, the china set was an entirety never attained. Not only was it a bridge from the past to the present, but it was also a barometer of love, whereby each aunt could measure *la* Tía Piedad's fondness for her. Whoever the china set passed to ranked first.

It was too much pressure for such delicate porcelain.

It's a Girl!

There was a ponytailed blond man walking ahead, a midfortyish woman coming out from a store that sold used furniture, a girl with too much makeup and a top that left her tummy open in this windy weather, a young mother with three kids talking to a young mother with two kids, and at the entrance of Brookline Booksmith, a couple that either had just quarreled and stopped talking to one another or were frowning at the same time at *The Poems of Mao Tse-tung*. After a clipped doubt, Ömer chose the midfortyish woman to ask the time, and when given the answer, in panic he realized he was late again. He pressed the play button to start Queensryche's "Suite Sister Mary," and hoped to be at the Sizzling Mandarin before the song was over. Only after the third round, however, was he able to reach there. Not a negligible delay, given the song's duration: eleven minutes, thirty-three seconds.

It was all because of that crazy Vinessa behind the counter in the record store in Jamaica Plain—a badly lit burrow of a place with a wonderful punk collection that he visited every other day, lingering longer each time. Vinessa knew all the lyrics of each and every one of Joe Strummer's songs, and to prove the depth of her area of specialization, during her shifts she kept playing The Clash at highest decibels, singing at the same time, singing even louder than Strummer, regardless of the customers' preferences or possible reactions. Like all aspiring singers, she pined for an outstanding band of her own one day, and in the meantime, capitalized on the one at hand. The band at hand was called Rock Smear. Ömer had always enjoyed chatting with her, but today he was further delighted to notice the glint of flirt in her large, black, starry eyes. This being no good excuse to tell to Alegre for being late to her birthday dinner, however, he tried in vain to think of a better one as he scurried. He encountered a glaringly bored Arroz, tied to a lamppost outside the restaurant, his chin on the pavement, eyes wide open, suspicious of every shoe passing in front. "When I come back, I'll bring you Chinese," Ömer wheedled as he bent down to scratch his stomach, and received a not so enthusiastic but still animated tail tapping in return.

Inside it was swarming with people who seemed to have either no time to eat, for they were talking ad infinitum, or no time to talk, for they were eating ad infinitum. Toward the left corner at the back, he first spotted Piyu's wide smile, then affable faces circling a round table centered on what looked like a fluffy debate, and finally heard a familiar mantra explode: "But that is *precisely* what I am arguing against!"

"What's Abed *precisely* arguing against this time?" Ömer smirked as he slanted toward the empty chair next to him.

"Hi!!!" they thundered in unison.

Being the birthday girl, Alegre must've felt she shouldn't leave the question unanswered but forgot to introduce Ömer to the two girls at the table in the meantime. "Abed was saying this restaurant should not claim to be both Japanese and Chinese because—"

"Because these are two different cultures that we are talking about," Abed intervened with the self-assurance of a defendant rejecting the lawyer so as to make his own defense. "Two different, two ancient cultures! And when you mix them so easily, turning it into *ChineseVietnameseBurmeseJapanese cuisine*, whether you intend it or not, you are saying: Pile them up! No problem, because in the final analysis, they are all the same. All yellowfaces, teensy eyes! That is the implication."

Ömer grabbed a menu and hid klutzily behind the page of appetizers, as he snatched a glance at the strangers he was going to dine with. There were two hitherto unseen girls at the table, neither of them very beautiful. The one sitting next to Alegre had almost tomato-red hair close cropped in a boyish way, with a funny cowlick in the front, and two gargantuan wings of ears she had decorated with tiny earrings that somehow gave the impression of being stamped for eternity on her earlobes. Her emerald-green velvet shirt gave her a reserved, if not austere look. The other girl wore a black chemise, a black vest, and an even blacker bush of hair around her head. Speaking of which, she had a spoonlike silver thing sagging from that bush. But before Ömer could make any further observations about her, he caught her watching him, and instantly lowered his eyes back to the menu, spotting inadvertently "*Pupu Platter* (for two)."

Piyu turned to Abed, tossing a comforting glance that said: "We understand your point," and then turned to Ömer, this time for a scolding memo, but met instead a barricade of menu on the latter's face. "Now that *everybody* is here," Piyu emphasized *everybody* to make sure *somebody* got the message, "I suggest ordering different dishes and share each."

That, however, turned out to be a tough task, less because of the things they desired to eat than those they refused. Everyone at the table seemed to have at least one thing he refrained from eating, and these hardly coincided. Abed wanted no pork, nothing piggy inside; Alegre's girlfriends were strict vegans who refused to eat meat, egg, butter, and even imitation meat. Piyu would have none of those bamboo shoots because they made his teeth slither and when his teeth slithered he felt like he had touched a knife, and Ömer had eaten no fish since he was a child. Only Alegre seemed to have no particular reservations. She suggested the Seven Stars Whirling Around the Moon, which seemed to fall into a neutral zone, the stars being broccoli, asparagus, red pepper, green pepper, garlic, and eggplant, all fried in the chef's special brown sauce, but to their dismay, the wait-ress declared the seventh star had to be either duck or pork.

The waitress had both eyebrows pierced and an apparently low level of tolerance toward life. Or maybe it wasn't life that she couldn't tolerate but Abed with his questions. He wanted to learn whether the names of the dishes were originally Chinese, or if they had been renamed for the American consumer, and if that was the case, who on earth had chosen these names. The waitress had no answer to that, and no patience for further questions. Meanwhile, everyone else seemed to have decided to order her own food and to share none.

Once the fuss was over and the waitress had hated them all, Ale-gre deemed that the task to unite the table fell upon her. "Gail and Debra Ellen Thompson have a chocolate store," she beamed. "They make their own chocolates! Can you believe it?"

Sincere was her joy. She had been in the store, and had seen and smelled them all. Dark cashew turtles, peanut turtles, coconut truf-fles, milk filbert clusters, walnut butter creams, rum balls, mocha mushrooms, maple sugar candies, nut caramels, dark cranberry jells, peanut butter fudges, marzipan, wintergreen thins, white almond barks, milk pretzels, cherry cordials, peanut butter meltaways, cashew brittles, red twizzlers, pistachio chunks . . . A bulimic's castle of shadows.

"How come you girls own a chocolate store and are still so thin? Don't you gorge on your sellable items?" wondered Abed.

"I guess it's like being a gynecologist."

It was the black-hair-black-chemise girl speaking. Now that he could look at her closely, Ömer noticed her hair was incredibly black for a white girl and that silvery spoonlike thing next to her ear was . . . a silver spoon!

"I mean, pretty much like a male gynecologist, a heterosexual one, of course, or a lesbian gynecologist all the same. Both see and touch the object of desire all the time, and simply do not desire it for that's only an object now, and has nothing to do with desire any-more. Do you see what I mean?"

They did not, actually. They were looking elsewhere. Abed and

Piyu had rolled their eyes, each in a different direction. But then instantly Piyu rolled his eyes back with a quirky smile of relief as if he had just realized that things could have been far worse, that spoon in the girl's hair, for instance, could have been a pointed knife. Alegre had lowered her head, inspecting a reddish stain on the carpet beneath her feet. Debra Ellen Thompson was gawking at the serviette she kept twisting and twisting. Ömer meanwhile was scanning the restaurant, especially the tables at the other end, in an attempt not to chortle. That's how the waitress found them all, when, to their relief, she came back with *food*!

To open up another topic, one that Gail couldn't zoom into, Alegre asked about the fasting practices of Muslims. They began to chatter languidly and yet warily about the types of food prohibited by different religions and the logic behind the barrings. More than chitchat, it resembled vigilance, each on the alert like a sentinel on duty, each spying behind graceful curtains to see what the person at his door looked like, so tentative and cautious but not necessarily uninviting. For among groups of each-of-a-different-identity that meet for the first time or do not know each other well enough, to start up a topic necessitates an excursion beforehand. You need to map out to what extent the others are aware of your cultural background, how receptive they'll be, and where their biases will start, because there are *always* some gummed somewhere. With such prudence, Abed talked about the holy month of Ramadan, keeping the information more at the cultural level than at the religious one. He told them about the dishes cooked throughout this month, the lovely smell of *sebbakiyas*,* and how even the simplest olives or dates taste toothsome after a day of fasting. He finally deduced that though the whole thing might appear to be primarily about abstaining from food, it was essentially far more intangible than that, being a matter of taming greed and desire, and a matter of learning *sabr*, submissive patience. He prattled graciously while the others listened tentatively. Piyu was the most supportive and understanding of all. He gave resonating examples from Catholicism, likewise keeping it at a more

*Ramadan cookies

cultural than religious level. A breeze of geniality canopied the table, now garnished with six different dishes and six distinct soups, a breeze tenderly ferrying them from the Muslim concept of *sabr* to the verb *aguantar* in Spanish. From pious surrender they glided into mundane endurance, the need to carry on in life, no matter what, *aguantar la vara como venga.** A pretty much serene conversation, sparkled now and then with praises for and comments on each dish tasted, and the continuous sound of chomps. All was moderate, modest, and mellow, until an abrupt exclamation clutched the gossamer cordiality hovering in the air and yanked it down.

"With all due respect to you, I'll have to disagree bitterly. There is a thin line, I believe, after which all you have been talking about ends up in pure plain fatalism!"

It was the black-hair-black-chemise girl. She took a nervous bite from the tofu Szechuan style, and pouted inside as she chewed, as if suspicious of meat rolling up among the ingredients. Getting rid of her suspicion, she gulped down the whole piece, looked everyone in the eye, and spoke:

"If labor-intensive sweatshops can be so easily built in the free-trade zones of Mexico, it is not only because labor is cheap there but also because of that *aguantar* or *sabr* thing you are talking about. Mexican, Filipino, Salvadoran women and children are hired because they are more exploitable, plus they are thought to have nimble fingers. They are made to work fourteen hours a day, with only two bathroom breaks of ten minutes each, so that bourgeois consumers in Europe, Japan, and the Middle East can buy a greater variety of Nikes. And you know what's so sad, what's so hopelessly sad about it all? Most of these factory workers are thankful for being exploited. That is what's so sad! They endure gratefully. There is a whole system of thought and faith that teaches them to endure gratefully, no matter what. If those Nikes can be produced at such low costs with so much suffering, it is because of these cross-cultural fatalistic teachings . . . *aguantar* or *sabr* . . . whatever!!!"

---

*A term used in reference to bullfighting: to endure the blade from whichever way it comes

Deep silence. Dumbfounded silence. Deep and dumbfounded silence.

"How is your lamb, Abed? Is it good?"

Even though it was, even though this dish somebody had named Happy Happy Lamb was pretty good, Alegre's skimpy attempt to save her birthday dinner couldn't prevent Abed from looking daggers at Gail as he asked: "So tell us what is *your* suggestion?"

"I don't know." She smirked. "How about exchanging our names for a start?"

Alegre sighed, delicately carrying another chubby cashew with her chopstick from one part of the plate to another. Debra Ellen Thompson shot Gail an edgy, cryptic glance. Nobody at the table noticed, but an auburn-haired, once-a-child-star-now-a-real-estate-agent-woman two tables crosswise caught sight of it just when she was tilting her head up in order to find the best angle to disguise that double chin she hated so much, before exclaiming firmly and aloud: "Yes!" Out of reflex the woman looked at the target of the glacial glance she'd just spotted, only to find there some dark-haired girl with a . . . spoonlike . . . thing . . . a spoon in her hair. In the confusion it took her three seconds, maybe five, or eight, to dehook her eyes from that peculiar table of peculiar people and focus back on the worried face of the man sitting across from her, who in the meantime had inferred her unexpected delay to respond as a sign of a latent hesitation to accept his marriage proposal.

"You want us to exchange our names?" Piyu fluted.

"Names, yes, metaphorically if you will. Rather than taking pride in being born what you have been born, try being instead what you have not been born."

As if with a sudden command, Alegre stopped playing with the cashews and ate one, then another, and then all the cashews, and all the shrimps one by one, not alarmingly rapidly and definitely not loutishly but almost robotically gulping all the Empress Gourmet.

"It's something like . . . I mean if you were born a Mexican, try living like an Arab for one year, and the next year be something else, choose another from the 'Other.' Change your name and your identity. Have no name and no identity. Only if we stop identifying ourselves so much with the identities given to us, only if and when we really accomplish this, can we eliminate all sorts of racism, sexism, nationalism, and fundamentalism, and whatever it is that sets barricades among humanity, dividing us into different flocks and subflocks."

"Well, it is easy for *you* to say that," Abed grunted. "You are not the one who has to fight against discrimination all the time. Have you seen *Casablanca* the movie? Such a magnetic man Humphrey Bogart! But you know what they say in the movie about Moroccans? *Those walking bedsheets!* That is what my grandparents were in the eyes of the colonizers. A walking bedsheet! That is what I still am according to many! How can I be expected to forget that and change my name?"

In the ensuing silence, Alegre asked permission, and with quick, dexterous, sliding steps she walked diagonally among the tables glancing at what other customers were eating as she headed to the restrooms downstairs.

"Abed is right," Piyu exclaimed irritably as he suddenly noticed his teeth grating, and guardedly inspected the House Special Duck on his plate, which was supposed to be not only boneless, but utterly devoid of those ugly yellow bamboo shoots. "Besides, I sincerely believe there is a reason for all the suffering and pain that we as human beings have to undergo from time to time. Sometimes God tests our faith through such difficulties. Encumbrance never comes without a cause."

"Geez, who wants to be tested? I definitely don't!" Gail croaked, her face glinting sharper than her tongue. "If anything, I would prefer to remind him how much he needs me. Just as Rilke wrote: *What will you do, God, when I die? You lose meaning, losing me.* Be it God, nationality, this or that religion . . . whatever you deem *the* most important, all we need is to tell to it: *When I—meaning this little little ant among billions of little little ants—when I die, what will you do without me?*"

Inside the restroom, Alegre smiled awkwardly via an egg-shaped mirror at the auburn-haired, contented-looking lady washing her hands, for a moment had the impression of having seen her but couldn't figure out where, inhaled the intense, syrupy coconut aroma in the air and wondered if it was the woman who smelled this way or just the air freshener, chose the farthest toilet, closed the door behind, leaned on the stall, waited in that position until she heard the woman leave, and pushed a finger down her throat. The surge was quick to come, as always. While the first tide of vomit came out, she flushed the toilet to suppress the sound. As she gagged, her eyes watered as if her face cried independently, for she felt no sorrow, not even the slightest worry about what she was up to. If she felt anything at all, it must be a bottomless numbness.

"But that is precisely what I argue against," Abed squawked, hunting around for a euphemism. "Look, Gail, in the past, there were lots of Muslim mystics who uttered similar words. They said things that sounded radical, or even blasphemous. But the problem is they were not radical, and not at all blasphemous. They were men of sincere faith . . ."

The second tide was stronger, far more stuffed than the first one, bringing out all the weight burdening her stomach, torturing her soul. When it was out, that pinky puddle, time was rewound, a burden erased, she lightened. Alegre stared at the pasty color Empress Gourmet had acquired once it was fired from her body. If as she stood stiff and silent in that toilet smelling of tropical islands and coconuts Alegre had one of those color brochures for home decoration in her hands, she would find out that the color she was staring at now was numbered there 52-E and named It's a Girl!

". . . it was not their mouths that spoke radically but the ears of others that heard them wrong. Esoteric wordings have to be perceived within their own system of thought. It would be a gross mistake to take their words literally. Like trying to read a text in Chinese with only knowledge in . . . in the Cyrillic alphabet. You need to be acquainted with the Chinese alphabet to be able to read anything written in it. In every message you can find two meanings: one outer and one inner. The Sufis, mystics, they all spoke the language of the inner. They were in a totally different state of mind when they said all those things. Ecstasy, reverie, frenzy, trance if you will, in their love of God."

"Probably golden mushroom!" beamed Ömer speaking for the

first time. "They must be on some kind of hallucinogenic drugs, like mescaline or LSD or something!"

"What?" Abed scratched the cleft in his chin, looked in awe at his Muslim brother, and scratched the cleft in his chin as he always did under tension.

Alegre pushed for a third wave but only bitter water came out this time. She took a roll of toilet paper and carefully cleaned the pinky stains scattered on the toilet seat, and flushed again. When water had disappeared down the drain, it had taken everything with it, leaving no trace behind.

"LSD," came the reply. "Short for lysergic acid diethylamide, a drug which overstimulates a section of the brain, and thereby distorts responses . . ."

"I know what LSD is, you idiot! How can you muddle up the reverent Sufis with your rotten junkies?"

"Well, the symptoms are the same." Ömer shrugged. "People on hallucinogenics see objects with extreme beauty and rare brilliance. The doors of perception open up. Nothing new. It's a pretty old technique. I don't see anything bad in it."

"But I do," Abed sniped. "Those dervishes were men of deep wisdom, they spent long years to tame their earthly desires and attain esoteric knowledge. They had no interest in this world, absolutely no interest in its material offerings. But here you are, informing us they were like hippies on marijuana or something, basking in the sun and having visions! Everybody can be a mystic then, as long as they have the money for the drugs!"

"Not *everybody*, of course," objected Ömer bobbing his head thoughtfully. "It is more a matter of bringing together the right people with the right hallucinogens."

"Ah! Just in time . . ." Piyu's glasses sparkled, and his cheeks blushed with relief as he saw Alegre coming back, apparently expecting her to draw a buffer zone between Gail and Abed, Abed and Ömer, and salvage whatever there was left to save from this wreck of a birthday dinner. "Just in time for the desserts! Doesn't anyone feel like a good dessert?"

"I sure do," Alegre's face radiated with joy.

Now that the sum total of calories lumbering in her stomach had been reduced to nil, genuinely *nada*, she could start eating anew, devour whatever she wished, even the heaviest desserts on the list, even an entire thousand calories. For the bulimic is one capable of savoring the never-ending freedom of zero, which is, by no means, an ordinary numeral among numerals. It is, in fact, pretty dubious if zero is a number after all, or a numinous gateway to another sphere, if not a sphere in itself, most definitely another ecosystem, a higher consciousness, where everything is possible, nothing irreversibly lost, where there are no endings, and thereby no beginnings. What the bulimics know and experience today, old Babylonians knew, too, and wisely refrained from experiencing. It's no idiosyncrasy that nowhere in their inscriptions and calculations did they utilize the number zero. At any rate, the world became a more difficult place to live in after the first Babylonian dynasty.

"Powdering your nose, Alegre? I'll never understand how much time you girls spend in restrooms . . ."

Piyu must have hoped a gag could be a beeline for the way out of the ongoing squabble, but noticing the impact of his last words on Debra Ellen Thompson's face, he instantly cut it out and instead tried to find in the menu a dessert sweet enough to redress all the sournesses.

But a Chinese restaurant, after all, is not a great place with respect to desserts, even if it's a *ChineseJapanese*. After inspecting the menu, asking the waitress if that was all they had (no cake?), and trespassing into the kitchen to ask the cook couldn't he do anything special (but it's her birthday!), all Piyu could obtain was three melting balls of green tea ice cream.

"Look how beautiful it is," Alegre twirped when Piyu returned, frustrated from his excursion.

In her right hand was a present she'd just got from Abed and Ömer collectively, a pearly cross at the end of a golden chain. As he looked at the swinging necklace in a hypnotized haze, Piyu felt several things, including guilt, resentment, and pity. Guilt he felt toward Alegre because as her boyfriend he should have bought a present surpassing *this*. Resentment he felt toward his housemates for not telling him anything about *this*. And pity he felt toward the wrapped snow globe in his pocket, which could not outshine the glory of *this* no matter how hard it snowed.

The ice-cream balls were not bad at all, but Piyu wasn't interested in providing Alegre with a decent birthday dessert anymore. When asked, the only Chinese waitress on earth with both eyebrows pierced to eternal frowning brought the check instantly, saving them all from additional moments of company.

Before they left the restaurant, Alegre asked permission to go to the restroom again.

"Normal" the Antonym

"The word is *Gail*." Piyu smirked with a broom in his hand, hunting crumbs under the breakfast table.

"Snooty/snobby/sneering/sniping/scornful . . . and all the *S* words are synonyms," Ömer crooned. "And my exemplar sentence is: The other girl is even more *S* words. Did you hear her boast she doesn't eat even imitation meat because that, too, is part of an *omnivorous* lifestyle?"

"*Normal* the antonym," said Abed. "And my exemplar sentence is: Where on earth did a normal girl like Alegre meet these weirdos?"

They shared a bawdy chuckle and headed to the fridge to add their new scores. They kept the scoreboard there under a violet dinosaur magnet, among phone bills, Joe's takeout menu, discount coupons, a recipe for Glazed Beef with Pineapple Salsa (Alegre's), a warped woozy face (a picture of Ömer deep in the throes of yet another swoon—photo taken by Piyu to prove to him the pernicious effects of alcohol on his body and soul), the discounted album cover of an L.A. punk band found in Ömer's room by Abed and instantly made a scene of because of a note at the bottom of the order form promising a 15 percent discount to all those who sent a nude Polaroid, a coupon from Starbucks (Ömer's), a photo of a stunned Arroz in bath suds head to toe, a color scheme in purplish hues where the eggplant tone was named "Enduring," an article titled "Are Hispanics As Good Lovers As They Say?" (which everyone thought belonged to Piyu, and Piyu thought belonged to Alegre, of unknown origin).

As they recorded the scores, Abed seemed to be on the verge of another joke but was instantly shushed. Alegre had just come in, her skin paler than ever.

"Hey guys, it is so *cold* out there." She came in almost yelling, carrying a small box in one hand and waving an envelope in the other. The former she handed to Piyu, the latter to Abed: "Morning news! You should check the mailbox more often."

A strong, stirring odor filled the kitchen as Piyu unwrapped the box. The smell of garlic bread swallowed the smell of coffee, ruining Ömer's pleasure.

"Drink hot chocolate instead," Alegre bellowed, noticing the war of odors.

"Yeah, she is right. Stop drinking that mud, it makes you nervous," either Abed or Piyu snorted, inviting him to share a cup of either mint tea or hot chocolate.

Ömer gave a saintly smile as if pardoning them all for this fatal sin.

"I gotta rush to the office. Just came in to tell you guys thanks for yesterday." Alegre thoughtfully caressed the pearly cross now swinging above the slope of her gaunt, pale chest before turning to Piyu. "Did you tell them what occurred to *us* afterward?"

Piyu gave her a sheepish look as he clapped his hands to draw Arroz's attention toward himself, toward the other counter, anywhere other than garlic bread. The look on his face slyly hinted that whatever thought they were talking about, it had occurred to *her* rather than to *them*, but Ömer and Abed pretended not to notice that detail.

"Piyu and I thought it might do us all good to give a Halloween party at the house. What do you think?"

Ömer shrugged, scratching his head, Abed rumbled a throaty

sound, his mouth full of garlic bread. "Good!" Alegre smiled her thanks, interpreting both gestures as affirmative. "So you guys better start thinking of a costume!"

"Abed, why don't you think of a costume to protest Moroccans being called 'walking sheets' like you told us the other day?" Ömer hollered, suddenly cheering up.

"Like what? Be a walking pillow instead?" Abed groaned and seemed ready to groan more had his glance not been hooked by a sentence in the letter he had just begun to read. He fixed his eyes on the line, muttering in a sagging voice: "This is from my mother. She says she wants to see me."

"Oh, do you have to go?" Alegre asked incredulously, sounding as if she'd relished the idea of a walking pillow, but was surprised to see it walk away so soon.

"No, she says *she* will come." Abed looked up, his large, dark eyes clouded with anxiety. "She's coming!"

"But that's good news, isn't it?" someone faltered aloud.

"Sure," replied Abed, though his face had visibly crumpled. "It's just that . . . how's she gonna come? She . . . she . . . never got on a plane in all her life. She has no idea about America."

"Well, she will *now*, why are you worrying, man?" Piyu said, trying to console a friend, control a dog, and chew garlic bread at the same time, with not much success in any field.

But Abed heard no more. Said no more. Breathed no more. Lifting his chin, together with his cleft, tilting his forehead up, like some soldier swollen with pride though enslaved now by the enemy, he trampled stiffly, and then stopped walking altogether, started running instead. His nose had begun to drip. Before Ömer could realize where he was heading and the possible consequences, Abed had already scurried upstairs and darted straight to the bathroom, only to be rammed back by the locked door. As he halted there stupefied, the door opened and a young, tall, black girl with the shiniest coal-black eyes and the widest smile he had ever seen came out.

"Sorry, it was me in the bathroom." She gave a shy smile with a voice full of oomph. "My name is Vinessa. And you must be . . . *Abdoul?*"

Abed looked away dramatically, but since there was not much of a way to stare in front of bathroom doors, in a few seconds he'd glance back at her. "Actually it is Abed," he corrected, sniffing and snuffling while he spelled it for her.

When he was finally in the bathroom, three thoughts occupied Abed's mind in the looming quietude of postnasal angst. First of all, had she said her name was Vinessa or Vanessa? Second, what had happened to Lynn?

Third, Zahra was coming!

His nose started running again.

"We shouldn't have left poor Arroz alone. Didn't you see how miserable he looked? *Pobrecito!*" Piyu grieved.

"But don't you know that, then, we'd have to leave him at the entrance?" Alegre exhaled—almost a sigh.

"I know, I know!" Piyu squawked.

What he could not squawk was his wish to be treated on purely equal terms. He tried to imagine a scene at the hospital where they'd find this notice at the door strictly forbidding his entrance, something like: *Ni perros o piyus!* In that case he could stick to the comforting legitimacy of this excuse and wait happily outside, wait until Alegre paid her visit and came out. But equal opportunity was no more feasible in the zone of daydreaming than here in actual life. No matter how hard he tried, all Piyu could come up with was the vision of a "hospital scene" in which Arroz looked dejectedly at him, pleading to be taken inside as Piyu looked dejectedly at Arroz, pleading to remain outside, each so badly craving to be in the other's shoes.

"Let's go to the florist first. *La* Tía Piedad loved those scarlet roses last time."

"Alegre, *por favor*, don't make it harder," Piyu wailed, suddenly recalling tedious memories of the last hospital visit, memories pertaining less to the scarlet roses than to their piercing thorns—like how much they'd cost, the embarrassment of carrying that mountainous bouquet, etc.

"Why don't we buy something nice and simple? Why does it have to be so . . . so? . . ."

If only he could find the right word, that exclusively multitalented word that would both express his anger and manage not to sound angry at all. The word that would knock Alegre off the ground without hurting her back. Certainly *ostentatious* would be too obnoxious, *snobbish* even more so, and *flamboyant* not harsh enough. He decided to give *overgenerous* a chance and exclaimed: "But why does it have to be so *overgenerous*?"

"Don't be so mean." Alegre shook her head patiently like shushing a small child. "Certainly we can spare a few bucks for *la* Tía Piedad! You penny-pincher!"

Piyu did not object anymore. Certainly *overgenerous* had missed the point.

They did not quarrel. In point of fact, they *never* quarreled. Not today, not in their worst moments, not even once ever since they had begun dating. After all this time, Piyu had finally conceded, Alegre would by no means have any sort of direct confrontation be it with him or with anyone else. She seemed to have developed supplementary methods to express her exasperation or bitterness. Serving a soup hotter than normal, adding to hot chocolate more sugar than required, or leaving the faucet dripping, the bed undone, furniture in the wrong place . . . Alegre had manufactured a remarkably subtle modus operandi to articulate her sentiments. A proxy vernacular typical of *las tías*.

Alegre's relation with *todas las tías*,* Piyu construed, was reminiscent of a yin-yang shape, only this time the black half was to be named "You are not like *us*, you should have a better future" instead of yin, and the white half "You are not like *them*, don't forget you are one of us, don't forget your roots" instead of yang. Alegre's double seclusion, in turn, could be likened to the small balls of opposite color inside each half of the overall circle. As such, half of the time she struggled to convince *las tías* she couldn't be expected to be like

*All the aunts

them, for she was essentially different, and the rest of the time, she struggled to convince them she shouldn't be expected to be so different for she was essentially like *them*.

Before anything else, her language was different. She hadn't visited Mexico—not even once in her entire life. Though all in all her Spanish was not mediocre, she usually felt more comfortable in English, and spoke an authentic version of Spanglish with both Arroz and Piyu. And yet in one prominent respect, Alegre spoke basically the same idiom with *las tías*. She, too, was a native speaker of the language of the gaze.

Not that they didn't speak. Sure they did. But, even when they were *conversando, charlando, chiflando, platicando, hablando, murmurando, turuquiando, chinchorreando* . . . they never gave up the language of the gaze. It was through this particular vernacular that they'd been shuttling the most elaborate messages to one another all their lives. Amid strangers *las tías* were able to talk without being heard, without uttering a word. No need to articulate speeches. No need to craft fastidious utterances. Why burden yourself with such niggling? Why cripple your mind under the pressure of an avalanche of words that no matter how hard you try to bestow their precise meanings and possible connotations, they will always be able to unleash much less than they were originally aimed at. Accordingly, *las tías* had replaced words, English and Spanish alike, and not only words but even sounds, including snorts, giggles, and guffaws, with a series of wanton movements whereby the eye took myriad shapes, merely through winking, goggling, or squinting, and not necessarily at something or somebody. It was a visual gymnastics in which the gaze spinned round and round in a whorl of lingering looks or flickering peeps, depending on the content of the message conveyed.

It was this indirect language and its plentiful dialects that Piyu found peculiarly mind-boggling. Deep down in his soul he wished, so badly wished, Alegre could be more . . . more womanlike . . . cry and nitpick and shriek like *womanlike women* did all the time. Decoding Alegre's cryptogram from the heat of the soup, some clue buried among the lines of a book left open on the bed, or the saltiness of enchiladas was nerve-racking. Nowadays Piyu had begun to suspect the flowers they bought for *la* Tía Piedad each time, either in their color (why scarlet?) or type (why roses?), were included in this circumlocutory language he could never follow.

Once again, the florist was extremely stylish, pretentiously polished, and annoyingly slow. She glided in ballerina steps between the roses and decorative greens, choosing twelve of each with extreme gracefulness as if they weren't a bundle of plants bound to die in a week but antiquated papyruses with a vow to eternity. As the pair of scissors in her hand drew circles in the air, Piyu felt he was going to faint. What were all these razor-sharp objects doing in a florist store? Scissors, knives, stilettos, blades . . . the whole place was some sort of an arsenal. He ran out and waited outside.

Back on the road again, Alegre's face looked pleased, Piyu's face didn't tell much, now concealed for the most part behind an overgenerous bouquet with a small card attached to it: *"A la mejor tía en el mundo!"**

La Tía Piedad had been taken to the hospital the day before. "She had a backache since early morning, very painful!" Alegre had informed *las otras tías* over the phone, making a call to each from Piyu's room, retelling the incident with nondeclining enthusiasm though repeating exactly the same words each time, and apparently hearing exactly the same comments back. According to what she had told, the day before at the dinner table everything seemed pretty normal. *La* Tía Piedad had scolded the youngest maid for the disgrace of the green pea soup she served, gone to the kitchen to turn the *thing* in the cauldron into something *edible*, compelled the guests at the table to stop eating and wait for her to come back, and then simply hadn't.

When she had gathered the courage to reenter the kitchen, the youngest maid had found the soup boiling in a green trance on the stove and *la* Tía Piedad lying motionless on the floor, with a wooden spoon in her hand. She was immediately taken to the hospital, to the only doctor she trusted on the surface of the earth: Ricardo Aguilera. His nationwide reputation as an excellent doctor, his

---

*To the best aunt in the world!

half-Mexicanness ("There is no half! *Si la madre es Chicana*, so is he,"
la Tía Piedad would argue each time), his kindheartedness toward
his patients . . . but above all, that charming porcelain smile of his,
Piyu suspected, lay behind the great-grandaunt's zealous *Ricardo
Aguilera-nism*.

Each time she was taken to the same hospital where the same
scene was repeated with minor changes here and there. *La Tía*
Piedad would be half sitting on a bed in a pinkish nightgown (or
cherry or ruby or burgundy), *todas las tías* marshaled around her bed
(in rotating orders each time), in a luxurious room saturated with
flowers and more flowers, a frame of San Camilo, the patron saint of
the sick, placed on the side table. The moment she spotted Alegre
enter, *la* Tía Piedad would exclaim, "*¿Dónde está tu Piyu?*"[*] Not even
once had she skipped the question. Correspondingly, not even once
had Alegre skipped taking Piyu with her, though she knew too well
hospitals were full of pointed objects.

"Don't worry. It won't take long, I promise." Alegre gave him an
encouraging smile as they approached the building. "You know *la
tía*. The same mishmash every time, before we all make it to the hospital, she has already recovered. Sometimes I can't help thinking she
does it deliberately, to bring us all under her power, jumbled and
poached."

Piyu offered a shaky curtsy of a nod. By now he recognized that
a substantial part of Alegre's vocabulary was gastronomic, directly
derived from cookbooks and recipes. She had a daily jargon
whereby human relations of all sorts of packaging could be spiced
up or heated until completely baked through. Likewise, love could
be sliced and finely chopped, stirred to dissolve and sautéed until
tender, roasted over low heat and the ribs removed, tossed with a
creamy sauce and marinated, simmered and allowed to cool down,
or garnished with fluffy filling and served with extra sugar, if desired.

They recognized *el* Tío Ramon in the parking lot, calmly smok-

[*]Where is your Piyu?

ing a cigarillo. His drowsy face gave a bob of grim salute as he watched them draw near. "She is fine. No need to worry," he repined with a voice that sounded painfully bored.

As usual Piyu tried to avoid eye contact with him, and failed, as usual. It was something between them; some entirely abstract, hazy tension going on for more than a year now. Every time he caught *el* Tío Ramon's eye, that piercing glint he saw there was incomprehensible to Piyu except as sarcasm. He couldn't help suspecting *el* Tío Ramon was silently, persistently, and grimly making fun of him, of whatever he saw in him, perhaps his own mirror image. It was as if he were saying, "Once I was a different man, this meek *el tío* of a man you see now I've waned into after becoming part of this crazy family."

If that indeed was the message, Piyu took the implications seriously and personally. At those times he tried hard to think of a countermessage. He would never be like *el* Tío Ramon, never fritter away his personality, his independence, his . . .

"Let's go, Piyu, *vámanos*!"

A smile cracked *el* Tío Ramon's humble facade. They left him there and walked inside. As they searched all through the sixth floor, Piyu listened to the echo of Alegre's footsteps, each reverberating at full volume through the empty corridors though she, thank God, never wore any of those pointed heels. The walls on both sides were painted in faint green at waist level. If Piyu had one of those color brochures for decorative items with him, he could find out the color he stood staring at just now was numbered 35-E and named Choice Land. Somewhere along the corridors of Choice Land, they encountered the right room. Alegre entered first.

"*¿Dónde está tu Piyu?*"

Piyu corked his head up behind the bouquet and saluted everyone. *Todas las tías* were standing in a horseshoe around the bed. They saluted him back in chorus and went on with their *charlando, chiflando, chinchorreando*. In the midst of this familiar but still as alien as always rubble, Piyu picked out the great-grandaunt's voice: "Last night, in my sleep, I hear someone call my name. I wake up here in this room. Then I see a light, very bright, rising on my bed. I understand I'll die soon. Before I breathe my last, I've decided to bequeath the china set to Alegre!"

What transpired after that was an itchy, profound silence that in a few seconds muffled everyone, every gesture in the room. *Las otras tías* tried not to look affronted, Alegre tried not to look thrilled. Piyu plowed through slowly, knowing too well he could take advantage of the situation. Once outside, he found a machine that served hot chocolate for a buck. There was no one around, no patient, no doctor, no sign of life. It gave the impression that everyone in the emergency room had run out for an emergency. But if there was no one on this floor, who was in control of all the scalpels and lancets that should be all over the place? He tried to breathe more, panic less. Breathe more, panic less . . . Fortunately, Alegre showed up just on time, for he had almost begun to confuse the order by now: breathe less, panic more.

"¡*Vamanos, Piyu!*" she twirped with an ear-to-ear smile.

Outside, as they passed by the parking lot, to Piyu's relief, *el Tío* Ramon wasn't anywhere around.

The Leftovers

At 7:08 p.m. as Alegre and Piyu got on the T, Ömer got off. As soon as he started walking down the avenue, a grief creeped into his mind for some reason clear to itself but unknown to him. He started looking for a good reason for his despair, found more than he wanted, and chain-smoked five cigarettes while listening to Lagwagon sing into his ears "Coffee and Cigarettes" seven times. Around the corner of Prince Street, he almost ran over a young man who looked remarkably similar to his cousin Murat back in Istanbul.

"Oops, pardon me!" the guy caroled, though there was nothing to pardon. Even that funny tickly smile curving on his shadowy upper lip was exactly the same as cousin Murat's. Annoyed by the coincidence, Ömer shot the stranger a cutting look, which helped him to detect that the guy had less hair than his cousin, and in a year or so would most probably go bald. Relieved that there was no carbon copy of his cousin in the city where he lived, and he hoped nowhere else in the world, Ömer tried to redress the acidity of his earlier glance with a sugary smile, which, unluckily, was instantly misinterpreted by the other guy.

Now frowning more than before, Ömer replaced Lagwagon

with Lou Reed and kept on walking with "Stupid Man." Two minutes, thirty-one seconds. But before the second round of the song, it
occurred to him that maybe his cousin, too, had lost hair within the
time they hadn't seen each other. It must be more than a year now
since they'd stopped talking, and at least five months since he last
saw him. It was sad the way things had turned out. It was sad because everything was so different once. Their mothers being not only
sisters but also neighbors who spent more time in each other's
houses than in their own, and they being of the same age, it was inevitable for them to pass all their childhood glued to one another.
Back then they had so many things in common, or maybe, perhaps,
each merely echoed what the other voiced. They collected the same
things: stamps, foreign coins, and girls' hairbands. In principle, the
hairbands could not be bought from stores; they had to be jerked
from the heads of girls they knew. That's why every piece in their
collection had an identity and story behind it. Their mothers' simul-
taneous and tumultuous objection upon learning about the collection
had shattered that particular project but certainly not the lengthy list
of their common interests. In camaraderie they dreamed of the same
professions (first tavern owner, then baby doctor, woman's doctor,
and then tavern owner again), read the same books (*The Kids from
Pal Street*, *Around the World in Eighty Days*, *The Adventures of Tom
Sawyer*), supported the same team (Fenerbahçe), and favored the
same silly swearing which made them snigger each time they
whooped it (eat that watermelon ass of yours!) though the connotations were a little blurry in their imagination. They were like peas in
a pod then, with interests, accomplishments, and even failures so
much alike, and to continue the resemblance, they started dating
girls that were close friends, and once even fell in love with the same
girl, and then months after, found out they had both slept with and
been duped by her . . . anyway, it was a sore story, but even then
they hadn't broken apart. Such was the density of their camaraderie.
     But the first discernible split had ensued shortly after, when the
porn omnibus housed under Ömer's mattress was discovered, appro-
priated, and annihilated by his mother. The magazines in fact belonged to cousin Murat. This, of course, Ömer had not broken to his

mother. He didn't have to make any explanation anyhow. His mother had first destroyed all the magazines, then pretended there never had been any, and hence, nothing to talk about. That was her archetypical way of solving conflicts, an incredulous conviction that if you pretended hard enough, belief would turn real. It was this style of covering filth with florid patchworks, this harmonious hypocrisy of hers that annoyed Ömer so much.

"Are you out of your mind? You should be grateful she doesn't say anything. My mom would make life hell. You are so lucky!" cousin Murat had rasped.

It must have been then that the first crevice appeared on the surface of their comradeship. A trivial, ethereal fissure, nothing much in itself, but definitely a harbinger of the cleft to come. And as the cleft had extended and widened, Ömer had dourly realized that all this time cousin Murat and he had been as close to one another as two trains stationed side by side at some transitional station, only to discover that the direction they'll head for when the moment of departure comes will be opposite.

The day they heard the news that both had scored so high in the university entrance exam that they had been admitted to the department they mostly aspired to (which happened to be the same, METU, Industrial Engineering), their mothers had cried in joyful unison. A house was rented in Ankara, small but comfy, for the boys, where they were supposed to take care of one another. Before they left, their parents had vowed to have an exceptional celebration together upon the boys' graduation. The improbability of that, however, was soon revealed. In their first two semesters as wannabe industrial engineers, Ömer fell in love with an anarcho-socialist girl, stopped attending classes, started reading Marx, continued reading Marx, enjoyed the poet in Marx more than the theorist but kept this to himself, mealymouthed with his new girlfriend the poverty of socialist tradition in late-capitalist societies, the poverty of oppositional movements in socialist countries, The Poverty of Philosophy, but also the poverty of their sex life that had come to an end when she had suddenly, unilaterally, mind-blowingly declared that their relationship should remain at a platonic level. In what followed Ömer became a confused lover, an even more confused Marxist, joined the student union, broke up with his girlfriend, had a terrible quarrel with the leaders of the student union, participated in numerous demonstrations, got arrested, failed all but one course . . . while cousin Murat solely, unswervingly, unfalteringly studied . . . and studied . . . and studied.

Once released from custody, Ömer had found everyone at home, and myriad dishes at the table, all his favorites, all in mountainous amounts as if it weren't only two days of custody but years of starving imprisonment from which he had returned.

"You've been in bad company! I didn't know these leftist *things* still continued in this country," his aunt had pouted at Ömer as she served the yogurt soup.

Ömer had observed his mother fidgeting on her chair upon hearing the issue being brought up, searching for an alternative topic and upon failing to find any, heading toward the kitchen to stir the sauce, to decorate the desserts . . . whatever.

"These leftists are only leftovers, Ma," cousin Murat had replied with a scowl on his face to make it obvious to his mother and to everyone at the table that he did not approve of *them*.

Ömer had raised no objection. Cousin Murat was right in actual fact. That is what they were: "leftovers," the still limply politicized, young and middle-aged and old alike, unable to fully recover from the deadening depoliticization of the military takeover of thirteen years before. Today's resistance was nothing but the remnants, the scraps of that potent, profuse, and mostly vivacious opposition that used to thunder during the 1970s, when Ömer was a child, thunder until the 1980 coup d'état.

Some of the leftovers came from traditional families. A few others, on the other hand, were the children of once-leftist parents, quite a number of whom had even named their children Revolution (boys and girls alike, for revolution was supposed to be androgynous), only to bitterly regret that decision as soon as the military came to power, and in the ensuing years, raised these children in the most depoliticized way they could to redress the balance. That's why, sardonically, most walking Revolutions in Turkey happened to shine among the most fervent supporters of the status quo.

The parents of these Revolutions, meanwhile, had never repeated the same mistake. Some parents had come up with a better name for their second children: Evolution. And then after a few more years, if there was a third or fourth child on the way, they chose some other name completely devoid of any far-reaching connotations, possibly a flower or a star or anything, as long as it was cute and shiny, and above suspicion. Ömer wondered where else on earth but in Turkey could one find siblings whose names ranged from Revolution to Evolution and from there, to Tulip or Gentlewind.

As to the estrangement between the two cousins, it would remain more or less the same in the years to follow, wherein Ömer oscillated to and fro, decided he did not want to be an industrial engineer anymore, retook the university entrance exam, this time to be educated in the Department of Political Science in Bogazici University in Istanbul, and to everyone's surprise, including his own, managed to get a high score, left his cousin behind and moved back to Istanbul, and once again fell in love with the chaos of the old city, met other girls there and other groups, became extremely successful in the classes, amazing everyone even further, including himself, though he failed enormously in all his affairs with the other sex. At the same time, he moved away from Marxism toward situationism, from Marx toward Guy Debord and from there, cantered toward a blend of hedonism, pessimism, and cynicism, after which he'd galloped straight into abysmal nihilism, drank too much, vomited too much, flirted too much, screwed too much, lamented too much, and consistently staggered up and down, down and up in life. Cousin Murat, in the meantime, had studied . . . and studied . . . and studied . . . graduated, found a good job, and got married. And today the more he thought about him, the more likely it seemed to Ömer that cousin Murat could be a bald man by now, and the more, accordingly, the chances of a replica of him sauntering the streets of Boston.

In front of 8 Pearl Street, he took his headphones off, and shushed Lou Reed before entering the house, or actually, failing to enter, for the door was blockaded by an ecstatic hail: *"Welcome! Welcome! Welcome!"*

Behind the porch door skipped and hopped the vast bulk of a painfully bored and desperately hungry Arroz, his tail beating drum and bass. Once he'd managed to sneak into the porch, and overcome the soggy, sloppy squeezes, Ömer made five sandwiches. Arroz gobbled down three, he ate two. Then they both sank onto the couch, listening to Sugarcult's "Stuck in America." Three minutes, twenty seconds. They were in their third round when the phone rang.

Ömer remembered telling Vinessa he'd come to pick her up after work, but now he didn't feel like going out again. He tried to think of a nice excuse, could only come up with: "There is no one at the house. If I, too, go out Arroz has to stay alone! He'd be depressed." It was true, at least to some extent. Confident with his excuse he picked up the phone. But it was a distant call, from a distant love.

"What time is it there?" Ömer asked her the first thing, as if that had to be clarified before they could go on speaking.

"You mean here or there?" Defne chuckled with a tinge of nervousness in her voice. There was an echo in the line, which made her sound even more nervous.

Ömer paused. It was not the sort of pause one gives in moments of deep contemplation. It was more like the sort of pause one gives at the sight of something unexpected, something irksome, and yet so familiar, like seeing your own worn-down image on the tinted glass of a car passing by, and suddenly facing the truth about yourself. It was a similar tremor that helped him to realize whichever way the question was asked, she'd still be giving the wrong answer. For whatever the port or destination, her "here" would remain his "there."

Behind the window display of Squirmy Spirit Chocolates, Gail was busy dripping caramel dots on the eyes of the cobras around the necks of a trayful of chocolate Shiva the Destroyers, when she spotted the woman pass by the store again. Every day unfailingly at

11:45 a.m., she passed by the store and half an hour later she walked back with a paper container in her hand. She went to a soup kitchen nearby, Gail was almost sure, and inside the paper container there probably was soup, chicken noodle, she guessed. Every time she saw her pass, she couldn't take her eyes off her. Actually, every day at this time Gail stood waiting for this homeless woman to wobble down the street pulling a tattered suitcase on wheels, breezing by in a gust of rancid smells. Sometimes she stopped the pedestrians, only the ones she picked out, Gail had observed, to make the same statement as always: "Jesus told me you had a spare dollar . . ." Apart from that she almost never uttered a word.

As she passed by, Gail fixed her gaze with an uncanny blend of alarm and admiration on the woman's hands—fingertips of the color of sour cherries, nails buried behind a veil of mire, big, crumpled, and callused hands tainted with dark blood clots though they bore no discernible wound. Gail did not know, but barely sensed, what it was in these hands that attracted her attention so much, or what it was in this homeless woman that enthralled and troubled her simultaneously.

One thing Gail both feared and hoped was that the *Jesustoldme-youhadasparedollar* Lady was aware of her, too. Though not even once had she turned her head and peered inside the store, Gail couldn't help thinking that as she strolled across the street, from the corner of her eye she was looking at her, deep down into her soul. *Jesustold-meyouhadasparedollar* Lady knew too well why Gail was mesmerized by her presence, and drawn into her orbit. And yet, so did Gail. She, too, could see that in actual fact, she and this woman were not so far apart. As she watched her from behind the shop window, Gail couldn't help thinking that the frontier separating them was as thin and frail as this barrier of glass.

While she watched the *Jesustoldmeyouhadasparedollar* Lady, Gail also watched the ways in which this homeless woman was seen by others, including herself. She observed her being sneeringly avoided, lavishly pitied, grotesquely helped, and systematically ignored. Those who shunned her as if she were infected with some sort of disease, Gail thought bitterly, did have a point in fact, because, indeed, she was contagious but not in the way they supposed. This was a contamination that only affected those already affected. Those that had already, and for entirely diverse reasons, carried the virus—that specific malady that did not impede them from living in society, not even from being successfully a part of it, but still at the same time, even at the peak of their accomplishments, kept them on the verge of tergiversation, excommunication, and derangement. Gail feared she might have nothing to fear because she, too, might already be infected by the lure germane to those that destroyed their own plumage.

For Christmas, along with taffy Santa Clauses, praline reindeer, candy-corn bells, honeycrisp angels, and nougat-bar cherubs, and I-Believe-in-Santa marshmallows, Gail was planning to make a set of *Jesustoldmeyouhadasparedollar* Lady bonbons. She would sell these to happy families, or those with the ambition of becoming one, so that they could transfer, without knowing it, this shadow of a homeless woman into their buoyantly decorated homes, wherein every night too much light secreted the darkness out-of-doors. She would make them delicious and delicate. Each *Jesustoldmeyouhadasparedollar* Lady bonbon would be covered by bitter chocolate outside, a solid, dark armor that, once bitten, would leak out the soft and sweet fondant silently waiting to be discovered inside.

The Hole

Once they started to consider making the house ready for Zahra, it didn't take them long to realize what little they knew about her. Was she *traditionalistic*? Would she be annoyed by the consumption of alcohol, for instance, or of bacon, or any other thing that wouldn't even occur to them? How much of themselves could they reveal and how much should they conceal? What did Zahra like? What was she like?

"What shall I cook for her?" Alegre asked from the chair she had stepped on to look for a fondue set she was sure she'd put somewhere in the cupboards.

By now Abed was tired of everyone questioning him about Zahra's ways. Tired and somewhat edgy: "Why do you have to cook all the time? Maybe you should take a break!"

But the moment these words flooded from his mouth, he regretted saying them. "I'm sorry, Alegre, I didn't mean that. It's just that, it makes her happy to cook for me, you know. Would you mind not cooking while she's here and let *her* do it?" Abed asked in a droning voice, swiftly realizing the sacrifice he demanded from her. "It's only for two weeks . . ."

Alegre nodded affably, though without giving full-length attention and thereby not comprehending that the implications could be
complex for her. At the moment all she wanted, along with the fondue set, was to ease Abed's worries. Zahra's arrival had generated a
firm and flawless comradeship at 8 Pearl Street, as if they'd now
united in stalwart solidarity vis-à-vis a globally renowned figure that
though she came in different packs and sizes was still in her intimate,
ubiquitous, eternal figure familiar to them all: mother!

"Alegre, come down please," Abed moaned, holding her chair
tightly as if scared that if she did tumble down, she'd shatter to
pieces, for that's how tiny and fragile she looked from down here.
Had she lost more weight these days? he wondered. But instead he
asked: "What do we need a fondue set for? Zahra needs no such
thing!"

"Aha, here it is," cheeped Alegre, pulling out the fondue set, and
handing it piece by piece to Abed below. "I need everything to be
perfect. There are gonna be too many people to please. Zahra is
coming. Party people are coming. Friday is *the* big day!"

"You mean *Thursday*," Abed corrected grimly. "Halloween is on
Thursday!"

"Yup, but the party is on Friday." She passed down the enam-
eled pot, but Abed was not there to hold her chair anymore.

Instead of arguing with her, Abed ran out of the room and kept
running until he found Piyu in Ömer's room, both pasted to the computer screen, admiring the scintillating animations in a newly built
Canadian Web page.

"Piyu, *amigo*, you gotta talk to Alegre. Do something!" Abed
dashed in with fondue forks in each hand. "Alegre says the party is
on Friday. That's the day Zahra arrives. Look, we cannot postpone
Zahra's flight, so we have to make this party thing some other day!"

Having some difficulty in diverting his gaze from the luminous
animations to Abed's utterly dull face, it took Piyu a few seconds
more than usual to fathom the meaning of that soliloquy. Once having decoded the message, he bit the cuff of his shirtsleeve, only to
let it go to wail: "I can't do that, she invited so many people!!"

"If Halloween is on Thursday, how come she is having a

Halloween party on Friday?" Abed moved his hands nervously. A few more moves were enough to block Piyu's mind as he stared hypnotized at the sharp-edged fondue forks drawing circles before his eyes, while his face grew paler and paler, acquiring an ashen tone toward his cheeks—adding a cross expression tinged with desolation.

Ömer jerked his chair backward and goggled at his two housemates in double amusement: "Why don't you two cool down? I don't see any problem here. Party on Friday. Zahra comes on Friday. So what? What's wrong with that?"

"What's *wrong* with that?" Abed pointed a fork at him while hopping forward like a fencer making balestra. "That woman has lived all her life in this small town where everybody knows everyone down to their tiniest sins. She has no idea at all about American culture. She wonders what my life here is like, and she is deeply worried about me, OK? So she dares to do this journey, to see how her only son is doing, and her first impression of my life in this country should *not* be Iggy the wigworm and a bunch of drunk monsters tumbling on her!"

In the ensuing minutes, Piyu made two attempts to ask Alegre to alter the date of the party but in both, he caught her talking on the phone, inviting new people for *Friday*; Abed searched the Net for alternative flights from Morocco but common sense stopped him midway through; and Ömer stayed still in his chair, watching neither getting anywhere, and privately amusing himself.

"Would you guys like to know what you're gonna eat this Friday?" Alegre swished into the room with the wrong mood at the wrong time.

Creepy-crawl cinnamon bites, grave-shaped brownies, skull-shaped mozzarellas, eye-popping stuffed tomatoes, eye-shaped meatballs, ghoulish lime salsa, giant chocolate cockroach, strawberry-twizzler-spider, Iggy the wigworm, Wanda the wiggle worm, Sammy the swirl worm, liposuction leftover loaves, brain surgery salad . . . and so on went the Friday Special Menu, tweaking Abed's nerves further and further with each item on the list. It was then that Piyu came up with an idea, a middling resolution: to change their rooms!

On Friday evening, around 8:30 p.m., Abed would be back from the airport with Zahra. The party would have hardly commenced by then. Not too many would've shown up yet, thus making it relatively easy to keep everyone in the living room, doors firmly closed, so that when Abed appeared with Zahra, he could take her directly upstairs through the back door, preventing her from peeking at unwarranted monsters. During the rest of the night she would stay and sleep in the bedroom on the third floor, and would be safe and sound there.

The plan requiring numerous modifications, that's what they'd been busy doing during the rest of the afternoon. Particular items were carried down from the third floor to Abed's room (*New Jerusalem Bible: Saints Devotional Edition*, a glazed porcelain Jesus carrying the cross, Blue Madonna nightlight, a sixteen-by-twenty Guardian Angel frame, Piyu's sheets and pajamas, Alegre's private notes and love letters to him, and several items belonging to Arroz, including Buddy Biscuits, and a radiant Frisbee he was supposed to catch in the air but usually didn't bother to). Then, of course, several other things had to migrate from the first floor to Abed's new room (the Holy Koran, a picture of Abed's father, a leather amulet against the evil eye that Zahra had made him promise to carry wherever he went, a music box in which he kept Safiya's letters, and clothes, sheets, books, and all sharp-edged objects in the room, including safety pins).

Watching the bidirectional exodus of religious objects in the house with increasing amusement that he had increasing difficulty in hiding, Ömer, too, was ready to make his share of concessions by giving a break to his daily libidinal routine with the other sex. But the greatest concession, no doubt, was Alegre's. She was going to cede *her* kitchen to Zahra.

Preparations done, concessions made, objects temporarily sent to exile, by late evening, Abed had eventually calmed down. He kept Ömer company as the latter chain-smoked on the porch, and then, surprisingly, borrowed a cigarette from him. Abed smoked in a puffy funny way, too smoggy, too smoky; the way people not used to smoking do whenever they try to have a cigarette. Ömer suppressed a smile. Silently and stiffly they sat there, facing the street, their eyes fixed on the maple tree in front of the house.

"So your father died last year . . . were you in the States then?"

"Papa passed away right before I came to the States." Abed puffed another altocumulus. "I had received my acceptance from Tufts and had everything ready by June. Two weeks before my flight, Papa died. His heart stopped in his sleep. A peaceful death, they said. After the funeral I decided to change my plans, I didn't want to leave Zahra alone. You know the condolers kept saying to Zahra she should still be glad that her husband left a son behind. I mean that is the kind of mentality there. When the father is absent, it's the son's duty to take care of his mother. But Zahra refused, no way! Let me tell you, Omar, one thing about my mother. If she has made up her mind, there is absolutely *nothing* on earth that can convince her to the contrary. So she sent me here and instructed me not to come back until I'd got the degree."

A balmy, caramel-like scent stuffed the dense silence that ensued. "That smells wonderful, Alegre," Abed yelled back over his shoulder, still feeling bad about scolding her this afternoon.

"Creepy-crawl cinnamon rolls!" came Alegre's vivid voice from the kitchen, having long ago forgiven him. "They'll smell even better when fully baked."

A car passed by, illuminating the porch for a few seconds, in concert with the branches of the maple tree. Recently the leaves had tinted an amazingly bright crimson, and right on time, Abed was glad, for Zahra to see. If he had one of those color brochures for decor items at this instant, he'd see that the color he was looking at was named Cherries Jubilee.

"Don't you find uneducated women's fascination with education astonishing?" Abed asked, lowering his voice to an almost inaudible timbre. "I mean, my mother had little education herself, you know, and with all her heart she wants me to have a Ph.D. in a branch she can't even pronounce. What good will catalysts and hydrogens do her? But all the same she believes in my vocation more than I do."

They did not speak for a while, both peering thoughtfully at the arboreal silhouette outside.

"When the eye disappears, the place remains a hole."

"What?"

"That's what Zahra said to the condolers." Abed stubbed out the cigarette. "She said, when the eye disappears, its place should be kept empty. If you try to fill a hole with clay, all you'll have is clay in the shape of a hole. My son will go to America because a son's presence cannot fill a father's absence. A hole has to remain a hole."

Zahra and Iggy the Wigworm

Thursday night Abed woke up sweating in fear in his new room upstairs on the third floor. After being absent for one full year, she had returned: the woman of his nightmares. As sinister and scary as always but this time even more menacing. Abed felt he could not go back to sleep again, and yet his body disproved him. In the morning, no matter how hard he would try to remember the dream, all he could recall was only one scene from it, wherein they were all gathered in the kitchen, except that this kitchen was a huge, cavernous hollow in the ground. On a single stove at the corner there was a boiling cauldron. Alegre was calmly dipping fondue forks into it. Abed then learned in panic that the hollow they stood in was in fact a swimming pool and soon there'd be a swimming contest there. Scared that water might fill in anytime, he warned everyone to pack and leave, but Alegre did not want to go without the cauldron. Piyu and others meanwhile were studying at a mammoth wooden table at the other end of the pool, completely unaware of what was going on. Then all of a sudden, somebody yelled that the faucets were being opened and water was coming. When he turned toward that direction, however, Abed could see in awe that instead of water, it was the dream woman coming his way.

Shooting him a fleeting glance in her long waxen dirty gown, she had drawn a circle around the boiling cauldron and then simply vanished. She had said nothing, done nothing, changed nothing; obviously she had no specific role anywhere in the scenario. Next morning as he ruminated about it, Abed had this strange feeling that he was having this fully autonomous dream but then, wherever it might be from, this woman had popped up, trespassing, traversing, and transmuting his dream zone.

But Friday was no day to lose time brooding over a dream. Abed had other things to worry about all day long, too many arrangements to wrap up. Finally, at 5:05 p.m. he walked out of the house, made a beeline toward the scruffy Volkswagen in dire need of being washed, focused his gaze on an amorphous stain on the windshield, the stain turned out to be nothing important, he got into the car, inadvertently gaped outside, and froze up. The maple tree had disappeared. In its place, mockingly, stood a gaunt, dull, wooden figure, like a tarnished effigy of the arborescent splendor that once coruscated there. The Cherries Jubilee was kaput, alas, that stunning crimson had withered away with each leaf abandoning its branch, like blood callously draining away from the veins of a wounded animal bleeding to death. Abed felt a tension descend. He started the engine, hurrying to get away from this mood as quickly as possible. It was odd that such sudden sadness grabbed him on the day of Zahra's arrival.

Even if this cryptic misery had accompanied him to the airport, he would have forgotten about it entirely the second he caught sight of Zahra, there among a fussy bunch of passengers incapable of standing for ten more minutes in the customs line as if it weren't they who had sat motionless for ten hours of flight, and after a while had become so accustomed to it they could simply keep on flying forever. Unlike them, though, Zahra looked resplendently serene in a pasty white head scarf and a long silky taupe manteau that either made her look more shortish and plump than usual, or she'd gained weight and shrunk a bit in the meantime. But that hidden scent of hers was, Abed would quickly ascertain, the same as always. While she hugged him and cried, kissed him and cried, hugged and kissed him, and then cried, Abed savored the syrupy scent now canopying him like a gauzy silk scarf, and once deep inside that dearly beloved shelter, he, too, felt about to cry. But then followed the usual hustle and bustle of airports, the hassle of orbiting around baggage carousels, getting back all the suitcases but one, waiting for the missing suitcase, stop waiting and start worrying about the missing suitcase, and keep worrying until you spot it placidly standing somewhere at the back, long before pulled aside from the lane by God knows which one of the passengers. Then came the traffic. There must've been an accident somewhere, Abed informed Zahra, for the road back from the airport had never lasted so long. Not to his knowledge.

Thus, when the originally golden-brown, currently less golden, more brownish Volkswagen finally parked in front of 8 Pearl Street, four hours and ten minutes had passed since Abed had frozen there, gaping sorrowfully at the nudity of the maple tree under the evening sky. Four hours and ten minutes is more than enough for several changes of significant value to crop up. To give an idea, the female mayfly, beautifully named Ephemeroptera, or *Dolania americana*, lives less than five minutes after its final molt. It is within this period that she mates, lays her eggs, and then dies. Four hours, ten minutes is quite a lengthy time on the surface of the earth, and the surface around a party house is no exception.

"Hey, Abdoul, yahoo . . ."

Once they got out of the car, Abed and Zahra squinted in the direction of the voice, detecting first the blurred frame of the house (an image of 8 Pearl Street under the dim light of half a dozen jack-o'-lanterns and flimsy candles decorating the house but shadowing the multitude inside) and then, somewhere in the precincts of that frame the faint periphery of a moving subject (a girl waving and windmilling gleefully from an open window as if she'd wound herself up into some delirious wobble of a dance she'd just invented, simultaneously holding an empty wineglass in her hand, and two other glasses on her head. It looked like Vinessa. It was definitely Vinessa. If not, it was Vanessa).

"How come she doesn't drop them?" Zahra exclaimed admiringly, walking toward the open window.

She had just started distinguishing some other items standing equally firmly on the head and body of this teetering black girl, first an alarm clock, next an ashtray, and a faucet—and could perhaps spot some more items, had Abed not seized her arm, grumbled something, and almost pushed her around the house, never stopping till they'd reached the back door. But there was no back door anymore. Instead, there were three exasperated-looking guys, and a cavewoman, all unfamiliar faces, all guzzling beer, and either on a vigorous verbal galloping to get to the bottom of some edgy topic of too tortuous and tormenting ramifications, or simply chattering in Spanish. They made no attempt to give a break, not even a fleeting pause, but did gently lean back to let Abed and Zahra pass through, inspecting curiously the short plump woman's costume in the meantime. Abed glared back at each one of them, at the laces on his shoes, at the knob of the door, at his meek mortal existence in this hectic world . . . and leaving all ontological considerations on the doormat, rammed Zahra into the dim corridor.

Inside, trying to be cordial and commanding at the same time, he grabbed Zahra's hand, guided her through the corridor, which was not a corridor anymore but a suffocating tube of swinging and sweating bodies. Soon he gave up cordiality and opted for command, left the hand and seized the arm, shoved his mother's bulky body through the slope of the staircases right up to the bedroom on the third floor, and closed the door behind. Once there, he had to wait several minutes for Zahra's respiration to turn back to normal, every second adding up to his augmenting guilty conscience. Ashamed of the fuss he had made, Abed attempted to make a reasonable explanation but only could come up with: "They are all good people, Ma!"

They were all, he said, good friends, and had gathered for a small celebration, no big deal. Some sort of an American party that'd be over in a couple of hours.

Still struggling with her breathing, Zahra looked around inquisitively. The room was pleasant and tidy, and to her relief, the windows looked eastward, to welcome the sun the first thing in the morning. She wondered which way Kibla was, but as she turned back to ask, catching a glimpse of the shades spinning in Abed's eyes made her ask instead: "Son, do you sleep well? Any more nightmares?"

"No, Mama, I don't see them . . . *her* anymore," Abed stammered, deciding to keep his most recent nightmare to himself.

One by one, the suitcases were opened, carefully wrapped boxes and secretive gift packs scattered around, first invading the bed, and from there moving in every direction all over the carpet. Apparently, Zahra had brought almost nothing for herself, everything she carried all the way here being for Abed.

"And how is your nose?"

"My nose!? My nose is a calamity!" Abed bellowed, all of a sudden losing his confidence. "Never stopped flowing since I came here. It's killing me!" But then a chirpy, almost childish, cheerfulness crept into his voice. "My nose doesn't like being away from you, Ma."

Zahra held his face between her soft, tepid palms, and smiled at this handsome but always somewhat squeamish son of hers. A bosomy kindness enveloped them until Abed inquired:

"So tell me, Mama, how is Safiya? Didn't she . . . send me anything, or her greetings?"

Swinging instantly to the very other end of the mood spectrum, Zahra's face cramped. Stiff and silent, she stood away from Abed awhile, but then she nevertheless pulled out a package, not missing in the meantime any single gesticulation to display the extent of her disapproval. Abed pretended not to get the message, took the package instead, and let out a lengthy yawn, the only way he knew to ease escalating tensions, at least his own.

"You must be very hungry. I'll go downstairs to bring you something to eat. There is so much stuff, you'll love it."

Before heading toward the kitchen, however, he stopped on the second floor, where he found the bathroom occupied, knocked on Ömer's door, didn't like the sounds coming from inside, ducked into the small room next door where they kept all the junk, sat on the floor with his legs tucked under him, and opened the package Safiya had sent. There was a letter inside, a picture of her with her elder sister's son, and a small, scented decorative box. When he'd finished reading the letter, Abed had to start reading again, not for the sake of a more meticulous assessment or in order to read between the lines this time, but mainly because he'd rushed through the letter so much that he had understood absolutely nothing from it.

After the second reading what he needed was privacy and silence to contemplate awhile, but once downstairs, party people were quick to remind him this might not be the right time or the right place for that. As he passed through the corridor bumping into all sorts of people in all sorts of costumes, Abed's despair left him—a little flustered, a little tired, and also now a little curious to distinguish who was who or *what* at this party.

One such puzzle was a tall, hefty girl in a pinky pink bathing suit that had a huge candy-shaped cushion attached to her butt.

"Guess what I am!" she yelled downward to Abed, narrowing her ferrety eyes as if hunting for the appropriate punishment in case he gave the wrong answer.

"She is a candy-ass!" somebody trumpeted from behind, sounding delighted and gratified for having illuminated yet another party fool. After that, Abed did not feel like wondering who was who or what anymore. But they informed him, all the same. Everywhere he turned, he kept seeing Arroz, dressed as either a pirate, or a pirate's dog. He looked for Piyu, but couldn't find him anywhere. To his relief, there were no walking sheets or walking pillows around. Debra Ellen Thompson was here, wearing a long, pea-green dress, with a basket of plastic fruits in her hand, and an olive laurel on her head that somehow had made her hair look redder than ever and her ears even bigger. "I am Mother Nature," she said. But Abed wasn't paying attention to her anymore; his eyes now focused on his mother's welcomer, busily assessing the details of her costume that he'd missed the first time. Apart from those two glasses of wine, several other items were hanging from Vinessa's costume, which consisted basically of a white box wrapped by a stained bedsheet to which she had glued an ashtray, an alarm clock, and condoms of every color, some filled with a pretty dubious substance. Abed groaned nervously trying hard not to curse Ömer, who had now appeared behind his girlfriend's shoulder, dressed in a torn cat costume with tire tracks and blood splashes all over him.

"I am the cat crossing an autobahn, and she is a one-night stand," Ömer beamed with tequila pride. Abed cursed Ömer. Ömer twirled and scurried back to play "I Kissed a Drunk Girl," and kept kissing Vinessa until the song was over. Three minutes, twenty seconds. When the song was over, he played it again, and then again, and then . . . everybody cursed Ömer. That was the start. The whole lot went into tumultuous hyperspeed, everyone fighting over the CD player to be in command of the banging music. Abed cursed everybody.

When he had finally found his way to the kitchen, "Hellooo, Abed, isn't this a great party?" the skinniest scarecrow on earth saluted him jovially. "How is your mother? Here, I prepared a yummy tray for you to take to her."

She had indeed. Brain surgery salad with saliva dressing, icky sticky sugar snakes, meringue bones, stomach-churning bile-green mashed potatoes, eye-popping stuffed tomatoes, all were here, ready to be carried upstairs. Abed gaped at the witch-finger cookies, trying to grasp how come they were oozing blood under their nails. With all due respect to her culinary talents, he extracted several items from Alegre's menu, and replaced them with slices of cheese and bread, the most basic of all food on earth, and for good measure, added a glass of milk.

On his way back, proceeding among an ever-hungry crowd with a tray of comestibles proved to be quite hard. But he didn't have to go very far, anyway. There, ahead of him on the couch, next to a hair-straightened-up-in-rigid-gelled-bolts-and-clothes-torn-and-burned Gail that looked like a lightning victim, ardently recounting how or why (or both) in *Blade Runner* Zhora had smashed through glass windows to a girl dressed up as Zhora in *Blade Runner*, and a couple passionately transmitting a chocolate spider to and fro on each other's tongues, Abed caught the sight of the flabbergasted, disquieted, but still-smiling face of his mother.

"Ma! Zahra!" he hollered as if these were two different people. "What are you doing here?"

Zahra shrugged her shoulders. "I was thirsty. I called out for you, but you didn't hear."

"Ma, please take this tray and go to your room, I'll fetch your water, you *must* be tired," Abed gulped, perspiring, struggling, scrambling for a justification. "Tomorrow we'll go around the city. You need to have some rest now."

"Where is your costume?" Zahra wondered. "Why aren't you wearing a costume like your friends?"

"Well, actually I *am* wearing a costume. I am disguised as *the-only-normal-and-sane-person-in-the-room*!" Abed grinned. "Don't you think all this fuss is stupid, Ma?"

"Every country has its own people," murmured Zahra. "All people have their own customs. If you are in their land, you should be more agreeable. The guest eats what the host offers."

Abed gazed at her in wonder.

Abed gazed at her in wonder and all night long continued doing so, as he observed his *not-even-a-word-in-English* mother: lighting the burned-out candles in jack-o'-lanterns; assisting a scarecrow in the kitchen; serving round platters of sugar skulls and trays of werewolf claws; inspecting the embroidery on the skirts of Mother Nature's long dress; supplying extra beef-and-garlic flavored potato chips to a head-chopped-off-body, and extra of everything to a dog with a black bandanna and an eye patch; repeatedly gesticulating to apologize over and over to a girl in a pinky pink bathing suit for crashing into her with a bowl of grisly spicy soup; helping a one-night stand crawling on the floor to find an alarm clock lost while bopping and hopping; boiling mint tea with lemon for a tottering cat with tire tracks all over his body now vociferously vomiting in the bathroom; taking the mint tea back and making a pot of dark coffee for a tottering cat with tire tracks all over his body still vociferously vomiting in the bathroom . . .

The next morning . . . actually, there was no next morning.

Though each for a different reason, neither Ömer (headache), Piyu (stomachache), nor Abed (nightmares) could wake up the next day before the sun had made it halfway through a breezeless sky. And even when they had woken up, none wanted to get out of bed, less due to fatigue than to avoid the impossible postparty mission of cleaning up the wreck. By 3:00 p.m. when they could no longer twiddle their thumbs in bed, one by one they showed up in the kitchen, the last place you want to enter alone after a tortuous get-together night but somehow cannot help heading toward the first thing in the morning. But to their amazement, there were no heaps of muddy plates on the counter, no stinking swamp of suspicious contents in the sink, no piles of leftovers already ossified and gone putrid, no repulsive remnants . . . the kitchen was as clean and sparkling as it had ever been (even Piyu would concede), and either it had enlarged overnight, or had simply become more visible.

The kitchen proved to be only the beginning, however, a tangible port to embark on an overseas expedition, doggedly ambitious despite the vagueness of the final destination. In the ensuing hours Zahra's deluge of hygiene expanded in every possible direction and into every perceptible crevice of the house, moving with the velocity and fortitude of the red and blue arrows illustrating the sea and silk routes of the Tang dynasty over an intercontinental map in a BBC documentary.

As the arrows moved to and fro, hygiene entered into every corner of the house, and so did Zahra necessarily, seeing things she wasn't supposed to see. Thus she took notice of a hidden plastic bag in the kitchen full of grapefruit peelings nibbled down to their skins; detected in Ömer's room the glow-in-the-dark condoms and the faux-leopard-fur–lined leather cuffs produced with a large O-ring on each cuff to provide plenty of bondage possibilities; secretly rejoiced at finding a Koran in a drawer next to Piyu's bed, but was deeply worried when a pendant of a Christian saint appeared in Abed's room; and finally discovered Arroz's fleas, for which he was soaped and washed, resoaped and rewashed, shampooed and rinsed, powdered and combed, groomed and perfumed during the rest of the day.

Then there were some other discoveries she'd have to make, because to everyone's surprise, Zahra simply could not identify any of the characters she'd met with the ogres and creatures she'd socialized with at the Halloween party. Hence, some people had to be introduced to her for the second time. Although Zahra had liked her so much, Vinessa was not included among these mostly because two days after the party she and Ömer had broken up, in a mysterious and impetuous way that had stunned no one in particular.

When Zahra remet Alegre, she generally liked her. Though too skinny and inclined to interfere in *her* kitchen, still she seemed cute and could, why not, be a perfect wife to Abed. When Zahra remet Debra Ellen Thompson, she liked her, too. Though her hair was as red as hell and no longer than that of an abstemious dervish, and the freckles on her arms were no less than the number of fish and fowl swarming in the army of the prophet Suleiman, still she seemed nice and could—why not—be a good wife to Abed. When Zahra met Gail, she did not like her at all. Though the girl was neither skinny nor freckled, though her nocturnal hair was plentiful enough to flow in every direction, and she obviously had no interest in the kitchen work, there was something in those eyes of hers that bitterly annoyed Zahra: They were blue!

"*La ðjûwuj l-mra 'aina zarqa âlu tkun 'anða ð-ðrâhim f ðonðôqa.*"*

"What does she say?" asked Gail.

"She says you are beautiful." Abed smiled affably.

He had, indeed, distorted. And it wasn't the first time if truth be told. Now and then he did apply some makeup on the blemishes of the words he translated, or simply skipped words to do so. But Abed can't be said to be the only one. For each and every translator is, no matter how minute or voluminous his task, an accomplice in some thievery. Just like the fine merchandise transmitted from one place to another via caravan routes, words, too, are habitually plundered on the way, not by cinematographically head-to-toe black hordes of troglodytes but by cultivated personas in the shape of writers, poets, publishers, and *especially* translators.

Despite Abed's periodic prevarication, however, in the days to follow, an unexpected intimacy would flourish between Gail and

---

*"Don't marry a blue-eyed woman, even if she has money in her box."

Zahra, an amity streaming a course of its own, giving birth to its own lexicon. Accordingly, Gail had started to spend long hours at 8 Pearl Street, eager to learn more about Zahra's life and culture, especially about the notion of *"baraka."**

"Could you ask her, Abed, can food have a *baraka* of their own?" Bread and water sure had, and so did figs.

"Could you ask her, Abed, can places have a *baraka* of their own?"

Mosques and saints' tombs sure had, and so did wells.

So it went. At first Abed had reckoned Gail's company might be of interest for his mother but with that expectation fulfilled, it had started to become an annoyance for him. Part of his exasperation, sure enough, stemmed from his having barely any sleep these days. The woman of his nightmares had appeared every single night in the last week, just like she used to do in the past. Yet, it was different this time. Her visits had turned into a series, of which he watched one episode each night, only to wake up sweating and never able to sleep again until dusk.

"Oh, Abed, come, will you please ask her about these scars, is this some kind of a treatment?"

On the morning of his third sleepless night, Abed found Gail and Zahra sitting side by side at the kitchen table, with an amazingly similar expression of polished serenity on their faces, glittering like some Benetton ad.

Rather than transmitting the question, Abed preferred to answer it himself this time. "Some sort of a scarification." He waved his hand as if wielding a knife in the air.

Back in the past, women used to organize bloodletting gatherings with *serratas*, venerated women related to the saints. *Serratas* made superficial cuts around wrists and ankles, and then these were rinsed and smeared with a tincture of saffron, henna, or *akr*. "That was long before," Abed added with a tinge of authority, "you can't see such things in Morocco anymore."

Baraka: divine blessing that can be transferred from one person to another, or from an object to a person

The youth of aged societies that have undergone tumultuous transformations to modernize, which concomitantly meant to *West-ernize*, repeatedly utter this mantra when a Westerner with scant information shows some interest in a single facet of their cultures that they themselves are barely interested in and in actual fact, wouldn't want to appear, or flatly refused, to be associated with: *"Oh, that?"* they'll reply. *"But that was a long time ago. You can't see such things in my country anymore."*

Thus proceeding onto the very next question gyrating in her mind, Gail demanded: "What about the henna, Abed, will you ask her about it?"

"It is a fuckin' henna that you put on your hands! There is nothing to ask about it," Abed exploded. "Why are you asking all these things? Why do you make her believe that you are really interested in . . . in *her*?"

Gail gave him an edgy, scowling look: "Well, maybe because I *am*!"

"Yeah, I guess," Abed smiled sardonically. "What an exciting culture! Exotic! Erratic! Despotic! Embrace your third world sister!"

"Jeez, you wicked mind! Why does my curiosity disturb you so much? Are you ashamed of your own customs?"

As if simultaneously attracted by two different magnets situated at opposite poles, they yanked apart from one another leaving Zahra wondering what was going on, sighing, whining, brooding by herself alone in the kitchen. After spending some time in motionless angst, she came upstairs to check how Abed was doing, and found him under a thick blanket from head to toe, trying either to suffocate himself or merely to get some sleep.

Hesitant to ask but unable to push back her distress anymore, Zahra awkwardly sat on the bed and whiffed out the question in her mind: "So, what does Safiya say? Was there a letter in the packet?"

"Nothing much," the blanket replied in a gruff voice. "Her father's illness, the weather's volatility these days, her little sister's wedding . . . that kind of thing . . ."

But every text can be read on more than one level, so says the hermeneutical tradition. The archives of haruspication fully testify that even texts that seem to be fairly commonplace are capable of hiding esoteric messages. Safiya's letter, too, bore the mark so often encountered in hallowed texts: *May the initiated explain this to the initiated, and the uninitiated see it not!*

True, Safiya's letter was small talk, *that kind of thing* in the outer stratum, the *zahiri.* Nevertheless, down through the inner layers of the *batini,* it conveyed a different sort of message, one that said that her father wanted her to get married before too long, for he feared he'd die soon, and she, too, felt it was time, even her little sister was getting married, though it was obviously her turn. The letter further divulged that her mind was confused, her mood volatile these days. Safiya would apparently not, the *batini* layer whispered, wait for Abed too long.

Zahra lifted her chin, furrowed her brow in an endeavor to hint at the magnitude of what she was going to say, though her only spectator might not be able to see the arrangements from underneath that blanket.

"Safiya is no good for you, let her go her own path." Even though Zahra had expressed her disgruntlement about this affair in a variety of ways up until now, it was the first time she was voicing her objection so directly. The atmosphere in the room got viscous under the weight of a sudden strain ballooning between them. It was hard to breathe, hard to contest until Zahra unleashed her next line: "You should marry the blue-eyed!"

Abed's head corked up from the blanket, his eyes all pupil: "You want me to marry Gail the witch?"

"Yes, why not?"

"Why not? Because her mouth pukes rage and . . . and claptrap!"

"It's good that she talks." Zahra smiled. *"L-hauf men bnadem s-sâket."*[*]

Abed snorted a laugh, and then a series of laughs. "In case you haven't noticed, she is taller than me," he growled, lifting his gaze

[*]Have fear of people who are silent.

toward the ceiling, as if to point out *that* tall she was or simply expecting some celestial redeemer to fall from there to finish off this conversation.

"She is no taller." Zahra shrugged. "You are a bit shorter, if anything. The camel does not see his own hump."

It was then that Abed decided to try a bigger shot: "Ma, she is *Jewish*!"

A look of placid inquisitiveness passed across Zahra's face. Disbelief, Abed thought at first, but couldn't help identifying as recognition at the same time. "Oh really? Ask her not to kill the spiders in the house! Tell her the spiders saved the life of the prophet," she murmured with composure as she left the room. "Now, why don't you get some sleep?"

Unfortunately, he did. After several nights of tormented slumbers, it didn't take him too long to fall asleep. But the nightmare woman was even quicker to come. Two large charcoals of eyes shone on her deadly white face, pretty much like a snowman's vapid gaze, only here the eyes had sunk inside like two dark, dazzling, jagged holes. Abed woke up in panic, only to find her again, standing on his chest, even nearer this time, even fiercer. While beaming from the dream into whatever reality this was supposed to be, she had shriveled enormously, now reduced to doll size. A macabre Barbie, a zipped horror.

Abed tried to make a move though he knew instinctively she wouldn't let him. He opened his mouth to call his mother, someone, *anyone*, but only a drag of breath came out. She had rendered him motionless, soundless, almost anesthetized. As she crushed his chest, Abed tried to scream again . . . and again . . . tried harder and harder each time . . . until the door of the room banged open:

"*Habibi* . . . Abed! . . . Abed!!"

He woke up into a shaking cuddle, Zahra squeezing him in panic. Behind her stood Gail, Piyu, and Ömer, all three lined up with the same fretful expression on their faces. "Abed, what is it?" asked either one of them in a collective voice, or all of them at the same time.

"A bad dream." He paused for a split second, decided to narrate the rest. "It's the same old nightmare as always, ever since my child-hood it comes and goes. Apparently the season has started again. Only this time she looked too real. She sat on my chest, and didn't let me move. *Ouaghauogh* . . . she scared the shit out of me."

Abed turned aside to translate their dialogue to his mother, but the look on her face said she already *knew* what they were talking about.

"What's this nightmare woman like?" wondered Ömer.

"She's young, and has long, extremely black hair . . . actually, she looks like Gail."

"Thanks man!" Gail grinned.

They chuckled briefly, and might have chuckled some more, had they not noticed Zahra's face grimacing. In the ensuing silence, Zahra gave them a piteous squint, and walked stiffly out of the room before her son could even make an attempt to console her.

Smokeless Fire

First, let's differentiate them from other *bêtes crépusculaires*. Extraterrestrials, elves, hobgoblins, fairies, or even vampires . . . you may or may not believe in any of these, but someday one of them can crop up on you all the same. To sneak into your life, none needs to be recognized in advance, not necessarily. That, however, is not exactly the case with those created from smokeless fire, literally known as "the jinni," who would rather be not only recognized beforehand but also identified exclusively. For the basic rules of diplomacy are also pertinent to the affairs of human beings vis-à-vis the jinni: here, too, the recognition of the other's existence as a separate entity is a *sine qua non* for relations to develop between the two sides—relations not necessarily implying peace.

"*Some of them are righteous,*" says the Koran, "*and some are otherwise.*"

Therein lies the menace. Not in the *righteousness* part apparently, and yet, not in the *otherwise-ness* part necessarily, but in the very pendulum restlessly oscillating between these two, in the possibilities that this teeny tiny "or," might *or might not* entail.

At some point in their personal trajectory, all jinn should make a choice between good and evil, which most of them are said to have done but there are a few others that have still not picked a side. And yet, even with regard to those that opted for the evil, it is not solely their malice that renders them so daunting, but their unique talent to appear otherwise. Every jinni is perfectly capable of giving the impression of being virtuous when in actual fact vicious inside, or vice versa, or even much worse, capable of changing sides in time, to become vicious though initially virtuous, or vice versa. To top it all off, just as in the world of humans, so, too, in the world of the jinni, gender is *the* determinant.

Female jinn are said to be far more whimsical than the male, and thereby more mercurial. They like to be adored and complimented in eloquent ways. Failing to do this properly may turn you into the target of their hatred, whereas managing to do it properly may turn you into the object of their infatuation; hard to say which will be more menacing in the long run.

Even *sheytan* is not as nerve-vandalizing as the jinni. The devil is evil, and pretty consistent in that. One will always fear the worst from *sheytan*, and will probably get even worse than that, but at least there'll be no ambiguities. The jinni, on the other hand, may be friend or foe, or foe when friend, friend when foe, and it is precisely this may-or-may-not-be pendulum that turns every encounter with them into some sort of a mind-ransacking jigsaw puzzle that may not (or may) ever complement into a telling whole. The jinn are notorious for ambivalence.

And human beings are notorious for their fear of ambivalence.

"Don't you worry, Ma," Abed slurred the words softly when he had finally found Zahra sitting on the porch solemnly contemplating the maple tree, or that amateurish facsimile that had now replaced it. "I know why this is happening. I haven't been watching my horror movies lately, if I start sleeping downstairs with the TV on, like I did before, everything will be all right."

Expressing disbelief and clearing her throat simultaneously, Zahra gave a scooping snigger—a noise that proved to be only a prelude to a convoluted speech. When she had finished talking, Abed staggered off the porch slightly concussed. *She* stayed taut. She did not make a single move. Two hours later, not much had changed.

Zahra was still on the porch, stiff and silent, Gail and Arroz coming now and again to check how she was doing.

"What's going on?" Ömer and Piyu wondered in unison.

"What's going on?" Abed growled. "She comes to America, and her third day here she loses her mind. That's what's going on!"

Finally, he got tired of hooting and revealed the story. Tardily, tiredly, in words and details that were not his, he told them when Zahra was very young and a newlywed, she had this nagging encounter with a jinni, an *encounter* that still to this day kept on encountering them.

It was more than twenty-five years ago, sometime in mid-February.

On a frosty and gusty day, Zahra was alone in the kitchen, making wildberry jam. Though never a bad cook in all her life, she must have been still inexperienced at that time, for she had gorged the cauldron with far more sugar than needed, and now the more she boiled the jam, the more she spoiled it. In despair she crossed her curvy fingers on her womb, and breathed pensively—almost a moan. Neither her hands nor she was aware of this at that particular moment but Zahra was pregnant. Pregnant with Abed.

Zahra's lack of information on this subject was more revealing than it seemed to be because if she weren't at such an early stage of her pregnancy, she wouldn't have been left alone in the house, since pregnant women are counted among the favorite preys of the jinni, especially the female ones, and should therefore never be left alone. But wrapped in a cardigan of wool and the bliss of ignorance, on that cold morning in February, the new bride that Zahra was had no reason to be afraid of the jinni. She was too strenuous for that, so young and carefree. All she was concerned about was the wildberry jam acquiring a bizarrely mottled color and exceedingly sugary flavor as it boiled on and on in the dark cauldron. After a while, she heard a knock, and though always wary of strangers, ran to open the door with no hesitation whatsoever.

At the door stood a woman in tattered clothes but with the most beautiful black eyes she had ever seen. Even though the bowl in her hand verified that, she didn't look like a beggar at all. "Good day," she mumbled. "I'm very hungry and very thirsty. Nothing has entered into this mouth of mine since three long days and longer nights."

Though she had heard perfectly what was asked from her, Zahra did not make a single move and kept staring almost mesmerized at the nocturnal whirls in those black jewels of eyes. Watching her bewilderment, to make her intention clear, the beggar raised both hands to her mouth — or to where her mouth would have been if she had one.

Between her cruelly perfect nose and pointed chin, there was nothing reminiscent of a mouth. No upper lip, no lower lip, not even a pinkish line, but only a carmine void — a greedy cavity ready to engulf anything. Looking at the woman with hindsight after all these years, all Abed could tell was she must've had either a ghastly accident or some fatal illness, probably leprosy. Whatever it was, it had carved out and swept away her mouth.

"If you can give this soul of mine a slice of bread, I'll bless you," the carmine hollowness echoed. She then tilted her head slightly as if helping her nose to catch the strain of syrupy smell leaking from the kitchen. "And if you put anything sweet on that slice, some of that wildberry jam perhaps, I will bless your male child on the way."

Then she flung herself onto the threshold as if attempting to intrude. It was at that instant that the young, callow girl Zahra was panicked, and out of reflex closed the door, banging it harshly on the woman's face. For God knows how long she stood there, congealed in dread and regret, listening to every little sound outside. When she'd finally found the courage to reopen the door, there was no one there, except for the cloak of ice sullenly melting on the narrow, filthy road. She returned to the kitchen, only to find the wildberry jam hopelessly spoiled.

Still she was quick to ward off the incident from her mind and actually never gave it serious thought until the day Abed was born. For when Abed was born, he came with this carmine stain on his tummy, which, startlingly, looked exactly like a mouth.

"Wow, that's cool. Do you still have that tattoo on your tummy, you sexy thing?" Gail smirked, lashing her black lion mane from side to side.

"It's not a fuckin' tattoo that we are talking about," Abed sniped, and took a deep breath, determined not to let Gail annoy him. "Zahra believes that the beggar was, in fact, a jinni. But that's not the issue. The issue is whether a jinni or not, what she did to her was wrong because you should never refuse a piece of bread and a cup of water to any of God's creatures. Besides the moral lesson, the jinni has cursed us, especially me. Zahra thinks I'm the one in danger."

"Aha! Is that the woman in your nightmare?" Ömer asked, his face lighting up with curiosity. "The jinni femme fatale?"

"She is no woman to fantasize about, you pervert! Don't you have jinn back in Turkey? You should know what this is all about!"

Fortunately, to both Gail and Piyu's relief, they did not indulge in some sort of jinni nationalism. Instead, Abed told them in a discomforted voice fainting toward the end, about Zahra's firm belief that if the she-jinni had so far been unable to harm Abed as much as she sure would want to, that was thanks to the alms they'd given and the sacrifices they'd made in the past. These had visibly diminished her power, preventing her from aging (after all, elder jinn were more powerful than young ones; female jinn were more powerful than males; and hence, elder female jinn were the worst of all), and turning her into this young woman that sporadically visited Abed. Alms and sacrifices kept her toothless. And yet, this year, though Zahra had made a solid oath to sacrifice a ram the day Abed received his scholarship, she had not been able to fulfill the pledge, postponing it for a variety of reasons, and then she'd totally forgotten about it upon her husband's death. As the debt lingered, the she-jinni had slyly aged and became more powerful, getting hold of Abed's nights and nightmares each passing day.

"Wow!" Gail nodded broodingly, as if scrutinizing a genuine solution, but when back from whatever contemplation she had made, all she came up with was another: "Wow!" She thought about making a new set of milk chocolates in the shape of the jinni but prudently kept this idea to herself, heading back to her store.

The moment Gail got out of the room, as if identical buttons on their remote controls were pressed at the same time, Piyu and Ömer attacked Abed, pulled up his sweater, and pointed to his tummy. He was right. It was there! Right on his abdomen, a carmine mouth that looked like some tattoo of a Gothic letter from a heavy-metal album cover, no matter how much he might dislike the comparison. Once they'd seen what they desperately needed to see, they helped Abed, still snarling on the floor, to stand up, and then, all together, headed to the living room to watch *The Sopranos.* When the episode was over, one by one they peeped out, only to find Zahra still sitting on the porch, still in the same position, with Arroz next to her feet, completely faithful to some sort of a mission he had apparently bestowed upon himself.

"Isn't she going to sleep?" Alegre whispered fretfully when it was her shift to spy on the porch territory.

"How would I know?" Abed grumbled inconsolably, shuttling between the two kitchen doors. During the rest of the evening thrice he ducked onto the porch in an attempt to convince her to come inside, but each time he came back alone and flushing crimson. After the third attempt, he could no longer hold back: "She's lost her mind! She wants to sacrifice a ram and she wants to do it now!"

"What do you mean *now*?" Piyu asked in pointless panic, the word *sacrifice* bringing to his mind the sharpest of knives.

"Not *now-now*, you dummy, *as-soon-as-possible-now* . . ." Abed rolled his eyes to the kitchen ceiling, right to the spot where water dripped sometimes from the bathroom tub upstairs. "God . . ." he wailed, "we are in Boston," as if God had lost his whereabouts, and he was giving the coordinates all over again.

But the coordinates did not help much to bring Zahra back, who now seemed to trust the simulated maple tree and Arroz more than anyone in the house. All of a sudden, she'd developed some fear of life, expecting something ghastly to happen at any moment. The world had become a lottery of calamities, tormenting her with the odds of what her son might win in the next round. Her sudden fear of flight was only a tiny part of this overall fear. Taking a plane for the first time in her life had not been an issue for her, but taking that plane for the second time was becoming impossible to imagine. Making the trip back home, leaving Abed alone here in this foreign country, hoping for the best . . . whatever the next move, she didn't want to make it before giving something in return. Such is the arithmetic of alms. Though those guided by reason, and reason alone, might run into some difficulty in empathizing with this numberless math, a calculation of pluses and minuses is essential in any conciliation with the supermundane. Before expecting anything affirmative, something must be forfeited to balance the equation.

Reggae Alms

Next morning Alegre fixed a delicious breakfast with a huge glass of fresh orange juice, which Abed carried to the porch on a tray. Half an hour later he brought back the remnants, all consumed down to the last scrap except for the orange juice, that being of no interest for Arroz. Zahra meanwhile had not touched anything. Ömer attempted to convince her to have some morning coffee, but that didn't work either. He kept the whole pot to himself.

"If you are determined to glug down so much coffee, why don't you at least turn it into *café con leche*?" Alegre frowned, arms akimbo, her voice muffling the hum of the refrigerator she stood beside.

Ömer's face lightened. "*Café con leche!*" He beamed. "Hey, can you teach me a few sweet words in Spanish?"

"Disgrace!" Abed yelled back from another abortive visit to the porch. "Teach him how to say *disgrace* in Spanish, Alegre. I bet there is some Hispanic girl on the list. Is that so, my true friend, Omar?"

Ömer shrugged his shoulders. "I have always been interested in learning Spanish."

"Abed, why don't you tell Zahra to make donations?" Alegre proposed, hoping to soothe him a little. "She can donate that poor ram's money to our charity. It is a Catholic organization, but we serve food regardless of faith."

"*Muchas gracias*, but I don't think your chicken-noodle soup will meet my mother's standards of sacrifice." Abed heaved a sigh, glancing out the kitchen window. Hard to say there was much to watch, though. Zahra still on the same chair in the same position, her eyes still fixed on the same leafless skeleton of a tree. The only sign of vitality could be observed in Arroz, now twitchily flipping on the floor every two seconds or so, apparently torn between being faithful to his mission to guard this woman who, unlike the other housemates, smelled of jasmine and musk, and going back to the house to check if there was any more breakfast left.

Arroz was not the only one fluctuating between two poles. Late in the afternoon Abed got tired of shuttling back and forth and finally decided on an action to solve the problem for once and for all. With such decisiveness he knocked on the door of his Muslim brother.

"Omar, my brother. You should help me. No matter what, you are a Muslim, right?" Regretting the question instantly, he guzzled off without waiting for an answer. "At least you come from a Muslim country. You are the only person in this house who can help me. I'll meet Jamal in half an hour and we'll visit the imam to get some advice. You, meanwhile . . ." he pointed a finger, "should be looking for a butcher."

"Why not the other way round? You look for a butcher, I do the rest."

"Well, for one thing, I am not sure you are the right person to talk to the reverent imam," Abed replied. "To tell the truth, I don't think your paths should ever cross."

Convincing enough, each did his part.

That day they got nowhere. True, there were various Muslim butchers in Boston, selling halal meat. Yet, when it came to having a ram sacrificed instead of buying it in parts and pieces, that info was subject to change. Two butchers said they might be of help but the nearest appointment they could give was next month. Nobody at 8 Pearl Street expected Zahra to survive on the porch that long.

More daunting than the hardships of probing how a Muslim woman could have a ram sacrificed in the middle of Boston in one week's time, was the embarrassment that came along with them, the tacit discomfort as to what American friends would be thinking if and when they heard about this. Strikingly, Abed had had no difficulty in revealing the matter to Alegre or Piyu. Hispanics were on the same side, he felt, especially Mexicans, though he couldn't exactly tell why. Apart from these two, however, he'd rather not tell this incident to any one of his non-Muslim friends. Especially not those two vegans, one of which even opposed imitation meat. No, neither Gail nor Debra Ellen Thompson should be informed of this *crime*.

Two more days passed. Many times more they heard the same answers: There were several Muslim butchers that slaughtered sheep and rams in a slaughterhouse, in accordance with both the American standards and the Islamic requirements, but in any case, this would take time, unless, of course, one of the housemates volunteered to do the slaughtering himself.

Time being his foremost foe in life, it was at this point that Ömer felt he should start playing his part in this scenario. There must have been a reason why, he concluded, Abed had pulled him into this biz—a reason obscure to Abed himself but probably clear to the rims of his subconscious. Having too much faith in religious sacraments and too deep of a love for his mother to lie to her, there was one particular thing Abed could not possibly accomplish without delegating the case to someone like Ömer: treachery.

Ömer knew he could not possibly slaughter the ram but could instead be of help in other respects. After all, killing an animal might be beyond him, but deceiving a human being was certainly not. Hence, when on the fourth day he scampered into the kitchen with a cauldron full of fresh meat that once belonged to a ram—actually to two, maybe three rams, parts and pieces a Muslim butcher had sold him and helped him to complete into a ram in total—Ömer did not feel even a morsel of shame for telling Zahra what seemed to him his most innocuous lie.

"It was a beautiful ram." He nodded cheekily. "A good Muslim butcher slaughtered it in a slaughterhouse. I couldn't take you with us because according to the rules in America unauthorized people cannot get in there."

As he translated Ömer's words to Zahra, Abed feared she wouldn't be convinced, mainly because he himself wasn't. But this kind of fraudulence being nowhere in her book, Zahra's face had already buoyed up with relief. She abandoned the chair she had been pasted to for most of the last four days and instantly set out to work. To her dismay, she couldn't find the head, the hoof, the stomach, or the intestines of the animal. As she asked over and over where all these had gone, Abed translated none of her demands to anyone.

Reserving very little for them, Zahra divided all the rest of the meat into seven plates to be distributed to seven different people.

"Distribute them to seven neighbors in need," she decreed.

What seven neighbors, Ma? Abed wished he could ask her while he scanned in his mind an array of vegetarian bohemians residing in East Somerville.

One of the seven pieces, Alegre decided to take to their youngest maid, Marta. If Marta didn't want the meat, she would cook it for *la Tía Piedad*, pretending it was bought from the market. Three of the remaining six, Abed distributed to three Muslim friends, two from Egypt, one a Pakistani, all studying for a Ph.D. at Tufts, none poverty-stricken perhaps but all suffering considerably with their grad incomes. One other he reserved for Jamal. Finally, Piyu took a portion for two staunchly carnivorous friends of his that he knew would welcome most any kind of meat as long as it was good and fresh. That left them with one more share to distribute.

"Be sure to give it to someone poor," Zahra repeated the instruction.

Tired of socializing for charity, Abed delegated the task to Piyu, Piyu to Abed, and then they unanimously delegated it to Ömer.

Ömer, in turn, was convinced that for alms to merit virtue, they should be given to utter strangers in need, rather than to gluttonous friends. Hence, he started with the panhandlers and bag ladies in the neighborhood, only to be shaken by the lack of interest he encountered there. *Jesustoldmeyouhadasparedollar* Lady turned out to be a vegetarian, *Gotnopennyforacupofcoffee* Chap was extremely distrustful of the offer because he suspected the mayor had given orders to poison all the homeless on the streets. A few more attempts, a few more rejections, and Ömer decided he got all the excuse to ask for help from an ex-lover. Besides, for once in his life he wanted to prove that yes, why not, the intricacy of love and hate should on no account be denied, ex-lovers could still resolve their basic animosities and be mature enough to help each other at hapless moments, becoming truly good friends in the fullness of time!

Down in the record store he found Vinessa singing another Clash song behind the counter, under the diagonal gaze of several new-to-the-place customers, half enjoying, half sneering. When she saw Ömer coming, her voice escalated: "Somebody got murdered / His name cannot be found / A small stain on the pavement / They'll scrub it off the ground."

When the song was over, without bothering to lower her voice, she asked all the customers inside whether it wasn't bizarre that a relationship could be ended in just one day when it was going on pretty well, and that this guy named Ömer could all of a sudden announce, "This thing between us did not work." Looking back at their unashamedly unromantic romance now, she had every reason to conclude that he had never loved her, and since he had *never* loved her, Vinessa howled, he had better go and find himself another store to buy punk and postpunk CDs.

Ömer in response swallowed hard, lowered his voice to almost a whisper, said he wasn't here for punk or postpunk CDs, and told her about the ram. When he had finished with the story, Vinessa remained thoughtful for a minute. She wouldn't stir a finger to help him, she then decreed, albeit now in a normal tone; besides, she was against the killing of animals no matter what, but on the other hand, she sincerely wanted to help *Abdoul* and his sweet plump mother whom she had liked so much at the Halloween party that night.

Vinessa had a number of Jamaican friends singing on a different corner of Huntington Avenue every day, and she could tell for sure, they'd welcome fresh, good rib.

Hence, the seventh piece of Zahra's unsacrificed sacrificial ram was curried and cooked in coconut milk by a bunch of penniless reggae musicians, who were later going to report to Vinessa that it was quite good and they looked forward to being donated to again.

Three days later, Zahra said farewell to each in a different way and took the plane.

To Piyu she said: "Fresh milk is for friends and buttermilk for the sons of palmetto bags."

To Ömer she said: "The country where the stones know you is better than the country where the people know you."

To Alegre she said: "If you meet one who has an evil eye, turn your tongue at once and say to him: 'Stomachache for a long night.'"

To Debra Ellen Thompson she said: "If your friend is honey, don't eat it all."

To Gail she said: "To go in the night with a lantern is better than with clouds in the day."

To Arroz she said: "If people have eaten with you they betray you, if a dog has eaten with you, that's because he loves you."

Finally, to Abed she said: "You are lucky you've got good friends here. Don't forget that your friend who is near is better than your brother who is far away."

And then to herself she reminded: *L-farh seb'a iyam u l-huzn taul l-'omor.**

*The joy lasts seven days and the sadness all the life.

Winter

At 11:33 a.m., a scrawny, hunchbacked, half-toothless woman who had been looking older than she actually was for the last forty-two years of her life, and selling corn kernels to feed the pigeons in front of Sultanahmet Mosque for the past six, sheltered her eyes with a bony, crinkled hand as she pensively pouted at the distant sky splintered by a flock of pigeons that had suddenly taken off. She bobbed her head from side to side, unleashing a reprimand, something that resonated like "Chtz! Chtz! Chtz!" Her wrinkly face giving no clue whatsoever, it was hard to tell at which one of these three was that sound particularly addressed: the sun, for letting its radiance be so easily shattered; or the pigeons, for making a fuss over nothing; or the mob of young protesters pouring from the ages-old mosque with angry slogans that chased the pigeons into the cloudless sky wherein they'd sliver the serene winter sun into fragments of perturbed rays. For, depending on which one of these three the pigeon feeder had referred to, the implication of that "Chtz!" might change considerably, and so could she be deemed to have a different personality.

If it were the sun up there she had Chtz-ed at, then she might be making a celestial plea, perhaps asking God to peer from that roof-less sky down at the chaos she was left in.

If it were the pigeons she had reprimanded, then she could be more preoccupied with the mundane affairs, like how many of her pigeons will die this year, will the price of grain swell, or how long will she be able to survive on the scantiest of incomes.

If, on the other hand, she had unleashed that "Chtz!" at the ful-minating mob, then perhaps she'd be a secularist grain vendor, pro-testing the Islamist protesters in her own way.

But maybe it's too late to wonder anyhow. For it is already 11:35 a.m., and her Chtzs cannot be heard anymore, muffled amid a ruckus of shouting and slogans, the steady march of the police squads approaching, the honks of the cars stuck in the traffic jam behind the police buses, and the raucous voices of vendors selling water, *sahlep*,* rice, chickpeas, amber rosaries, or anything to the protesters, pedestrians, tourists, police officers, or anyone. It was this rumble that had muffled the third "Chtz!" of the scrawny, hunchbacked, half-toothless pigeon feeder. Amid the confusion, no pair of ears, celestial or earthly, was able to hear it, not even her own.

At 11:36 a.m., a sinewy police officer with ferrety eyes under a black helmet, and cheeks that went red whenever he got furious, and very red when very furious, drew a roundish shape in the air with his club and started walking toward the rabble, as if that circle would be the very gate from which he'd enter into the scene. It was precisely then that the two ocher-bearded protesters in front of the mob, so exceedingly similar that rather than two different men they looked like the replica of the same person, launched a new slogan, evoking the ones behind them to join in the second round. Exactly at the same moment, an agile photographer working for Reuters, fi-nally satisfied with the luminosity and clarity of the frame he had ob-tained, focused his camera and started shooting. In the succeeding fifteen shots, this was the sequence he caught: A sinewy police offi-cer with ferrety eyes in a black helmet and a black shield approach-ing two protesters from behind; the police officer's club drawing a

*A hot drink made of milk, sugar, and cinnamon

circle in the air; the two protesters shouting slogans without any notice of the police officer behind; the club wagging to and fro, hitting
the closest protester several times on the forehead; the two ocher-
bearded protesters in front of the rabble not looking alike anymore,
with blood covering one's face . . . all pictures, backgrounded by the
serene splendor of the old mosque, and foregrounded by a gaunt pigeon feeder pouting over the tumultuous crowd into some distant
sky. The Reuters photographer held his breath, pleased with the
fineness of the pictures, and took the roll out to replace it with a new
one. That lasted eight seconds.

Within those eight seconds, Zahra back in her house in Marrakesh poured melted lead into a pan of cold water to protect the apple of her eye against the evil eye. The lead sizzled sadly. At the same
time, a coyote in the empty horizons of Arizona smelled a dubious
plant that had flourished at the spot where a Buick had crashed into
a caravan parked by the road at this time eight years ago. The plant
did not taste as good as paloverde, but the coyote ate it all the same.

When the camera had paused clicking in Istanbul, the lead
stopped sizzling in Marrakesh, and the coyote gulped down the
plant in Arizona, the clock in Harvard Square moved from 3:37 a.m.
to 3:38 a.m. That was precisely when winter came to Boston.

Winter came to Boston so incredibly swiftly, in a blink of an eye.
It wasn't there a minute ago, and then it was *everywhere*. For among
four seasons, only winter is capable of being so clearly visible in its
forewarnings but still catching you by surprise.

By the time the police had begun to disperse the mob in Istanbul, Zahra's lead had molded into a shape of a pierced eye floating
on water, of the plant by the road only the roots were left behind,
and winter had already conquered the whole city. When she had
every little thing and everyone in the city under her control, she as-
cended to her throne, cracking it under her enormous weight. Unlike the Chtz in Istanbul, the sizzling in Marrakesh, or the coyote's
gulps in Arizona, the "crack" in Boston did not go unnoticed.

The instant he heard that peculiar crack, Arroz leapt from the
bed, squeezing the pair of feet in deep slumber next to him, opened
the door, sniffed the air as if that was one way to hear better, and

then, as swift and decisive as an arrow destined to its target, slid down the stairs, passed by the bedroom on the second floor, ignoring the slippy sloppy noises coming from inside, rushed to the first floor, paid no heed to the screams of a thriller coming from the living room, headed toward the kitchen, opened the door of the porch, and once there, stood looking outside with wide-opened eyes.

Outside, it was winter everywhere, dancing in raptures. The only true pantheist in the pantheon of seasons, winter connected every diminutive entity to every other; covering earth and sky, part and whole, the small and the big, under the one and the same pure white mantle of quintessence. In a flash, Boston had been shriveled into a toy city, zipped inside Alegre's snow globe. And a pair of hands must be shaking it nonstop, for it snowed and snowed.

Abed was the next to discover winter's arrival. But he couldn't remain as calm as Arroz. For seeing the entire world canopied by snow first thing in the morning has a socializing effect on human beings. In a split second, Abed beetled up the staircase, stayed away from Ömer's bedroom, and just in case from the bathroom, headed to the third floor, and dragged Piyu out of bed.

Even Ömer was enthusiastic and did not slip into one of his morning tantrums when he came out of his room and found out why his two housemates had been tapping gently albeit persistently on his door. Back in his room, he gave a sloppy kiss to Marisol, and whispered in her ear: "Wake up coffeebunch, take a look outside!" It was a term of endearment, praise to the skies in Ömer's book, but even though she knew what coffee meant to this tall and clumsy new lover of hers, there were times when this dulcet, elfin, and always cheery Puerto Rican girl—a student in sociology who waitressed at Rao's Coffeeshop in her spare time—didn't feel honored by the term. On those occasions, Ömer added a further dash of savor to his compliment: "*Mi morena café con leche y mucha crema.*" Marisol giggled at the silliness of the compliment and ran to her house before the roads were clogged.

After a long breakfast the three housemates, now much less agitated but still spirited enough, stood looking out the windows of their rooms, each with his own favorite hot drink in his hand, watching this American winter restlessly twirl and twirl amid their lives.

That zing, however, would not be there to last. Before long, winter deenergized them with its dreary dynamism. It snowed incessantly on the first day, gave brief pauses on the second, but recovered for the time lost on the third, and definitely burned the candle at both ends on the fourth day. Laundry, grocery, Blockbuster, CVS, tobacco store . . . had now all evolved into remote islands of questionable reality, the routes to which were sated with perils even if they themselves did exist somewhere in that engulfing blankness. They listened to NPR advise them not to go out in the blizzard sometime in the afternoon of the first day, and once having heard that, remained anchored, just in case. If this weather was too chilly even for native New Englanders, it sure was ultrachilly for the Mediterraneans that they were.

One bad thing about lethargies of this kind, however, is not their beginning, but their end or, more to the point, their failure to come to an end. Inertia is blood cousin to dipsomania. Once you plunge into it, you might go on submerging forever, losing track of where to stop, and, more glaringly, *why* to stop anyway. So the three housemates stayed safe and sound and sluggish at home, while it snowed on and on outside, getting tired of each other, but even more of themselves, during four long, white days of voluntary incarceration.

To ease the indolence that initially they themselves had created, and then exaggerated out of all proportion, each clung to his habitual joys. Piyu vacuumed, mopped, and polished the house, hunted for crumbs, made endless phone calls to Alegre, played with Arroz, thanked God for Arroz, thanked God, nibbled potato chips, read the *New Jerusalem Bible: Saints Devotional Edition*, studied in bed under blankets, swept the crumbs, chatted with Alegre on the Net, studied, and got bored. Abed rewatched every single movie in the house, lamenting deeply he hadn't more in supply, made mint tea, wrote too many letters to Zahra, and many times tried writing a single letter to Safiya, studied with the TV on, designed a Web page, got hurt by the tone of discrimination against Arabs and Muslims looming in several articles he read and more than several TV programs he came across, made mint tea, studied, and got bored. Ömer, in turn, decided to keep things at a minimum level for maximum efficiency in terms of energy and time. Since the best way to accomplish this end was to enter into a loop, therein he went. He listened to David Bowie's "I'm Deranged" over and over, wishing somebody would be kind enough to bring him coffee, ending up making his own, and musing on new reasons to quit smoking as he chain-smoked in his room. Now and then amid the rounds, he had phone calls, too.

"What happened to AIDS Janice? Did they arrest her?"

"What AIDS Janice?" he thundered a smoker's morning cough, though it wasn't morning.

"You still smoke, don't you?" his mother wailed.

"Yes, but not as much as before." He swallowed hard as if disgusted by his own lie, less for the ethical burden of having lied than for the cerebral frustration for having lied no better.

Next, he learned and promised to be careful about this woman with AIDS skulking the streets somewhere in the United States, sleeping with as many men as she could to spread the disease, and hence her name. Though Ömer's conscience grilled him as to why on earth did he keep on making oaths on matters he couldn't have cared less about to a mother he could only love with a tainted affection, by this time he had scored so many of those oaths that another one was scarcely news. He hung up the phone, kept listening to "I'm Deranged" and drinking coffee throughout the day. The pattern remained more or less the same in the hours and days to follow, until he noticed, in shock and anguish, there was no coffee left at home.

"Hey, are you going out?" Abed tried to chase him but ran into some difficulty stretching his legs, paralyzed after three days of immobility.

"Outside, yes, definitely!" came the answer. "I am sick of this! I need some fresh air."

Piyu scampered toward him, more successful in this than Abed. "Fresh air? We don't need fresh air. There are more urgent things. Just wait, OK? Don't go anywhere, wait!"

Along with the list handed him, Ömer took three CDs; decided to start with Anita Lane's "Sex O'Clock," put his headphones on, and his cap on that, pressed the play button, urgently needing fresh air "Like Caesar Needs a Brutus." Four minutes, thirty-four seconds. As the song made its rounds, he felt better at each step, watching people shoveling snow in front of their stores. To his amazement, there was life outside. The city was leading its life as usual, though somewhat more somnolent and clumsy, perhaps. Snow had slowed down all action—motions, ambitions, passions—as if a glaze of suspicion had covered everyone. Ömer observed in surprise babies and kids not minding the cold at all though their noses had metamorphosed into small, red buttons; New England children who had no idea how utterly mind-blowing their cold tolerance could look to outsiders.

After he had bought every item on the list, Ömer stood in the middle of Cambridge, not knowing where to go with three bagfuls of silly stuff in his hands. He walked to a music shop but it was closed, called Marisol but could only get to her answering machine, lingered around, without any specific aim in his mind but with no desire to go back home. It was then that he recalled he must be close to Gail's store. He could get Piyu some more chocolate from there, and it'd be a nice walk. He put on Banco de Gaia, and started walking along to "How Much Reality Can You Take?"

Ahead of him there was a burly woman in tattered clothes shuffling her feet at an enormously slow pace. She wore a cerulean velvet hat, and pulled along a dirty, badly tattered suitcase on wheels. "Jesus told me you had a spare cigarette."

As Ömer nodded, taking a cigarette out of the pack, she watched him warily. "Nice weather, huh?"

"Yeah, but too cold for me, I guess," Ömer prattled, lighting her cigarette.

"Where did you bring that accent from?" she asked between puffs in a bright, chirpy tune, almost girlish, he sure wasn't expecting to hear from her. Her voice was younger, and no doubt less damaged, than her features.

Ömer had liked the way she had put the question. As if it were our accents that belonged to nationalities but not necessarily us. "Istanbul," he replied without expecting any real comment in return.

Inside the store, Gail was busy wrapping fat-free dark chocolate owls for two Wiccan customers when she stood in amazement and peered outside. She was astonished to see *Jesustoldmeyouhadaspare-dollar* Lady chattering with someone, and even more astonished to see that someone being Ömer.

"Istanbul . . . Istanbul . . ." she slurred the word in every possible way.

Ömer nodded contemplatively, as if with that everything was drawn into a meaningful conclusion and there was nothing left for him to say. He threw the stub, thought this could perhaps be a good opportunity to quit smoking, turning the cigarette he had smoked with this homeless woman into his very last, and with this venture in mind, he was about to say farewell, when he heard her murmur: "I have been to your country."

"Oh really?" Ömer asked automatically.

"Yes, we did." She gave a smile miles away. "We passed from Chios to Athens, then to your country. Stayed in Istanbul for three days. I have good memories. I remember this child had showed us the way when we were lost in some borough. He had beautiful eyes, that little boy. I wonder what happened to him. Do you think he is a happy grown-up now? Or do you think he might be suffering? Maybe dead already?"

Back in the store, Gail's curiosity as to what these two were talking about had reached the zenith, when finally she noticed Ömer saying good-bye to *Jesustoldmeyouhadasparedollar* Lady, and coming her way.

The chimes on the door tinkled joyfully as Gail and Debra Ellen Thompson welcomed him, smiling, though the latter with a glint of dislike in her eyes. They offered him something to eat, he preferred something to drink—*coffee, for instance?*

They had coffee to put inside all these nougats, truffles, and bonbons and all that stuff, but none to drink. Ömer looked at the chocolates on display in increasing amusement. There were chocolates in the shape of horoscopes, Celtic love knots, Gothic dragons, Runic pentacles, Egyptian ankhs, Kokopellis, peace signs, and white chocolates in the shape of peace doves. There were sitting Buddha milk chocolates, moon goddess fudges, brittles in the form of peacock feathers. They even had toffees in the shape of empty vessels for Taoists interested in the art of being an empty vessel, but nowhere among this chocolate gallery did they have a damn drop of coffee to offer him.

"Do people buy these things?" Ömer said.

Gail laughed. Recently some Indian psychic claiming to be the Wisdom Keeper of Nature and Culture had ordered fifty trays of Buffalo Eye butterscotches to send to his best customers. There were even people who wanted to have chocolate statues of their departed relatives, but, Gail added energetically, they were not in that kind of biz.

That afternoon as he watched her dust Eight-Spooked Pagan Wheel marshmallows with powdered sugar, Ömer felt an unexpected wave of composure descend over him. The sight and smell of this placid little store had a schmaltzy effect on him; that morose sense of fleeing the present tense, the tenseness of the present, toward a familiar memory, an auspicious vacuity from childhood. He recalled this feeling or this feeling made him recall a time when he used to enjoy being with his cousin Murat at home, nibbling the pastries their mothers prepared for a bunch of guests, all women (all married, all mothers, all enthusiastic to talk about the lives of others, but tired of theirs) who gathered every two weeks. Ömer remembered how much he liked, back then, to peer into the living room ogling that feminine aura, so iridescent, so curvaceous, listening to their laughter, too jarring, too joyful, but also unexpectedly voluptuous. Those indeed were the days, he loved to be entrapped at home, and now that he came to think about it that must have been the last time he felt comfortable with the mother and the family he had been given.

Still smiling at that distant memory, he thoughtfully took a sip from the soothing Zen tea herbal medicine Gail had made . . . and immediately put it aside. The placid expression on his face scrunched up like crumpled paper. In haste, he took a bite from the colossal chocolate-filled croissant on the plate in front of him. That was better.

"Croissants!" Ömer squeaked, happy to get rid of the tartness of the tea. "They changed the course of history, some say. In the seventeenth century, Ottoman armies besieged Vienna, but they couldn't capture the city. So they decided to proceed under the ground. They started digging these tunnels that'd take them right into the heart of the city. To keep it secret they only worked at night. But it happened that Viennese bakers worked at night, too. Down in their bakeries, they heard the sound of spades and spread the alarm. Hence, depending on which side you were, some people must have been thankful to croissants while some others gnashed their teeth to them."

"Oh, then we shouldn't have offered you any croissants, you must be unhappy with that in your past and this on your plate," Debra Ellen Thompson blurted with a wavering smile on her face, and an unswerving sourness in her voice.

"It was just a story . . . from the past . . ." Ömer did not disguise being offended. "Do I look like having intentions of conquering Vienna?"

Observing an elusive tension balloon between the two, Gail chewed her lip, nibbled a femina-shaped truffle, chewed her lip some more, and then suddenly turned toward Ömer, her face mysteriously glowing, almost iridescent in its vivacity: "Hey, why don't we go out and get you some coffee? It's time for my lunch break."

Once outside, the first thing each did, entirely unaware that the other was doing the same, was to search around to see if *Jesustold-meyouhadasparedollar* Lady was still here. But she wasn't. Where she stood smoking half an hour ago was now only a cluster of newly shoveled snow, thawed at the bottom into some sludge in shades of gray. As they walked without a word for a while, the wind fluttered dryly on their faces, wavering every which way the black shrub Gail carried on her head. Today she had a silver spoon with an amber stone. It must be part of her work costume, Ömer mused, somewhat surprised to see himself enjoying her company so much.

"I'm hungry," she exclaimed. "What about you?"

"As hungry as wolves!" came the answer.

So the Turks got *hungry as wolves*, Gail wondered. She did not tell him, of course, that Americans got as hungry *as a bear*, *as a pig*, or perhaps *as a wolf* but did not usually get as hungry *as wolves*. The devil is in the details, they say. Perhaps true, perhaps not. But the proof of foreignness is certainly there. Gail wouldn't correct anything as she listened to him dabble in English. After all, native speakers enjoy hearing those teeny tiny imprecisions that the former produce as if there were money in it. Seldom do they intervene, and when they do, it is too often with an affectionate vigilance like parents taking joy in the mistakes kids make.

They dashed into a deli nearby, where Ömer noticed the multiplicity of his choices, and Gail noticed the limitedness of hers. "It's because of the eyes," she murmured looking contemplatively at the bowls of spinach with chicken, salmon carpaccio, spaghetti with tuna, wild rice with beef, and every-thing with every-meat. She did not eat anything that had a pair of eyes because she couldn't help thinking that it was through those eyes that they had watched their slaughter, witnessed the unfairness of death at the hands of humans.

A queasy scooping of a cough came from Ömer. Having lived his entire life feeding mostly on bleating, mooing, gobbling, or cackling beings, he didn't know what to say. Like most of the staunchly carnivorous, he relished eating meat simply because he relished eating meat. Plain and primordial. Too oafish, no doubt, blushingly barbaric when compared with the poetic delicacy he had just been told. Vegans will never realize how much and how often they risk their own lives, provoking nonvegans with their sermons against the killing of animals. Eating-healthy people are not necessarily talking-healthy people.

But standing in the deli line with her that day, Ömer, to his own astonishment, felt little desire to strangle Gail. "You must be having a hard time," was all he uttered after a dawdling pause.

"I dunno," she grumbled tucking a whorl of hair behind her ear. "I guess I might be *atrabilious*, from time to time, like I've been told in the past."

They talked about the past, Ömer more than Gail, once he had happily gorged on his angel hair pasta with chicken. He talked speedily as they walked slowly, while Gail munched her angel hair pasta without chicken and unleashed a cascade of psychological, philosophical, rhetorical, and personal questions. Questions that could get on his nerves but startlingly did not. Comments that could normally wind him up but somehow did not. This Ömer didn't recognize at that moment, but part of the reason why talking to Gail had turned into such a pleasure was because it was essentially and exclusively "talking to Gail," nothing more than that. No open-ended flirtation, no prospects for dalliance. Like too many men accustomed to either start flirting with every woman they happen to chat with for more than half an hour or to chat for more than half an hour with only the women they'd like to flirt with, he, too, had felt lightened as if suddenly he'd jettisoned a burden when he caught himself conversing with a woman that both was and was not . . . a *woman*. Not that he hadn't paid attention to her breasts when she bent forward to lift up a tray of chocolate pretzels back at the store, not that it had never occurred to him what'd it be like to kiss her, not that he wouldn't want to sleep with her—maybe, probably, realistically, why not—but none of these had anything to do with their chatting at this instant. Flirt was not the basic motive here. Actually . . . he doubted if there was one at all. Conversation was all there was behind their conversation.

He told her his stories—past and present, most of which he had so often told to so many people—women, more precisely. But also, now and then, he found himself uttering new info, doubts he didn't know he still doubted, fears he didn't know he feared so much. A gauzy curl of smoke followed them as he chain-talked. Frantically, obliviously, and in words that were lacking to him, he talked about what bothered him most in life: pretending.

"It's so weird," Ömer said. "Before I came to this country, I refrained from asking myself why I was going abroad. The answer is, obviously, to get this degree. But then again, why? Only after I arrived here did I start asking the question I should have asked myself long before. The question wavers like a delayed echo, coming from behind."

Gail tore her gaze away from Ömer's face toward a pair of olive-green gloves somebody had left on a bench. The right hand was on top of the left, with its fingers slightly curved as if begging or trying to reach out for a hand. She decided to take this as a good sign and gave Ömer a heartening smile.

"I guess I envy Piyu and Abed. They know so well what they would like to accomplish in life. *Why did you come to America? What will you do upon graduation? Where is home?* They know the answers! But me . . . I am only pretending . . ."

Gail's smile verged on recognition, but when she spoke it was a new set of questions that came out of her mouth rather than her own remarks. Every question she asked about his life and his past, Ömer answered in increasing eagerness, enjoying her being close enough to ask to learn more about him but then also distant enough not to be disturbed by the answers she got, enjoying, to his own surprise, every minute of this walk.

"I can't help thinking how badly your soul needs clarification and composure," Gail gasped as her eyes slid toward the plastic bags in Ömer's hand, where she spotted beef-and-garlic chips and a VHS that read *House of 1,000 Corpses*. Hard to figure if these had any impact on her thoughts but as they turned around the corner she said: "Maybe you'd like to come with me to tai chi sometime. Give me a call if you'd like to try."

In need of clarification and composure! Ömer chuckled as if sharing a joke with himself but did not object. After all that talk they had, it was sort of odd the perturbed silence that descended on them once they were back in front of Squirmy Spirit Chocolates. In a flash they had become estranged, and their promenade a bout, a momentary lapse in the continuum of their lives. And maybe it was exactly that lapse that had made their talk possible, and so profuse, some sort of a "strangers-on-a-train" effect—the relief of knowing there'd be no expectations, no commitments at the moment of parting. They smiled awkwardly at one another, squelched their boots in the snow, exchanged a few more words now more of courteousness than consideration, shook numbed fingers, smiled again, and squelched their boots in the snow some more.

"Hey!" Ömer's face lightened with a puerile smile as he noticed the placard swinging above the store: "You've got dots up there!"

Side by side they stood gaping up at the three dots on the "i"s of Squirmy Spirit Chocolates, prompting Debra Ellen Thompson inside the store to wonder what the heck they were looking at.

"When I write my name in Turkish, it has dots. In English, I lose them. It sounds stupid, I know, but sometimes I lament losing my dots. Therefore, those dots up there must be mine, take care of them."

Gail gave an unconditional nod, seeing no need to reveal to him that what he thought to be dots were, in fact, chocolate bean pictures, that were amateurish even back in their most glorious days but had now turned into russet stains worn out by wind, sun, and snow.

Sliding his gaze from the placard, Ömer caught the shadow of Debra Ellen Thompson behind the window display. "I guess she doesn't like me much," he snarled.

"Well, I guess you are right," Gail replied, looking him directly in the eye. "But that's because I do."

Because she had said this with the tone of someone asking if the bus had left or which way was the main plaza, it took Ömer a few seconds to be able to unknot the prospective trysts in her words — only a few, maybe just three or two seconds, but even that was enough, perception had fallen behind action. He didn't know this yet but that lack of synchronization between perception and action was going to be the quintessence of whatever liaison they would have hereafter. Similarly retrospective, so tenaciously Kierkegaardian would their relationship remain, to be lived always forward but understood only backward.

"*Pasa el pollo a Alegre*," *la* Tía Piedad decreed from the other end of the table.

She had been brought back from the hospital this afternoon and had missed homemade food. Yet since the moment *todas las tías* had gathered around the table, she seemed to be concerned more with what Alegre was not eating than with what she was. The chicken drew a semielipse, passing from one hand to another until it reached Alegre's plate.

It was different when her parents were alive. Then she wasn't forced to eat more but to eat less. Her mother didn't want her to get fat, to reduce her chances for snagging a well-mannered, well-heeled man for a husband. Alegre had always suspected she was slightly ashamed of her. Not at the beginning, no doubt. Not when she was a child, but much later. When it had become clear that she was not getting rid of that plumpness that had descended on her at puberty, and looked cute then but not now, not anymore. Though looking back Alegre could detect no precise commencement for her weight concerns, she could more or less evoke "puberty" as the time when she started dieting. Back then, too often she'd pass the whole day without eating anything, but then when she started eating, she'd eat too much. She took regular overdoses of acetaminophen, and the more weight she lost, the more verbally abusive she became toward her parents. The docile girl Alegre had always been, had now turned into this furious teenager, her mouth refusing to take anything in, puking anger out.

Then came the accident. The parents she had always loved so much, but cursed so badly in the past two years, the mother she wanted to make proud of her but made instead ashamed, vanished all of a sudden.

"Hija, coge mas frijoles de olla!"

Upon her parents' death she'd become extremely interested in sanity and health, in a system of thought entirely abysmal to others but clear and sensible to her. Calories, carbohydrates, dietary fiber, soluble fiber, insoluble fiber . . . she knew them all. A pack of baby carrots contained only seventy calories. This she could eat, as much as ten, fifteen, twenty packs a day, and nothing else. Her palms were orange, her feet orange, her gaze orange. She had become a thin and delicate effigy. Thin and delicate and orange.

Orange is the color of that callous limbo between girlhood and womanhood.

"*Hija, toma flan de coco!*"

Then, she had begun to skip periods. Three months she'd skip her period, and then it'd come back again as if to assure her she didn't have control over her body, but her body had control over her and that her womanhood could just come and go the way it pleased.

Pork chops, buñuelos de viento, chambergos, cicadas, yemitas, capirotadas, flan de coco . . . eat and binge / gorge and vomit / gorge and fast / fast and gorge / vomit and gorge / vomit and . . . *pork chops, buñuelos de viento, chambergos, cicadas* . . .

Half an hour later, she heard *la* Tía Piedad call in front of the bathroom door: "*Alegre, quieres te, hija?*"*

"*Sí por favor!*" She shot a final glance at the ruins of the dinner, at the sludge that was once *flan de coco*.

She flushed the toilet.

Tai chi was the last thing on Ömer's mind in the following days. Sometime that week he suddenly recalled two truly interrelated albeit not necessarily complementary facts about himself. First, he was a grad student. Second, he had not been studying. A file titled "Blood, Brain and Belonging: Nationalism and the Intellectuals in the Middle East" was patiently waiting in his laptop, waiting for the day he'd start writing his thesis. By the end of December, Ömer had to realize how little he had accomplished in all this time. His appointment with his mentor was daunting. Spivack gave him an additional three weeks and asked him to do his best to revise that fiasco of a first chapter.

To compensate for all those months he had failed to study, during those three weeks Ömer switched to the other pole, working at an enormous speed and energy, at the expense of tattering his nerves and bodily functions. He ate little, slept little, drank too much coffee, shouted at his mother when she asked him about the fate of a serial

*Would you like some tea, my child?

killer, distanced himself from Marisol, and kept drinking too much coffee.

"How can you so easily split?" Marisol murmured, managing not to cry. Ömer said it wasn't easy. "We could have worked it out." She turned her head, still not crying. Ömer said it wasn't easy. "You never loved me," she sobbed bursting into tears. Ömer said nothing.

"I wish you heaven," she said.

"*I wish you heaven*" is a lover's curse written on the mirror. As it is with mirrors, here, too, what is on the left is in fact on the right, what is *heaven* is in actuality *hell*.

At the end of those three weeks, Ömer finally handed Spivack an entirely revised chapter, which the latter soon returned with too many comments and emendations but apparently satisfied.

Pain in the Chakra

"So what are the typical dishes you eat in Turkey on religious occasions?"

Behind the rickety flicker of Sabbath candles, Ömer politely smiled as he gulped down a piece of chicken. He didn't feel like talking about Turkish cuisine, not in this way. Yet, Pearl's mother being always so nice, the last thing he wanted was to be rude to her. All her questions, he answered, naming a number of dishes, sketching a few customs, and giving some carefully selected information on Istanbul, growing more and more exasperated by the wheedling tourist guide he knew by now he had become an expert at. Just like those tourist guides, he didn't even consider taking his audience into the side streets of the city, the streets where real rotten life throbbed.

By now he had concluded that the mothers of the girls he'd been dating in America fell into two camps:

a. The Surprise-Me! Mothers
b. The Nothing-Can-Surprise-Me! Mothers

The Surprise-Me! Mothers were those who were inherently displeased to see their daughters dating a Turk, but pretended not to mind it up to a certain level, as long as it didn't get *serious*. Not that they treated him badly or anything. To the contrary, though visibly reserved, they were always welcoming and elaborately polite, embracing him in a condescending, almost aristocratic courtesy, as if giving him a chance to do something, *anything*, to win them over, as if expecting him to *surprise* them. The Nothing-Can-Surprise-Me! Mothers were, on the other hand, liberal Mater Cosmopolitans determined to embrace every cultural variety whatsoever in exactly the same way and with exactly the same interest. With them it made no big difference whether you were a Muslim or a Zoroastrian, or worshiped the great Kali, or a bevy of gods, or even declared yourself one, for they would equally enjoy seeing you around, except that when you were around, it wasn't you that they saw but only a vapid silhouette of a foreigner as reflected in the misty mirrors of such unconditional open-mindedness. With both types of mothers, Ömer suspected, the least to have an impact on what was thought about him was his *personality*.

Falling into the second group, Pearl's mother was easy to get along with. Things, however, did not run as smoothly between Ömer and Pearl herself, not even on the surface. Pearl was not the crazy hedonist Vinessa was. She was not the sort of person to waste her time echoing Joe Strummer behind the counter of a scruffy music store frequented by punks. To the degree that Vinessa was carefree and joy-oriented, Pearl was indomitable and goal-oriented. On the road to the bright future she pined for, every piece was to fall into a functional place, including her boyfriends.

"Ma asked me what were your plans after the Ph.D.?" Pearl muttered to Ömer as the two of them were washing the dishes after the dinner. "I couldn't give a *satisfactory* answer."

Ömer knew perfectly well it wasn't her mother but Pearl herself who ached for that satisfactory answer. Even if it didn't work out between them for too long, still, she needed to hear about their *future* in order to be comfortable with him *today*. Talking about their future, however, was the least Ömer wanted to do. Not because he mistrusted this affair, which he did, but because he mistrusted life, which he thought was fundamentally unpredictable. You could work hard to shape the future, and succeed in that, and you could even lead a good life, but you should never indulge yourself in the delusion that *life can be planned ahead*. Hallucinations you could have, hallucinatives plenty, but not future plans, not them.

Nonetheless, it wasn't Pearl's fault, he knew. It was ultimately his. For with Pearl, Vinessa, or Marisol it made no difference, it was always the same old pattern: His was a plea to be loved without ever loving in return.

As December was coming to an end, along with his affair with Pearl, Ömer decided to take the new year's approach as an opportunity to do something about this prolonged problem of his. The new year is, after all, a recurring commencement to end the recurrences in your life. Ömer decided to stop dating from this day onward, and in order to prove how determined he was, he chose to spend New Year's Eve alone. So, when he told Piyu not to worry when at dinner at *la* Tía Piedad's house because he would gladly stay at home and keep Arroz company, he really meant it.

At 5:00 p.m. he started drinking, a few cans of beer, which he was quick to replace with rakı after Piyu left the house, and then accompany with a spliff after Abed headed out to meet with his Muslim brothers. As to what kind of music to listen to on this special evening, after a few flips, he decided on Cypress Hill's "I Want to Get High," and achieved that end in no more than an hour. With that state of mind it suddenly occurred to him to write a farewell note to each and every one of his ex-girlfriends. As soon as he opened his inbox, however, an unexpected e-mail stopped him halfway through. It was from Gail. She had written his name in capital letters and made the dots a pair of hieroglyphic eyes.

Dear ÖMER,
I wonder how you are doing. I can't help worrying for your health these days, mainly because twice this week, first on Wednesday night and then today in the afternoon, I felt

connected to you in my trances. In the first, I got connected
to you through my crown chakra, which made me wonder if
you were having a headache. And today, I felt this spark of
light and pain in the umbilical chakra, which made me
wonder if you were having any problems with your
stomach.

If your stomach feels bad, do not drink coffee. Not
tonight. Try herbal calming tea. If you don't have any at
home, have nothing but lukewarm water. The pressure in
the umbilical chakra is too severe. If you can't avoid alcohol
keep it to a minimum.

Take good care of your soul and body and your dots.

Gail . . .

Ömer thought about writing a "thanks-for-your-concern-but-I-
am-fine" message, with a P.S.: "I-am-fine-but-you-are-nuts." But he
did not. He did not write to his ex-girlfriends either. Instead, he read
all the past year's Turkish newspapers on the Web, learned about in-
cidents long forgotten, news from a distant time, a distant place, and
felt miserable and too lonely. He made a huge pot of Sumatran coffee to sober up but kept drinking the rakı at the same time. During
the rest of the night, he went on testing Cypress Hill songs on Arroz,
smoking, grimacing, and frenziedly mixing the two drinks at hand to
such an extent that after a while he started sobering up with every
sip of rakı, and fuddling with coffee.

At 11:59 p.m. they heard the fireworks outside, Bostonians celebrating the new year's arrival. Ömer kissed Arroz. Arroz licked
Ömer. The room cuddled them both. The phone rang. His father,
his brother, and his mother wished him a happy new year, each
with a tint of wonder in his voice, surprised to find him at home
tonight.

"If you go out to celebrate with your friends, be careful with the
sniper!"

"The sniper is in Washington, Ma, I'm in Boston . . ."

"No, he is not there anymore. They lost his whereabouts," she
said softly and warily. "I love you so much, we all love you, but it is

difficult because you are so difficult, we don't know how to love you without annoying you with our love . . ."

Ömer's face marred with confusion as he stood silent, unable to utter a word. He felt slightly ashamed for not being a better son. He knew he should feel more ashamed than that but because he couldn't, he ended up feeling deeply ashamed of feeling slightly ashamed for not being a better son.

The moment he hung up, bubbles started dancing in his stomach. A funny way to get drunk, he thought. You never stop learning. In a few seconds, the bubbles were replaced by bile, and then, the bile by pain.

At 3:15 a.m. when Piyu and sometime after Abed returned home, they found Ömer struggling with distension. Assuming he must be in one of his usual episodes of crapulence, they brought him coffee, as dark as he liked. Ömer guzzled it, then fell on his knees vomiting blood spots resembling coffee beans.

At 3:45 a.m. he was taken to a hospital decorated with Santa lights and sparkling reindeer, where he would be be diagnosed with severe bleeding in the stomach.

In Need of Clarification
and Composure

They ran a tube through his mouth down to his stomach, wrapped a cuff around his arm, checked his temperature and blood pressure and pulse and respiration, put a mask on his face, gave him extra oxygen, placed a pulse oximeter on his toe, hooked him up to machines, placed a tube in his vein, made him swallow medicines the names and side effects of which remained a total mystery, shot him bitter glances to remind him all this was his fault, and told him, at the end, how lucky he was that it didn't turn out to be much worse. But "lucky" was the very last thing Ömer felt he was, especially as he came to realize what it meant to be sick and with limited health coverage in the United States. Only one of the doctors gave him a pinch of sympathy, but that, Ömer suspected, stemmed less from anything akin to kindness than a technical interest in his *case* as the youngest patient with one of the most drained stomachs.

Two days later, Ömer called Gail.

"How you doin'?" He tried to fine-tune his hospital-tattered voice to sound not cheerful perhaps, but no more cheerless than usual, screwing up all the same.

"I'm sorry I couldn't come to visit you yet. Did they take good care of you there?"

That she already knew what had happened did not surprise Ömer at all, since by now he was entirely convinced that Gail was this peculiar being who somehow knew everything about him. "Yeah, I'm much better now, thank you. Listen . . . I've been thinking about what you said the other day . . . about this clarification and composure thing . . ."

"You mean tai chi?"

"That's right, tai chi!" Ömer echoed brightly. "I wonder if I am still invited?"

"No . . . I'm afraid . . . I mean I'd love to but I quit that last month. I started Reiki in the meantime. I'm already in the second level. You are more than welcome to join . . . if you are interested in Reiki, of course."

Yes . . . sure . . . Reiki . . . whatever . . . definitely!

The day Ömer was liberated from tubes and machines, Abed and Piyu came to take him back home. Though they never put it this way, Ömer noticed a puckish glee in their eyes, as if they were glad 99 percent at seeing him recovered and much better now, but also 1 percent for this misfortune, which they secretly hoped would henceforth correct his ways. Outside, in the drive, they bumped into Alegre, who had a mammoth bouquet of scarlet roses in her hand. She was talking to a scruffy, dour-looking man.

"Wow, I'm flattered," Ömer hollered. "But you had already brought me daisies."

"These are not for you." Alegre smiled apologetically. "They are for *la* Tía Piedad. She was taken here again."

"But it's nothing to worry about," groused the man who was introduced as *el tío*, exhaling a puff of intense, smelly smoke.

"Are you coming with me?" Alegre signaled to Piyu.

While the others politely said good-bye to *el tío*, Ömer reverentially said good-bye to *el cigar* in the latter's hands, a sullen farewell to an old pal that he was told to strictly refrain from. As he walked out of the hospital, he placed the bans on cigarettes, alcohol, coffee —and though the doctors had not said anything about it, presumably on |weed|, too—in imaginary boxes each, and hung them loose in the air, wondering which one of these epicurean piñatas he would have to shatter first. Until that day, however, he could give a nice little try to a healthy lifestyle.

When Ömer made up his mind to holiday at the *Clarificationand-composureland* that Gail had so highly recommended, he was expecting the place to be remote and uninhabited. After days of perusing leaflets, journals, ads, and papers, he would be surprised to discover that it was neither. If anything, it was too "popular" and "populated." America was jammed with people in search of clarification and composure.

Gail was right. There was something called Reiki, and those who practiced it looked better off. But then there was also shiatsu, shambala, feng shui, Tibetan bowl healing, yin-yang eight energies and five elements therapy, Shen therapy, body-centered Gestalt therapy, aura cleansing, chakra balancing, Nuji chi gong, energetic reconnection therapy, craniosacral therapy, vibrational healing, spirit transition therapy, aromatherapy, hypnotherapy, light therapy, past-lives regression therapy, intuitive spiritual psychotherapy, somato respiratory integrative therapy, chi kung, Ayurvedic pulse balance, Rasayana therapy, danskinetic workshops, Vedic music therapy, and raindrop therapy techniques. For those interested in moving their bodies along with their minds, there were tours to Siberia, India, and Mongolia. Those with less money to spend had alternatively innumerable summer camps all around the United States. There were even time treks that took you to a particular place and period in world history. There was one agency that transported its customers to India's Vedic past, and promised to return their money if on the way back home they still felt like they had not been able to attain all the ancient secrets. Speaking of money, Ömer would soon notice, there was too much of it circulating in the boulevards of spirituality.

Then, there were the leaders. All these techniques claimed to be self-healing, self-birthing, self-transforming, and self-empowering, but then they ended up submitting you to another self, the spiritual

teacher. One among these, a midfortyish Bostonian, was highly eulo-
gized in his brochure for having gone to the East to attain illumina-
tion with regard to three questions: "Who am I?" "What is my place
in this universe?" and "What will happen to me afterward?" He had
gone there to find the answers to these questions, and had come
back with more than he had wanted. Ömer wondered where exactly
this man had gone and for how long, but neither the destination nor
the duration of his trip was stated in the brochures. Suffice it to say
"East." Somehow, the East was like the tax office, you went there
with questions you were sure had no answers, and came back with
answers that rendered meaningless your original questions.

There was a woman called Marla Master of the Wind, another
one named Betty the Painkiller, and then, a Princess of the Night, a
Black-Rose, and an Abby the Abyss. Ömer noticed the names these
spiritual teachers chose for themselves resembled heavy-metal song
titles, but he didn't quite know how to interpret this. Another
woman, a spiritual surgeon in her own words, had published the list
of the celebrities she had healed. Her surgery consisted of opening
up the patient's heart under hypnosis, singing a song of felicity, and
then closing the heart again. After that, the patient went on with his
daily life, humming the same tune whenever he felt under stress.
Ömer reckoned he could try this technique as long as he himself was
allowed to choose the song to be played into his open heart. If so, he
wanted the Patti Smith song "Citizen Ship" to sink into his pores.
But he doubted if this song would be in the repertoire of the spiritual
surgeon.

As he roamed this new territory that Gail had pulled him into,
Ömer would gradually discover that there were people in the United
States who regularly, systematically, and of their own free will as-
sembled to create mandalas, erect sacred circles of stones, communicate with angels, dowse for their missing, visit their previous lives
under hypnosis, weave meditative baskets, get in trance in public
parks, receive divine channeled messages, cleanse their office of
ghosts, dance in full-moon circles, take courses to chat with their
pets, swim naked with dolphins, and organize trips to collectively

watch cows give birth . . . all in the name of awakening their authentic self and opening the meridians in their bodies. These were people who chewed Amazon herbs at breakfast and took showers with sage soaps.

"Is this what you call clarification and composure!" Ömer frowned to Gail when the two met again for their first Reiki session.

An hour later he was repeating the same question just to be shushed each time, and pushed back into the intense incense silence canopying the cozy, miniature room at the back of the chocolate store. The process of attunement to Reiki was not supposed to take that long but because of Ömer's blatant intrusions, Gail seemed to be running into some difficulty in awakening the talent dormant in him.

"Put your hands together, straighten up your back," she commanded, this time more stridently than before. "Let the burdens of life *ooooze* away."

Ömer straightened up, knitted tighter the fingers he had just briefly loosened, and let another inflated huff *ooooze* away. The room smelled pleasant, a balmy combination of sandalwood and the mellifluous aroma of caramel-colored candles drawing flippant shadows on the walls.

"Gail, do you really believe this is going to work out?" he asked incredulously, though he sure would have asked the same question with an extra topping of cynicism a week before. They both knew that he would be somewhere else now had his stomach never rebelled against him in a bloody mutiny and scared him to death.

"Try not to speak!"

Ömer inhaled through his teeth, listening to what the snow says outside as it melts under the winter sun, the snow melting as always, the sun shining as always, everything being itself, everything but him, only he unable to be his usual self. So grievously he craved for just one cigarette, a cup of coffee, those trifling daily delights entirely lost to him now. He regretted having consumed those joys so joylessly in the past. He lamented being such a heavy smoker, and a heavier drinker all that time. How superb it would be to erase all those years of overconsumption. If he hadn't been drinking or smoking in the past, he could be doing both profusely today. Next, in his twisted penitence, he regretted being where he was. Evidently, this Reiki thing was getting nowhere.

"Try not to regret!"

If at least he could put on his headphones, and listen to "Better Things" a couple of times, maybe he could feel better.

"Try not to resist being here!"

That didn't sound good. What was the use of it all, what did Dasein mean without resisting being *here*.

"Shush . . . try not to fear," Gail said. "It is all about fear."

Fear? Ömer drew back, he sure didn't fear. He could be bored, or suffering in his own way, but fear, no way. This Reiki was a mistake, obviously. "Maybe we should try it some other day, Gail. Sometime later . . ." he stuttered.

"Shush . . ." she said.

"*Karma* is the word!" squealed Piyu the moment he saw Ömer enter into the house late that evening.

"*Waste-of-time* is the synonym!" Abed yelled back from behind the stove, a book in one hand, a scoop in another, stirring lentil soup while studying what looked like Photoshop 5.0. "This world is full of ironies," he went on yelling as he skipped a page, stirred the soup, all at the same time. "Here is our brother from the Eastern world discovering spirituality in the Western world! It should be the other way round, you pervert, you got everything wrong!"

They sniggered and chortled and chuckled, then chuckled some more. Ömer endured their attacks with a saintly smile, ran inside to the CD player, and in a moment filled the kitchen with Nico's opiated voice singing "These Days."

"Yes, Omar, tell us more about 'These Days,' " grumbled Abed. "Did Gail ask you to tie anything these days?"

"Like what?"

"Like what? *You* tell us like what! That trance thing is no good."

"Reiki!" Ömer corrected with all due respect.

"*Reiki!*" Abed slurred the word over his tongue as if it would soften like one of those quesadillas Alegre topped with extra cheddar. "Listen, *dostum*, try to remember, OK? Did she ask you to knot a string or anything? If she hasn't already, just be careful, don't tie anything that she asks you to!"

That evening, bombarded by his housemates' pleasantries, Ömer sat stiff and silent in the kitchen, sipping puke-green organic peppermint tea from his majestic COFFEE, EVEN BETTER THAN SEX mug.

Watch the Herring in the Ebb

Gail glided down Huntington Avenue amid employees rushing to lunch, the usual Chinese food suspects. She wondered how come they all carried exactly the same umbrella above their heads—large, ashen black umbrellas with ecru wooden handles—as if around the corner somebody was distributing these like free pamphlets. Having no umbrella and being in no rush, she slithered in utter bliss, enjoying the rain tinkling over the spoon in her hair, enjoying the walk, this brief solitude, the joy of getting away from the chocolate store, and the caring yet incarcerating gaze of Debra Ellen Thompson. There was too much of a past between them, many a stream that once flowed with the vim and vigor of a rather one-sided friendship, then after a long wait, briefly flooded with mutual love, and, finally, turned into these muddy waters that were neither love nor friendship but only an itchy coexistence.

Their past was a battleground of two armies that had actually never waged war but had still ended up with an avowed victor. Being that victor in the eyes of Debra Ellen Thompson, it was easier for Gail to acknowledge the fact that no one had gained much in this unfought warfare, and that, if not losses, too many resentments were left behind on each side. She had tried to tell her in different talks, some of them completed, many abandoned halfway, that their past was too overburdened to let them start afresh. Their past had lived more lives than one, and this dead end that they were stuck in now simply didn't have the language to resurrect any one of them. All they survived on were odds and ends that yet diminished little by little with each passing day, like the echo of a wail long gone.

Like two elevators going opposite ways they had been so far, meeting at the same eye level only for a short time. At the outset, back in their college days, there was no doubt as to which one of them was looking at the other from a distance far below. But once the inertia was shattered and each started to move, surprisingly enough, it worked out that the one below was encoded to ascend whereas the other to descend. It was only much later, when Zarpandit had become Gail, that they had stood side by side along this parallel yet reverse movement, looking directly into each other's eyes, astonished by the multitude of things they had failed to see there before. What followed was love—sharp, short, and implacable, less because it had ended so soon than because it had ended for only one of them.

Then, somehow, somewhere, their relationship had gone all the way through a tunnel of deconstruction, and when they'd finally come out from the other end of the tunnel, a bit ragged, a bit flummoxed, their roles had been reversed, and so had they. Today, it was Debra Ellen Thompson standing where Gail had stood once, looking at the other from a distance far below. Powerful and privileged might the dominant be over the dominated, but is equally dependent on the latter. Losing a *Gail in need of her* had made Debra Ellen Thompson more and more in need of Gail.

When she was a child, on a trip to Cape Cod with her parents, Gail had watched the herring in the estuary at the time of the ebb. With no more water left to swim in, hundreds of fish had turned into one big mouth breathing in morbid panic, flapping tails as if applauding their own death. Gail recalled that morose scene very often these days. The initial submissiveness of that meek Zarpandit that she once was, had for such a long time been the waters in which

Debra Ellen Thompson swam freely. Then came the ebb, and the sea diminished inch by inch, leaving Debra Ellen Thompson suffering, scuffling, and desperately clapping for her past performance.

Of Zarpandit the subservient magpie no visible traces were left, replaced by this tumultuous young woman that Gail had turned into, always in some sort of a melee even she herself found difficult to tolerate. In a way, she was a walking miracle, the dream of the suppressed. She could plausibly glower, Gail mocked to herself, in one of those "success stories" where people perused their pasts from the spectacles of their current personality, sometimes belittling, sometimes pitying, but almost always distancing the self they had once been. Women winning the fight against breast cancer, battered housewives establishing their own businesses upon getting a divorce, mentally deranged children doing miracles at school . . . hers, too, could be accounted among those stories so profoundly appreciated by the average American. Her story could be titled "From Humble to Intrepid." With such a title nobody would possibly guess that the reason she was intrepid today was not because she wasn't humble anymore, but because being humble or intrepid made no difference to her any longer.

All the same, she kept shifting between two poles, one of outermost glumness, the other of hectic energy. When the pendulum swung toward the former, the only thing that mattered was that suicidal lure. Her first memory on this planet was as fresh as before, always hooked somewhere in her mind. And today, as she glided down the avenue wondering how come everybody carried exactly the same umbrella above his head, once again she felt time had ripened to give death a try.

Half an hour later she was walking vigilantly beside the railroad, and then on the railroad tracks. When tired of walking, she halted and lay down. The rails were cold and clammy, but it was OK. She lay there waiting patiently, letting the rain sink into her pores, her eyes firmly closed, as she listened to the shriek of the train coming closer . . .

But trains, after all, do not shriek.

"Hey, don't you hear me? Deaf or dumb?"

Gail grudgingly opened her eyes into an accusatory ray of sun shining right on her face. She shadowed her eyes with a hand and gawked at the giant shadow yelling down at her with a thick Boston accent. "What you doin' under my feet, you little worm? Get up!"

To double the impact of his words he thumped his umbrella right onto her stomach. "Get up! Get up! Stupid girl!"

His was a different sort of an umbrella. No doubt a good sign, Gail deduced, and holding the hand he offered, she rose to her feet, bashfully thanking the vagabond, on whose face compassion now replaced anger.

"Are you all right, miss?" he bellowed, his voice still fuming. " 'Cause you better be. Don't you ever lie on this railroad again, or on any other road for that matter! You hear me?"

Gail softly smiled at this homeless man who introduced himself as Joe, and who, behind that tart stare of his, had the shrewdest eyes she had ever seen.

On her way back to the chocolate store, Gail came across a bouncy bunch of reggae singers in shades of purple singing "Mellow Mood." Just at the moment she leaned forward to put a buck in the amethyst bonnet in front of them, a crinkled leaf alighted onto it. She looked up quizzically to see where it had come from, but there were no trees nearby. No doubt a good sign, she thought to herself. A good sign . . . Suddenly, she felt happy for having failed to die.

A Dormant Talent Awakened

How long he had been staring at this paper, chewing wintergreen gum, he couldn't tell in clock time. In music time, though, it was Primal Scream's "Out of the Void" times sixteen. In chewing-gum time it was tantamount to four packs approximately, twelve pieces each, forty-eight in total. He gave each piece ten seconds, replacing it with a new one before its flavor had barely eroded. Chewing so many gums numbed your tongue after a while, he had discovered, though startlingly there was no warning on the packs as to that. Unlike his tongue, this paper in front of him defied any transformation whatsoever. Empty it had been and empty it still was.

"Write down your *most important reason* for quitting smoking and look at it often," instructed the navy-blue brochure he was given at the hospital. So far, he hadn't been able to make much progress as to the first part but had run into no difficulty in the "look-at-it-often" part.

"You've got to be determined," the navy-blue tips went on, "and it always helps to set a date to quit and tell your friends, family, and co-workers."

No problem. He had been doing this already. He had been fully determined each time he quit, and not even once had he failed to inform his housemates about his decision, except that they didn't seem to have faith in him. Be that as it may, so far, quitting had never been a major issue for Ömer. He would simply quit . . . and after a while find himself first smoking, then quitting again. However, the process was entirely different and more grueling now. Going through that torment of a New Year's Eve must have played some role in the impasse he was suffering at the moment. For he knew that this time, he had to quit once and for all.

The touch of death, he presumed. Not the acquaintance, not the intuition, not even the fear, but the touch of death. It wasn't like gaining knowledge of what you always knew, that sooner or later you would die. What he had experienced there in the hospital bed, listening to his mind mutter while Ken, an accommodation service manager poisoned by Lobster with Wild Mushroom Risotto, prattled in the bed next to his, was far less cerebral than corporeal. It was as if death, not in some sort of an abstract notion, but Death, liquid and acidic, stabbing and sprawling, had run through his veins, traveled up and down in his body, and then still let him live not because he was too young to die or his stomach not that wrecked after all, but because Death herself had gotten bored of playing with him, and hurled his body aside like a dreary, broken toy.

Then, of course, one other reason that quitting smoking had become so excruciating now was that along with cigarettes, he was advised to quit almost everything that made life worth living. All his pleasures were trimmed and wrapped into a single package, and deemed to be sheer, rancid rubbish. No cigarettes. No coffee. No alcohol. He had been given a distinct brochure of quick tips for each. Navy blue for cigarettes, taupe for coffee, and God knows why, lilac for alcohol. With a phone number at the end of each brochure, twenty-four-hour motivational messages, available in Spanish and English.

Ömer had twice called the number in the navy-blue brochure.

The English version sounded as alien as the Spanish after a while. In both you were expected to be motivated by the mechanized voice of a woman who sounded like she had never ever smoked in all her life, and was completely unaware of what she was talking about. A female tone intended to make you hate tobacco but if you listened to it a couple of times, was more likely to engender hostility toward the female sex.

How could he quit a bad habit, if he had to quit each and every one of his bad habits at the same time? Until now, whatever ephemeral success Ömer had accomplished in every new episode of his quitting-smoking series, he owed to the solace of his supplementary addictions. It was like working in shifts, wherein distinct addictions filled in for each other on off days. When cigarettes weren't around, coffee made extra hours of work. Alcohol both did and did not help, whereas sex was always the best alternative for any kind of craving except that he always ended up smoking in the aftermath. Best of all was weed, which at no stage of his personal saga had he considered giving up since he was nineteen. Now, having renounced all his addictions, with no crutches whatsoever, he didn't know how to put one foot in front of the other. He figured people in similar situations compensated themselves with other means of distraction. But he didn't feel like taking bongo lessons, turning shrubs into bonsai trees, making jugs of polymer clay, or learning the art of ribbon design for that purpose.

So, when on the fifth day of his quitting journey, the fifth day of the new year, Ömer initiated an unnamed ritual, some sort of a spiritual clutch was all he was looking for. He turned off the lights, chased Arroz out, lit the candle, burned the incense Gail had given him, and opened the Mother Nature Music Web site she had told him to listen to throughout the process. At the bottom of the page there were two lotuses in blossom, one gauzy white, the other rose-tinted. When you clicked on the white one, you heard an array of sound effects, all *natural*. As to the other lotus, it was either designed to provide a profound meditative silence or was still under construction. He stuck to the white one.

First, he heard water dripping, birds twittering, and then a sudden clamor as if dozens of glass jars had been rolled down a slope. There was a minute of irksome silence, torn by a baby's jarring cry. Ömer placed each hand crosswise on each ankle, closed his eyes, and waited. The rest he needn't worry about much, Gail had informed him, because the "Reiki was an amazing energy that had its own intelligence, its own instincts, and it just knew where to go, what to do." That is exactly what had happened to Mikao Usui as he was fasting on the holy mountain of Kurama Yama where his spiritual journey had guided him, after spending three years investigating ancient techniques of healing.

He started reading Gail's handwriting. *"I put my right hand on my heart . . ."* He put his right hand on his heart. *"I relax my body. As I breathe in, I go inward . . . entering the world of my thoughts and feelings . . ."* A pigeon cooed. *"I say to myself, I love you . . ."* Ömer said this while bees buzzed. *"I say to myself, you are a good person, doing the best you know how . . ."* He paused. *"I think of someone with whom I want to create a loving relationship."* Wolves ululated in the background. Female faces popped out from the annals of past years, the most recent ones standing closer than others. Ömer decided to skip this part altogether.

"I think of the other person as a mirror . . ." With no person to think of, there was no mirror. *"Whatever this person is not giving to me is a reflection of something I am not giving myself."* He decided to go the other way around, designating the things he failed to give to himself rather than those he couldn't get from that occult lover. "Coffee" came to his mind first, and then "patience," "resilience," and "composure." *"I honor myself in all that I do . . ."* He stopped. His mind refused to go on like this. A field frog croaked.

He crawled out of bed and shut down the Mother Nature Music site. If music was needed, then so be it. He put on "It Takes Blood and Guts to Be This Cool but I'm Still Just a Cliché" on the CD player, and decided to give this attunement biz five shots of Skunk Anansie. If at the end of that nothing significant happened, he'd give up the whole project. In an attempt to wipe the noxious effects of the forest orchestra from his ears, just for five rounds, he saw no harm in giving the CD player full blast.

"From now on, I'll keep the relations that do honor me, and I'll let go of those that do not honor me." He closed his eyes and let his troubles waft away in the flurry of a past that, he knew too well, had not honored him much so far. *"I'll know when to stay in a relationship . . . and I'll know when to leave."* Yes, he admitted he was afraid. Afraid of really, truly loving someone, and then losing that person, afraid of settling down and belonging to somewhere, be it family, country, or marriage, afraid of the irreversibility of life, and the sternly linear flow of his eternal enemy: time.

"Ya basta," Alegre exploded upstairs in Piyu's room. "I can't stand this anymore. Go, tell him to turn it off!"

"Why don't *you* go and tell him, you are the one who is complaining."

That wasn't true. He, too, was complaining. And yet, it wasn't solely the noise downstairs that made Piyu so tense. Since late afternoon they had been in this room, playing Scrabble, Spanish edition. Then, out of the blue, Alegre had pushed the board aside and asked for a kiss, then another, next a tongue, next an earlobe to bite. After that, she had rolled on top of him, took her cardigan off . . . it never stopped anywhere. *"Un besito,"* she said each time and ended up with her scrawny breasts exposed . . . and afterward, her heart broken.

"Well, fine, if you are not going downstairs, then *I am*!"

Alegre slid out, buttoning her cardigan on the way as she bit her bottom lip, that discontented lip of hers kissed with affection and love but never with passion or craze. It was because of her body, Alegre was certain, that Piyu did not want to sleep with her. Too rotund she was, maybe not fat but corpulent for sure. It was her body that pissed him off. Alegre tried hard not to cry but still might have failed in that were her thoughts not shattered by the sight she came across downstairs.

Ömer's door was ajar. His arms around Arroz, his long legs in lotus position, his shoulders quivering, and his mind *Godknowswhere*, Ömer was sobbing on the bed. Alegre closed the door on them, and made no explanation to Piyu when she curled next to him again. Oddly enough, Piyu did not ask anything either. Without a word they kept listening to Skunk Anansie spinning around, taking each of them to the pits of their own thoughts.

If this is what they called a "trance," Ömer concluded, coming back from there the next morning was a real pain in the neck. First, he found himself in a suffocating reverie, then in a perturbing awakening, equally anesthetized in either stage as if compressed under some sort of a weight, a tepid, smelly, arduous gravity. His eyes still closed, his mind still stunned, he tried to fathom how come he had cried like that, for no reason at all, deep, deep sobs as if he had long run out of space within him to take in anything else. How it all started, he couldn't recall. All he remembered was this sudden sorrow attacking him like some crook in a grimy, dark street. What the assailant wanted from him he had no idea. What he had stolen from him eventually, however, was clear enough: his energy! He was enervated, crashed under this tepid, smelly, arduous gravity. He opened his mouth to take a breath but got instead a tang that smelled—and actually *tasted*—like dog.

"*Arroz, çekil üstümden.*"*

Bizarre but true. With animals, plants, and babies, foreigners speak in their native tongue when there is no one around.

In any case, Arroz got the message in Turkish and leaped off the bed. Once the smelly weight on his chest had gone, Ömer didn't feel any better, however. He shuffled his feet to the bathroom, got in the shower, but feeling too tired to struggle with the water he let it flow over his body for a few minutes . . . or maybe more . . .

"Omaaar! What you doin' there, man, get out, I'm late."

The door opened, and out came Ömer wrapped in towels, too drained to dry the water dripping from his hair. As he waddled to his room in a mummy walk, Abed's lips quirked as if he were going to say something, perhaps grumble a little, but whatever it was that he noticed on Ömer's face dragged him instead into a fretful silence.

*Get off me, Arroz.

Neolithic Goddess

"No, Gail, I'm afraid he cannot come to the phone . . . He's sick! Very sick! His face is as yellow as lemon. Yes, we made him tea. No, he doesn't eat. No, he doesn't sleep well either." Abed's voice rolled monotonously but suddenly gained vigor, as he felt the need to ask: "For God's sake, what have you done to him?"

Gail gave a nervous laugh, asked him what on earth made him think this illness had anything to do with her. But since it was time for *The Sopranos*, Abed cut the squabble short.

"Do you think it's his stomach?" asked Piyu, hastening to sweep under the couch before the theme song was over.

"I've no idea, man, either he is secretly drinking coffee and killing his stomach or . . ." Abed paused, his eyes fixed on the screen, "it's something else. We better find out soon. Wise men make trenches before the flood comes."

After the episode, Piyu ducked into Ömer's room, found him still lying on the bed, staring at the ceiling, shoveled vitamins into his mouth, and played him the Primal Scream song he had asked for, "Don't Fight It, Feel It." Half an hour later, Abed walked in with a bowl of beef and onion soup. Ömer thanked each of them over and over, but when it came to eating, he merely kept glaring at the bowl of soup, which didn't look like food anymore, but a pair of innocuous eyes of a cow that had witnessed death at the hands of humans. "I'm gonna miss the next Reiki session," he wailed.

"Re-i-ki!!" Abed threw a fit. "Why don't you instead worry about your Peee-H-Deee? Remember you have a dissertation to write? What about your next appointment with Spivack? Or maybe you're gonna tell him you've changed the topic and decided instead to write a thesis on . . . Re-i-ki!?"

Before the next appointment with Spivack, though, came the one with Gail, or more precisely, Gail herself came. On Tuesday she mushroomed in the kitchen in black pants, black jacket, black everything, looking like a punk vocalist just down from the stage, carrying along books and notebooks in one hand, a huge box of white chocolate peace doves in the other, the latter offered to Abed as a sign of amity.

"Well, aren't you guys gonna offer me anything to drink? What happened to that famous third world hospitality of yours?" She grinned.

They sat around the kitchen table sipping mint tea, eating their doves, contemplating Ömer's situation. But before Abed could fully concentrate on the topic, he had to be able to take his eyes off the cover of one of Gail's books.

"What's that thing?"

"What? Oh *that*!" Gail said heartily. "That is the goddess Ishtar."

Abed nodded broodingly, looked at Gail, then at the picture, and back at Gail again. "Sorry to inform you about this," he muttered with soft caution, "but that woman of yours has a *beard*!"

"Yup!" Gail beamed. "That's because she is bearded Ishtar."

Piyu and Arroz bent forward over the table, the former to share Abed's surprise, the latter to share the box of white chocolate doves.

"It's because she is a hermaphrodite. That's how the ancients portrayed her, having both breasts and phallus. She was served by

bisexual priestesses and by eunuch priests who had castrated themselves. For the castration process, these priests first had to . . ."

"All right! All right! We got the point." Piyu blushed and moved
the box of white chocolates away from Arroz.

But keeping her quiet was impossible today. She must have
slipped into one of her manic moods for she kept on talking, scattering on the table those eerie idioms of hers. "Matrifocal," "Phallocentric," "Mother Nature against Father Logos" . . . brain-brandishing
concepts drizzled on the table over the mint tea glasses and half-
nibbled doves.

"They were in search of the woman in them so that they could
surpass their bodies and attain the mystery of creation. All religion is
about woman." She gave an assuring smile. Piyu and Abed gave a
consoling one in return. "That's why in Siberia, for instance, male
shamans wore symbolic breasts on their robes. No need to go that
far. Don't you realize that women's robes are still the official priestly
garbs? Priests function as mothers to the believers. Priests are
women, too."

Piyu coughed nervously, Abed sighed.

"There are so many examples from different cultures. Why do
you think, for instance, Taoist priests used to pee sitting? They
wanted to turn into women!"

To conclude the argument, however, she had to wait a few minutes, for the sudden burst of sniggers to wane. While Piyu and Abed
chortled, Gail calmly watched a wisp of mint swimming on the surface of her tea. The mint swam counterclockwise, drawing unruffled
whirls of its own. She decided to take that as a good sign.

"Well, one should only be conscious of history," Gail went on,
her eyes aglow with zest. "Imagine what'd it be like living in a Neolithic city rather than living in Boston. A city that was a ceremonial
center for the cult of the goddess. Archaeologists found this city.
They excavated it, layer by layer. And you know what, nowhere in
this city did they come across any sign of warfare. No weaponry!
Nobody killed another human being. Nobody killed animals either.
No sign of animal slaughter . . ."

Abed coughed nervously, Piyu sighed.

"Most probably they were all vegetarians. It might be hard for us to grasp this with our minds long tainted with militarism and nationalism but let me assure you, these people lived in peace. The word *primitive* is misleading. They were civilized! We are primitive!"

Piyu and Abed stood silent, ossified in their "sure-tell-me-more-about-it" stare.

"Women and children were buried there under the sleeping platforms inside their houses. Buried with their amulets and icons. Everywhere in this city there were murals depicting women, and venerating the mother goddess. The Neolithic goddess . . ."

It was exactly then that they heard this voice, so faint and diffused that for a second it sounded as if it had no body of its own, rising from the handles of the pans on the wall, the pepper grinder, the baking cups . . . anything but a human being.

"*Th . . . pl . . . e . . . th . . . pl . . . e . . . ᴅ in . . . r . . . ey!*"

Three of the four pairs of eyes around the kitchen table simultaneously rolled toward the corridor. The fourth pair of eyes remained anchored on the box of chocolates.

"That . . . place . . . is . . . in . . . Turkey!"

Out of the corridor ghosted Ömer. As he leaned toward the kitchen door, unshaven, looking long unwashed, he kept glancing at Gail with a weird brittle look in his puffed and baggy eyes, his lips teetering on the verge of an impetuous smile, as if he had just made a confession, or was about to make one.

"The place you were talking about is in Turkey," he droned, and then nodded supporting his cause. "I know!"

Like the crushing majority of Turks, he had never been to Çatal-höyük, the Neolithic city of the Mother Goddess, never visited its museum, and never ever read anything about it. But there was one thing about this city he was certain of: It was somewhere in Turkey!

So they put him in his bed again, appointed Arroz his guardian, played him "Somebody Put Something in My Drink" from The Ramones, and went back into the kitchen to finish their mint teas and

white chocolates, but, it was hoped, not that voltaic discussion. Half
an hour later Gail left, taking her bearded Ishtar along. The moment
the porch door was closed behind her, Abed and Piyu scurried upstairs to check *how* Ömer was doing . . . and also, to ask *what* the hell
he thought he was doing.

"A million years ago there were Amazons in Turkey. By the way
I am Turkish, you know. Will you *coucher avec moi*?" Piyu warbled,
swinging back and forth, blushing garnet with each swing as if he
weren't the mocker but the one mocked at.

"You are a walking disgrace, Omar," sniggered Abed. "There
is nothing you won't do to sleep with women. All women in your
eyeshot!"

Listening to their voices from a distance, Ömer waited patiently
for the bulky guffaws to cease. But having once entered into the ex-
uberant palace of male pleasantries, Abed and Piyu did not seem to
be willing to come out of there before they had visited every room.
So they ridiculed and nagged, nagged and ridiculed, while Ömer
sighed and sighed, getting more transparent with each sigh, like a
floating shadow riding on puffs of air, his toes barely skimming the
rough rug of Reality.

"You don't understand, guys," he almost whispered ducking his
head timidly into the first crack of a silence to appear. "I'm going to
ask Gail for a date . . ."

"I knew it!" Abed hollered, pouring a cauldron of husky voice
over the flimsy void of silence Ömer was trying to inhale. "I fuckin'
knew it!"

Abed got up from his chair, and walked so stiffly toward him
that for a second Ömer thought he was going to slap him on the face.
Instead, however, Abed stopped briskly within a nose reach, looked
him directly in the eye, and bobbed his head thoughtfully from side
to side. "She made you tie something, right? A shoelace . . . her
hair . . . a string . . . can you remember what it was? You are be-
witched, *dostum*. You are fucked up! *Ouaghauogh!*"

Abed and Piyu stood inspecting Ömer with increasing curiosity,
as if he were some sort of dotted mushroom they had brought back

home from a serene saunter into the woods but now doubted if it was edible.

"But Gail is a *lesbian*," Piyu interrupted with the penitent yet absolute tone of someone long contemplating a hitherto unsolved mathematical formula, finally arriving at the conclusion that no way, it will never be solved. "She doesn't *like* men!"

Actually, he had no particular evidence on this particular point. They had never talked about it before, and never heard anything resonating from either Gail or anyone else. But that kind of information was not necessary to make this sort of a conclusion. To the contrary, it was precisely this ambiguity that made Gail's homosexuality all the more probable. *Nature abhors a vacuum*, they say. *Men, too, abhor a vacuum*, any rift of indistinctness in their classification of women and thereby in their encounters with the other sex, they pigeonhole, pigeonhole, pigeonhole.

"Did you know she wants us to piss like women?" Abed ran to Piyu's help in this futile attempt to clarify Ömer's blurred vision.

"You don't . . . understand," stuttered Ömer faithful to his "you-don't-understand" mantra. "I . . . have reached . . . the point of no return. Hereafter it makes no difference whether she is a *witch, lesbian, alien* . . . I just couldn't care less." His left eye blinked in seven or eight subsequent spasms of exasperation, which made him look either like he was trying to secretly convey to his housemates not to worry, that TRUTH in capital letters was other than the one they had been dabbling in but that he couldn't say it aloud at the moment for there were bugs all around the room transmitting their talks to some bad guys parked outside . . . or simply, like he had developed a tic in his eye overnight. In the ensuing silence of confusion, Ömer winked at them again and added gallantly: "If she wants me to pee-pee like a woman, that is fine with me. I will gladly piss that way all my life!"

"Omar, my friend, you are not well these days," Abed rattled on trying not to sound nervous. "Listen, you want *aaaaaall* the women you meet. Ever since you started living in this house, toothbrushes come, and toothbrushes leave. Last month it was Marisol, today it

is Gail, we couldn't even understand when was it that you broke up
with Pearl. You see, this day next week you will be fussing over
someone else."

"That's true," Piyu nodded, careful to choose his words so as
not to hurt Ömer's feelings. "You are always *interested* in women. So
many girlfriends . . ."

Ömer lowered his eyes, staring for a suspicious length of time
at a sky-blue sock on the floor, and then scanning the room all
over with a sanguine look on his face as if when he found the other
one, he'd have also found the solution to his problem. "You don't
understand . . . this is entirely different. Until today, I've been dating women I knew I did *not* love. But with Gail it's diametrically
opposite. I didn't try to date her because I didn't know I loved
her."

Abed and Piyu chorused a rueful moan.

"It's different this time." Ömer emitted a new attempt of clarification. "You don't understand . . . I'm falling in love."

"You are not falling anywhere!" Abed quacked. "You with the
memory of an aquarium fish! Somebody should remind you that you
didn't meet that girl today. She was here all this time, right in front
of your eyes. Remember what you said the first time we met
her? You thought she was snooty, snobby, sneering . . . and all the *S*
words . . . remember? You clearly disliked her. This is a momentary
lapse of memory, that's all. Maybe a side effect of those yellow pills
they gave you at the hospital, huh?"

"You don't understand," yowled a voice that sounded strangled
at the onset, only to mount toward the end. "I am in LOVE . . ."

What transpired after that was a collective awakening on the
side of Piyu and Abed, which started as an endeavor to laugh aloud,
tumbled halfway through, and lost vim toward the end, drifting instead into pure amazement. It wasn't particularly the word itself but
the way he had articulated it that shushed his housemates. Ömer
had pronounced the word *love* as if it weren't just another word. For
God's sake, *Cambridge Advanced Learner's Dictionary* had 170,000 of
them but he still had to make a hopeless defense, all alone by himself,
in a court notorious for its injustice, a court whose laws were alien to

him, and in which he knew there was no way he could prove his in-
nocence even though he himself was so sure of it. He had spoken
with that kind of a distress, as if he had long run out of hope for better, and had already accepted the worst of verdicts for this crime he
was put on trial for: love.

Not **Love**, not even **LOVE** but **LOVE!**

Quantum Mechanics
and Cupid

Alegre narrowed her eyes at the page open in front of her, emitting a chortle that was meant to sound like *mockery* but resonated only as far as *dissatisfaction*.

> DID YOU CRY WHEN YOU LEARNED YOU WERE PREGNANT? According to a recent study a whopping 61% of moms shed happy tears on that special day.

Sitting right across from her, Manuel tilted his head and stared at her suspiciously. The couple in the waiting room must have heard her, too, but they simply ignored her. Having been told that their daughter suffered from attention deficit disorder, and having no idea what that might mean, they had come here for clarification, but Alegre suspected they would be even more confused after seeing the doctor. She gave Manuel an *everything-is-OK* smile, which the boy met with an *if-you-say-so* gaze.

> On whose shoulder did you run to cry on? 48% of women shed those happy tears with a close friend, 34% with their husbands, and 28% with their mothers.

Eight years before, she, too, had shed tears when she had found out she was pregnant. To this day she hadn't told anyone, not even the father, a slothful Ukrainian teenager whose family owned a fruit stand across from the school and with whom Alegre had slept only two times. The only person who knew about the abortion was *la* Tía Tuta, the less chaste, the most secretive among *todas las tías*. On the way back from the clinic, she had cuddled Alegre, asking: "Did you learn your lesson well?" Alegre had sobbed, and that was the only time she had cried over the incident. "Good," *la* Tía Tuta had squeezed her hand tight, "and now that you have learned your lesson well, you should *unlearn* it all. Erase it. This has never happened. *Lo comprendes, corazón?*"*

This had never happened. Not to her. After so many years, it was still buried deep inside. A couple of times she had given serious thought to having her phone call taken live on the Catholic Families Radio Show like many women in a similar situation did. But even then, she knew, there would be one thing about the whole incident she could never reveal. Nobody knew that within her tightly woven fabric of morality resided a separate thread, blatantly corporeal. For the very first thought that had occurred to her when she had learned about her pregnancy was the fear of gaining weight, swallowing inside, and ballooning into a fat body, the fear she had never been able to share with anyone.

What did your husband do when he learned you were pregnant? According to the same study, 52% of the husbands of those 34% of 61% women had hugged them, 36% of husbands had opened a bottle of champagne, and 18% had called their moms.

After that day she had grown cold toward *chicos*, toward sex, and refrained from any affair until the day she met Piyu. Today, every time Piyu refused to sleep with her, Alegre couldn't help fearing he somehow knew about the incident, not knowingly but intuitively, as

*Do you understand it, dear?

if his body knew what his mind did not, and thereby refused to sleep
with this woman who was neither female enough, skipping her periods, nor a good prospective mother, worried more about her body
image than the baby she had lost.

She skimmed the pages until a familiar face popped up. It was
the girl who couldn't stop reading. Her parents had thrown this huge
party to celebrate her four-thousandth book. There was a jaunty
photo where she stood beaming with all the guests next to a mammoth cake in the shape of a book. Alegre skipped the rest, and dialed
Piyu's number. She wondered if Piyu had read the message she had
given via the fluffy pumpkin cheesecake pie, which was baked less
than enough and was, therefore, far fluffier than it should have been.

"*Hola amor.* Did you eat your fluffy pumpkin cheesecake pie?"

"No! I haven't," came the gruff answer. "But somebody here *did.*"

In the background Ömer smiled dully as Piyu looked at him
scornfully over the receiver. After days of starving, his appetite had
proclaimed its independence, and ever since that moment Ömer
had been eating nonstop.

"Yes, of course, I'm hungry. No, don't worry. Abed and I are going to arrange something now. I don't know, we haven't decided yet.
Maybe spaghetti. *Que no*, the casserole is finished, too!" Piyu yam-
mered. "He also ate that. How would I know? OK . . . I'll ask
him . . . I'll call you back later."

Piyu turned to Ömer. "Alegre wants to know if you have noticed
anything *unusual* in her fluffy pumpkin cheesecake pie."

"The pie?" Ömer pondered going through the plentiful records
of all the food he had been devouring since early morning, until
finally somewhere underneath the pile he found the required information: "Oh, the pie was great, thank you, just what the doctor
ordered."

Piyu and Abed inspected him under cross fire. After days of clot-
ted stupefaction, Ömer had all of a sudden become too vigorous, and
definitely too ravenous. While it was hard to tell which particular
state was more nerve-wracking, before or after, they could sense this
sudden change had something to do with the talk they had had the

day before. After all, confessions of love long suppressed are capable of inflaming a chain reaction.

1. The impact of declaring love on the subject of love.
2. The impact of declaring love on the witnesses of love.
3. The impact of declaring love on the object of love.

Such being the general framework, each effect in turn may assume a variety of forms depending on the case at hand. In this particular one, it happened more or less like this:

1. The impact of declaring love on subject Ömer Özsipahioğlu: Positive. A feathery, wispy sense of relief like a burden taken off his shoulders.
2. The impact of declaring love on witnesses Abed and Piyu: Negative. A cramming, harassing sense as if that missing burden was now placed on their shoulders.
3. The impact of declaring love on the object Gail: Zero impact. Having no idea about what was going on, no change could be observed in the object.

Looking at the scene with the benefit of hindsight, perhaps it was this imbalance and the wish to go halves in their burden that incited his housemates to pressure Ömer to declare his love to Gail. But perhaps it was inevitable for them to intervene in the process. Some sort of a *Cupidean Interpretation of Quantum Mechanics.* "Conscious observation is," Bohr assumed, "what causes real events to happen." Once having learned about somebody's secret love, witnesses might find themselves in constant and conscious observation, which entails a dose of intervention, pretty much as any attempt to trace atomic processes involves a fundamentally uncontrollable interaction with their course.

Hence, Observer 1 (Piyu) and Observer 2 (Abed) spent that evening observing Ömer. Late at night Piyu called Alegre and told her what was going on. But it took some time to integrate Observer 3 into the process, for Alegre refused to believe that anyone, even if that person be Ömer, might fall in love with someone like Gail. Still, she tried to help: "Flowers! Make him buy her a gorgeous bouquet. White lilies and a single red rose."

Alegre and Abed were sure that flowers would be a romantic declaration, and after a little prompting, Piyu was sure, too. Nevertheless, when his two housemates, serious and sure, came downstairs to his room to inform Ömer about their project, the latter's answer between chomps wasn't so enthusiastic.

"I don't think she'll like that kinda stuff." Ömer blew out a mouthful of hummus, his most recent plunder. "She's probably against the massacring of roses to please cockamamy bourgeois lovers. She's not your typical woman!"

The only reason Abed and Piyu did not strangle him instantly was because, as good scientists, they knew they shouldn't destroy the entity under observation. That evening the three of them went out for a walk and paid a visit to a store on South Street that seemed to have everything *not your typical woman* might enjoy. Tibetan singing bowls, tempurpedic pillows, Native American jewelry, dried botanicals, gel stones, talismans, wind chimes, essential oils, charm bags, herbal candles, Wiccan items, and a green substance that looked like ordinary grass, and was actually, as they'd learn in a minute, *organic grass*.

"Do people pay nine bucks for a bag of turf?" Abed squealed.

The Nordic-looking salesgirl slit a condescending smile.

"Anyway, Gail does not need turf," Abed nasaled in the middle of a sudden attack of allergic rhinitis. "What she needs is some sort of a tranquilizer, to make her less aggressive and more . . . normal. Do you have an herb that helps to normalize?"

"Then I should give you some ginseng," the salesgirl chirped, bobbing her flaxen locks. "Anemia, general debility, nervousness, neurasthenia . . . It cures all. Actually that is what it's called: Cure All!!!"

So they bought a big bottle of Ginseng Vegetarian Capsules, Ginseng Tea in bags, and Ginseng and Astragalus Extract Sipping Ampoules. And thus furbished, twenty minutes later they dropped by Squirmy Spirit Chocolates, ruining Debra Ellen Thompson's day. Gail, on the other hand, looked pleased to see them.

For a second, the three housemates stood staring at the spoon sagging from her hair. *How strange!* thought Piyu. *How stupid!* thought Abed. And Ömer thought: *How lovely!*

The pattern showed little change when Gail offered them obese Mother Goddesses of almond-chocolate. *How strange!* thought Piyu as he politely bit into a huge breast. *How stupid!* thought Abed jawing a goddess's head. And Ömer thought the usual. "*We* were out to buy some ginseng, and on the way back *we* thought *we* could stop by to see what you girls were doing," he then stuttered, sheltering his tall, klutzy body behind the barricades of "*we*."

"Ginseng . . . the miraculous Panax!" Gail's face crumpled slightly. "Cure All's Cure Nothing, I'd say. I hope you don't expect much from it. Did you buy it for a specific purpose?"

A *purpose* for ginseng? Ömer stared back traumatized as if he didn't even have one to live. How could he reach her when she was so unreachable? How could he make her love him when she so obviously disliked everything he did? After that, he barely spoke, and to keep his mouth busy, during the rest of the visit, he mostly, enormously, hysterically ate as if determined to wipe out as many Mother Goddesses as he could from the face of the earth. He ignored all attempts on the part of Piyu and Abed to open up increasingly meaningless topics to pull him out of the ingestion loop, while Debra Ellen Thompson, Gail, and the mint-chocolate Laughing Buddhas on the trays watched all three of them in wonder.

Attempt to Declare Love — II

Beadwork in Iroquis Life; Tradition and Innovation in Meiji-Period Prints; Reproducing Ancient Tombs Using Digital Technologies; Photographic Chronicle of Hazardous Work in America; The Art of Chinese Calligraphy; Surreal Light Installations; Exhibition of Tapa Cloths from the Pacific Islands; Book-signing: *The Mysteries of Ancient Egypt*; Norwegian Couple Dance . . . To keep track of the cultural activities in Boston, Piyu had already deduced, was merely impossible. "Maybe we should find a good restaurant," he heaved a deep sigh over the Boston City Guide. "They could have a nice dinner somewhere."

"Keep going, Piyu, don't lose hope," Abed's voice rose from behind the Arts Calendar of *The Boston Globe*. "Dinner is too dangerous, he'll be under the spotlight. A cultural activity is less risky. We need to find something that Gail will take pleasure in."

There was a photography exhibition called "Divided Self," which looked highly interesting, but it required too much energy for it was displayed in three different galleries in three different parts of the city. Music was, of course, another possibility where Ömer could reveal his specialization. But then, his housemates were afraid that his musical taste might be too outrageous for Gail and spoil everything.

A Video Installation on the Depictions of Female Nudity; An Exhibition on the Masks of Africa; A Talk on "Is Unmasking the Faces of the Orient the New Face of Orientalism?"; A Panel on the Depictions of Female Nudity in Video Installations . . .

When the phone rang Piyu picked it up with visible relief, glad to find a moment's break.

"Is he still in the bathroom?"

Piyu smirked to Abed over the receiver. "It's Alegre. She asks if he is still in the bathroom!"

"Tell her the bathroom is his new house."

Too much chocolate. The curse of Laughing Buddhas. Back from the chocolate store, Ömer had ended up in the bathroom.

"Tell her we need to help him," Abed volleyed, suddenly getting serious. To convey the message better, with no intermediaries, he grabbed the phone from Piyu. "I think this diarrhea problem is more symbolical than physical. It's all because he couldn't confess his love. It's as if when the soul cannot be revealed, the body starts to discharge."

Alegre had other suggestions, natural activities for the most part. Whale watching, for instance, not a good way to confess love perhaps, but you never know. Tours and excursions of which there were plenty in the region. Watch sea lion pens in the New England Aquarium; learn more about stuffed birds in the Museum of Comparative Zoology; see baby dinosaurs in the Harvard Museum of Natural History . . . Gail would surely enjoy these. A romantic promenade through the arboretum sounded even better . . . All looked plausible, had Ömer looked more energetic. Diarrhea had not only enervated him but had also anchored his body to a circumference around the toilet. He couldn't possibly spend much time outdoors.

"I gotta hang up now, the doctor is coming," exclaimed Alegre. "Good luck!"

Connoisseurship and the Graphic Arts in Eighteenth-Century Venice; A Lecture on the Crisis on the Korean Peninsula; An Exhibition on Handkerchiefs and Bandannas from American Presidential

Campaigns; Images of Colonial India; Byzantine Women and Their
World . . .

"Wait! Wait!" Abed quacked. "That sounds good! Women and
Byzantine . . . Byzantine and Women . . ." he repeated slurring each
word with utmost fervor. "That can be a common ground, don't you
think? It is related to both of them in a way."

The exhibition covered a period from the fourth through the
fifteenth centuries, and displayed ivories, toiletries, coins, seals, amulets . . . two hundred objects in total. Looked more than enough to
declare love at some point.

By this time Piyu was so tired of searching he'd have jumped on
any suggestion. They came downstairs and chorused in hearty unison in front of the bathroom to inform the observed entity of his very
next move. "Byzantine Women?" the bathroom door rumbled incredulously. But to their relief, no further objection came.

Ömer spent the next day resting in bed, seemingly working on
his dissertation but actually making some inquiry into this new topic
on his agenda before he found the courage to ask Gail out. Originally, his intention was to make a brief excursion into "Byzantine
Women" but the excursion became more of a voyage as he delved
into the topic with an increasing interest. After several hours of research, he had concluded that Byzantium might have been a joyful
place if you were an upper-class man but you might need to recon-
sider living there if you were a woman, especially one from the lower
class. But then, fascinatingly, there was Theodora, the charming
daughter of a bear raiser, growing up in the slums of Byzantium, to
become a sparkling full-time actress, then the empress, and one of
the most potent women in world history. In order to marry her,
Justinian had to abolish all regulations preventing actresses—who
were categorically treated like prostitutes by law—from marrying
into the senatorial class. So profound was her impact on him. After becoming the empress, she had enormously furthered women's
rights, passing laws to help prostitutes, banning brothels, protecting
unfortunate women . . . never forgetting her background, never
turning a blind eye to the sufferings of her sisters. The more Ömer
read about Theodora, the more he likened her to Gail. By late after-

noon, he was absolutely sure that Gail would do exactly the same things Theodora had done if rather than being a chocolate maker in Boston, she were given a chance to ascend to the Byzantium throne.

With this impetus, he made a call to Squirmy Spirit Chocolates, and after some trivial talk, tentatively asked Gail what she thought of this exhibition he had heard about by chance.

"The exhibit on Byzantium Women and Their World?" Gail crowed with joy, or so it sounded to Ömer. "Yeah, that's a great exhibit!"

"I was planning to see it tomorrow. Maybe you'd like to come with me."

"Oh . . ." her voice faded. "I've already seen it. But you should definitely go."

When he hung up the phone, Ömer stared nervously at the large fawn mosaic eyes of the Theodora he had downloaded from the Web and turned into his wallpaper, eyes which on second thought, didn't look so enchanting anymore.

Attempt to Declare Love — III

So far every day of January since New Year's Eve might be said to have been a tough one for subject Ömer Özsipahioğlu, but it looked like this Saturday was going to outscore the rest. To double the effect, the day started too early, ended too late. Early in the morning, in what was neither the first nor the last in a chain of toilet visits running amok all through the night, he stood staring at an image the mirror said must be familiar. He gave himself a tired smile. Got one in return. While the smile kept bouncing to and fro between him and his image, growing more tired at each rebound, imperceptibly, indescribably but inexorably, an air of indifference descended over him. For an indefinite instant, he felt like he had found a fissure in time, and through that crack had slipped out of the condition he was dawdling in. The sensation rose in his stomach, quickly passed the rib cage through the lungs, moved up the throat, never pausing until it was propelled out in a suffocated sigh. Everything seemed so meaningless. This endless hassle to be given "more" of everything, this urge to make Gail fall in love with him, and even Gail herself . . . lost their coronas as they faded one by one into this euphoria that had come over him. Not that he didn't love her anymore. On the contrary, he sensed he loved her even more. More but differently. This love was *all about* but also external to her. With this feeling, Ömer deduced, he could go on loving her even if she didn't respond to his love emotionally, physically, and even sexually. He felt so elated.

He had no idea where this bliss had come from. All he could tell was that it felt great! It felt ginseng! If right at this instant one of his housemates were to dash into the bathroom and ask him to name this exceptional feeling, Ömer wouldn't hesitate in answering back: "Ginseng!"

The feeling Ginseng! was definitely Ginseng! but it was doubtful that it was a feeling at all. It made you feel nothing. Absolutely nothing. Pretty much like having a shadow but not "having" it, that kind of gentleness, almost companionable. He washed his face, started to foam all over his chin but stopped halfway through. The feeling Ginseng! asked him why he was doing this. What was the use of shaving every day, with the same compulsion and tenacity, when it kept coming back, and you knew that it would, that tomorrow morning another shaving would be scarcely news. If that's what your beard wants, why not let it grow? Why this persistent need to intervene in the course of life? Ömer went downstairs to inform his housemates that they, too, should stop struggling for him, stop being so pushy about his love, and instead let everything be what it simply is.

Ömer clomped toward the kitchen. Since Abed had taken Arroz out for a walk, and Piyu was in the living room sweeping the floor, that constant clatter coming from the kitchen could only mean one thing: Alegre at work.

"Good morning! Today is the great day, are you ready? But you haven't even shaved yet." Alegre frowned and smiled at the same time. "Tell me how I should cook this Zucchini Squash Strudel. With walnuts or raisins? Which way do you think Gail would like it more?"

Zucchini Squash Strudel . . . It sounded like a cryptogram. *Walnuts . . . or raisins . . . or both . . . or none . . .* What difference would it make after all? This was just the outer form, shadows on the surface; he wanted to go beyond, deep down into the essence. "*Why do you all want me to confess my love? Do we always have to inform the beloveds of our feelings for them? Doesn't this declaration imply a request to get something in return? Is not every proclamation of love a statement of selfishness?*"

"Oh, you poor little thing, don't worry, it's gonna be a fabulous dinner. Trust me, she'll love it," Alegre consoled him, missing the philosophy altogether.

"*But why all the rush? What's the use of appearances but to prevent us from seeing the reality behind? Why are you all investing in me when I am not that sure of myself? Who am I, what do I want, do I really have to want . . . someone, something . . . do I really have to be . . . someone, something? Maybe love does not need to win the beloved but to lose yourself in her. When you lose yourself, and raze your tower of ego, what difference would it make if you were loved in return or not? The moment you start giving without expecting to be given to in return, the whole universe would be Ginseng! Ginseng! Ginseng!*"

"Ginseng no! This-is-TO-FU," croaked Alegre pointing a finger at a plate in front of Ömer. "But-you-do-not-worry," she added, switching into this caringly instructive idiom reminiscent of a White Colonizer chatting with Mowgli in the *Jungle Book*. "The-dinner-will-be-so-splendid-she-will-ask-to-dine-here-every-day."

Ömer gave up, and writhed in discomfort toward the bathroom, his only haven nowadays. He took his Walkman to listen to The Smiths sing "What Difference Does It Make?" Three minutes, eleven seconds.

The truth is, Alegre was a bit overwrought this morning as cooking for this special day had turned out to be extremely and unexpectedly frustrating. In order to fix a splendid menu she had done some preliminary research on vegan cuisine, and found out in awe that she would have to refrain from not only meat, but also butter, eggs, milk, cheese . . . and everything that made food savory and cookery enjoyable. For the first time in her life, Alegre was feeling uneasy in the kitchen. That's why when, back from an invigorating stroll, Abed and Arroz scurried into the kitchen to see what she had been up to, it wasn't very sensible of them to react so callously to the menu, which had been so painstakingly concocted.

THE MENU

Soup:
mushroom cauliflower leek
potato corn

Main dishes:
carrot cabbage pea puree
carrot squash casserole
marinated & grilled tofu
stuffed tofu roast
zucchini squash strudel

Side dishes:
mushroom pancakes with potato filling
breaded tofu
scrambled tofu
tofu salad

Desserts:
carrot pie
pumpkin pie
carrot and pumpkin cookie bars

"What's this? Are we celebrating a greengrocers' festival?" Abed protested. Alegre hated Abed.

But perhaps before solving the problem of *what to eat*, they'd better solve the problem of *how to eat* because it soon turned out that Ömer was not coming out of the bathroom. Most of the afternoon he had been anchored there, not only because watching his wobbly face in the mirror induced him into a new set of ontologically Ginseng! questions but also because he was still physically unwell.

In the echelon of illnesses diarrhea is disparaged down to the lowest level. It is the only illness that is so common and yet so marginalized at the same time. To save Ömer from the shame, the three observers tried to think of a cure that would work its wonders in the couple of hours before the dinner. Since they knew of no such cure, but had heard of numerous less miraculous ones (for when diarrhea is the issue everyone has some fuzzy cure either heard from someone else or remembered from childhood days), they decided to try all at the same time. Thus, in the following three hours, Ömer was made to consume a potato soup with coconut juice that neither looked like soup nor tasted of potato (Alegre's cure); blackberry juice (*la* Tía Piedad's suggestion); apples (Oksana Sergiyenko's suggestion when she dropped in to say hello before going shopping); a bowl of boiled oatmeal (Piyu's grandmother's cure); a bowl of rice porridge (Zahra's cure over the phone); bananas (everybody's suggestion); yogurt and peaches (Zahra's cure over the phone); blackberry juice and wine (*la* Tía Piedad's suggestion on second thought); more apples (Oksana Sergiyenko back from shopping with a bag of Granny Smith apples); a family size Coke (everybody's cure); and lots of garlic in lieu of antibiotics (Abed and Piyu's medication). When everything was devoured and gulped down, his stomach ballooned into a barrel, Ömer shuffled his feet upstairs, not to the bathroom, not there anymore, but to his room, to take a nap, and also to organize all his Reiki powers to send Gail a telepathic message begging her not to come.

Alas, the message must have been lost on the way.

At 7:15 p.m. Gail and Debra Ellen Thompson were downstairs sitting at the table with everyone, praising the menu, a bit surprised but content no doubt. Alegre had made Gail sit across from Ömer, but since the latter did not tear his gaze away from the piece of leek swimming in his soup, it was hard to tell whether he was aware of it or not. Every now and then a harsh, gruntlike sound was heard from his stomach, but to the three observers' relief, Ömer didn't seem to be in need of running to the bathroom anymore. The cures had worked out, at least one of them.

Once bitten twice shy. No one at the table seemed to have forgotten the tension over the last supper. In order not to have similar friction again, they tentatively prowled the streets of potential conversations, searching for light, inoffensive topics to chatter on. Within such multicultural groups, sensitive not to offend anyone, eager to have some fun without any vilification, one good dinner topic being "urban legends," that's what they talked about for the next hour.

Though from different countries, they had heard exactly the same stories with minuscule changes here and there. The man who'd found a finger in a jar of pickles bought from a supermarket nearby was equally Moroccan and Spanish and American. So was this young couple who had left their newborn baby with the new nanny, and when they came back home late that night, found him in a large platter roasted and garnished with potatoes. Then there was this other couple whose car was stolen on the night of the earthquake in San Francisco and weeks later found under the ruins of some building, with the body of the thief inside crushed beyond recognition. And then, of course, there was the story about this scuba diver who had died endless deaths in every place where there had been a forest on fire. From helicopters with large buckets, urban legends had thrown him over and over into flames all around the world.

Urban legends are the free citizens of the world. They need no passport to travel, no visas to stay. They are verbal chameleons, absorbing the color of the culture they come into contact with. Whichever shore they reach, they can instantly become a native of it. Urban legends are free souls that belong to no one, and yet are the property of all.

"Do you have similar urban legends in Istanbul?" asked Alegre, turning to Ömer, and instantly smiled an apologetic smile, for she had never meant for the question to sound as blushingly naïve and obvious in its intent as it apparently did.

Do we have urban legends? What difference does it make? The story of the thief who crashed in a stolen car in the San Francisco earthquake also circulated after the earthquake in Istanbul, as if in order to be able to endure, people needed a dash of divine justice in each and every worldly disaster.

Yet, he didn't say any of these things. As he kept his head tucked down, "Yup," he gasped, paused for a few seconds, and then, amicably came to an agreement with himself: "Yup."

Between the first yup and the second, Gail gawked fixedly at Ömer's face, seeing there one other thing she loved about him: system failure! He relished, almost symbolized in his very own existence, not only the possibility, or even the proclivity, but the very inevitability of a system failure. In a success-oriented world,

where everyone knew so well exactly what he wanted and where
he was headed, this permanently perplexed guy, this walking self-
destruction, was different than the rest. How could she ever tell him
that she, too, was familiar with the muddy waters of misery that
pulled him deep down. Gail smiled at Ömer as if she were on the
verge of saying something but didn't know how to put it. "Stop it,
baby," she'd like to whisper to him. "This is all about fear, this sorrow that I see in your eyes every time I look at you, this sorrow that
was already there before we met, and long before you started loving me."

But fear no more, for I will be with you as long as you want me to.

None of these things she could say aloud. She swallowed all her
words with a forkful of carrot squash casserole and listened to what
the others were saying. They were talking about this urban legend professor of every nationality who had in a philosophy/physics/
political science/genetical engineering exam asked just one question:
"Why?" and failed all students but the one who had replied: "Why
not?" Then there was this legendary spider visiting every country,
laying her eggs under the skins of vacationers. There were tons of
satanic stories, appearing in one country the moment they disappeared elsewhere, creating panic and mayhem wherever they went.
Listening to all these rumors and legends circulating around the
globe, Gail felt she, too, should say a few things.

"My favorite is this all-time urban legend," she blurted out, "of
some Virgin Mary shedding blood tears in the altar of some remote
village church . . . Crying Marys, Winking Marys, Whispering
Marys . . . Oodles of them!"

Now that she had started to talk, the group was all at once semi-
paralyzed, torn between letting her say whatever she had to say and
then getting annoyed, or being prudent enough to get annoyed right
now, and save the burden of hearing all the things she had to say. A
glint of resentment, in differing shades, flickered in the eyes of all—
all but one. Though his gaze was still glued to the carrot cabbage pea
puree on his plate, Ömer's lips cracked with a tender smile. It was so
naïve of her, if not so sweet, and so so *lovely*, to make this gaffe in

front of visibly religious people, where Catholics happened to compose the majority.

"There is a whole lot of money in the miracles biz, I'd say," Gail enthused, failing to perceive the whorls of irritation she had begun to stir. "I mean, if we were to sell chocolate Crying Marys we'd be wallowing in money, don't you think so, Debra Ellen Thompson?"

Debra Ellen Thompson gave a tired smile; Gail continued all the same. "This Crying Virgin Mary tourism must be the most profitable urban legend of all times."

"Hah! Here we go again!" Abed slumped in his chair belching out all the pressure accumulating all over his nervous system since they had sat around the table, mostly because of this herbal menu he was compelled to enjoy, but also partly because everyone's extreme conscientiousness not to create any tension was a tension in itself. "They asked the baking-oven, 'How did fire enter in you?' And do you know what her answer was, Gail? She said: 'Through my mouth!' "

"Hey, you said that before!!" Piyu beamed out of reflex, unable to control the enthusiasm of having at last heard a familiar proverb from Abed's lips, familiarity not necessarily entailing lucidity. But then immediately he turned to Gail, unable to suppress his resentment: "Maybe you are right, Gail, maybe some people try to make money out of others' beliefs. But this doesn't mean that the miracles you are talking about are phony."

A breeze of silence, a gauzy tension, a transitory estrangement . . . all interrupted by a long resonating stomach growl.

"It is in itself a miracle that *Virgen de Guadalupe* left us her image as proof of her apparition, and also left us some important messages," Piyu muttered, his gaze blurring behind the glasses while his cheeks flushed deeper. "We do not think that message can be confused with an urban legend."

With a grin set to her jowl, an eerie twinkle in her eyes, ready to prove she was not going to backpedal so easily, Gail opened her mouth. At the same instant, Ömer raised his head, and for the first time in two hours managed to look at her directly. There, in the shadows of her open mouth, he heard the swish of what was yet to come, like a pre-echo. He heard her talk about a world that massively exploits every wee hope in people's hearts. He heard her propagating about living this life like a human boat floating on the seawater, never having anything solid beneath your feet, ready to sail anytime, ready to sail anywhere. He heard her mentioning going to sleep every night fearing that the very next morning you may wake up in some stranger's shoes, or in some strange land from which you might never want to return. He heard her talking about death, and the only way to immortality being changing names, places, abandoning who you are, dying before death. "Stop it, my love," he wanted to whisper to her. "This is all about fear, this rage in your tongue that I come across every time I listen to you, the rage that was already there before we met, before I started loving you."

But fear no more, for I will be with you as long as you want me to.

None of these he could say aloud. He tried to swallow all his words with a forkful of puree. And yet, he had listened long enough to others talk in order not to have to hear the voices in him. He suddenly felt he, too, should say a few words.

"I think we all pine for a miracle, though in different ways. It's not only the Catholics doing that. We all harbor similar expectations. It comes in different names but it's the same basic longing underneath: a miracle that can brighten up our flat lives. A miracle, or a savior, or a lover . . . all the same. I never thought I'd share in the same expectation, but . . ."

He being the very reason for this occasion, and these being his very first words in hours, Ömer had in a flash become the center of squirming attention. It is to this awkward audience that he uttered the following speech:

"I've been watching myself change. Now, I've started to think that falling in love is pretty much like falling for a miracle. Love, too, is about expectations and beliefs. You hope there still is a salvation for you and that someday someone special will make this possible. Isn't this a longing for a miracle? Even when you know you should not expect much from this world, still something inside wants to resist . . . and keep hoping . . . that you might be loved by the person you love."

Deep silence. So deep that it made Arroz nervous. Tap tap. Arroz thumped his tail twice. No one cared.

"Just like the way I feel for you . . . Gail!"

Tap tap. An anonymous sigh. Or maybe it was a piece of tofu perspiring as it languished untouched on Abed's plate.

"Maybe we should be together, live together, we should even dare to *marry* and see what this miracle is about," said Ömer, or someone at the table who looked like Ömer. Having nothing to lose at this point, he added tenderly, "just like lovers do . . ."

Her mouth being full of mushroom pancake with potato filling, and having forgotten to chew for the last four minutes, Gail could only unleash an incomprehensible sound at first. A few seconds later, she stammered between chomps: "Did you say like lovers do?"

Everyone was terrorized with the fear of what was coming next, with the horror that she'd now bark something excruciatingly arctic, if not irretrievably merciless, and smash Ömer's delicate carafe of a heart into a thousand shards. But when she had finally gulped down the mushroom pancake with potato filling, all that came out of that baking-oven mouth of hers was: "I love you, too."

Deep, deep silence. Then a sigh. This time definitely not the tofu.

BIRDS OF
A FEATHER

Number Zero

They had become a loving couple in the blink of an eye. And like all those who become a loving couple in the blink of an eye, they soared full speed up there into seventh heaven without realizing how profoundly annoying they looked from down below. They were nonstop touching and kissing, cooing and tickling in some eerie language they had just developed but spoke so well, as if they'd been practicing it for ages. Theirs was a balloon puffed up with rapture. A balloon suspiciously watched from earth, continually seen but itself incapable of seeing; hence the supposition that *love is blind*.

Lovers are pathetically charming, and exceedingly full of themselves, *itself* more precisely, for one of the plentiful troubles with loving couples is that the minute two autonomous selves develop themselves into a duo, instead of "two" (as in one plus one), they somehow become "zero" (as in one minus one). Likewise, before anyone could follow up, Ömer and Gail had germinated into a totality. They were not "Ömer plus Gail" any longer, but a consummate zero, a mutant of a *Gailömer* or an *Ömergail*, all the same.

Love was okay, even sweet, whereas *lovers* were bothersome. And if that was too much, marriage was sheer overindulgence. More than anyone else, perhaps, Alegre was the one most ticked off. After all, with marriages, as with train schedules, one has every reason to expect first the ones scheduled to arrive first. Alegre and Piyu had been dating for two and a half years by now, talking about what it would be like if and when they got married, where they would live if and when they got married, and even what they would cook if and when they got married. They were waiting for the right time.

"Each day there is a moment when a man cannot say no to his woman. A smart woman should know that moment," the great-grandaunt advised.

For some reason, Alegre sensed, that special moment escaped her. Sometimes she doubted if Piyu really wanted to marry her, but *la Tía Piedad* assured her there was nothing to worry about. "*Con los hombres*, it's always the same riddle. First, they think their life will end if they get married, and once they are married, they think they cannot live if it's over."

So here was Alegre, meticulously pondering for more than two years now, waiting for the right moment to come, giving serious consideration to having a family and everything that required serious consideration, and then, out of the void, the two dodgiest characters in her habitat came up with the idea of getting married. How could they dare to marry so speedily, so heedlessly? Besides, it wasn't right ethically. Both Gail and Ömer, the former more than the latter, were notorious for bad-mouthing society on every occasion, condemning every single deed every normal person did. After all of that, how could they act so outrageously *normal* now? Alegre's infuriation had a double effect on Piyu, and Piyu's double-infuriation, in turn, irritated both Arroz and Abed. Before long the whole house was shaken, not to mention Debra Ellen Thompson's distress. Only that peculiar organism of a *Gailömer* remained unperturbed, spinning serenely in its gyroscopic reverie.

Hence, the duty of reminding Ömer of the gravity of the situation fell upon his housemates. The next evening, Abed found Ömer lying tipsily on his bed, thinking of Gail, listening to Portishead's "Only You," under a dense fog of arrant bliss and also some tobacco.

"Aha! So you have started smoking again." Abed frowned, but as there were more perilous concerns to frown about, he couldn't frown for this particular one as much as he would have liked to, stuck in a dilemma reminiscent of a father who had caught his son smoking in his room the day before he would join the army and head off to war.

"Have I?" Ömer's eyes darted from a faraway world of delightful dreams. "I decided to treat myself to a cigarette, but I don't know if I've started smoking again. I make no plans for the future, *dostum*." He valiantly hailed his new Ginseng! philosophy.

"No wonder you make no plans for the future. You've proposed marriage to Gail. You think you have a future anymore?" Abed rasped. But then he drifted into an unusual silence, fixing his gaze on the finger where he could have the same ring as Safiya, if only she would wait for him. His gaze grew dim as he scratched the cleft on his chin. By now, Ömer had known him long enough to recognize that this gesture meant they were going to have some "serious talk."

"Omar, you know me, I talk too much perhaps but that's because you are my friend. Plus, I've always respected your privacy. I mean, how many times have I seen you get drunk, or gobble down pork steaks. Then all those girlfriends coming and going. These wouldn't make you a good Muslim but did I ever question it? It's your life, man, none of my business. But this time it's different. This is about . . . *marriage*!" Abed emphasized the last word while inspecting Ömer's face, as if to check if he was aware of its meaning. "Please don't get me wrong. I have nothing against Gail. This isn't about her. Well . . . of course, it is . . . she is so . . ." Abed rose to his feet, drew a nervous semicircle around the bed looking for the *mot juste*, finally found it, and yelled: *"Difficult!"* He completed the other half of the circle, apparently dissatisfied with the word he had come up with.

"She is so *difficult* . . . Well, I'll be completely honest with you. Ever since the day I met Gail, I thought, 'Boy, if this girl gets married one day, may God give her husband patience!' And now, that husband is *you*! Look at *you*!" Abed flapped his hands ostentatiously toward Ömer like a magician does onstage just before he opens the

cabinet where someone in the audience was locked up a minute before and has now vanished.

"Marriage is serious, man." Abed sat on the edge of the bed
again, his voice now dwindling into a cordial, confidential whisper.
"You know what I mean."

Ömer nodded wholeheartedly. Yes, he did.

"Only You" had made another round when the door was
knocked on again. "Cooome iiin!" Ömer chanted, ready for what
was to come next. The door opened cautiously, and in slipped Arroz,
walking in his sluggish rhythm, and right after him came Piyu.

"You know me, I don't talk much perhaps, but I really care for
you. You are my friend." Piyu cleared his throat, pushed back his
glasses, wrinkled the ridge of his nose, and blushed a carroty tone.
By now, Ömer had known him long enough to recognize that this
particular hue meant they were going to have a "serious talk."

"Love is a wonderful thing, of course, but . . . is it enough in itself . . . to build a family . . . a lifelong relationship? You can only
achieve such stability . . . with . . . someone of your own kind. Of
your own . . . *kind,*" Piyu repeated, running low in vocabulary this
evening.

"I know," Ömer sighed. "You think I haven't tried? How many
times I searched for someone of my own kind! But nowhere could I
come across another twenty-six-year-old Turkish guy who was born
on the last day of October, and writes a dissertation titled 'Blood,
Brain and Belonging: Nationalism and the Intellectuals in the Middle East,' and lives in Boston with the funniest Spaniard and the funniest Moroccan in the world. The day I find that guy, I promise, I'll
leave Gail right away and marry my own kind."

"I'm not joking, man, this is serious." Piyu blushed an even
deeper carrot. "You know what I mean."

Ömer nodded halfheartedly. Yes, he did.

He knew what they each meant. Being intuitively irrational by
definition, some sort of a tolerable madness, love did not require
one to be enamored of someone of the same background, although
no doubt that would be the ideal. When it came to getting married,

however, things changed drastically. The unwritten laws of wedlock required every bird to mate within its own flock.

Somehow marriage between two of a distinct kind incited in people a fear of tragedy, a primordial fright, almost religious, as if even if the couple managed to get along flawlessly, when they tumbled deep down into their own slumber each night, their gods would start fighting till dawn.

Flee the Moment

- Pick out your wedding theme and wedding color.
- Announce your engagement in hometown newspapers.
- Plan the atmosphere you'd like at your wedding.
- Sign up for dance lessons months ahead.
- Order rings and engraving.
- Help mothers choose dresses.
- Purchase a guest book and make sure all guests sign.
- Make a detailed list of all the gifts you received.
- Never type or computerize your thank-you notes. All thank-you notes should be handwritten. Show your style by selecting a beautiful note card.
- Mention the gift by name and even tell how you plan on using the item: "Thank you for the beautiful navy towel set, they'll go perfectly in our bathroom."
- Pack an emergency kit for the wedding day containing a sewing kit, extra nylons, bobby pins, and Kleenex.

"What are you doing?" asked Piyu when, back from Ömer's room, he found Abed sitting in the kitchen, with the *American Wedding Day Sourcebook* open in front of him.

"Making sociological observations." Abed tilted his head backward, widened his nostrils, blocking a chain sneeze just in time. Pleased with the achievement he grumbled: "What kind of a woman would take an emergency kit with extra nylons to her wedding? Who on earth would want to marry her?"

The two of them spent an hour in the kitchen skimming through wedding sourcebooks, at first out of curiosity, then with escalating wonder. An hour later, they had arrived at the conclusion that American brides were control freaks. Their aspiration to be in command of everything down to its smallest detail left little room for what many women outside the United States were rather accustomed to: fortuitousness.

But Gail was quick to defy any generalizations on American brides when on the day of her wedding, around three o'clock in the afternoon, she walked into the kitchen in shades of purple from head to toe. If someone in the room had one of those color charts with him, he'd see that the color of her dress was numbered 57-A, named Wild Grapes; and of her shawl numbered 60-D, named Proud Tradition. There were lilac feathers in her hair and in today's honor she had replaced the small silver spoon with a bigger silver spoon.

"Wow!!!" Piyu said, his voice lilting with amusement. "You look like a purple tree!"

Gail smiled bashfully as if flattered. "Where's the bridegroom?" she asked.

The bridegroom was upstairs listening to Sex Pistols scream "Something Else." He was safe and sound, only on the brink of losing his mind. Since early morning he had been busy putting on and taking off all the clothes in the wardrobe, getting more and more tired of the clown in the mirror. He was nervous. In order not to look the least bit so, he had made a decision not to dress any differently than he usually did. The difficulty with calculated informality is, however, that it's basically an oxymoron. The harder you try to be casual, the farther you sway from it.

Such was the bridegroom's state of being when the phone rang.

"Aren't you gonna ask me what time it is here?" Defne's voice tinkled as cheerfully as the chimes on the door of a boutique swarming with people could be.

"What time is it there?" Ömer said, albeit in a voice as husky as the door of an adjacent store that had long lost the competition with the other.

"Well, right here, right now, it is 3:33 p.m."

"Oh, yeah? And how's everything?"

"You silly!" she chirped. "You are so silly."

Ömer didn't know what to say to that. Instead, he faltered: "Listen, I'm glad you called. There are gigantic changes in my life. I need to talk to you."

"Oh we'll talk, don't you worry." She giggled in a mysterious way. "Listen, I have to go now. Don't move anywhere. We'll have plenty of time to talk!"

Before the line was cut off there was a ripple of laughter, so awry and unlike her that Ömer wondered if it were someone else tricking him in her voice. He put on Manic Street Preachers' "Suicide Is Painless" and threw himself on the pile of trousers and sweatshirts mounting on the bed. Three minutes, twenty-six seconds.

"What's this music now? What's he doing upstairs? I thought it was the bride that spent hours getting ready." Piyu frowned. Just when he had finished frowning, he spotted a few crumbs underneath the TV set.

"Leave that broom, come here, eat a chocolate," Gail consoled him. "Ours will be an unusual wedding."

Theirs being an unusual wedding, they wanted no authorities, no showy ceremonies, and as little bureaucracy as possible. They wanted no relatives, either. Abed and Piyu did not hide their discontent, especially about the "no relatives" part. Still, they brightened up during the wedding service, which was performed by a rabbi who was unrivaled in Boston, and possibly in the world, for having no reservations in his heart toward anyone. Rabbi Mark performed services for people from every walk of life, including gay and lesbian, atheist, agnostic, or interfaith couples, as long as they loved each other.

Back at home the first thing the newlyweds did was to open a beer can.

"We have developed a Newtonian theory of matrimony," Ömer caroled as he put an arm around his purple wife. "We believe that if all marriages start differently but end up in the same way, one reason for that is the number of people involved. Knowledge in this context is definitely power. The more people know, the more power they have on your marital affairs. In other words, if you don't want your marriage to fail, keep it a secret."

Still, a wedding is a wedding, and even though the newlyweds refuse to take it that way, all the more reason to celebrate. True, there were not many guests (twelve to be precise), but the ones that were present desired to rejoice all the same. Catering was provided by Alegre, and the wedding cake by Debra Ellen Thompson. This time she had been prudent enough to keep Gail away from the cake business. But hers wasn't the only dessert. Somehow everyone seemed to have agreed that whatever it was that this wedding lacked to make it look like a proper wedding could be compensated for with extra desserts. The good old Oksana Sergiyenko had brought strawberry Romanoff, Jamal brought baklava, and a couple of friends from the Political Science Department brought raspberry tortes. Spivack, too, had stopped by with a box of cream puff shells, and had even smiled as he handed it to his infamous student. Some girl had brought a pink cake. The color reminded Abed of a distant memory, and after one more look at her, he recognized the candy-ass from last Halloween, now learning she was a friend of Alegre's from the soup kitchen. With people, food, alcohol, and after one good reason to celebrate, the rest came by itself.

Amid the steadily swelling racket of the party, Debra Ellen Thompson and Gail sat side by side, their eyes fixed on a half-nibbled frangipane someone had left. A rickety silence strove under their words when they started to speak.

"Are you in love with him?"

"No," Gail said, "but he's the closest I can ever get to that."

"You don't even know him," Debra Ellen Thompson murmured

in a barely audible voice. "He's a stranger, Gail! Do you think he can understand you? Do you think he can understand you better than me?" Her face crumpled as if the question had left a sour taste in her mouth.

Gail felt her face burn as she regarded Debra Ellen Thompson with a blend of guilt and compassion. For a moment she stood looking at the red cowlick in the front of her hair, the austere expression on her face, to find there the young girl who had once saved her from a tense man with a goatee and a mob of giggling girls. This was the face she knew so well, in every gesture. These eyes, how many times she had seen them in the past ten years glimmer with delight, pride, and verve but then also crinkle with despair and torment. A face that was so utterly beyond her reach at the outset, and then, astoundingly dependent on her.

"I hurt you bad, I know," Gail faltered with velvety caution. "I'm so sorry."

"No, don't say that," Debra Ellen Thompson answered with totality but also with a tacit resilience. "I can understand it perfectly. In the past, I mean at the beginning, I was so harsh with you, I guess. But tell me, between my harshness with you and your subsequent harshness with me, there was another time when we really loved each other. Is that right?"

Gail tried to fight back the despair descending on her, with little success. When she started talking again her voice had diluted, her eyes clouded with angst. She took Debra Ellen Thompson's hand, gripped it affectionately. "That's right," she mumbled. "That's so right, my dear *Debra.*"

Debra Ellen Thompson's face was composed now, serene even, though the next words she said with averted eyes. "I hope you'll be very happy with him."

Out of reflex the two of them turned toward Ömer, as if to see if there was a morsel of hope for that. Ömer, meanwhile, was playing Chumbawamba's "Amnesia" for the sixth time, at a higher decibel in each round. Already stoned, he had stepped up on the couch to orchestrate the merry gang below, for whom the line between modestly having fun in a modest wedding party, and shouting at the top of their voices had been by now noticeably blurred. As Ömer mouthed the lyrics, his choir sang jovially: *"Do you suffer from long-term memory loss? I don't remember."*

Abed was in the kitchen preparing mint tea for those he knew would shortly be wallowing in inebriety, when he heard a girlish voice from behind. "Hello, can I come in?" the young, elegant woman standing at the door panted with a melodic accent. She pulled a suitcase on wheels, took a deep breath, and then carefully, very carefully, stared at Abed. Her face lit up. "I know who you are . . . Don't say your name . . . You . . . must be . . ."

Abed looked at her in stupefied amazement.

"Abed!" she almost jumped. "You are Abed, am I right?"

"That's me," Abed said tentatively, his body taut and his face marred with puzzlement, as he couldn't help wishing she had gotten his name wrong, or better, confused him with someone else, confused the house, confused the cities, hoping she was not the one he suspected her to be. He asked with caution: "And who are you?"

"This is Defne, from Istanbul. Perhaps Ömer has mentioned about me," she added, her voice wavering with verve. "He doesn't know I'm in America. It's going to be a surprise. Is he at home?"

Abed swallowed hard, trying to make up myriad lies, then swallowed harder, unable to come up with even a single one. It was then that he noticed the gift box in her hands. It looked like some sort of sweets from Istanbul. He couldn't help wondering if it was a dessert familiar to him. As he stood there perspiring, Defne shot him a fretful glance, suspected something inauspicious was on the way, left her suitcase in the middle of the kitchen, and with slow, staggering steps plowed toward the dining room, where she froze, staring at the crowd thundering inside.

"Do you suffer from long-term memory loss?"

Still swinging on the couch, Ömer shouted down at his orchestra: *I don't remember . . .* As his lanky, long body swayed to and fro on the couch, so did his gaze, scanning the room until his eyes slid toward the kitchen door and glommed onto a box of chestnut sweets.

He'd never had a sweet tooth, and that was the only dessert he used to eat back in Istanbul. With some difficulty, he tore his gaze from the box to stare at the woman holding it.

He did remember.

What transpired after that would remain somewhat different in the memories of each spectator. Alegre would later recall Gail walking out, but the character that went out running in Piyu's memory was Defne. According to both Abed and Piyu collectively, after that Ömer had come down from the couch in panic, stumbled toward Defne, but then immediately stopped and writhed toward Gail, trying to convince both women of utterly opposite things, not scoring much on either side. Abed would even assert that at one point in the muddle he had been floundering in, Ömer had spoken Turkish with Gail and English with Defne.

Ömer, in turn, was not able to refute any of these allegations on his side for, startlingly, of that ill-fated experience only one sight would be hooked up in his memory: the box of chestnut sweets, and on it, inscribed with a stylish lettering, the name of the store where it was bought: Demdenkaçaroğulları.*

"Hey, shame on you, Arroz!" Abed said. "And double shame on you, señor Piyu. How can you eat the poor girl's chestnuts?"

The party was over, people had left. Alegre had taken the leftovers to the charity, Debra Ellen Thompson had gone back to the store, and Gail had disappeared. Ömer had gone out with Defne to have a talk in private but shortly afterward he had returned, alone and depressed.

"Why shame on me?" Piyu objected. "Shame on him, not me!"

"Well, yeah, you are right!" Abed immediately snapped a reprimand. "Shame on Omar, long-legged walking disgrace of our house! Scandal stork!"

Ömer's mouth drew into a line as he sneaked an affronted glance at each.

*Those Who Flee the Moment

"What did your girlfriend in Istanbul say?" Piyu wondered, transferring the chestnut sweets to the other end of the table, away from Arroz.

"Ex-girlfriend," Ömer corrected uneasily.

"Yeah sure! Except that she didn't know she was an ex," Abed mused.

"She wished me heaven," Ömer grumbled.

"It is a catastrophe to be cursed by a woman." Abed shook his head, quick to get the message. "If men swear to do you harm, spend your night sleeping, but if women swear to do you harm, spend your night awake."

"What did Gail say?" Piyu wondered, relocating the chestnut sweets as Arroz kept moving in tandem.

"Not much. I was so afraid that she would be furious or hurt. But she said I shouldn't worry about her feelings because she could *understand*. We all have a past, she said." Ömer turned to his friends in sore need of some elucidation. "That's a bit of a strange reaction, no?"

"*Strange?*" Abed croaked, rolling his luminous dark eyes while raising his voice as if addressing an invisible audience in the kitchen. "Did our dear friend Omar just say Gail is *strange?*"

They chuckled, Ömer frowned. In the ensuing disarray, Arroz eventually managed to steal a chestnut sweet out of the box.

Signifier-Without-Signified

The question as to where the newlyweds would live had remarkably never been a question. Having by now accepted this matrimony *as a fact of life*, Abed and Piyu had taken for granted that Gail would move in. Hence, when they heard the couple had been looking for a house with that measly income of theirs, their objection was sincere. Instead, they proposed living together, at least for a while. The second room on the second floor was not too spacious, but it still was some extra space that Gail could use. Not as attractive as the brick house in Davis Square that she had liked so much, but still a fairly nice dwelling until they were ready to move in there in the spring, or the summer, whenever.

On Thursday morning Debra Ellen Thompson drove Gail to 8 Pearl Street with six boxes, two hissing, four deeply silent. When all boxes were carried inside and piled in the kitchen, the Jeep Cherokee guzzled off in an indigo rush.

As Gail scrambled upstairs to see the small room, the three housemates stood in the kitchen, clearly worried about the contents of the boxes, not the silent ones, but the other two. The fourth housemate, the one expected to be the most troubled, meanwhile, moved around indifferently, not even caring to sniff the boxes. Arroz's indifference did not show much of a change when the two boxes were finally opened and out came West and The Rest, shaken, irritated, stiff, almost feral.

When the two fur balls walked out, Piyu grasped Arroz's collar in case it ever occurred to him to attack. Ten seconds later he had let go of Arroz and was instead trying to hold back the two cats. With brute force Gail and Ömer put West and The Rest back in their boxes and carried them upstairs, while Piyu took care of Arroz's bleeding nose.

The moving in was swift. Once all the boxes were opened and out came books, clothes, teas, and dozens of items of dubious content or function, Gail's presence was visible everywhere around the house, starting with the bathroom, to Abed's consternation. Two hours later, when back from shopping he ran to the bathroom trapped by yet another allergy attack that had caught him on the way, the transformation there was so whopping that he almost forgot about his nose. He stood looking around in confusion. Aromatherapy essences, oils, bath salts, herbal soaps . . . Abed was relatively used to seeing such foreign things in the bathroom but indeed none of Ömer's girlfriends had been so bold as to bring a whole store with her.

Next to the closet there was now a huge basket, and in it, a whole bunch of books and journals and articles. Among the pile Abed spotted the Dada Manifesto, a photocopied article titled "The Silence of Feminine Jouissance," Dorothy Parker's poems, a book titled *The Jew As Pariah: Jewish Identity and Politics in the Modern Age*, and a book titled either *For They Know Not What They Do* or *For They Do Not What They Know*. He hoped the content of the book would be more lucid than the title, and skimmed a few pages: *"The authority of the classical Master is that of a certain S1, signifier-without-signified, auto-referential signifier which embodies the performative function of the word."*

Abed skipped a chapter.

"If we progress far enough on the surface of the pure form, we come across a nonformal 'stain' of enjoyment which smears the form—the very renunciation of 'pathological' enjoyment brings about a certain surplus-enjoyment."

Abed closed the book.

Soon it'd be clear that the bathroom was only the beginning. In a breeze . . . in a gale . . . the whole house was under a whooshing invasion, and Gail was everywhere. Her invasion was more in terms of odors than in terms of commodities. At different moments of the day she burned distinct incenses; 8 Pearl Street smelled of jasmine and patchouli in the mornings, sandalwood in the evenings, and honeysuckle late at night. She burned cypress bark on full moons, and rosemary on moonless nights. And on the weekends the house smelled of curry but that had more to do with the vegan dishes she kept cooking to Alegre's dismay. West and The Rest were especially fond of these, being basically fed on grains and vegetables. As such, Abed and Piyu mused the two cats were a walking counterproof to the vegan credo that aggressiveness at both individual and social levels was a direct concomitant of omnivorous eating habits, and that we'd all be more peaceful beings if we stopped consuming meat.

But looking at the process retrospectively, perhaps more than books, seashells, and even odors, it was the words she spread out that made Gail's presence all the more conspicuous. It was through these words that she sniped, nitpicked, and regularly crucified her new housemates, sharp-shooting her verbal bullets with no caution whatsoever, as if when political correctness had gained pace in the United States, she had been snoozing somewhere else, and had never even heard of it.

Abed and Piyu had never talked about this, but at the beginning of their friendship there had been a stage wherein each had been on guard for an abrasive question or a biased remark from the other with reference to his religious background. The thought of the possible objections or questions a Catholic might raise against Islam had crossed Abed's mind several times, and he had in store more than a few answers, in case Piyu ever used them. Likewise, Piyu, too, had pondered the likely arguments that a Muslim could make against Christianity and had his answers ready. In the fullness of time, it had become clear that none of these answers would be needed, as both Abed and Piyu had been remarkably respectful toward each other's religion. Nowadays, however, this harmonious coexistence was badly shaken by tedious questions and thorny comments coming not from the neighboring monotheistic religion as each had originally expected, but from this heathen catapult of Gail hurling profanities at both sides simultaneously.

It wasn't only the things she kept saying, but also the way she said them. Somehow, Gail seemed to have failed to notice that none of the three people she shared this house with happened to be a native-speaker.

"Don't you ever consider changing your manners, Gail?"

"Not until I shuffle off this mortal coil."

Every passing day, Abed, Piyu, and Ömer absorbed her jargon like a dry sponge absorbs water. The argot they snatched from her, expressions they heard for the first time, they thrust into their pockets, and once outside the house, they instantly tried to use these new words, like a child eager to skate with his new skates.

Such were the contours of Gail's presence in the house. As to what that presence was like inside the two rooms on the second floor, neither Abed nor Piyu had any idea, having strictly refrained from entering in there. After the marriage, Ömer's bedroom had become a private zone they would rather not trespass. It was going to take them weeks to go in there. And when they finally did, the room had changed so much they forgot what it looked like before. Right across the wall, among posters and pictures and drawings was written in huge letters: DISTURB THE COMFORTED, COMFORT THE DISTURBED. For Abed and Piyu the slogan didn't mean much at this point, for they were already feeling both uncomfortable and disturbed here. This place wasn't connected to the rest of the house anymore; not only because of Gail's items but because it was a married couple's bedroom now. To avoid looking toward the bed and anything that might entail privacy, they fully concentrated on the walls.

"That is a love charm," said Ömer upon seeing their interest. He was alone in the room, working on the second chapter of his thesis. "There is a goddess sign right side up, and a god sign upside down."

Abed was the first to give up trying to see where the hell this god was and where the goddess was. He proceeded to the next symbol.

"That one over there is the Star of the Muses. Sacred female spirits came in groups of nine. They were the muses of classical Greece, and the nine moon maidens who created Scandinavian gods," Ömer churred, glad to share all this information he had learned from Gail and didn't quite know what to do with. "Medieval superstition called them mares, who dwelled in the wild woodlands and settled on top of sleeping men, choking off their breath and taking away their power of speech. Hence the word nightmare!"

"This is the motto of the woman you married! Choke off men's breath, take away their power of speech!"

"What's this swastika doing here?" Piyu interrupted.

"Piyu, you are so *lo-go-cen-tric*," Abed squawked. "If you weren't so hopelessly *lo-go-cen-tric*, and on top of that *phal-lo-go-cen-tric*, you'd see this swastika in a completely different light. I bet there is a hidden goddess somewhere here."

Piyu chuckled. Watching them furtively, fixedly from the pouf where she had been pretending to sleep the whole afternoon, West rose and approached them as if to share the joke. The Rest instantly followed. Together they sniffed Piyu's socks, in that irritating way that makes one feel alarmingly suspicious about his bodily odors.

"Actually, it's a swastika," Ömer explained heartily. "But a Roman swastika. Gail is particularly fond of it because it looks like a man kneeling with arms upraised in worship . . ."

"See?" Abed quacked.

West lost interest in them, The Rest wasn't interested at any rate. The duo walked back portentously. These days it was hard to see Arroz around. He had developed this habit of spending most of his time lying motionless under Piyu's bed on the third floor.

"Yes, but Gail says the shape has been a religious emblem since no less than 10,000 B.C. It appeared on the oldest coinage in India, and on images in Japan, China, Asia Minor, Persia, Greece, Britain, Scandinavia, and even Iceland. So you see, the Nazis do not own the swastika. Hitler adopted it on the supposition that it was a pure Aryan sign. This was not true. Gail believes we should get the symbol back from them," enthused Ömer, visibly inspired by his own speech.

It was then that Piyu muttered thoughtfully: "Come my friend, let's go!"

"Come my friend, let's go!" is no ordinary expression. If anything, it's some sort of a visceral, virile call back to the roots—one of the many signals bachelor men give to a married brother who has been too much engulfed by a woman.

"I'm so sorry," Alegre puffed.

"It's OK, Alegre, we'd just started." Connie smiled around the circle integrating everyone in her smile. When her eyes met Debra Ellen Thompson's, she caught a glint of scorn there but preferred to ignore that. "Amy was telling us what she felt when she saw Debra's journal of the past week."

"When I saw Debra's journal, when I saw the things she ate this weekend, I felt sad and angry . . ." Amy went on eagerly. "Look at her Tuesday. Her best friend Gail gets married, what would you expect her to eat on this special day? Pastries, sweets, nice food, you know, at least a slice of the wedding cake. Did she? No, she didn't. We all knew she didn't eat chocolate, or bananas, but now on top of that she doesn't eat the wedding cake either. Why not? I think she's protesting. In her mind all these foods are related with this best friend of hers, which I sincerely doubt is a friend at all. Just as Maureen's husband prevents Maureen from being herself, Gail prevents Debra from being herself, too."

"What about you, Alegre?" asked Connie as she leaned back and crossed her arms. "Do you think refraining from food can be a way of protesting things?"

Alegre's face paled under the weight of gazes. To avoid looking at anyone, she searched for something to focus her stare upon and chose Connie's necklace. Her stare fixed there, her voice subdued, almost a whisper, she said: "Maybe it is, I cannot know for sure."

Connie shot a pitying stare, Amy splayed her hands in exasperation.

"But I do know that," Alegre went on talking to the necklace, "like Jesus taught us, it is not the things that enter into our mouths but the things coming out from there that make a sin. The things we say. Our words."

Connie's upper lip drew into a thin line, Amy's eyes narrowed.

"Thank you for sharing your thoughts with us. Would you also like to share your journal with the group members?"

Alegre rose to her feet, looking at Debra Ellen Thompson. The latter gave her a nod of encouragement. Alegre drew a circle distributing photocopies of her *My Food Journal of This Week* to every member of the group, and lastly to Connie.

Monday 21st: I came to work decisive and energetic. Dr. Marc Victor Fitzpatrick had seven appointments. All day long, the doctor acted weird, as if he had something on his mind. I ate a turkey sandwich at lunch. Dinner at home.

Tuesday 22nd: I suspect the doctor is having a secret affair. When his wife calls he is extremely nice to her but then he is nervous all day long. Under these circumstances I get nervous, too, and I lose my appetite.

Debra Ellen Thompson suppressed a smile as she spotted a fissure of dread appear on Connie's patronizing facade.

Thursday 24th: I have finally learned the doctor's secret love. She came to the office this morning. She's so young, only nineteen. They went out together, kissing. Half an hour later the doctor's wife called. I had to lie. I couldn't eat anything all day long.

"May I start interpreting," Amy hooted with enthusiasm. "May I?" she had to repeat, for there was no answer from Connie for a long, dead minute.

"Oh yes, go on, please." Connie recovered quickly, but her mind was far too scrappy to pay attention to anything the latter might have to say.

Debra Ellen Thompson and Alegre exchanged glances—cool, calm, and composed glances, as they softly sank into the lagoon of contentment their souls needed so badly.

A Notion of Hell

"Abed, can I ask you a question?" Gail caught him in the kitchen fully focused on the sizzling pan, preparing one of his family-size sunny-Sunday breakfasts, although it was Friday. "Can you tell me about the notion of hell in Islam?"

"Why is it always worms and snakes and flames and torture that you want to learn about, Gail? Pass me the salt!" Abed bobbed his head from side to side with discontent, and because he kept doing that for additional seconds he ended up putting too much salt on the eggs. "What's wrong with the paradise, isn't it interesting enough for you?" he croaked in a husky voice as he gently poured mint tea in two small glasses. In this house only he was capable of being coarse in voice and tender in manners at the same time. Besides, he could give some extra credit to Gail in the mornings for being his finest mint tea buddy. He watched her hold the glass carefully between her palms as if it were a most precious thing, a gesture more than enough to wheedle him. When he spoke again, his voice had softened, and so had his stare.

"How come you don't believe in God? I understand Omar the infidel has nothing to do with faith. But you are not like that.

You're interested in the mystery of creation and the afterworld, you know . . ."

Gail let out a long, languid yawn. "But I do *believe* in God!" she almost yelled when she had finished yawning. "I believe God is a circle, whose center is everywhere and the circumference nowhere, just like an alchemical philosopher said in the past."

"I don't know which philosopher that is . . ." Abed had just begun to grumble when he saw Ömer enter the kitchen, still in his pajamas and typical morning daze, and turned toward him for the solace he knew he'd never get. "Omar, can you please explain to your crazy wife that God is no geometrical shape she can measure in her limited brain of a mortal."

Circumference . . . How come you people find the energy for these words as soon as you get out of bed, and if you can, why can't I? Ömer's drowsy eyes asked back.

But Gail was indomitable. She chased Abed to and fro in the kitchen with new questions, casting shadows upon the four sunny-side-up eggs painfully sizzling in the pan. In putting that fourth sun there, Abed cannot be accused of having forgotten that Gail did not eat eggs because he had refused to believe in that ever since the first day. That a person might, of her own free will, abstain from a breakfast of well-cooked eggs was simply inconceivable.

"At least tell me that thing about books again," Gail begged.

"All right, all right! I'll tell you the *thing about books*," Abed surrendered. "According to the Holy Koran, he who is given his book in his right hand shall have a blissful state in heaven in a lofty garden, with clusters of fruit and beautiful things within his reach. But he who is given his book in his left hand will be burned in the fire of Hell. Is this what you wanted to hear instead of 'good morning'?"

Gail squeezed Ömer's elbow as she echoed: "*He who is given his book in his left hand.* Don't you think it's lyrical?"

Lyrical . . . How come you people find the energy for such words as soon as you get out of bed . . . and if you people can, why can't I? followed the standard stare.

It was at times like these that Ömer longed most exasperatedly for his dark, hot beloved of the good old days. It had been eight months now, eight months of a hell without coffee and alcohol, though he had been now and again smoking pot and puffing a few cigarettes . . . or maybe more. He left them in the kitchen sipping their mint tea debates, rattled up the stairs longing more and more for a cup of coffee at each step. Back in his room, he first called the number in the navy-blue brochure, listened to the automated lady's ten key tips for quitting smoking, could only endure until the fourth, and hung up. Next, he called his mother.

"Is it still raining there?" she asked. "Six people died of lightning, and many more were hospitalized."

"It's been unexpectedly rainy in the past days." Ömer squinted at his left wrist as if suddenly wondering how come he never had a watch there. "But I'm OK, don't worry about me, the house is hot . . . and . . . dry . . . and, Ma, I got married."

She cried. Ömer lit a cigarette. The Walkman played an Elvis Costello song: "Home isn't where it used to be. Home is anywhere you hang your head."

This wasn't about his mother. This wasn't about coffee or this cigarette he couldn't stop smoking or even about Elvis Costello. This was about Gail.

Several times in the past, and more and more often lately, he had seen her drift away into sorrow before his very eyes. At those times, she tended to become extremely sensitive. A stupid politician's stupid statement, the killing of civilians in some part of the world, or a dead squirrel outside the window . . . all broke her heart and made her overwhelmingly sad. At first, Ömer had thought there was nothing to worry about as long as she was in control of her sorrow. In time, he came to realize she was not. Each time he tried to cheer her up, he felt like he was bumping into a wall behind which, he sensed, lay a burrow, a wormhole, some sort of a space where she retreated when she felt despondent only to come back from there even more so. It was that small but solid space that frightened him like nothing else, for he had learned by now that when she tumbled into that void, he could find no way either to get in himself, or to pull her out of there. What worried him even more was the fear that this might not be an enclosed space but instead a gateway into some other zone,

an existential underworld. Deep down into that Hades, too bur-
dened and intoxicated with the venom of the past, she fell in a bottomless perdition. When back from there she was usually so
energetic and daring that nobody could possibly guess what she had
been like in the past few days.

As Gail's visits to her underworld multiplied, Ömer struggled to
think of ways in which to protect her without ever giving the impression of so doing. If they moved into one of those brick houses on
Davis Square that had a private patio of its own, and had won Gail's
heart at first sight, he hoped, she could have more space to herself.
He knew they could not afford the house but now that his mother
had learned about this marriage, he also knew, after the first shock,
his family would send him money. His mother might be disappointed
with his getting married but now that he was, she would not want
him to be embarrassingly penniless. Telling them about the marriage
would provide Ömer with more money, though it clearly meant a be-
trayal of the Newtonian theory of matrimony. His parents would
definitely want to meet Gail in Istanbul as soon as possible.

Pillow Talk

Numbered 12-G, named Pillow Talk, was the hue on Piyu's cheeks when he came to Abed's room to confide a secret that he, and only he in this house could understand.

"It's about me and Alegre. You know, we've been together for quite some time . . ." Piyu said, his eyes fixed on the book open in front of them: *Advances in Molecular Bioinformatics*. "I love her so much. But I cannot . . ." Piyu closed his eyes and did not open them until he had unleashed the rest: ". . . sleep with her."

"Never?"

"Never!"

"Well, well, well," echoed Abed managing to pronounce the same word markedly differently each time.

"Any Moroccan proverbs?" Piyu tried to veer this difficult talk to an easier trail.

"There is one that comes to my mind. Roughly translated it says, 'Too much sleep with women produces blindness.' But then there is another one: 'If no sleep with a woman the eye sees no more.' "

Piyu nodded in vain.

"Proverbs are sagacious," Abed supported his cause. "I think, we tend to disparage them because we believe they are too simple whereas our lives are way too complicated. Today, in the modern world, it's trendy to make everything as complex as possible. But proverbs speak pure wisdom. Simple and clear. And in your case . . ." Abed rolled up his sleeves resolutely, and scratched the cleft in his chin to double his determination ". . . the message is crystal clear. It means going to the extremes is no good. There should be a middle road in between. Not sleeping at all is an extreme."

"Maybe you are right." Piyu hunched his shoulders in exasperation. "Maybe I am afraid of the results. But not for myself. Honestly, I am worried for Alegre. I want to marry her but what if I am not the best man for her?"

"Don't worry about that. Women do not marry the best." Abed tilted his head, slowly and solemnly. "They fall in love with the best, and then marry the second in line."

But that didn't help much to soothe Piyu's worries. Bemused and unnerved, he pushed his glasses back: "Don't you think there is a direct correlation between love and . . . sex?"

"Sure. We got another proverb for that. A more naughty one. It says if a woman loves a man, she will give it to him even through a hole in the door."

"What about you? How come you advocate this middle road and still got no girlfriend in America?"

"Girlfriend?" Abed repeated thoughtfully. For a minute he thought of confessing both to Piyu and to himself his interest in a woman he kept seeing at the laundry—a woman old enough to be his mother. What irritated him so much whenever she looked into his eyes was the straightforwardness of her desire. She didn't try to sugarcoat it with words or smiles. Pure and blatant was her desire. Pure and blatant and intimidating. Each time they met, Abed was torn between avoiding her gaze and returning it. "Well, you know, until today, there was only one woman for me. I preferred to wait for Safiya. Thinking she'd be doing the same . . ."

"Why are you speaking in the past tense?"

"I got a phone call from Mama yesterday. She says Safiya is getting married. Guess who is going to be the bridegroom: my cousin! Next summer, I'll probably go to their house and congratulate them. As the proverb says: 'Eye does not see, heart does not suffer.' "

"But then the proverb is mistaken . . ."

"Yes," Abed's voice lowered. "Sometimes they are . . ."

DESTROYING YOUR
OWN PLUMAGE

Eternal Spoon Provider

"I still don't understand why you are moving out," Piyu whined, looking crossly at the two high-speed Lebanese movers in blue uniform, as if they were to blame.

"You are not planning to have children, are you?" Abed asked suspiciously.

"Children? No way." Ömer laughed loud, too loud, perhaps, twice more than necessary. It's because he was lying, not only to them but also to himself, thereby the need to double. In the past weeks he had several times caught himself mulling over what it would be like if they had a child of their own. Not that he *wanted*, but simply *wondered*.

He wondered if a child could fasten Gail to this life, through a cord of love, devotion, and dependency, a tactful blend she would most probably dislike in other contexts, but might be passionate about in a child of her own. At unflustered moments, Ömer had a vision of a baby girl with a cute little nose, cute little hands, and a mammoth bush of black hair on her cute little head. That baby could accomplish what he had failed thus far: to breathe life into the death drive inside Gail. As the nihilist in him bitterly mocked the aspiring father he had all of a sudden molded himself into, Ömer kept this blushingly universal and conventional yearning to himself, never talked about it, not even with Gail, especially not with her.

"So have you guys been giving the garlic test?" Ömer asked to change the topic, but the moment he asked this question he feared the answer. If only he hadn't packed his CDs, in point of fact, one particular song: Dot Allison, "You Can Be Replaced."

"Yeah, this time we've also put application forms on the Net," said Piyu. "Already received some back."

"Oh really?" Ömer stopped momentarily. "Any good candidates?"

"Only the wackos," Abed said. "Either purely coincidental that only madcaps race to be our housemate, or every grad student in Boston secretly verges on insanity."

"There was one that I liked, though. A woman, very beautiful. She's a yoga teacher and can bend herself into a *pretzel*." Piyu blushed salmon as he pronounced the last word, making everyone wonder if *pretzel* had some salacious connotation unknown to them.

They idled over a lunch of garlic chicken and couscous. Alegre had been cooking less and less these days. Most of the time she was hanging out with Debra Ellen Thompson. Piyu had begun to fear she might turn into a vegan, too, and now, as he recalled his fear, he couldn't help groaning. Arroz instantly popped up by his side, putting his head on Piyu's knee, consoling human beings in the best way he knew: make them feel they are loved but make them also feel they are the boss. No problem. Of love Arroz could provide plenty today. Wasn't this a great day! He had been extremely engrossed in the hustle and bustle in the house, especially in the part wherein those snobbish furry balls were put back into their carriers. The cats had gone! Gail had headed to the new house with them two hours ago, so that they could sniff and feel themselves at home before the stir started over there.

With the Lebanese movers working even faster than they talked, everything was packed and ready to go in an hour. By 3:08 p.m., the three housemates were in the car, following the Galloping Horse Van

Lines van. Abed and Piyu spoke little, while Ömer put on his head-phones and kept listening to "Bleed for Me" by the Dead Kennedys, the only CD he had put aside, until they'd arrived at an apartment building steps from Davis Square. The building was visibly old from the outside and had a musky odor inside, definitely not a pleasant one but not necessarily bad either. A sour smell of its own, which Gail thought might mean it had a sour story of its own.

Gail herself was at home in the meantime. To be more precise, she was at the windowpane. Waiting here for the others to arrive, she had spent some time watching West and The Rest sniff around and tried to understand whether they liked the new house or not; paced to and fro and tried to understand whether *she* liked the new house or not; ate a banana, and then a nougat *Jesustoldmeyouhad-asparedollar* Lady—not one of her successful collections she had to admit, as so few customers had shown interest in these since Christmas. Maybe she should have made the bag lady from praline rather than milk chocolate. She could give praline a try next Christmas. But now, as she leaned against the window frame, less to watch the mist outside than to feel the coolness of the glass on her forehead, she decided she could do something else: die.

The windows of the third room at the back looked at a hushed, shady patio hemmed in by the neighboring buildings. At the heart of the patio there was a ligneous plant, most of its leaves abandoned to brisk winds. But maybe it wasn't the blustery weather that had stripped the plant of its vivacity. Maybe the cause of the drying up was somewhere inside and had little to do with the harshness of external circumstances. The plant made her sad. As she opened the window and pulled her body outside, Gail was convinced that some plants, just like some people, dried and shriveled inside.

"Miss! Miss! Will you please come down? No, no, don't! I mean from the other side, via the stairs, would you please come down using the staircase?"

Down in the patio there was an aged, morbidly wispy couple, both with a thatch of cropped flour-white hair, red cheeks, and a sharp pointed nose red at the edge. Actually they looked so similar to each other that, had they been dressed in the same way, it could have been really hard to tell at the first glance which one was the wife and which the husband.

"Oh, hi there! We are the new neighbors," Gail shouted down at them when it was clear there was no way she could escape from the potshot of their inquisitiveness.

"Are you all right?" the man yelled back.

"Don't you yell at her," his wife yelled. "Can't you see she is not *all right*?"

The doorbell came right on time, saving Gail from the pain of watching herself being dragged into life by such a lifeless couple. With visible relief she waved good-bye to them and, winching the right leg, then the left, almost bucking over the windowpane, she finally poked herself inside. Her feet bare, dewdrops on her hair, she opened the door and smiled affably at Abed, Piyu, and Ömer with the movers of Galloping Horse Van Lines lined up behind them.

"The small room at the back shall be your silver spoon room," Ömer said when everyone had gone, leaving them alone among boxes and more boxes. "We'll buy you thousands of silver spoons."

Gail's voice dwindled into a confidential whisper as if disclosing secret information: "That's too much money, you know."

"Then I'll steal them from fancy restaurants. I'll be your eternal spoon provider."

Eternal spoon provider. Gail liked the expression. Instead of expressing her approval, however, she heard herself object: "Eternal is such a big word. How can you be so sure you'll still love me tomorrow?"

Ömer grimaced for a fleeting moment, a sullen sparkle flickering out in his hazel eyes. "I don't think you can ever understand this because you don't love me the way I love you," he said without giving her a chance to object this time. "Don't you deny it, please. It's true. It's just the way things are. I hope . . . I keep hoping that one day you'll love me more than you do today. But even if you don't, my love for you is an independent, sovereign state, you know!" he assured her, like a good political scientist. "It doesn't depend on external aid to exist!"

Catching the barely perceptible tinge of trepidation in his voice, Gail couldn't help feeling bad and good, guilty and released, at the same time. She pulled him toward her, and gave him a kiss with a compassion that was quick to mold into passion. Ömer let her cuddle him, mommy him, embrace and engulf him . . . destroy and create . . . create and destroy him. There among the boxes on the floor and under the persistent gaze of the cats, especially of The Rest, they started making love. As he kept drawing circles around them, and then around West, just to be refused by her each time, The Rest's nervousness escalated bit by bit, so did his meows, making them burst with laughter within a schizoid sex oscillating between jollity and an eerie sorrow out of the blue, as if they would never be able to penetrate into each other like this again.

"Can cats ring or is that the doorbell?" Ömer whispered into Gail's ear.

It was the doorbell, and indeed, a very pushy doorbell. The Rest was going crazy, the doorbell roaring, and Gail constantly giggling . . . When he had to accept the sullen fact that under these circumstances his penis could no longer stay erect, Ömer rose to his feet, couldn't find his trousers among the junk, tried wrapping a towel around himself, tried wearing Gail's trousers, finally found his own and ran to answer the door, the cats running with him. Gail, meanwhile, lay on the floor giggling in her bald nudity.

"Who was it?" she asked a few minutes later.

"Some wacky couple!" Ömer scratched his head as he walked back. "Some Mr. and Mrs. Jones. They asked me if you were OK. Do you know them?"

"Me? No!" Gail meowed, winking at the cats still around her, and then pulled Ömer once again down to the floor.

The first two weeks in the new house were wonderful, partly because the first two weeks in a new house are always wonderful, but also because after living with housemates they were now discovering

how comfortable and unashamedly sexy was this conjugal capsule
they found themselves in. Living with Abed and Piyu for ten months
had its own gratifications and joys for sure, but also entailed a series
of restrictions, the weight and scale of which they realized better
nowadays. Bestowed with the liberty of cooking whatever they
wanted and eating less couscous, of not hearing horror-movie
screams at night, of brushing cat hair from clothes rather than
brushing both cat hair and dog hair, and the liberty of rambling the
house entirely naked, at least in theory . . . becoming a typical bourgeois couple was not, they concluded, as bad as it looked from outside. Moving to a place of their own brought, first and foremost,
freedom of decibels—the freedom to moan, come, coo, and quarrel
loudly, sonorously, deafeningly.

"Mrs. Basu is complaining," the Korean concierge said one evening as he blocked the entrance in a droning voice and with a brooding look that could be decoded as: *I couldn't care less about the thing I'm
going to tell you but I'll tell it anyway.* Having guessed the question to
follow, he quickly added: "Mrs. Basu is your next-door neighbor."

Subsequently, several liberties had to be curtailed.

At the entrance of the building there was a tiny brown mailbox
for each household, and on each box, an even tinier piece of paper
for the names of the household tenants to be written on. It looked
quite egalitarian, but like most things that look quite egalitarian,
only on the surface. This system, Ömer argued, and argued louder
when stoned, favored people with shorter surnames and disfavored
those with longer ones. Mrs. Basu next door was, no doubt, one of
the most favored, though probably she wasn't aware of this. There
was an inverse relationship between having knowledge and knowing what you had in hand. In order to know how privileged you
were, you had to be unprivileged first, but then, paradoxically,
you wouldn't be privileged anymore.

Dinner on China

Sitting side by side on the large sofa in the living room, shining with curiosity, *todas las tías* were lined together looking in the same direction like a bracelet of pearly, round stones. Both their smiles and stares were targeted at the redheaded guest that Alegre had brought for dinner, now fidgeting on the pouf, trying to smile back at each and every one of them, confusing the order. At the end of the row sat *la* Tía Piedad. She spoke less, smiled less, stared less. More power with less of everything.

"The dinner is ready!" Alegre's voice came from the dining room, and in a minute, she herself came, whispering to her guest of honor: "Bored?"

"No, not at all," Debra Ellen Thompson purred. That was no lie. She was so glad for being invited to this family dinner boredom had not even crossed her mind.

Everyone rose to their feet at the same time, walking in a languid convoy toward the dining room. But then, unpredictably, the march stopped, and a susurrus was heard, wafting from the front rows to the back. Next came *la* Tía Piedad's voice: *"¡Dios mío!"*

Alegre's face showed no surprise. She seized Debra Ellen
Thompson's hand and pushed her toward the dining room, where
they stood looking at what everyone stood looking at: the dinner
table.

On the dinner table, lit by soft yellow candles and embellished
with crystal glasses, gauzy serviettes, and two vases of white lilies on
each side, lay the china set—twelve bread-and-butter plates, twelve
soup bowls, twelve dessert bowls, three salad plates, a covered
casserole, a teapot, a coffeepot, platters, and cups and saucers . . . all
of them, eighty-seven pieces in total, taken out of their coffins after
so many years, apposed neatly on the table. Tens of fabulous Myosotis were now carrying *caldo de queso*, avocado salad, *enchiladas de queso*,
black beans, and *guisado de cerdo*.

"¿Alegre, qué significa eso?"* La Tía Chita couldn't suppress the
question any longer.

"They've been kept in boxes for such a long time," Alegre stuttered, her eyes glistening with excitement. "I thought it might be
good to bring them out and start using them in the way they were
originally designed for. Besides," she swallowed hard, trying to avoid
looking at *la* Tía Piedad, "rather than one of us having the whole set,
we may all have it this way . . . I thought . . ."

"But they'll be smashed to pieces in a few days," frowned *la* Tía
Tuta.

The curiosity as to how the great-grandaunt would react looming over every other concern, what followed was an itchy silence.
Fortunately, they didn't have to wait that long. In slow yet firm
steps, *la* Tía Piedad walked toward her chair at the end of the
table, unwrapped a serviette, and pouted at the soup on the china
bowl. "Is this *caldo de queso* that I am seeing? Did you do it better this
time?"

The young maid smiled apologetically.

One by one *todas las tías* pulled out a chair, and though still visibly uncomfortable, they started to dine together on the longest sur-
viving memory of the family that had come a long, long way without

---

*What does all this mean?

even a scratch. It was the past, it was always the past that cropped up in every aspect of their interaction. Even when they seemed to be talking about something else, they were always talking about the past, talking with and within the abundant conjugations of the Spanish language, while the future tense waited aside, barely used.

As *las tías'* words and sounds paradiddled over the china set, Debra Ellen Thompson plunged deeper and deeper into the warmth of this blatantly conventional, blatantly female air, feeling both like a small girl and a grown-up at the same time, glad to be among women, glad to be a woman.

Grammatical Errors

Dreams. It was dreams that bothered Ömer these days, bothered him like nothing else. In his dreams he tarried with Gail, roaming the streets of unknown cities, passing by plazas with fountains, houses that didn't look like homes, unfamiliar faces hardened with sourness, and here and there, marble statues with an arm, hand, or head missing, effigies of mutilated bodies. Somewhere in the dream sequels in a way incomprehensible to him each time, Ömer would lose Gail, start searching for her, fear for her, plowing back the streets they had walked together, alone and terrified this time. It was dreams that bothered him during the first two weeks of March, bothered him more than the term papers he had to write, and even more than hearing Spivack's disparagement each time he failed him in some way. Gail, meanwhile, did not seem to be taking much notice of Ömer's nocturnal troubles. She was exceedingly active and agile these days, full of zip and buoyancy, far too loaded, far more than Ömer could handle. In a week she had designed an entirely new set of dark chocolate figurines from the entire Hindu pantheon. She was also too busy with the details and arrangements of the upcoming trip to Istanbul. Her indefatigability was tiring at these times.

Three weeks before their flight, on a rainy Tuesday, Ömer made a call to 8 Pearl Street. For some time he found comfort in listening to Abed complain about the insipidness of the new housemate—an industrious grad student in the School of Management, with a thesis on "Stakeholder Management and How to Increase Profits in the Digital Age." Hearing that the new housemate had not replaced him in any way gave some solace to Ömer. What he needed was, however, a greater solace; if not, he needed a drink.

"Abed, I don't feel well today . . . I feel like I'm thrown into a well . . ."

When the two met in Davis Square Abed knew for sure that Ömer was out not for a walk but for a drink. Though it was hardly news that he had been smoking cigarettes and some dubious stuff from time to time, all in all he had managed to refrain from alcohol, and amazingly from coffee, ever since the hell of a night at the hospital. As they kept walking, Ömer tried to convince Abed that unlike other spirits raki did not upset the stomach, and Abed tried to convince Ömer not to start drinking again. Both failed.

It was the sixteenth of March, the night of The Laughing Magpie. It was, Ömer would construe much later, an ominous threshold after which Gail would softly yet inexorably ebb away from him.

Too many parts and pieces of that night would remain blurry in his mind, and even more entirely erased. Of the walk back from the bar he'd only remember scenes wherein Abed talked about magpies, he about Gail, Abed about *lost Muslims*, he about Gail, Abed about spiders, he about Gail . . . Likewise, he wouldn't remember how much time he had spent standing in front of the mailboxes, after Abed had watched him enter into his building safe and sound. Mailbox eighteen. There it was, his surname, once so familiar, now turned into a pastel of itself, with letters squeezed toward the end to make it fit inside this narrow frame: OZSIPAHIOGLU. A flimsy sense of continuity in this life of sudden ruptures, a rickety facade of identification he had been glued to at birth, and compelled to carry around wherever he went all his life, and expected to be proud of, and then even more proud of passing it to his son, just because some great-great-grandfather of his or perhaps an indolent clerk long-chewed and digested by the bureaucratic machinery, had in a fuzzy past for some reason now utterly unknown, favored this rather than any other combination of letters.

When the diligent O wears his reading glasses, it becomes an Ö; when the mischievous I goes out for a walk and wears a cap, it becomes an İ; when the gorgeous G lets her hair flutter in the wind, she becomes a Ğ . . .

The last time he had murmured this syrupy silly tune, he must have been a seven-year-old in Istanbul secretly suffering at the hands of a fortyish teacher whose idea of education was enjoyment, which was fine, if only her sense of humor had been more mature. As they learned the alphabet, the kids were forced to sing and expected to enjoy an idiotic song personifying every single letter. That the alphabet contained twenty-nine letters had indeed been a painful discovery for him.

And yet that night, twenty years later, and miles away from Istanbul, he came home drunk and dog-tired, and beyond his mind's ouzo-intoxicated rim, suddenly found himself watching the dimpled arms, meaty nose, and droopy mouth of his first teacher on this planet. Teachers, especially those early ones, are mortals with God-like tasks. Only they can destroy the yet-to-be-created.

He had searched for his fountain pen in his pockets, without realizing he had left it back at The Laughing Magpie, so that he could put the dots of his name back in their place. But what difference would it make anyhow? With or without the dots, such a surname was nothing but a shackle on his feet, too much of a burden for a nomad. It compelled one to belong somewhere, to settle down, to have a traceable past there, a family and a future worthy of the name. If given the chance, Ömer would rather possess a short surname, light and genteel, flexible and portable, one that you could easily carry along wherever you went, like the one Mr. and Mrs. Brown had.

Back in Istanbul in his high school days, the very first book he had read in the first English-language course he took was prosaically titled *Learning English—I*. That was the course book of the first semester of the very first year. In the second semester they had proceeded to another book, *Learning English—II*, and so it went. It didn't give the impression of making much progress and in their fourth or fifth semester, the kids were already making fun scribbling on the covers of the prescribed books *Still Learning English—XIV, Desperately Learning English—XXXV*. Their teacher had told them basically the same series was being used all around the world to teach kids English, and yet there were slight changes here and there as each book was adopted for a different country. Whatever the grandeur of the intentions of those who had planned this series, the title and content of the books were not much of a success. They depicted the English language like something you could never really, fully learn but merely dabble in; a slippery substance you could not take hold of but only lay a hand on. It was a swift hare you could not possibly catch no matter how hard you tried, an aspiration you could neither attain nor be given the chance not to aspire for.

And yet, despite the demoralizing elongation of their titles, the *Learning English* series could have been much more enjoyable had their main protagonists been other than Mr. and Mrs. Brown.

If high school kids back in Turkey spoke some sort of a crooked English with maximum attention to grammar rules and minimum competency in vocabulary, part of the blame could be put on Mr. and Mrs. Brown, and rightly so. In the *Learning English—I-II-III* . . . series, they roamed the pages doing the most simple things in the most scrupulous ways, never realizing, in the meantime, the extent of the damage to whatever creativity and ingenuity might reside in their young readers.

The couple had popped up in the very first pages of *Learning English—I*, smiling from ear to ear in the kitchen of their house. At that initial encounter, Mrs. Brown was standing beside the counter with a mission to teach "plate," "cup," and "a bowl of red apples," while Mr. Brown was sitting at the table, sipping coffee with no particular mission. The following week, Mrs. Brown was portrayed in the living room, still with the same smile and in the same dress, to teach "armchair," "curtain," or, to everyone's shock, "television." Mr. Brown was nowhere in the picture. The couple's teaching techniques had, like their clothes and expressions, showed little change in the weeks to follow. At each particular scene at their house, Mr. and Mrs. Brown defined and taught everything around them in terms of three fundamental criteria: color and size and age. Thus, Mrs. Brown cleaned a *green* carpet while Mr. Brown saw a *small* dog in the garden or Mrs. Brown made a *white* birthday cake as Mr. Brown sat in his *old* chair, and at those moments they decided time was ripe enough to complicate matters, they ran the vacuum over *small green new* carpets, or came across *big old black* dogs.

Be that as it may, it soon turned out that these indoor scenes were a temporary tranquillity, some sort of an intermediate stage, in the couple's life. Once that phase came to an end somewhere in the middle of the book, Mr. and Mrs. Brown launched a series of outdoor activities, never to be stopped again. They went to the zoo to name the caged animals; climbed the mountains to teach herbs and plants and flowers; spent a day at the beach to wear "sunglasses," eat "ice cream," and watch people "surf"; drove to local farms to look for "celery," "lettuce," "cabbage," and to shopping malls to buy "gloves," "belts," and "earrings," though for some reason they'd never wear them. One other activity they kept repeating every now and then was going on long, languid, *"it-was-a-nice-sunny-day"* picnics. There they taught "frog," "kite," "grasshopper," as they rested next to a "brook" flowing through the "hills." Though neither Mr. Brown nor Mrs. Brown seemed to be interested in what was happening in other parts of the world, on one occasion they went to Mexico to teach "airport," "customs," "luggage," and "sombrero." To many a student's dismay, they quickly came back, and were detected at their house once again, giving this flamboyant party to show friends and relatives their holiday pictures (each with a sombrero), while they taught the past perfect tense.

Though they seemed to be in restless motion all the time, there were certain places Mr. and Mrs. Brown would never set their foot in. They never went to graveyards, for instance; and nowhere in their habitat could you come across sanatoriums, rehabilitation clinics, mental asylums, let alone brothels, where most boys in the classroom had made a visit by this time but none had yet dared to go inside. Not that they expected to see Mr. Brown smiling from ear to ear in a penthouse, teaching words everyone craved learning, or Mrs. Brown recalling that she could do other things with her body than point at ducks or decorate big white cakes. But at least they could take a walk, be on the streets; this Ömer remembered expecting from them. As the world they depicted was so unreal and vague, the language they taught became unreal and vague, too, making it all the more difficult to speak English even when you knew what you were supposed to say theoretically—that is, grammatically.

Then preposterously, that ominous moment would come when the bad facsimile of a happy life taught in *Learning English I-II-III* . . . series would be grimly, glaringly tested by the unhappily real life, with its really unhappy people. Hearing their children talk in English was a mountainous pride for middle-class Turkish parents. They would miss no opportunity. Out of the blue, in front of relatives and friends, they could force their children to speak English, to say *something*, anything, as long as it was, it sounded, English enough. The parents' urge to hear their children speak English, even if with no definite content, for no definite purpose, was agonizing enough, and yet, how much more agonizing it could get would be unveiled the moment these parents bumped into a couple of tourists. "Why don't you speak," they would say, and elbow their children, "go and speak with the tourists, ask if they need anything. You've been taking English courses for two semesters now. You *can* talk!"

Sure they could. They could talk, even chitchat with those tourists, if only the scene had been a little different if rather than being accidentally located in the midst of horns, ambulance sirens, street vendors, and angst-ridden pedestrians scurrying on the broken pavements in this tumultuous city of Istanbul, they had been gently escorted to a-nice-sunny-Sunday picnic near a brook to fatten on conjunctions and interjections, while watching frogs croak and lilies blossom, and they had been asked to connect two independent clauses with conjunctive adverbs rather than answer the chillingly simple question of "how to go to the Grand Bazaar." Sure they could talk, but not now, not under these circumstances. By the time summer came to an end, kids would already hate their English teachers, hating Mr. and Mrs. Brown all the more. The next semester would commence upon this shaky basis of solid detestation, offering such little motivation to go on *Learning English—III*.

More than all the things they purported to teach, it was one simple point they declined to acknowledge that made these books so
ossified: that all their instructions were correct on paper and yet perfectly falsifiable in life. So deep was the deleteriousness of these
books that Ömer could still be struggling with their side effects, if it
weren't for his deep affection for cinema and music. It was cinema—
low-budget, independent, and unpretentious American/British/
Australian movies—as well as a multitude of punk/rock/postpunk
lyrics that had taught him far beyond all advanced English books he
was made to study.

Life, real life of blood and flesh, did abide by grammatical rules
and yet, incessantly, systematically, and luckily managed to deviate
from those. Life did construct sentences as grammar required but
then also punched holes here and there from which the gist of the
language seeped out to find its own way. It was precisely this distortion, and the matchless pleasure residing there, that *Learning English*
books forgot to teach.

Impossible Perfection

Every so often they pottered around together, Debra Ellen Thompson imitating Connie's gestures as Alegre giggled nonstop, or Alegre imitating *las tías* one by one, as Debra Ellen Thompson laughed heartily, sumptuously. It felt splendid to spend time together, just like it did today.

They entered a coffee shop on Auburn Street famous for its inventive sandwiches. Inside it was unusually tranquil, only a few customers here and there. They sat by the window, sipping their tea, gossiping about the cast in the reading group, watching pedestrians sail along, and then before they knew it, talking about themselves.

"When I'm at the office I skim through these weekly women's magazines," Alegre said. "All those perfect women are so annoying. Magazines, ads, TV . . . they are everywhere. *La* Tía Piedad likes to watch this soap opera where all the charming women are white, you know. If they are brown, they are either maids or nannies. What a great feeling it is to know *Virgen de Guadalupe* did not appear to some rich white man but to a poor Indian. And when she appeared to him, she was as brown as me. Nobody can change that. Nobody can snow-coat her because she is *la Virgen Morena!*"

"La-Veer-gen-Mou-ree-na," Debra Ellen Thompson repeated in a dreadful accent like that of a number of North Americans—so inflated and smashing that one cannot help suspecting that deep in the uncharted depths of their subconscious they foster some sort of resentment for the Spanish language that even they themselves might not be aware of.

In the ensuing silence they finished their tea—not one of those awkward pauses that float up in between two topics, but rather a velvety silence in fluid motion as if they were humming a common air, perhaps each in and by herself but still concurrently and in utter harmony. Whatever the tune, when it was over, Debra Ellen Thompson fished out of her bag two small gift boxes, handing one to Alegre, keeping the other for herself.

"What's this?" Alegre wondered.

"Open it."

Inside each box there was a chocolate woman.

"I asked Gail to make us a chocolate Connie and here it is! Though I have to admit it doesn't quite look like her." Debra Ellen Thompson smiled. "I wanted two Connies from her, one for you and one for me, but I didn't tell her what for."

"Why?" Alegre gasped. "I mean, *what for?*"

"Well, I noticed that for both of us chocolate was in some way . . . the forbidden fruit of our lives," Debra Ellen Thompson bumbled, fearing that Alegre might not like the metaphor. "I mean, chocolate is our cutting edge. Whatever the reason, we cannot eat chocolate. In a way, it symbolizes the 'impossible.' As to Connie, she symbolizes 'perfection,' that perfect woman we fail to be. Therefore, a chocolate Connie stands for 'impossible perfection.' "

"Impossible perfection." Alegre smiled a childish smile, relishing the expression.

"That's right," Debra Ellen Thompson enthused. "This solid little thing here," she lifted the chocolate statue to her eye level, pouted at it, and snarled, "is so shamelessly *wrong*. It's an awful burden on our bodies . . . and on our souls. This thing here is what prevents us from being true to ourselves."

Alegre repeated the mime, lifting the chocolate Connie up to her eye level, and pouting at it, though apparently with less vim and vigor.

"And do you know what we are going to do with this?"

Alegre almost held her breath.

"Eat it!"

"Eat it?"

"That's right. We are going to gulp down this impossible perfection we are fed up with. Eat it, devour it, digest it, and throw it out of our bodies like a piece of . . ."

"Shit?" Alegre asked politely.

"*Shit!*" Debra Ellen Thompson echoed at full volume.

A morbidly scrawny Japanese tourist with an MIT cap and the intention of going to the JFK Museum without knowing he was walking in the wrong direction stared in wonder at the two women inside the coffee shop. They were both frowning at the brown figures they held up in their hands. He kept watching them as he glided in front of the windowpane, walking far more slowly than he normally would.

"All of it?" Alegre gasped.

"Well, not necessarily," Debra Ellen Thompson answered, now hesitating. "Let's start with the head. Tomorrow we'll eat the body. But . . ." she added softly, "don't you vomit it, OK? Don't let Connie escape from our hands."

Alegre gaped at her with a baffling fusion of various feelings wherein the following three outweighed all the others: surprise, panic, and release. All for the same reason: Somebody had somehow discovered what she had so far been doing secretly. That somebody was both a friend and a stranger, both a woman and not a perfect female. As such, being detected by Debra Ellen Thompson was both cutting and somewhat not as cutting as she would have feared it to be. With a glint in her eye, grit on her pale face, Alegre sank her teeth into the chocolate and cautiously nibbled, enjoying the savory morsel as it melted in her mouth, watching Debra Ellen Thompson do the same.

What Alegre did next was not quite expected of her. She turned toward Debra Ellen Thompson, gave her a warm smile, and suddenly kissed her on the cheek. What Debra Ellen Thompson did next was not quite expected of her, either. She looked at Alegre for a few seconds, gave her a warmer smile, and suddenly kissed her on the mouth.

Having been informed about the right direction to the museum, the morbidly scrawny Japanese tourist was walking back the same way when he impulsively sneaked a look inside the coffeehouse to see what those two women were up to now. That is why he is still standing there, still peeking. He had indeed heard about the freedom of lesbians in Boston, but he was not quite ready to see them being so audacious in public places. Yet, being the well-mannered man that he was, after the pithy shock, he tore his gaze from the kissing women and gathered speed, scurrying this time far more swiftly than he normally would.

Inside the coffeehouse, Alegre flinched in deep panic and deeper shame, and rose to her feet, avoiding any eye contact with Debra Ellen Thompson. Not knowing what to say, she took her bag and walked out, almost running. Absurdly, the first thing that came to her mind was to find a restroom to throw up Connie's head. But she didn't do that. Instead she hastened her steps, almost knocking down the Japanese walking ahead, hating Debra Ellen Thompson more and more with each step. Actually, hate was only on the surface. Below that she didn't quite know what to think, or how she felt. What a fool she had been to believe they were friends. All this time Debra Ellen Thompson had pretended to be friends, whereas in actual fact, she was . . . she wanted . . . Alegre did not even want to say the rest. She streaked down the street with escalating speed, couldn't stand waiting for the traffic light to turn green, and jaywalked in a breeze of confusion. Two Turkish tourists who happened to be waiting at that crosswalk less because they thought one should stop at red lights than because everyone else did, instantly followed her example, thrusting themselves into the empty street.

Meanwhile, back at the coffee shop, being so harshly tossed out from the yacht of amity she had all this time been serenely, gracefully, happily sailing with Alegre, Debra Ellen Thompson sat anchored in stunned inertia. It took her a while to shake out of her daze, and even then she couldn't help trembling. In a way, she was acquainted with this pain, though never before had she experienced it so grimly. The same old inscrutable lesbian ache that you were bound to suffer when you fell in love with a woman who happened to be *straight*. If a heterosexual woman falls in love and is refused in return, she, too, will feel bad, but only about the consequence of her act, that's to say, about the "being refused" part. If a homosexual woman, on the other hand, falls in love with a straight woman and is refused by her, she will feel bad about too many things, including love itself, having asked her in the first place. The desire to love and be loved in return, the desire so amply approved and sympathized with in other contexts, will turn into a source of embarrassment.

Debra Ellen Thompson was no stranger to this feeling. She knew pretty well that Alegre could hate her if she ever exposed her feelings for her. And yet, this serene afternoon watching the sparkle in the latter's eyes, she could not, and perhaps did not want to, suppress any longer that for quite some time she secretly, inexplicably, and unequivocally loved her.

At first she had mistrusted her own feelings, suspecting that her interest in Alegre might be, as Gail had cynically suggested, a search for a submissive woman, the need for another Zarpandit. But the more time Debra Ellen Thompson spent with Alegre the more she was convinced that neither was Alegre as compliant as she seemed to be at first glance, nor was she herself looking for compliance anymore. Alegre had helped her to overcome the loss of Gail, not by being another Zarpandit, but by being just herself, her lovely self.

Down on the street, the first thing that came to Debra Ellen Thompson's mind was to take the box out and throw the chocolate away. But she didn't do that. Instead, she kept the now decapitated Connie in her box, and resolutely headed back to Squirmy Spirit Chocolates, the only safe haven she could think of. Halfway there, though, she stopped walking, stopped running away as if guilty of something, and started to cry.

The Advice of the Oracle
at Delphi

"The room might not be luxurious, but I was told it had a matchless view. Still, if we don't like it we can easily move elsewhere. My parents wanted us to stay with them, of course, but I convinced them it was kind of a honeymoon for us. And it should be. Tomorrow we can stay in our room all day long if you want to, otherwise we'll go to the Grand Bazaar, and the next day we should see the Sunken Cistern, I'm sure you'll love it . . . then there is Saint Sophia . . ." Ömer found himself bubbling to Gail on the elevator over the frizzy head of the bellboy who stood between them with an impish glimmer in his eyes listening to what this American couple was talking about. Although Ömer had talked with him in Turkish several times, the boy still seemed to refuse to take him as a Turk. This lanky, somewhat edgy, nonstop, gesticulating guy sweating in his baggy multihued clothes and this conversely composed young woman dressed head to toe in black, and with a spoon in her even blacker hair, being the most interesting tourist couple he had seen these days, the boy had fixed his gaze on them. From time to time he fluttered his incredibly long eyelashes in flapping sequels, as if amused by the things he heard.

"Then we should spend a day in the islands . . . Maybe we better take a trip along the Bosphorus before that. I want you to see the wine houses. There is a whole tradition of carousing in this city. You should definitely drink rakı. You should definitely eat the mezes they bring with rakı. And then we'll also go to the Galata Tower . . ." Ömer paused, squinting at the boy who had arched an eyebrow as if he was ready to say something, perhaps add a few suggestions of his own. But they were already on the sixth floor.

Room 606 was a typical three-star hotel room—so typical you could neither truly dislike nor possibly like it. On the walls there were half-fantasy drawings of the harem life, women reclining on soft cushions behind lattice windows, sketchy mass production for the sketchy tourist eye.

"Baby, will you please calm down." Gail sneered at him when Ömer had closed, well, more precisely *slammed* the door shut on the bellboy. "Stop worrying, OK? I'm sure she and I will get along."

"Who is she?"

"Your mother city, of course . . ." crooned Gail as she opened a suitcase and pulled out a black T-shirt and a darkened silver spoon, almost grayish. "You are remarkably abnormal, you know. You don't show any enthusiasm about me meeting your mother. But you get frantic about me meeting your mother city . . ."

Ömer felt he should say something to the contrary but just couldn't find out what that could be. Instead, he sighed. Why he had all of a sudden turned into a cut-and-dry tourist guide, he couldn't put in plain words. Preposterously, Istanbul had become a juicy, ambrosial, crimson apple he kept polishing and polishing before presenting it to the woman he loved. The more he polished, the more he felt the urge to titivate. Like catching cold, he had been exposed to a virus hitherto unknown to his body and soul, infected by some unnamed disease rampant among intercultural couples, especially where one of the partners came from a less developed country. Though he had not confessed this to himself yet, deep down in his soul Ömer wanted Gail to like the city, if not the country where he came from. Nevertheless, that longing had less to do with promoting Istanbul than with feeling better about himself.

Sitting on the bed with a brochure in her hand, Gail was trying to learn new things about Turkey while at the same time trying to unlearn some old things—*Midnight Express*, human rights violations, the Kurdish question, bits and pieces of tarnished information she had a sound feeling the Turks wouldn't like to be reminded of. This kind of inner censorship was not quite typical of Gail. Nevertheless, viruses being contagious, she, too, had been exposed to the unnamed disease rampant among intercultural couples, especially where one of the partners came from a more developed country. Though she didn't bother confessing this to herself, deep down in her soul Gail wanted, like too many Western women married to Eastern men, to like the city, if not the country, where her husband had come from. Nevertheless, that longing had less to do with discovering Istanbul than with feeling better about herself.

Hence, here they were, each sitting at one side of a kitschy twin bed in a mediocre hotel room with a brochure in their hands, one of them making plans as to how to *show* the very best side of Istanbul while the other was getting ready to *see* the very best side of Istanbul.

Meanwhile, behind the slightly ajar double door of the balcony, Istanbul was watching this couple with a silky smile and a sardonic sparkle in the amethyst abyss of her eyes. After all, she is no city you can wax and buff up, trim fancy on the edges, and then gift wrap in buoyant packets to cheer up your sweetie. She is no city you can serve with béchamel sauce on glittery plates to add a romantic tang to your faltering love affair. Istanbul is way beyond these trifling considerations, far too aged and yet ageless. She has long before arrived at the end of her time and yet she is endless. An ugly queen, the whimsical alma mater, an amorphous womb nonstop absorbing the semen of its newcomers but never in her history inseminated by anyone, home to the dispossessed but she herself owned by no one.

These, however, Gail would detect soon . . . in point of fact, she'd notice it in a minute, after Ömer had headed to the bathroom to take a shower, leaving her alone in the room. That was when she got up on her feet, and walked toward the shimmering light penetrating from the dreary curtains. Distractedly, languorously, almost dreamily she opened the double door, stepped onto the balcony, shielded her eyes from the sun, and the next thing she knew, she was standing still, almost astounded. At first and each sight, the city looked so *beguiling* to Gail.

How long she had been standing there staring at this most unlikely composition of a city is hard to tell, but when Ömer came out of the shower that was the state in which he found her. He, too, shielded his eyes from the sun; he, too, looked across languidly, but what *he* saw, in turn, was quite different, if not the opposite. His face crumpled while his lips heaved a groan. Either a mistake had been made down at reception or that talkative receptionist had deceived him. Certainly this was not the panorama he had been promised when booking this room. Actually, Ömer did not know this, but if they were given the key to room 607, what they'd see from their balcony would be the beautiful scenery he was after—a landscape of a sea of bottomless indigo with picturesque mosques and cute red roofs of houses arrayed far away with an algal shade of hills in the background. But from room 606 what he saw, over the jumbled roofs and under the wings of seagulls, was the havoc of the city, so threateningly close you could almost feel its pulse. Grimy, narrow, snaky streets, tangled, crammed, crumbled houses with windows wide open onto the life throbbing outside, and the hordes of cats on the streets, some incredibly august, some so miserable; this mess of history encrusted with not only the vestiges of the lives long withered away but also the signs of those yet to be born. At first and each sight, the city looked so *unsightly* to Ömer.

In point of fact, both could be said to be right. From the balcony of room 606, Istanbul looked equally *beguiling* and *unsightly*. Such is the complexity of her ugly majesty. Two adjacent houses, even the two walls of the same room can have an entirely distinct view of the city. Here unrivaled splendor and the grotesquely deformed exist side by side, the beautiful and the scrofulous are welded into a high-octane bedlam by the heat and pressure of ages. When *Istanbul* is the word, the synonym and the antonym are one and the same.

What Ömer didn't know, and could not quite understand in his tourist guide frame of mind, was that it was precisely this *concoction* that had mesmerized Gail. She had been rapidly captivated by

Istanbul—not the Istanbul Ömer was planning to show to her but, if anything, the one he was trying to hide from her.

"Come on!" Gail whooped all of a sudden getting out of her trance. "Let's go. There's a city to discover out there."

A city to discover? Istanbul sniggered. *Do you think I want to be discovered?*

But Gail did not hear this feminine voice. She was busy hearing other sounds. First and foremost, the seagulls! The very first thing every outsider will discover in Istanbul is that the roofs shriek here. Seagulls are amazingly complicated birds—or maybe far too simple. They are full of contradictions. They soar alone but always compose a collectivity; they are vulgarly clumsy and ugly but also possess a noble grace of their own; they look so dim-witted when they land near trash cans looking for something, anything to gulp down among the litter; but then nothing, no one can surpass their turgid wisdom while they rest on the roofs or rock pensively staring at the sea, utterly motionless, almost congealed under the weight of their contemplation. These white, sonorous, and jumpy birds perch on every roof in Istanbul—of rich and poor vicinities alike, residences and hotels all the same for they recognize no distinction between those who'll be gone in a few days and those who are firmly rooted here.

At the outset their screeches might be so niggling you think you'll never get used to it. Three days later the sound has become so usual and such a surefire proof of life that you'll start worrying if you don't hear it for more than ten minutes. Conceivably, the denizens of Istanbul are not bothered by this dissonant chant for they know too well that it is better to hear it than not to hear. Istanbul makes people wise enough to comprehend, not intellectually but intuitively, that there is something apocalyptic in the silence of seagulls.

So the roofs shriek in Istanbul, but it is the streets that talk. It is on the streets that life throbs in a mélange of fuming and frustrated, aching and buoyant voices; the squawk of horns splintered by the piercing yell of street vendors, emergency sirens, prayers from copious mosques, and the clangor of distant church bells; a hovering humming accompanied by the constant swish of the sea, as if it intended to wash away this pandemonium once and for all. It is a city of infinite quarrels—between men and men, men and women, and life and death. The hubbub is so dense that even the faintest click fuses with an outcry far away, absorbing, therefore, a touch of the overall tune. If you listen attentively, you'll notice there is an underlying rhythm. Streets are cadenced in Istanbul, far more harmoniously than the beat of the lives that slither upon them.

This city is a latticework of streets. It is as if all these monuments, age-old mansion houses, the swelling suburbs, or even the sea herself have been placed where they are just to make the streets accessible. Each street, in turn, is less of a thoroughfare into some passable track than a diversion from some historical road now entirely and irretrievably gone. It's the streets that matter in Istanbul, and not necessarily where they will guide you. Perhaps that's why the entire city is rampant with dead-end streets, unexpectedly cut in the middle as if it didn't really matter where they were initially leading to. If you ever wonder about the basic pattern, if any, underlying this urban fusion, you should ask the oracle at Delphi. It was her idea to have the city built right here, across the Land of the Blind.

Once there were two coasts ripped apart by the sea. They stood face-to-face in hidden enmity. There was an old settlement on one of the coasts but the other coast was uninhabited. Then one day came an oracle. "Those people on that coast over there must be blind," she pointed out, "for failing to see the beauty of this coast here." Following her advice, a city would be raised on the coast that the Tribe of the Blind had failed to appreciate. One of the multiple ironies of Istanbul, however, is that as it expanded in time, it ended up swallowing not only the coast it was originally built upon but also the Land of the Blind on the opposite coast. Ever since then, Istanbul is the negation of a negation. There, each sound is met with a disagreeing reverberation.

Gail looks surprised but it's hard to tell what bewilders her more, the city or seeing herself here. As to Ömer, he looks neither surprised nor attentive to the sounds. In point of fact, he is somewhat deaf at the moment. He can't really be said to be hearing anything except his mind's nagging voice as to where they should have lunch, will Gail be satisfied with the food, which sites should they visit first, which way would be better to choose so that they won't get stuck in the traffic for hours and Gail won't divorce him by the end of the day . . . Ömer is far too immersed in practical touristic matters to experience any philosophical or poetic abstractness whatsoever.

That day, and on the following ones, this was more or less their state of mind as they roamed the city, and the more they infiltrated it, the farther they swayed from Ömer's original to-do lists. Still, he remained firmly concentrated on practicalities and timetables while Gail remained interested in everything but these. What she found all the more surprising was to discover that the bellboy would not be the only one to take Ömer for a tourist. Somehow Gail's presence was sufficient to render them both Americans. And yet, Gail also sensed that behind this jumble of appearances wherein all unfamiliar ways and faces were deemed to be equally "foreign," there lay more of a structural riddle, some sort of a duality that divided Turkish people into two camps. On the one hand, there were the more educated, the more affluent, and far more sophisticated who were irrefutably Western and modern; and then there was a second group of people, greater in numbers, less in power, less *Western* in appearance. The discrepancy in between could transfer the members of the former bunch into "tourists" in the eyes of the latter group. A Turk could easily look like a *foreigner* to another Turk.

Interestingly, everyone spoke English in Istanbul, even those who didn't know any. This being her first visit outside the United States, Gail would be flabbergasted at not being subjected to what she was secretly prepared for: anti-American sentiments. This she hadn't told Ömer, but she was ready to confront a series of political, international, religious, and historical questions about American foreign policy in the Middle East, the *clash of civilizations*, ethnic conflicts in the Balkans, the West's delay in putting an end to the killings of Bosnian Muslims, prospects on the colossal issue of "Islam and woman," the war on Iraq, instabilities in the world oil market . . . and so on. Instead, as she would shortly find out, people here in Istanbul had an alternative set of questions in reserve for foreigners like her:

1. Where do you come from?
2. Do you like Istanbul?
3. Do you like the food?

It was as simple as that. Neither religious matters nor sociopolitical debates. The very first thing ordinary people were interested in learning from a foreigner was more basic: "How do I look from outside?"

Besides, Gail would be amused to discover, people in this part of the world did not quite expect an American to have the foggiest idea about what life outside America could be like. If you still wanted to discuss world politics with the natives, you had to pass some sort of a threshold first because the moment they noticed it was an American they were talking to, an uncanny flash traversed their faces—a flash that Gail had initially misinterpreted as recognition but then came to decode as: *Oh, then you must know nothing about us.*

Following the triple set of questions, or at times preceding it, one other mania people in Istanbul commonly showed when they met a foreigner was to shovel food into the latter's mouth as if to be a "foreigner" meant "to come from a land of famine." Everywhere they went Gail was offered something to eat or to drink, but usually both. Foreigners had to be fed! And fed she'd be, indeed, when on their third day in this city they'd visit Ömer's family.

As she handed her plate to Ömer's mother so that the latter could refurbish it for the fourth time with incredibly assorted food of incredible amounts, Gail moaned, which went totally unnoticed amid the jovial fuss at the table. On her left was the father, who didn't look like Ömer at all, and next to him was Ömer's brother, who didn't look like either his father or Ömer. On her right was the mother, an elegant, highly attractive woman who looked far younger than her age with her stylish haircut, bronzed face, and slender, lithe body. The house was located on a beautiful street with spick-and-span apartment buildings in an upper-class neighborhood. From the windows you could watch the sea roll, thick, almost jellylike in its dazzling blue, and Gail could swear this was not the same sea she had been watching from the hotel balcony. The living room was sophisticatedly decorated, upmarket and refined, svelte and chic but so calculatingly distanced from à la mode. There were a few photographs around, and in one of them Gail spotted the cute, serene boy with hurting eyes Ömer once was. The walls were embellished with numerous tastefully framed tasteful paintings, which Gail felt sure were authentic.

Stuffed grape leaves, marinated eggplant, artichokes in olive oil, chickpeas mashed in tahini, grilled red peppers in garlic, sweetened figs, and a massive amount and variety of pastries . . . The very best selection of Ottoman-Turkish cuisine, which, Gail had realized, could make a vegetarian delighted, and a vegan more than merry. Tea was served in small glasses with slices of lemon. Having the fatally wrong impression that whatever the offer it must not be turned down, Gail had already drunk twelve glasses. Ömer, meanwhile, remained at the other end of the table, paying no attention to her agonizing ballooning. His mind was too distracted to notice that. He was separately and yet simultaneously chatting with everyone at the table, prattling energetically but not quite like himself, trying hard not to look edgy, and harder not to pout at his mother as the latter spoke to Gail with excessive politeness.

On the way back to the hotel, they took the ferryboat to get to the other shore. Among the pedestrians teeming in Kadıköy Square, Ömer walked stiffly in storklike steps, Gail billowed behind, dragging her heavy body. When they had finally parked themselves on a bench at the upper floor of the ferryboat, Gail sighed in relief, enjoying the wind fluttering on her face, and unleashed the question long crowding her thoughts:

"I think your parents are nice. And your brother is wonderful. Why are you so harsh with them? What wrong did they do to you?"

What wrong did they do to me? Ömer didn't have any answers to that, and yet at the same time, he felt like he had loads of answers in store. His parents were not bad people. They had raised him in the best way they could, provided him with a good education, spent quite some money for his well-being, never beaten him or anything. Ömer could not possibly explain either to Gail or to himself where this bitterness of his came from. *What wrong had his family done to him?* None. But maybe the question itself was improperly formulated. Maybe this had nothing to do with *wrong*. Besides, his parents were too privileged, well-mannered, and posh to be *wrong*. Was he being unfair again? He didn't want the burden of guilt thinking *bad* about *good* people. He put on his headphones, and searched among his mixed punk-rock CDs for a song he felt he urgently needed to hear: "Overcoming Learned Behavior."

"There is anger in me, not only toward my parents but toward so many things and beings, including myself, you know . . . but then if somebody asks me why are you so outraged, I don't really know how to answer that . . . Do you think I should have an answer?"

"No, honey," Gail replied. What she didn't say was that Ömer's inexplicable rage was so similar to her inexplicable sorrow. *There was sorrow inside her, there always was, but if someone asked her the reason why, she didn't have any immediate answers.* Did she have to have an explanation, convincing and concrete, like the ones the girls back at Mount Holyoke College had tried to attach to her so that they could find her less peculiar. Would her constant despondency be more understandable if she had been harassed or beaten as a child or been subjected to all sorts of terrible things? What if none of these had happened to her and yet she still could not get rid of her sorrow?

Gail caressed Ömer's face with a compassionate smile. She liked, actually she admired, this unswerving sourness, vibrant and irate, almost juvenile, that detached Ömer from his class and their etiquette. She kissed him on the cheek, put her head on his shoulder, and started to watch the motley crowd of ferryboat passengers swaying around. Ömer inhaled the smell of her hair, loving being in love with her, and although a cold, silver spoon was entering into his mouth, he did not let that knock down the exclusive romanticism of the moment. Cuddling each other there they sat, watching the ferryboat embark. All along the hills on the other coast, mosques glittered like shards of broken glass. The water glistened with bubbling white foam, and so did the approaching city, so did life itself. As the ferryboat glided the waves chased it with no haste, and the sea rolled thickly, patiently, confidently, looking mucilaginous, gummy, almost edible.

"Ladies and gentlemen! A fleeting attention is all I demand from you. And in return, I provide you with everything you need in life, except for a lover, perhaps!"

It was a burly, swarthy Gypsy with astute hazel eyes, a giant bag on his shoulder, and an even bigger, flabby belly that looked like a separate organism somehow attached to his body. With both arms raised like a fully concentrated maestro he seemed ready to direct this hushed orchestra of drowsy ferryboat passengers. A few people chuckled but most stood stiff, avoided looking in his direction. They were sick of him. Either he or some other vendor, all the same. Every morning as they went to work, and every evening on their way back home, the ferryboat passengers in Istanbul found themselves the spectators of an inveterate farce that they watched each time partly with condescension, partly with ennui, and now and again, with a subtle envy for the itinerancy, archness, and baldness of these most unusual, most gifted, most tiresome actors.

The Gypsy vendor put his huge leather bag on the floor and pulled out a plastic tool of a yellow as bright and fatty as egg yolks, trimmed with pointed blades and an odd cap at the top. He lifted the *thing* in the air so that everyone could see this *miracle*. In the following three minutes, he peeled a potato, sliced carrots and cucumbers, squeezed a lemon, then an orange, and offered the juice to a few lucky people in the audience, sharpened a pencil, stuffed a wine leaf, and opened a jar of pickles, all with this "incredible Japanese innovation," as he named it. Nobody took it seriously.

"Although this miracle is in no need of promotion," the vendor yelled with a gruff voice rutted by smoking and yelling all day long, "the first three buyers will be rewarded with gratis items, including a lemonade maker" (he raised the lemonade maker in the air) "and an expanding trivet" (he expanded the trivet in the air) "and . . . a nut sheller" (he cracked a nut in the air) "and a fizgig for good fishermen" (he waved the pointed barbed implement) ". . . all on the house." Nobody chuckled this time. In fact, several people had begun to show interest. A chubby woman with a straw hat was the first to buy. Two other passengers were quick to follow.

"Congratulations, you lucky three. The campaign is over now, there won't be a similar chance," the vendor yelled this time even louder. "However, there's another campaign, one no less fascinating. If you buy two of these Japanese innovations instead of just one, you'll get a set of colored pencils" (he raised the set in the air) "and rubber gloves" (he waved a pair of gloves) "and an electric fan everyone sorely needs all throughout the summer" (he blew a fist-size fan toward a nonstop sweating man in front) ". . . and on top of all these, we give an egg beater for free!!!" A handful of passengers gestured to the vendor, then a few more followed their example. In three minutes all miraculous Japanese innovations in the bag were sold.

As he was packing his bags happily gorged on his sales, the man's hazel eyes caught sight of the tourist woman under a pitch-black bush of hair. In a flash he had appeared beside Gail. "For those of us who love spoons," he shouted full blast, and then pulled out first a set of cheap copper, next a set of stainless steel, and, finally, a set of plastic spoons. Each set being more ridiculous and shoddy than the one before, Gail found herself pouting at the vendor as if waiting for him to give a sign of joking, so that they could all chuckle together. But it was at that instant that the man pulled out another spoon, one utterly different from all the rest—an authentic silver ladle with an Ottoman tugra in its pocket, and an amber stone nested on the long, delicate, twisting handle. It looked pricey, and indeed old, very old. "For the lucky customer that buys these three sets of spoons," the vendor yelled, "this priceless antique spoon here is gratis!"

Then, they all disembarked—Gail pleased with her spoons, Ömer still shocked that she had bought them all, and the Gypsy

vendor already having forgotten about them, already off to his next
tirade on the next ferryboat.

They went to the islands once, and to the Grand Bazaar multiple
times; they visited Saint Sophia, and looked directly into the eyes of
Theodora, who now seemed to Ömer truly gorgeous in the warmth
of a distant memory. They came across startlingly dissimilar worlds
in parallel streets, roamed the most cosmopolitan, as well as the more
conservative parts of the city, and now and again found it all con-
densed in one spot. On each excursion, Gail came up with the idea
of a new set of chocolates. As soon as she was back in Squirmy
Spirit Chocolates, she decided to produce her new collection—one
set of white chocolate whirling dervishes, another set of bitter chocolate veiled women, and perhaps—why not—a set of ferryboat vendors made of truffle with a filling of brandy in their bellies.

In front of the age-old Blue Mosque, they bought grain from a
toothless woman and fed the pigeons. A tawny cat drew circles
around them, getting closer and closer with cautious but blatantly
ridiculous steps. The cat couldn't catch any pigeons. Gail took that
as a good sign. She was at the zenith of her manic moods lately,
which also meant that she was standing on the verge of falling down.
A fleeting stage of incipient insanity.

After rambling back and forth on the carnivalesque side streets
of Beyoglu, where an entirely distinct but equally loud music poured
from every single bar around, they stopped in front of a tomb
squeezed between buildings. Like many other tombs fortuitously
preserved among constructions, this one, too, belonged to a saint. By
now, Gail had discovered that the whole city was populated by innumerable tombs of countless ages, and that each had specialized in a
particular area. Some saints helped to find a husband, some others
not to lose the one you already had. Some tombs were visited by the
sick and the disabled whereas some others by the forlorn or those
who suffered from a broken heart. Then there were the ones visited
by women who couldn't have a baby. Whatever the differences between the saints, their visitors were almost always women.

Gail inspected the gravestone in an attempt to grasp what this saint had specialized in. But there was no clue as to that, only a sign that made little sense even when translated.

> **Do not light candles around the tomb.**
> **The saint is in no need of your light.**

"Tell me, my love," she murmured softly on the way back to the hotel. "Do you think I'm one of those that will have their book given from the left?"

It took Ömer the Infidel some time to grasp what she was talking about, and then some more time to realize she was serious: "Come on, you don't believe in *these* things!"

"Yeah, but you can still give an answer. I mean, if you were God would you give my book from the left or from the right?"

"If I were God," Ömer said and snorted a laugh, "I would throw it on your head."

A harsh ray hit her eyes as she asked: "But don't you think the metaphor is poetic?"

"No, I don't." Ömer offered her a consoling arm. "But you certainly are. You are the most poetic thing in my life."

The moment he heard himself utter these words, however, an unforeseen dolefulness got hold of Ömer as if *poetic* meant that which was no longer here. He remembered feeling this way before, with the same overtone, but couldn't possibly recall when or where.

The Hungry Mouth in Me

Night. Alegre is alone in the kitchen, the only place where she feels she is fully herself. The kitchen is her homeland. Surrounded by a long line of relatives and a circle of friends most of whom had been expatriated, deterritorialized, and even if willingly still painfully molded into foreigners in the United States, nobody will believe that the kitchen can be native soil, so she tells it to no one. Alegre does not know if being in the kitchen makes her happy or not. But perhaps that's not the point anyway. Homelands are not, she senses, about happiness after all. In any case, the only thing she can be sure of is that here, in the kitchen, she belongs. She comes here to cook for others, but every now and then for her and her alone. This is one of those moments. Tonight Alegre is not here to cook. This time she came to the kitchen to feed the hungry mouth in her.

Late. But time makes no difference. The hungry mouth is outside the timing of eating habits. People with normal eating habits erroneously assume that those with eating disorders are obsessed with food. But even if there is some sort of an obsession, more than the

quality or the quantity of the food to consume, it's the keeping up
with the order of eating that fails Alegre. That unwavering regularity
of eating, the steadiness of the sequels at exactly the same hours
every morning, afternoon, and evening . . . then morning-afternoon-
evening once more . . . again and again each and every day. Because
people get hungry at the same instants in the same sequence, they
are also perfectly capable of dining together. Alegre is not. Her
mouth gets hungry occasionally; once a month, once in a while, once
in ages. Other people's mouths are on their faces, drawn into a conspicuous line like in a child's painting, so discernible at the first
glance, an entrance opening from their body to the outside. Alegre's
mouth is erased from her face; it's down in her body, a wound in her
womb, a void churning deep inside. It's always in the background,
waiting guardedly in the dark, only to come out when it really wants
to. Because it's outside of time, it has no record of the past. This is
why, every time the hungry mouth starts to eat, it devours as if it has
never eaten before. Because it's outside of time, it has no conception
of the future either. This is why, every time it starts to eat, it devours
as if it will never have a chance to eat again. Unlike *la* Tía Piedad's
dinner china, the she-mouth in Alegre's body pines for a total blank,
an intentional amnesia.

Hunger. She shambled toward the fridge feeling all the more
ravenous after eating bowls of puffed cereals; first, of those crunchy
ones with walnut and raisin that belong to Piyu, and after that, of the
honey-frosted bite size that are Abed's favorite. Abed and Piyu eat
these cereals every day at breakfast. Alegre never does. They have so
many calories. But then on a night like this she ends up wolfing
down a whole box as if making up for all the mornings lost. One full
box with milk is tantamount to 1,880 calories, 75 grams of sugar in
total. It is too late to stop. The hungry mouth in her is fully awake.

She opened the fridge, peered inside absentmindedly, picked up
a slice of mozzarella, then another, closed the fridge, opened the
fridge, ate a gargantuan slice of cheddar quiche, closed the fridge,
and stood gaping at the white door no less absentmindedly than a
second before. There, among a bedlam of phone bills, take-away

menus, discount coupons, a picture of Arroz in bath foams, color charts for house decoration, and an old scoreboard for the game of English Vocabulary, which neither Piyu nor Abed had removed after Ömer left the house, she caught sight of a postcard that had arrived this morning.

Dear friends,
We are in the Grand Bazaar *(again!)*. Ömer is complaining because this is the third time I dragged him here. We write this postcard from a souvenir store *(shamefully Orientalistic, they even sell toy camels in belly-dancing costume)*.

In an incomprehensible way, Ömer talks like Abed these days (no offense, no offense, just kidding). Anyway, when he saw us buying this postcard, the owner of the store kindly invited us inside so that we could write here *(so that we could shop from here)*, and offered us tea and Turkish delight. *(Gail keeps eating everything they offer.)* Just now the man showed me two antique silver spoons, which he said belonged to a concubine in the harem. *(Now isn't this what Said calls the Orient's orientalizing itself?)* To my surprise, Ömer seems to have found great inspiration here for his thesis.

We wish you were here with us. Greetings from Istanbul . . .

Alegre turned over the postcard and pouted at the picture on it. It was a graceful silhouette of a mosque on a hill at dusk . . . the colors were beautiful, shades of orange and yellow, warm and delicate, like a spoonful of peach marmalade. Speaking of that, Alegre opened the fridge, peered inside to see what to eat next, bolted down a sausage, then another, swiftly closed the door and reopened it immediately.

Inside the fridge there were two dishes recommended by this week's women's magazine: Spicy Eggplant in Ginger-Tamarind Sauce and Mostaccioli with Spinach and Feta. She had cooked but not even tasted them, leaving it to Piyu, Abed, and the new housemate to enjoy. They were all asleep now. Only Arroz was awake, standing next to her with a surly beam spinning in the big, dark whirl of his eyes. He was so aware that something was wrong, he hadn't made even a single attempt to share any of the food Alegre had devoured in front of his eyes. Arroz knew this was not eating. This was something else, something frightening. This rite was about turning the order of things upside down; taking in what was outside and then giving back what was taken in. Eating and purging, greed and abstemiousness, sinning and repenting . . . this was about transcending impenetrable boundaries.

Alegre sat on the floor, staring at the containers with food marshaled on the shelves. All the eggplants and the entire mostaccioli inside the pan, and the cream cheese and sausages and sautéed mushrooms of the day before, and the baby corns and pickles in the jars and the whole gallon of butter cookie ice cream in the freezer . . . She finished them all, a spicy and sweet and sour and sore mixture. Alegre-style masala. Down to the minutest crumb, she bolted. She did not reckon the consequences of this outburst. Nothing worried her anymore. The act of gorging was devoid of all considerations. She didn't need to nibble in practiced courtesy now, and be the polite and docile girl she had always been.

She shoveled in another sausage, and after that, all the rest of the cheddar quiche. She smacked and smacked, while her eyes rowdily hunted for the next dish. She had just reached out for the peanut butter when a voice ripped the air apart.

"*¿Alegre, qué estás haciendo por Dios?*"*

Piyu was standing next to the kitchen door, flat-footed, arms akimbo, stone-faced in a stupor that verged on horror. His mouth dropped, not knowing what else to say, begging for an explanation. How long had he been standing there, watching her eat and eat and eat? Alegre shuddered as if caught naked before a crowd of utter strangers. She rose to her feet in panic, losing her balance.

Behind his sleepy gaze Piyu was so baffled and so sorely in need of a reasonable explanation, it'd take him additional seconds to grasp

*Alegre, what are you doing for God's sake?

the panic on Alegre's face. He looked around for his glasses, remembered they were upstairs beside the bed, and then blushed crimson as he swallowed his shock—caused less by his disgust of the repulsive appetite he had just witnessed than the tremor of coming to realize that his girlfriend was a bulimic and that he had failed to notice it all this time. Before he could start asking a series of questions, Alegre was already on the porch, rushing out. Just in time, though unconsciously, Piyu chopped forward, seizing her by the elbow.

"¡Déjame!" she yelled in a voice that belonged to someone else. "What is it to you anyway? You don't even sleep with me . . ."

The exclamation was so unexpected and out of context, Piyu's hands slackened as he paused to consider how to respond. In that slit of doubt Alegre found a chance to put a coat on over her pajamas and dash out only to keep running until there'd be no more air left in her lungs. When Piyu had managed to chuck out his confusion, grope for his glasses upstairs in his room, put on his shoes, and run after her, Alegre had already reached the avenue.

Night. Apart from them there is one more customer inside the laundry, a drunken man humming a drunken man's song. Abed and the woman are sitting on opposite chairs, waiting for their respective washing machines to give back their clothes clean. And she sure needs clothes, for tonight she only wears a gossamer blouse over her tight trousers, putting her large, white, bosomy tits under his nose. Abed is pretending not to look at them, not to look at her, and focus instead on the cheesy journal in his hand. Skipping a few pages, he comes across the picture of a comatose girl smiling in a hospital bed with an IV on one side and a pile of books on the other. The child is said to have fainted in the classroom while trying to finish her 6,667th book in life rather than listening to what the classroom teacher was saying.

Over the journal, Abed sneaks a quick look at the woman only to find her still fixedly staring at him with that bamboozling smile, with no pretensions at all, so straightforward and bold, so unashamedly shameless. When the light hits her face from this angle the wrinkles around her eyes and lips become apparent. Abed sees her age. She is old enough to be his mother and yet, how young is both her stare and her hands when compared to Zahra's. In increasing unease Abed rises to his feet, and without giving any thought to where he's running, why he's running, he scurries to the street, leaving his clothes in the washing machine, in dire need to get away from her lure.

A Bridge in Between

The day of departure. After staying ten days in Istanbul, Gail and Ömer are leaving the city. Their flight is at 3:30 p.m. The day before, they crossed to the Asian side of the city, to bid farewell to Ömer's parents. As usual, Ömer had planned the day, and the daily plan was not observed, as usual. Initially, the program was to have a late brunch with the family, then come back to the hotel at night to pack their suitcases and go to bed early for the next morning. Once there, however, the brunch had turned into a dinner and the dinner into a bout, and Gail into a balloon. Ömer's mother had insisted that they should sleep there, and be on their way early the next morning. When they had woken up, they had found themselves once again seated at a banquet table. Late to get out of the house, they had called a taxi to take them to the European side of the city, thereby committing the worst of errors in Istanbul: crossing the Bosphorus Bridge at rush hour!

Hence, here they are, dreadfully stuck in a traffic jam among in-finite convoys of cars neatly lined up on the bridge lanes, sitting in the backseat of a taxi under an agitated shower of a Brazilian football match broadcast and the even more agitated exclamations of the driver, a wispy little man with an amazingly gruff voice for such a minuscule body. It is 8:18 a.m. There is a balmy breeze outside and a beautiful mist, which is not mist, in fact, but a thin veil of air pollution that is still beautiful because it looks more like mist than air pollution.

Never really interested in football, and never having understood what it is that makes people of his sex so frantic about it, Ömer has put his headphones on and increased the volume, listening to PJ Harvey sing "This Mess We're In." From time to time he pouts at his wrist, as if angry with himself for not wearing a watch. If he had a watch or at least kept an eye on someone else's, they could have been on their way on time and be somewhere more pleasant doing something more meaningful now instead of being nailed to this congestion.

"*So we are in the in-between right now . . .*"

"What did you say?" Ömer took his headphones off.

"I said, *so we are in the in-between right now . . .*" Gail murmured looking ahead.

His mind galloping far away, in contrast to his body's compulsory inertia, Ömer was slower than usual in decoding the meaning of her words: With a sign that read WELCOME TO THE ASIAN CONTINENT on one side, and another sign that read WELCOME TO THE EUROPEAN CONTINENT on the other, the bridge they stood on was in the in-between.

That the city of his childhood was established on two continents being scarcely news to him, Ömer nodded sluggishly and put his headphones back on. Before doing that, however, he changed the CD for a new song. Iggy Pop and the Stooges, "Gimme Danger." Repeat track. Somewhere along the fourth round he noticed Gail's lips moving again but this time she seemed to be talking to the taxi driver. He took off the headphone from one ear to hear what the hell they were talking about. Over the wavering voice of the football raconteur, Gail was delivering a speech on the categories of saffron in the world, where to use which, and oddly enough, the driver was listening to her attentively. "If you are going to cook rice, it's better to use Indian saffron, but for the desserts, Persian saffron is much better."

"And no Turkish saffron?" the driver asked in broken English, apparently more interested in the *Turkishness* part than in the *cooking* part, as someone who had never in his entire life entered into the kitchen to cook anything.

But Gail seemed ready for the question. In a second, she was naming Ottoman-Turkish dishes made with saffron, widening the smile on the driver's face with each name she pronounced in her broken Turkish. Baffled by the grotesqueness of their ability to communicate all the same, Ömer plunged back into his music, increasing the volume. "Gimme Danger." To tell the truth, after ten days in Istanbul he felt exhausted—less from the city's hue and cry than from Gail's hectic energy. Repeat track. "Gimme Danger."

A minute later, Gail noticed moving in the right lane a pricey topaz car wherein a girl with pitch-black hair was sitting in the back-seat, peering out the window with a remarkably calm, irritatingly ashen face. The girl did not look happy. If anything, she looked despondent. Though she was gazing directly in this direction, somehow Gail had the impression that she could not see her. The child leaned forward as if she wanted to say something to the two grown-ups in front—a guarded-looking woman guardedly driving the car, and a pensive-looking man pensively staring outside his window—but she simply did not.

Watching what was going on inside the topaz car from her window, for a second or maybe more, in an incomprehensible way or maybe not, Gail shivered with this eerie feeling that the girl she was looking at was in fact she herself, and that right at this instant she was observing her past and present move parallel to one another but both clogged up similarly on a congested road. Her chest ached. Her mind was quick to enclose upon itself. Once again in her life, she started watching herself falling down, and the falling down accelerate at a bewildering pace, eroding her desire to live bit by bit, like blood oozing from a wound inside, except that there was no apparent wound, and, therefore, no apparent reason why.

Breathing heavily, and with some difficulty she managed to tear her gaze from the girl toward the gauzy mist canopying the bridge. Suddenly it occurred to her, and the next second she knew with certainty that this inbetweendom was the right place, and this very moment was the right time to die.

At 1:22 a.m. in Boston, 6:22 a.m. in Marrakesh, 7:22 a.m. in Madrid, and 8:22 a.m. in Istanbul, the back right door of a taxi stuck in the traffic on the Bosphorus Bridge yawned open. The door made a tinny sound, which went completely unnoticed by Ömer semi-entranced with Iggy Pop and the Stooges, and by the taxi driver double-entranced with that motherfucker arbiter showing a red card to his favorite player. The sound made by the door was something like *clack!*

At the same instant as that *clack!* in Istanbul, a sigh was heaved in Boston as Alegre pushed the door of the first place she found open at this hour. Puffing heavily and trying to look calm at the same time, one hand on the pearl cross sagging on her chest, one hand searching for whatever money she had in her coat pocket, she dashed inside, and zigzagged among the laughing, swaying, chattering bodies, each with a glass in hand. Toward the back she found herself staring at a pair of round, beamlike, crimson eyes frozen in a ferocious stare, shivered a little, realized it was not a toy but a dead bird, shivered more, and no longer able to suppress the urge to get rid of the weight in her stomach, she hurried downstairs to the restrooms.

Three minutes later, she had to accept the fact that she couldn't throw up any longer, though she still suspected there must be some more food left inside. She got out of the restroom and careened back upstairs. Just when she reached out for the knob of the door, she saw Piyu pass by right in front of the bar, writhing along in apparent discomfort, without taking a glance inside. A bar was, no doubt, not among the places he'd search for Alegre.

She flinched, deciding to wait here for a couple of minutes, trying to avoid the ravenous gaze of a middle-aged man standing at the bar. The man had a shadowed face, almost gray, and kept staring at her with fixed eyes reddened with alcohol. The very next moment, this chilly flush of blood passed through her body, moving to her tiptoes, then spread all over. Worried sick that the man might follow her on the dark streets, she scurried outside, ran to the T to catch the last outbound train. Tonight she didn't want to go to *la* Tía Piedad's house, and couldn't go back to Pearl Street, but she sensed that she could knock on Debra Ellen Thompson's door. In the chilly breeze, she looked at the name written on the napkin she had fetched from the bar. The Laughing Magpie. A funny name for a bar, she thought as she stepped into the train, and she wondered whose idea it was.

On the corner of Walnut Street, Abed stopped gaping at a shadow zipping past him at a breakneck speed. For a second he was sure that it was Alegre that he had seen. His logic was quick to correct that impression. No, it couldn't be Alegre coming out of The Laughing Magpie at this late hour. He slowed down and tried to clear his mind to fathom why he was in such a panic himself, why he had left the laundry like that. Though the answer was not clear to him, in a minute he turned back, slowly yet steadily, as if pulled by an invisible rope, all the way back to the laundry. He sensed but could never explain to anyone, no less to himself, that his loyalty for Safiya had been abstrusely interwoven with his devotion not only to their common past, but also to their country. The effect of losing bit by bit his connection to Safiya was a subtle loosening of the moorings that tied him to his homeland. Not that he felt less connected to Morocco now. But he somehow felt more connected to his life in the United States.

As he approached the laundry, at first he feared it might be closed, and upon seeing that it wasn't, he feared that she might be gone. But there she was, standing next to a washing machine, piling the clean and dry clothes in two baskets—hers and his. As she handed his basket to Abed, her smile was so embarrassingly victorious, and her victory so incredibly voluptuous, that Abed had to lower his eyes.

"She's going," the taxi driver said in a voice that was so paralyzed by disbelief that it did not sound surprised at all. Hence, he had to repeat, this time hooting: "She's going!"

Unable to make sense of what the driver was saying even after he had heard his words clearly, Ömer absentmindedly followed the man's gaze until he caught sight of Gail swiftly snaking her way among the vehicles stuck in the congestion, her long, black, bushy hair flapping hectically as she ran toward the barriers. He was so overwhelmed that only when he saw the taxi driver scuttle out and start running after Gail was his body able to move. His pulse rocketed to the beat of panic, Iggy Pop's voice still streaming "Gimme danger little stranger" from the headphones now sagging around his neck, Ömer rushed out of the car.

Piyu hung up the phone in deepening worry. Alegre could not be found, and Abed had not come home. More than the revolting greed he had witnessed tonight, it was the expression on Alegre's face that petrified Piyu the more he thought about the incident. It was as if Alegre's body had coalesced into a sharp knife he could not possibly lay a hand on. He paced to and fro in the kitchen, without realizing that at each nervous step he was deepening not only his own worries but also Arroz's, watching him from under the kitchen table, almost pasted on the floor as if looking for something solid to stick to amid this turbulence. Unable to figure out what wrong he had done to Alegre, his heart aching with despair, Piyu went upstairs to his room to pray. *Ruega por nosotros, Santa Madre de Dios, para que seamos dignos de las promesas de Cristo.* In the middle of El Salve, he suddenly shuddered. He could swear he had heard a pummeling thump like a heartbeat in fear, and a voice that warned: "Run, she is leaving you."

"Run, she's leaving you."

Once again in his life Ömer watches himself lagging behind the speed of time, unable to catch the cadence of life, except that this time it is the cadence of death he is running after. *Gimme danger little stranger.* Gail and the taxi driver and Ömer zigzag between the cars lined up on the bridge. Here and there, a few drivers watch them from inside their cars with an utterly perplexed gaze.

And I feel with you at ease. Some of them are just beginning to realize there is something extraordinary going on. They point it out to the others. *Gimme danger little stranger.* In a split second, all the people in all the cars are fascinated, almost delighted, to be the spectators of a live suicide attempt from the bridge. *And I feel your disease* . . . Ömer is running. In front of him is the taxi driver running. In front of him is Gail running. In front of her there is only a void.

Standing now at the other side of the barricades, with only one hand holding her into this life, Gail is unaware of her audience. She has turned her back to the bridge and to its mayhem, and her face to the city that looks unusually serene from up here. Strangely enough, the panoroma she sees at this instant is even more beautiful than the panoroma from room number 607. She breathes heavily as if getting ready to hold her breath. Once again she is at the other extreme, only this time she feels closer to the edge. This time she feels as if every moment in her life, every person she came to know, as well as every self she harbored inside is a letter in an alphabet soup. In her mind she stirs and stirs them all, until they lose their distinctiveness and mold into a delirious whirl. A pukelike puree in a bowl, the corona of her mother's raven hair, the taste of an omelet, and a piece of pepperoni, spicy and hot, unreturnable, unswallowable, stuck in her baby throat . . . an Assyro-Babylonian goddess worshiped at the rising moon . . . a sea of perennial borders . . . chocolate figures congealed on trays . . . birds flying high and alone, unable to remain within their flocks . . . Suddenly everything seems to be perfectly decomposable and yet a perfect component of varying totalities just like the letters in frenzy in an alphabet soup. Suddenly she feels falling with an enormous speed, and a swifter release, into some indigo vacuum where it wouldn't matter anymore what her next name would be.

Long behind her, long behind the time, a fleeting consolation crosses Ömer's mind. She won't die. No, she'll not. People do not commit suicide on other people's soil, and this is not her homeland. But did she ever have one? Who is the real stranger—the one who lives in a foreign land and knows he belongs elsewhere or the one who lives the life of a foreigner in her native land and has no place else to belong?

The bridge is sixty-four meters above sea level. A song plays on Ömer's Walkman. The song lasts three minutes, twenty seconds, but if you keep repeating the track it can last an eternity.

Gail's fall lasts only 2.7 seconds.